THE NEW ORDER OF FEAR

The Great Reset Trilogy: Book 1

Tom Quiggin

with Rick Gill

Dedication

The values that built Western society are vicious attacks from new forms of Marxism, progressivism, Islamism, and post-modernism. Western society is being assaulted, despite the fact that it was the first to ban slavery, give women rights, practice democracy and create a massive increase in lifespan for all. Western inventions have created a world where hunger is in retreat.

Christianity, in particular, is being harassed or forced to water down its values while billions of dollars are flowing into the West to create more anti-Semitism.

The so-called 'free press' in the West has capitulated on many fronts and will no longer defend its freedoms.

Even with these vicious and often violent attacks, many people are still willing to stand for freedom of thought, religion, conscience, association, mobility, and peaceful assembly.

This book is dedicated to those who maintain the fight and realize that freedom of speech is, above others, the most fundamental right.

Contents

Foreword

It is often necessary to use fiction to tell the truth the real world cannot accept. This is because fiction can be more accurate than truth in a world of deceit. As Hunter S. Thompson, channeling Faulkner, put it, "The best fiction is far more true than any kind of journalism."

The Great Reset Trilogy is a fictional work that explores how globalists will remake our world into a Marxian-inspired totalitarian system. The Great Reset is a rebranding effort for the globalist agenda where 'elites' determine outcomes. As stated by the World Economic Forum, "You'll own nothing, and you'll be happy."

As always, the elites say it is for "your safety," but what they mean is they want total control of you and everything you do. Consistent with previous resets such as the French Revolution in 1789 or the Russian Revolution in 1917, the elites have no concerns about the thousands or millions who will die in the process.

This fictional work raises an important question. Can a small group of well-informed citizens, using open-source intelligence, defeat the will of the globalists and their totalitarian agenda? Of course, they can, but the context of the future challenges will be one of massive violence.

The Great Reset

According to the World Economic Forum, the Great Reset plan will have three components. The first will be a 'stake-holder economy' which means that central authorities will make all decisions concerning production and consumption. The second component is the move towards 'sustainability.' This refers to 'building back better' and 'green infrastructure' spending. Part of this will be 'climate lockdowns,' which are advocated as necessary to achieve vague goals. The third component is harnessing the Fourth Industrial Revolution. Artificial Intelligence will monitor every human activity that will be approved – or disapproved – by invisible central authorities who will decide what standards will guide your lifestyle. Finally, it will be a social credit scoring system, much like Communist China has now.

The Great Reset is being advanced by individuals who regard themselves as elites, such as Klaus Schwab, Vice President Al Gore, President Obama, Prime Minister Trudeau, and President Xi of China. Make no mistake. You will suffer massive tax increases in exchange for a lower quality of life to meet the elites' climate, equity, and social justice goals. But the elites, like Senator Kerry, will keep their private jets while you suffer.

If you are wary of the 'Internet of Things,' examine the transhumanism concept of the 'Internet of Bodies.'

5

A Note on Sources

Unusual for a fictional work, this book has over 150 footnotes to help the reader understand the context and nature of intelligence, government, and what is happening in the world around us. Unlike academic work or documents for court, the sources were chosen for ease of accessibility and understanding. In addition, the bibliography contains a list of references for those who may wish to take a deeper dive into the subject matter.

Preface

This series of books came about for two reasons. The first is that we now operate in an era of increasing censorship, identity politics, and lawfare. It is no longer safe to speak the truth in many Western countries.

The other reason is the emerging threat from those who, once again, believe that the 'elites' must run the government because the masses cannot be trusted to decide for themselves what they want or need. In short, the same forces that brought us the evil twins of fascism and communism are trying for another totalitarian system.

The rebranding of this new form of totalitarianism has produced different names: Globalism, Progressivism, Wokeism, Islamism; The Great Reset; Building Back Better, and Agenda 2030. Unlike the previous attempts at centralized and totalitarian systems, the current crop of 'elites' has grander ideas. Not content to take over one country or one continent, they can force their ideas on the entire developed and developing world.

Those advocating the Great Reset are mainly older white males from Europe (think Klaus Schwab). Still, they have many partners such as President Xi of China and Islamist groups such as the Muslim Brotherhood and Jamaat E Islami.

7

BLM (U.S.)
Indigenous (can)

In this type of political and legal climate, the truth cannot be spoken as it may be offensive to groups who desire a cult of victimhood to advance their agenda. The situation today is so severe that even asking questions has been forbidden.

As has been frequently stated, "In a time of universal deceit, telling the truth is a revolutionary act."

So how does one ask the right questions today?

The truth may be stranger than fiction, but fiction can often do a better job of telling the truth.

The Great Reset Trilogy is a work of fiction, but it is not a flight of fancy. The Muslim Brotherhood is funded in Europe by Qatar. France has some 1,100 no-go zones, some 800 of which are under the influence of the Muslim Brotherhood. Incompetent politicians have ravaged the financial system of the West. The Great Reset program itself is genuine in more ways than many realize. These books are based on what the future might look like, given the forces at work.

The story, all names, characters, and incidents portrayed in this production are fictitious. No identification with actual persons (living or deceased) is intended or should be inferred. The only real characters in the book are President Erdogan of Turkey, Prime Minister Trudeau of Canada, Trudeau's brother Alexandre, Minister of Transport Omar Alghabra of Canada, Mississauga Mayor Bonnie Crombie, and Klaus Schwab.

8

Acknowledgments

Given the current climate of cancel culture, lawfare, and violence towards even fictional works, we have chosen not to name the many persons who have helped prepare this book. Free speech of any sort is under attack, especially in Canada, and we are now at a point where personal safety of anyone who speaks out is at risk.

A number of those who assisted have positions in the finance, intelligence, and law enforcement world. Others are retired military. In each case, those who helped review the work offered their expertise on content and style.

As always, any faults in the text are the responsibilities of the authors.

Introduction

The ultimate weapon of the politician and the terrorist is fear. Not the gun. Not the bomb. Fear.

This first action/thriller book of the Great Reset trilogy reveals how the artificial construction of fear by ruling elites is all-pervasive. The path towards the Great Reset has been shaped by the pandemic, the recession, and the climate crisis. Planning for the Great Reset must be accelerated, and the violence necessary for this action is of no concern to the plotters.

In Book One, the believers in the Great Reset are desperate. They must act soon to launch their Great Reset, as the hangover from years of government mismanagement is being exposed. They will use the Islamists in Europe as their tool to create the fear and violence necessary for their plans.

One of the leaders of the Great Reset is Enrica Leclercq. As the High Representative for the European Union for Foreign Affairs, she initiates the Great Reset's violent events. Contracted terrorist attacks in Europe and the murder of Canadian Prime Minister Trudeau confuse the political situation. But as the violence unfolds, so do other problems. Enrica does not understand it, but one of her main co-conspirators has plans of his own. While the co-conspirator is a disciple of the Great Reset, he believes that others lack the iron will to make it triumphant.

10

As the violence unfolds, a self-emerging group of citizens pieces the puzzle together. They ask questions. Can the Great Reset be stopped? Can they expose the globalists who enabled the Islamists in their bid to gain power? Can the West be saved?

On many occasions, the readers will ask what is real and what is fictional in the book and today's world of fake news and generated realities.

Books Two and Three of the Great Reset will follow the fight for freedom as the action moves through Europe and crosses the Atlantic. Will North America be called to defend freedom? Of course, but is it too late? Or have North American leaders already sold out in pursuit of the globalist ideology. What of China and Iran? Will the fight for civilizational freedom end with a clash of wills? Or with the whimpering sounds of soy-infused social justice warriors?

CHAPTER 1: WORLD WAR I AND FEAR

LOCATION: Sarajevo, Bosnia and Hercegovina, Austro-Hungarian Empire

DATE: 28 June 1914

TIME: Just after 10:45 AM

Gavrilo Princip fired his FN pistol twice at Archduke Ferdinand. The gurgling noise from the Archduke's throat panicked the driver, who then headed to the Governor's residence for medical treatment.

By 11:30 AM, the Archduke was dead.

By 11:00 AM on the 28th of July 1914, Austria declared war on Serbia, and the *War to End all Wars* was underway.

By 11:00 AM on the 11th of November 1918, nine million combatants were dead, along with 13 million civilians.

Nineteen-year-old Gavrilo Princip had carried out the June 1914 assassination with the vague hope of ending Austro-Hungarian rule in Bosnia and Herzegovina. He and his Black Hand terrorists had no strategy. No follow-up plans. Like most terrorists before and after them, they were incapable of defining a strategy to exploit fear and violence as political tools.

Instead, Gavrilo Princip triggered a series of events that started World War One, bringing multiple empires to their knees. Moreover, the war weakened Europe, leaving it more vulnerable to the Spanish Flu, killing tens of millions in 1918 and 1919.

Their assassination mission was a failure as it did not accomplish its goal – the independence of Bosnia.

CHAPTER 2: NEW EUROPE AND FEAR

LOCATION: Residence of Clement Raes-Javier, Managing Director, The International Monetary Fund

DATE: 27 June

TIME: 7:00 PM

Clement Raes-Javier was in a buoyant mood as he checked the news on his iPhone 13.

Tomorrow would be the 28th of June, the anniversary of the assassination of the Archduke Ferdinand of Austria. Only a limited number of people would note the day at its outset. Few people read history, and fewer still understood the significance of the day.

But future historians would remember tomorrow. It would be every bit as significant as 9/11 in 2001, D-Day in 1944, Pearl Harbour in 1941, Bastille Day in 1789, and the Battle of Hastings in 1066. Songs and poems would be written about this day.

As the Managing Director of the International Monetary Fund, Clement Raes-Javier, known to the world as CRJ, knew he would change the course of history, having learned from it.

Tomorrow would be the start of a new campaign for the control of Europe. This time, the application of political violence would be guided by strategy and intelligent planning, unlike the dim-witted Gavrilo Princip.

Victory would follow.

More pleasing still to CRJ were his colleagues who were working so diligently towards the Great Reset. Initially, they would be pleased with the violence as with the pandemic and the recession that had followed. The situation, they thought, would catapult them into the new order they so desperately desired. Later, the shock would hit them when they found out what CRJ had planned for them.

CHAPTER 3: THE FIRST SHOT OF FEAR

LOCATION: Brussels, Belgium

DATE: 28 July

TIME: 00:10 hours

Ilhan's Benhaddara's head exploded. Her body crumpled to the ground from the no-reflex kill.[1] Tarek Raman, her handler, stood frozen on the spot. He was initially unable to understand what had happened, even though he had her brain matter on his shirt and face. The 7.62 x 39 caliber round had entered her head just behind the left eye. With the round having traveled some 250 yards before hitting its target, it moved at close to 2300 feet per second. Most of the right side of her head splattered on the hotel door, and she was dead before she knew it.

Tarek Raman began to recover. When Ilhan's body hit the ground, the thump brought him back to reality. He glanced down long enough to confirm what he already knew. She was beyond dead, and nothing would help her.

---

[1] A 'no-reflex kill' is an informal military term that refers to an individual who dies immediately from a gun shot wound and did not have a reaction to being shot, other than simply dropping in place. It infers that the victim was hit directly in the head or at top of the spine.

Tarek looked to the north on Boulevard Charlemagne towards Square Ambiorix at what he thought was the direction of the shot. Nothing. He looked south towards the traffic circle, rotated on his right heel, and headed into the hotel. Few in the lobby noticed him. They fixated on the screams coming from those who had witnessed the burst of red as it painted the rotating glass door. He moved past the sign-in desks and towards the stairs at the back of the lobby. Every instinct told him to run, but he took the ten stairs one at a time. He had no desire to draw attention.

Upon returning to his second-floor suite, Tarek's first order of business was getting Ilhan's brain matter and blood off his face. As he was running the water in the bathroom sink, his still-intact brain was racing. He had to make phone calls, cancel meetings, and make new plans.

Tarek was thinking through the implications of her death when it struck him. It was not just death. It was a targeted assassination. He was standing next to her, less than an arm's length away. He had remained frozen for two or three seconds before looking around. It was probably five seconds or more before he moved into the lobby. If someone had wanted to kill him, the opportunity had been there.

Inshallah, he was still alive and would remain that way. But why?

Regrets would have to wait. Tarek wondered briefly about the threatening letters that had been sent to Ilhan Benhaddara. As head of the UK-based Islamic

Assistance Transnational, hate mail was standard. Yet, these recent letters were different. The security staff believed the letters had a specific feel about them. Whoever sent them knew too much about Ilhan Benhaddara, her residence, and her movements. As a result, Islamic Assistance Transnational typically ignored acting on such letters. Still, given the specificity of the threats, the decision had been made to send all five letters to a high-priced private security agency for analysis. The agency had assessed that this was not the work of some gormless chav or nutter. Instead, the letters had to be the work of a right-wing group with organizational and observational skills.

Now that the adrenaline rush was fading, Tarek began to think through the totality of the situation. Ilhan's assassination on this day, of all days, might cost them everything. Islamic Assistance Transnational, caught as they were in the multiple crosshairs, could ill afford the attention and scandal that the investigation into the assassination would bring.

At stake was all the work of the Islamists in Europe since 1955. Blood. Money. Pain. Suffering.

In the last 65 years, much had been accomplished, and the Islamists were within a decade of reaching their first political goal – a series of mini-caliphates in Europe that would be under the Muslim Brotherhood's control and ideology. The caliphate would then lead to the greater caliphate of Europe, once the Kingdom of Christendom. This caliphate would operate under the rules of the hallowed organization of Hassan al Banna[2] and the holy writings of Sayyid Qutb.[3]

A possibility existed that the project could be deflected from success by a single shot. Of course, Ilhan Benhaddara was irrelevant, but the optics and repercussions could be severe.

What to do now?

Tarek Raman realized that Allah had already provided the answer. When Ilhan Benhaddara's body had hit the ground, he had moved without thinking. He had fled the scene when he should have stayed. It would not take the police long to figure out that the two had checked in simultaneously, albeit in separate suites on different floors. Then the questions would start. By themselves, the questions would not be wrong. For the first time in many years, it was a high-profile Muslim who was the victim. But the event would draw attention to himself. The few reporters, damn them, who still did investigative journalism would ask too many questions about his role and background. The last thing he needed was someone like the authors of the *Qatar Papers* on his tail.[4]

---

[2] Unknown Editors, "Hassan Al-Banna," Wikipedia (Wikimedia Foundation, June 1, 2021), https://en.wikipedia.org/wiki/Hassan_al-Banna.

[3] Unknown Editors, "Sayyid Qutb," Wikipedia (Wikimedia Foundation, May 10, 2021), https://en.wikipedia.org/wiki/Sayyid_Qutb.

[4] Christian Chesnot and Georges Malbrunot, "Qatar Papers: How Doha Finances the Muslim Brotherhood in Europe," Qatar Papers: How Doha finances the Muslim Brotherhood

Tarek accepted the role that Allah had chosen for him.

It was time to go underground.

From the shadows, he would continue the inevitable struggle. He would use the Muslim Brotherhood's vast array of followers in the 800 neighborhoods they controlled in France, which the French government politely called 'Sensitive Urban Zones.'[5]   Others had been less kind and called them no-go zones.[6]

Tarek did not care what the infidels called them. In the civilizational struggle, he and his brothers were the foundations of the new European caliphate to which they were ordained to control. They had lost Cordoba in 1236. Another defeat was at the Gates of Vienna in 1683, but now was the time for the dreams of al-Afghani.[7]

Tarek burned the pages of his genuine passport, and the ashes fell into the toilet. He gathered some clothing, his fake IDs, and the Euros he carried for just

---

in Europe. eBook: Amazon.ca (Amazon.ca, March 25, 2020), https://www.amazon.ca/Qatar-Papers-finances-Brotherhood-Europe-ebook/dp/B086DSMKFY.

[5] Unknown Editors, "Sensitive Urban Zone," Wikipedia (Wikimedia Foundation, March 9, 2021), https://en.wikipedia.org/wiki/Sensitive_urban_zone.

[6] Unknown Editors, "No-Go Area," Wikipedia (Wikimedia Foundation, May 27, 2021), https://en.wikipedia.org/wiki/No-go_area.

[7] Unknown Editors, "Jamal Al-Din Al-Afghani," Wikipedia (Wikimedia Foundation, June 7, 2021), https://en.wikipedia.org/wiki/Jamal_al-Din_al-Afghani.

such an event. He removed the battery from his phone and flushed the SIM card down the toilet as well. Tarek would toss the phone down a drain along side of the street later as he walked towards the station.

As he headed down the fire escape and exited the hotel, Tarek took a moment to bless the European Union and its Schengen Agreement. Free passage in Europe with no borders meant he could enter France unhindered. Islamists, terrorists, drug dealers, and human smugglers were the silent supporters of a system that allowed them to ply their trades without the nosey officials of sovereign states asking awkward questions.

By the mid-morning hours, Tarek would be in Paris, entirely at home amongst his beloved Ikhwan.[8] To sustain his courage and actions, he recited the credo of the Muslim Brotherhood in his head.

> *Allah is our objective.*
>
> *The Prophet is our leader.*
>
> *Qur'an is our law.*
>
> *Jihad is our way.*
>
> *Dying in the way of Allah is our highest hope.*[9]

---

[8] Unknown Editors, "Muslim Brotherhood," Wikipedia (Wikimedia Foundation, May 23, 2021), https://en.wikipedia.org/wiki/Muslim_Brotherhood.
[9] For more background on the Muslim Brotherhood, see the Investigative Project on Terrorism report at https://www.investigativeproject.org/documents/misc/13

In France, and under the nose of the hated Macron, he would be the one to lead the Islamist struggle in Europe.

Inshallah.

5.pdf .

Chapter 4: A Fire Below the Waterline

LOCATION:	Bay of Biscay, off the Spanish Coast
DATE:	28 June
TIME:	03:00 AM, Local Time

The Captain of the cruise ship MS Nordsee Bliss woke with a start. Meyer Jager had left strict instructions just two hours earlier that his ship should maintain a steady course and speed throughout the night transit. Course and speed changes were *verboten* unless something was seriously wrong. The Officer of the Watch could have avoided a collision with another vessel with a minor course change.

Yet, the increase in the rotational speed of the ships' two Azipod thrusters had roused him. Most passengers and crew were asleep, and even those awake would likely not have noticed it. Meyer Jager, however, was fully awake due to the vibrational changes. He arose from his bed fully dressed, minus his jacket and hat hung on the back of his cabin door. As he reached for the jacket, he heard a discrete tapping on the door.

It was Andre Ramos, his steward. Calmly, but with apprehension in his voice, Andre told the Captain that his presence was requested on the bridge. The presence of Andre Ramos was unusual. Something was wrong. Why didn't the bridge just call?

The Captain listened as they walked. Andre informed him that another cruise ship had issued a distress call due to a fire. The MS Nordsee Bliss was the closest major vessel, and the Officer of the Watch had given instructions for a course change and the ship's speed to increase. He had also dispatched the steward, who had just brought coffee to the bridge, to retrieve the Captain, telling the steward to brief the Captain on events.

The Officer of the Watch dispensed with formalities and immediately reported to the Captain. The MS Fulfillment of the Seas had sent a distress call at 02:57 AM. The Nordsee's computerized navigation system had identified the vessel's location and identified it as 12.5 nautical miles away. A five-degree course change would make for an intercept. At 02:58, the MS Nordsee Bliss's radar confirmed the contact. On his authority at 03:00, the Officer of the Watch had changed course and increased speed. He told the Captain that the course change and speed increase were gradual not to alert the passengers. The Officer of the Watch then told the Captain that he had worked out a course and the time required to place the MS Nordsee Bliss at the exact location as the MS Fulfillment of the Seas.

Without answering, Captain Jager moved to the V-shaped command console and made his assessment of the situation. He glanced down at the twin sets of gauges for 'engine revolutions ordered' and 'engine revolutions actual' and then took a glance up at the screen for heading and speed indications. Without a flicker of emotion, Captain Jager walked back to the port side of the bridge and scanned the horizon. For just a moment, he looked through the glass panel built into the deck that allowed the bridge crew to look straight down at the water's surface. All he saw was darkness.

The bridge personnel had frozen in place. Their eyes followed the Captain's movements. For the Officer of the Watch, time had stopped. He stood for what seemed to be an eternity watching the Captain.

Finally, the Captain's head turned in his direction. One phrase, clearly enunciated, came out of his mouth.

"This is good."

The Officer of the Watch willed his heart to start beating again. Everyone on the bridge took a breath at the same time.

The Captain stared at the Officer of the Watch for about three seconds and then asked if they had established communications with the MS Fulfillment of the Seas. The Officer of the Watch pointed to the communications console, and a junior communicator held out the handset to the Captain.

"Fulfillment of the Seas, this is Captain Jager of the MS Nordsee Bliss, over."

"Captain Jager, this is the Officer of the Watch on Fulfillment. Stand by for Captain Warren Martindale, over."

Captain Jager formed a picture in his mind. He had briefly met Martindale when both ships were in Miami. Quiet. Competent. He had toured the Nordsee Bliss, asking intelligent questions and avoiding useless small talk.

"Captain Jager, this is Martindale, over."

"Martindale, this is Jager. We have an intercept course laid in and will be alongside you in thirty-six minutes. Status report."

"Captain Jager. We had a fire break out on deck two, port side aft, in a machinery compartment. It burned for an unknown period as the fire detection and fire suppression systems appear to have both failed. The fire was reported to the bridge at 01:30 by a crew member. The fire spread fast. Initial fire fighting efforts failed due to non-functioning fire hoses. Multiple teams are now engaging. Have turned the ship to the wind and maintaining steerage way only. Unclear if we can isolate the fire and prepare crew and passengers for the worst-case scenario. I am requesting immediate assistance. Over."

Captain Jager pointed at his young helmsman, whom he knew to be an online gamer and a massive Star Trek fan.

"Warp Speed Mr. Sulu." Mr. Sulu, better known as Anderson to the rest of the crew, nodded his head in affirmation and wondered to himself if the propellers would see their maximum design speed of almost 150 RPM on this day. He had seen this happen in a ship simulator, but never for real.

The entire bridge crew was, for the second time that day, shocked into silence. Not only was it clear that the MS Fulfillment of the Seas must be in severe distress, but it appeared that their Captain might have not only a personality but an awareness of the cultural world beyond his ship and the deep blue sea. Such a revelation was new to the crew.

"Martindale, we will contact you again when closing in and will have fire teams and medical assistance prepared. Have your Officer of the Watch keep an open line with mine for further information. Godspeed. O ver."

Jager was shocked by what happened next. Captain Martindale's voice had been calm. Flat. It sounded like he was reading a grocery list. But Captain Martindale's voice suddenly dropped in tone, and his formal reporting style disappeared. No longer was he a Captain addressing a peer in rank who was senior to him in service. This was the voice of one sailor to another.

"Meyer, this could get worse. Fulfillment out."

"Mein Gott," said Captain Meyer Jager to no one in particular.

Chapter 5: Snake Eaters on A Plane

LOCATION: South East of Iceland (Toronto to Frankfurt Flight)

DATE: 28 July

TIME: 03:30 GMT

The explosive device looked innocent enough. It was attached to the cockpit door of the Boeing 777, just above the latch area on the left side. Activating the device, Ali stepped back, entered the washroom, and pulled the door closed.

Once in the washroom, he pulled out his cellphone and called up the Bluetooth option. One quick push of the finger and a loud crunching noise followed. The overpressure, caused by the C4 explosive device on the cockpit door, created a sharp pain in both of his ears.

Ali paused, counted deliberately to ten, and then opened the washroom door. As planned, Qassem had rushed past him and burst into the now open cockpit. He slashed the pilot in the left seat in the neck and turned to stab the co-pilot the same way. Neither offered any resistance, having been stunned by the explosion.

Ali stepped into the first-class area and calmly stabbed a cabin attendant in the throat. The attendant's run towards the cockpit ended when he hit the floor. That would hold the first class and business class passengers in their seats for a short time.

Hossein, who had an aisle seat in the last row of the business class section, rose and faced back to see the startled faces of those in the economy seats. "Silence," he yelled while waving a Skorpion machine pistol in the air.

Ali entered the cockpit as Qassem was undoing the pilots' seat belts and helped him drag first the pilot and then the co-pilot out of the cockpit. They dumped them on the floor at the front of the first-class section. Qassem jumped into the left seat while Ali turned and looked at the passengers in first class. "Any questions?" he asked with a pleasant smile on his face.

Ali headed back to the business class section. "Chicken or fish?" he sarcastically asked the British businessman in a port-side aisle seat. "Not hungry just now," said the Brit, much to the surprise of Ali.

Further back, Captain Andrew Davies (British Army SAS/Royal Welsh) was seated on the aisle on the aircraft's starboard side. He was about halfway back in economy class. Next to him in the middle and window seats were two soldiers from his troop. Both had started to move when the explosion occurred, but Davies had put his arm out and stopped them. When he saw the Skorpion machine pistol a second later, he knew their best immediate plan was to do nothing. "Steady, lads," he told them. "Watch and learn before we even think about trying anything."

Davies was worried. He might be able to pass for a businessperson or bureaucrat with his longish hair and suit, but his two soldiers looked like − well − hardened soldiers wearing civilian clothes.

Hossein walked back into the economy section and yelled again at the passengers, telling them to remain seated and try nothing. Davies remained calm and looked straight ahead. His two soldiers, God Bless Them, slightly lowered their heads and looked at the seat pockets in front of them, trying to look as inconspicuous and submissive as they could. Training pays off.

Hossein, satisfied that his passengers were now under control, slowly walked forward to the business class area and talked with Ali. After that, he regularly turned to observe the economy section.

Davies tried to talk while moving his mouth as little as possible. "I make three of them so far, with at least one Skorpion pistol and maybe a knife. Not sure if the other bloke is armed or not."

"Weird," mumbled Staff Sergeant Allen Crosby, as quietly as he could with his head still down. "I was just going to visit the head when I noticed two blokes lined up, and then a third came out and nodded to the others. It struck me as strange because all three looked Middle Eastern, maybe Iranian, or something like that. But I am sure it was the same three guys."

Davies, who had dozed off before the explosion, was impressed with the observation. Were these well-trained attackers who thought a quick trip to the loo was a good idea before launching an operation, or was something about the washroom important to the plan?

Trooper David Skiffington had his thoughts. "Would someone of superior rank and intelligence please explain to this lowly trooper how three Middle Eastern-looking terrorist types got a bomb, a gun, and some knives onto a Western airliner in this day and age?" The Captain and the Staff Sergeant did not answer the question, but both arrived at the same thought. Whoever planned this attack had done so rather well. Somewhere, the attackers had well-placed accomplices with good access to airplanes.

The Captain wanted to lean out into the aisle to see where their troop commander was sitting in business class - rank and wealth hath its privileges. But he could not risk leaning out and drawing the attention of the man with the gun. Therefore, he could not see Major Roy Berikoff, Special Air Service, who had just told Ali he was not hungry.

The Captain put his head down slightly with one eye on the guy with the gun. "We need a good assessment of the situation, an objective, and then a plan. We have three bad guys, but we have to assume a fourth exists who could be sitting anywhere in the airplane. This hijacking has some sort of larger goal, or we would all be dead by now."

The passenger areas of the 777 were silent. The engines and the air vents were the only sounds. The plane had remained straight and level throughout the whole incident. Most everyone stayed still and looked at the floor or the inflight entertainment system while others started to look at each other. You could read the thoughts. Are we about to die? Is this a hijack for ransom? A hijacking for politics? A hijacking to turn the 777 into a guided missile?

Trooper Skiffington carefully raised his right hand, flipped the entertainment unit in front of him over to the mapping function, and stared at it for a few moments. "We are south and east of Iceland. Even if the bad guys want to land this thing in Ireland or the UK, we still have at least three hours to a landing. They want to take the airplane somewhere, and they want it intact. If they were going to use us as a guided missile like 9/11, they would have hijacked us just after takeoff, or they would have waited until we were closer to the target if it is in Europe. This flight probably does not have the legs to get to Russia or the Middle East without refueling, so we are headed to Blighty[10] or the continent."

"Meanwhile, folks are going to want to use the washroom. One of us must have a look inside that washroom where the three bad guys went. Maybe we can learn something."

---

[10] Unknown Editors, "Blighty," Wikipedia (Wikimedia Foundation, March 30, 2021), https://en.wikipedia.org/wiki/Blighty.

Captain Davies remained silent and motionless as Hossein did another visual scan of the economy cabin. "Probably best if I go. I have the aisle seat and will draw the least attention. You two look like squaddies, even in the nice shirts." Trooper Skiffington tried to put on his most wounded face and look hurt. But he knew the Captain was right.

The tension was rising in the passenger cabin. The shock of the explosion and gun-waving in the economy class cabin was starting to wear off. People began to talk among themselves, and Hossein had made two more walks through the cabin, waving his gun and yelling at random passengers.

Captain Davies watched and waited. Then, finally, something would happen, and when it did, they would start to react. He forced himself to breathe slowly and release the tension in his body. Conserving energy and maintaining focus would be the key to survival.

Hossein turned to do a scan of the cabin and began to yell, this time pointing at someone who was just behind the Captain. He ran back with the gun-waving in the air and was screaming, "Sit. Sit. Sit." Captain Davies decided to turn and see what was happening. Hossein was focused on the female passenger who had stood up, and almost everyone was looking as well.

The situation with the passenger was an opportunity.

The woman was in her late 20s and pregnant. Davies, a father of two himself, guesstimated she was seven months gone. She was pointing at the washroom and said she had to go now. Her rapid breathing worried Captain Davies. The everyday stress of pregnancy, a long flight, and a terrorist hijacking were bearing down hard on her.

Hossein pointing a gun in her face was not helping. Captain Davies decided now was the time to act. He slowly rose and said quietly, "Sir." Hossein pushed the gun into the woman's face and turned to the Captain. The Captain put his hands out slightly from his sides with his open palms turned towards the man with the gun. He looked in the direction of Hossein but did not stare directly into his eyes. "Sir, the woman is in distress and is seven months pregnant. You do not want her to give birth now, with all the mess that would make. Let me take her to the washroom and get her calmed down.

Captain Davies did not say he was a doctor, but his willingness to help and his assessment of a possible birth led Hossein to assume that he was a medical type of some sort. Hossein was momentarily worried – this was not a scenario for which they had planned. He had been ready to shoot anyone who resisted, but a woman giving birth in the middle of the aisle was not a problem he wanted.

Hossein pointed the gun at Captain Davies and said, "I will kill you. Do not do anything stupid."

Captain Davies put out his hand to the woman and led her up the aisle to the washroom. Hossein followed. Captain Davies guided the woman into the restroom and closed the door on her, leaving himself standing in the aisle. Hossein passed him and went back to his post, standing between the business and economy class. The gun was trained on the Captain the whole time.

Captain Davies stood motionless, staring at the door handle of the washroom, waiting for it to move.

In the meantime, Sergeant Crosby turned his head slightly towards Trooper Skiffington. "Our newfound friend has a Skorpion machine pistol. It looked to me like he had the fire selector on safe rather than on semi or full-automatic. That seems a bit strange."

Skiffington nodded his head. "It seems to me that he does not want a misfire. They think that the explosion and the mere presence of the weapon should keep the passengers compliant."

"Either way, I think he has one short magazine in the weapon and two long mags in a pouch on his belt. So, one round up the spout, ten in the mag, and forty more rounds for backup. Fifty-one rounds in all."

The Captain heard the toilet flush. Then he listened to the paper towel dispenser. His moment was arriving. He needed to get the woman to leave her purse behind so he could have an excuse to return to the washroom. Now was the time. The door handle began to turn. The Captain held it in place as the woman attempted to turn it. He held it until she stopped trying and then opened the door himself and pushed quickly inwards. He pointed at her and motioned with one hand to sit down again. White-faced, she sat. He smiled as politely as he could and told her to relax for a minute and breath deeply. He looked around quickly to see if anything was out of place. The Captain had earlier noted that this Boeing 777 was almost new, and the washroom was squared away and clean. Nothing jumped out at him. Why had the three terrorists felt it necessary to enter the restroom before starting the attack? Something was there. It had to be.

Hossein yelled again. It was time to move. Captain Davies reached out with one hand and helped pull the woman to her feet. He guided her to the aisle and, at the same time, reached across, took the strap of her purse off her shoulder, and slid it down, allowing it to drop silently to the floor. "Let me get that for you, Ma'am." Without thinking, she agreed and began to walk down the aisle towards her seat. She sat down and smiled weakly at the Captain, who smiled in return.

"Oh drat. Silly me. I left your purse in the washroom. Let me get it."

The Captain walked back towards the washroom, and Hossein began to yell again. Finally, the Captain put his hands out again in a sign of submission and said, "I forgot her purse in the washroom. Do you want to get it, or should it be me?" The Captain was betting that the hijacker would not want to walk down an aircraft aisle holding a woman's purse. Hossein waved while rolling his eyes.

Once in the washroom, the Captain got down on both knees and leaned forward. Hossein began moving back. "Get to your seat. Get up. Move." The Captain pulled the purse off the floor and stood up, with the purse dangling from its strap. He smiled weakly, headed back, gave the purse to the woman, and returned to his seat.

Trooper Skiffington glanced over briefly, and he did not like what he saw. The Captain, whom he had followed into some rather tense situations, was a bit white in the face. The situation was not good.

Hossein continued to stare at the Captain and finally turned away, scanning the rest of the economy class cabin before moving forward again.

"What? You saw something." The tone coming from Trooper Skiffington was almost accusatory. Sergeant Crosby stared as well.

The Captain put his head down and took a deep breath, and then slowly let it out. Then, with his voice as low as possible, he began. "There is a panel in the washroom. It is behind the toilet and forward. It has been pulled out a bit but not quite placed back correctly. Judging by the curvature of the panel, a void space must exist behind it." He stopped and looked forward.

The two soldiers also sat motionless as the message sank in.

The bomb.

The gun.

The knife.

Trooper Skiffington broke the silence. "Once again, does it fall to me to point out the obvious? The weapons were smuggled into the plane while it was under construction. The airplane is new, so it was done at the factory and not at a first- or second-line maintenance facility. If they did it once, could they have done it again? Do other planes have a terrorist hijacking kit built into them? Whiskey Tango Foxtrot! We have to tell someone."

The Captain put his head down. Despite everything, for the first time since the bomb exploded, he was beginning to feel good. 'Excellent points. But first, we have to get down to the business of killing a few hijackers."

Chapter 6: The Cash Heist

LOCATION:	South Amsterdam Industrial Park, The Netherlands
DATE:	28 June
TIME:	03:40 AM

Gamal al-Badawi took a shallow breath and increased the pressure on his trigger finger. The police car, with lights on and the siren blazing, was entering his kill zone. As the vehicle slowed to enter the cash center parking lot, Gamal increased the pressure again and heard the roar of the .50 caliber rifle. The length and weight of the weapon made it awkward to handle in close quarters, but Gamal wanted to be sure that any approaching vehicle would be stopped. The round, with less than a hundred meters to travel, found its mark. The engine block of the BMW cracked, and the engine died with an ugly rattle. The car came to a halt while two junior police officers tried to plan their next move. Should they stay in the car with the limited protection it provided, or turn and run - a rather unprofessional activity? Gamal helped their decision-making process by putting another round into the engine compartment of their now immobilized car. Then, as though running on the same program, each officer opened their respective car door and ran as fast as possible for cover.

From the top of the cash center, Gamal surveyed the scene. The heavy night fog had not dissipated so that no police helicopter would be disturbing them at the crime scene nor during their escape run. Darkness, once again, would be his friend. The sunrise was due at 05:21 AM, and the first light would start around 04:50 AM. Time was not a critical factor as everything was on schedule.

The dust had cleared from the bomb, which had exploded at the front of the cash center. Upon arriving at the cash center in two Audi A8 cars, Gamal and his team moved quickly. Gamal himself climbed up the side of the building on a ladder designed to allow workers access to the roof. At the bottom of the ladder, the wire cage had fallen away quickly when he cuts the lock with the cutting shears he had in his bag. Once on the roof, Gamal had taken up an overwatch position from which he could see the entrance and exit to the building's only access routes.

His other team members had moved in precise accordance with the intended plan. Two of them, Amin Attia and Yassir Haddad, had planted explosive charges with short fuses on the front of the building. The bricks had imploded into the building, scattering the few staff members who had just opened the cash vaults not five minutes earlier. The staff had just begun the laborious process of moving the heavy cash carts towards the distribution and loading zone when bricks and mortar began to fly around them. Gamal had heard Amin and Yassir yelling *Allahu Akbar* as they charged through the hole their explosives had created. He counted the rounds as each of them fired five planned rounds into the air above the staff. They should have 26 rounds each if needed, having started the operation with a 30-round clip and one round 'up the spout.' The intent was not to wound or kill but rather to terrify the staff into submission. Gamal knew a bit about creating terror.

Gamal inwardly laughed to himself about his men yelling *Allahu Akbar.* That had been part of the plan. Gamal had no time or interest for those who believed they were the soldiers of Allah and were serving the cause of Jihad. Gamal thought that only the weak-minded, the brain-washed, or the desperate thought that Jannah or paradise waited for those who died in the service of political Islam.

But those who hired Gamal had said they wanted someone yelling *Allahu Akbar*, so yell they would. When you were getting paid the kind of money Gamal was for this robbery, you did not ask questions.

As the shooting inside the building stopped, Gamal's two other team members had also entered the building carrying several sizeable black duffel bags. Following directions from Yassir, they scattered the duffel bags around four of the cash carts. The carts identified by Yassir had either fifty or one hundred Euro banknotes, all of them stacked in impeccably neat rows. All four team members began to stuff the bags full of banknotes as they had earlier practiced.

Gamal's last team member was positioned behind a concrete block at the end of the parking lot. His job was simple. He was to 'discourage' anyone from entering the parking lot or building area by spraying them with automatic fire from his PKM machine gun. He had waited patiently and silently as the police car arrived and did not fire at it precisely as directed. However, once the two police officers had retreated from their vehicle, he did fire several bursts of rounds in their direction. The investigators would only note that all the rounds fired from the PKM had hit the neighboring building about three meters above the ground. These rounds were intended to frighten and not kill the police officers. Gamal watched and listened as the PKM fired. Each burst, fired on the fully automatic setting, had consisted of four to five rounds. That created noise and confusion but did not use up the 100 round magazine attached to the underside of the receiver. Even on a bipod rather than a fixed mount, the expert hands of Gamal's gunner would have a spread of 7–10 cm at a range of 100 meters. Thus, the shooting was perfect for this night.

Gamal rechecked his watch. They had arrived on the scene precisely at 03:40 in the morning. The police car had taken only six minutes to arrive after the explosion, responding to a panicked call from a staff member who had retreated to the safe room. The Dutch police were, as Gamal had studied, able to respond in a reasonable time. However, they were not able to withstand the fire from the .50 caliber rifle and the PKM. Gamal also believed it would take some time before a second police car would dare enter the parking lot of the cash center. No doubt, the two retreating officers had told their shift commander that all hell was breaking loose in their quiet southern Amsterdam industrial park area.

Looking down, Gamal could see that four of his team members were now dragging the first set of heavily loaded duffel bags into the waiting cars. One car was an Audi A8 estate wagon, and the other a conventional four-door. The team would need more trips to move the cash-filled bags. As the team members moved the second set, Gamal blew two loud bursts on the whistle around his neck, a sign to all team members to prepare to leave the scene.

As planned, each of the team members jumped into one of the cars. Gamal was the last, taking only a second to look behind him and see that none of the cash center staff members were following him. As he entered the car, Gamal nodded his head at the driver, and the car shot ahead towards the end of the parking lot and the two waiting police officers. It would only be a short run to the A5 Autoroute.

Chapter 7: Fear Is the Greatest Weapon

LOCATION: Brussels Office of Clement Raes-Javier

DATE: 28 July

TIME: 03:00 AM

Clement Raes-Javier felt like he was floating on air. He had risen early to watch the news that he knew was coming. He was not disappointed. A variety of mainstream and social media outlets were already reporting the shooting death of Ilham Benhaddara. In addition, rumors and unconfirmed reports were emerging as to a possible fire on a cruise liner off the coast of Spain.

Clement Raes-Javier knew what had happened, and he knew what was coming. He was fully aware that more attacks would soon occur.

CRJ was quite confident that further attacks were coming because he had planned them. He was the mastermind behind the campaign of violence that would propel the European Union into the Great Reset. It was about to begin. Although many of The Great Resets' long-term proponents were unaware of where all of this would take them, the spilling of the first blood had occurred.

He saw the Great Reset as an opportunity. He would be the one who would trigger the early implementation of the Great Reset and then use that moment to turn his dreams for power into a concrete reality. The tool for his grand strategy was none other than Enrica Leclercq, the **High Representative for the European Union for Foreign Affairs and Security Policy.**

CRJ had believed for years that the European Union was failing. From the war in Yugoslavia to the financial crisis of 2008/2009, it was clear that the EU could not take the dramatic steps necessary to achieve greatness. However, the Brexit events of late 2020 had sealed this discussion as far as CRJ was concerned. If the UK could walk away and still stand on its own, other EU members would start making their demands.

The 2019-2021 pandemic had been the final straw for CRJ. It convinced him to move up his dates to go from planning to action. The leaders knew about the coronavirus by November or December 2019. It was public knowledge by January 2020. But what had the leaders of Europe and the West done?

Had they acted collectively?

Had they seized the day?

No. The leadership had fumbled the play. Dropped the ball. Missed the boat.

The EU was rotting slowly, burdened by a technocratic leadership class who were experts in bureaucracy and organizational matters but lacked imagination. They had neither the vision nor the will for Europe to triumph as a great power. The EU was, in his opinion, too weak to form another "Concert of Europe."[11]

As the current managing director of the International Monetary Fund, CRJ was painfully aware that change was needed in Europe and globally as well. Debts were overwhelming, and crony capitalism had changed the rules in favor of the bankers. Synthetic derivatives were an unmanageable nightmare. Money printing could only solve so many problems before it began to fail. Long-term low interests were reshaping the economy and the workforce – and not in a good way.

To him, the beliefs that were driving the Great Reset were little more than fantasies.

It was time for a revolution.

But it was not just that.

The Great Reset had to happen before the opportunity passed.

CRJ returned to the task at hand. Over the past several months, he had spent two hours every day

---

[11] Stanislas Jeannesson, "Concert of Europe (The)," Encyclopédie d'histoire numérique de l'Europe (Sorbonne Université, June 22, 2020), https://ehne.fr/en/encyclopedia/themes/europe-europeans-and-world/organizing-international-system/concert-europe.

writing his masterpiece. His work would be the first history of The Great Reset and the New United Europe. He had learned from Prime Minister Churchill of Great Britain. Churchill had said that history would be kind to him because he intended to write it. So CRJ would do the same. By the time the chain of revolutionary events was in motion, he would have his history book on its way to being published.

Enrica Leclercq would be cast as a visionary leader, albeit with the tragic flaws of a Shakespearean figure. Nonetheless, she would set in motion the revolutionary events for the Great Reset. In CRJ's book, however, Enrica's revolution would be sidetracked. She would not foresee or understand the social unrest and violence that would overtake her planned events.

The door would then open for CRJ. He would be the Grand Saviour who would emerge from the dust and smoke of violent conflict. He would be the Metternich of the 21st Century. It was he who would weld together the factions and establish a new order. CRJ would bring the EU and Western civilization to the brink and then offer it salvation. *Novus Oder Seclourum* – A New Order for the Ages.

Or, as he thought of it, a new order born of fear.

CRJ looked up at the small bookshelf on his desk. Arranged there were Klaus Schwab's *Covid-19 and The Great Reset,* Thucydides' *Peloponnesian War*, Sun Tzu's *Art of War*, George Orwell's *1984,* and *Animal Farm*. Next to them was Joseph Conrad's *Lord Jim,*

Machiavelli's *The Prince*, Robert Michels' *Iron Law of Oligarchy*, John Maynard Keynes' *The General Theory of Employment*, and Thomas Kuhn's *The Structure of Scientific Revolutions*. Finally, at the end of the shelf was Adam Ferguson's *When Money Dies: The Nightmare of Deficit Spend*ing.

He did not agree with all the writers, but CRJ believed that you had to understand power and ideas to conquer.

The Great Reset would not just be his work or that of Enrica **Leclercq**. It was the work of the minds of such great leaders such as Metternich and Charlemagne, who had sought to unite Europe.

In the mind of CRJ, Europe now had figures such as George Soros, Federica Mogherini, and Ursula von der Leyen. They were partially competent technocrats, but none of them would move history.

Decades had been required for CRJ to gain the knowledge and influence to identify his objective and plan the necessary strategy. It had taken years to formulate the operational plan. Months of work had been essential in developing the tactical details of the attacks. More work had been entailed to write the first three sections of his manuscript describing his view of history. But it would take only weeks for the last act of this historical moment to play out. In the end, only a few days would be required for him to rise to the position that his family deserved, and Europe needed.

CRJ ran his hand over the draft outline of his work, sitting on his desk. He rather liked the four sections. He had finished the first three. The fourth was about to play out in the real world, and he would record it as it happened.

The Great Reset: A European Declaration of Unity and Liberation

THE VISION: Progressivism, Diversity, Social Equity, and Climate Justice

THE OBSTACLES: Middle Eastern Christianity and Judaism, The Family and Private Property

COMPLICATIONS: The Islamists and Right-Wing Extremists

THE SALVATION: **Viribus Unitis – With United Force**[12]

* * *

CRJ had his views of history. To him, Gavrilo Princip barely deserved the title of 'terrorist.' His attack on Archduke Ferdinand had inadvertently unleashed a chain of events that started World War One. But Princip was a political fool. Like an arsonist who had intended to set one house on fire, he wound up burning down the entire city. Princip had no plan for what would happen after he murdered his target. To

---

[12] Unknown Editors, "SMS Viribus Unitis," Wikipedia (Wikimedia Foundation, March 26, 2021), https://en.wikipedia.org/wiki/SMS_Viribus_Unitis.

CRJ, political violence had to be followed by political action. Such was the failure of many terrorists. In the eyes of CRJ, Osama bin Laden had carried out one of the most extraordinary surprise attacks in history, yet he had no plan to exploit his victory. Bin Laden was a strategic failure, if not a half-bad tactician.

To Clement Raes-Javier, Gavrilo Princip represented the lowest form of a political activist. CRJ believed in the application of violence as a political tool. But for CRJ, the stupid application of violence was worse than no activity at all. Princip was every bit as foolish as Osama bin Laden and his 9/11 attacks on America. In both cases, the attacks were ultimately failures as there was no strategy.

CRJ had inwardly raged at bin Laden in the weeks and months after the 9/11 attacks. He hated the Islamists and their backward-looking ideology. But bin Laden and his al Qaeda force, with only 10 or 20 people, could have unleashed Holy Hell on America in the days after 9/11 if they had done any planning. A mall shooting here. A fake bomb there. A white powder attack with homemade Ricin a day later. A vehicle full of gasoline cans set on fire in an underground parking lot of a prominent office tower. America could have been run ragged. It was an overly confident society that had been filled with fear in just a few short hours. Bin Laden was too stupid to exploit his success. He had filled America with fear and then walked away. Bin Laden had not read Sun Tzu.[13]

---

[13] Unknown Editors, "Sun Tzu," Wikipedia (Wikimedia

Neither of these fools was any better than the Imperial Japanese Admiral Chuichi Nagumo, whose First Air Fleet had attacked Pearl Harbor in 1941. Following his masterful act of tactical and strategic surprise, the Admiral's fleet had sailed away, seemingly afraid of its success. If he had remained, one or two more days of attacks from Nagumo and the US fleet would have been out of the war for months.

CRJ understood that fear was the greatest weapon of the terrorist — not the bomb or the gun. Or the airliner. If the fear was not exploited, then the opportunity was lost.

This time would be different. First, CRJ would orchestrate the terrorist attacks and their follow-on violence. Then, when Europe turned to anarchy and fear, he would ride into the battle and save the day.

Were Europe's leaders even capable of taking collective action?

Europe's leaders had managed to exploit the pandemic crisis to their benefit at the tactical level. Still, all told, the performance of the technocratic leadership class had been worse than a disappointment. Not only had they not used 2020 as a springboard to decisive action, but they had also watched the problems grow. The UK's Brexit had further weakened them. President Macron of France had announced he would pursue the Muslim

Foundation, June 10, 2021),
https://en.wikipedia.org/wiki/Sun_Tzu.

Brotherhood and the Islamists, who were vital to CRJ and his plans for The Great Reset. The puppy who called himself the Chancellor of Austria had followed Macron. Hungary and Poland had gone toe to toe with Brussels over the immigration policies required to weaken them. Again, with all of this, the European Union leaders had collapsed in the face of opposition.

CRJ had initially conceived an action plan in the early 1990s. Europe had struggled to be relevant as Yugoslavia had collapsed into genocide in its backyard. The best Europe could produce was the European Community Monitoring Mission (ECCM). A bunch of observers with no power or influence and who dressed in white uniforms. On the battlefield, white was the symbol of surrender. To CRJ, it was entirely appropriate. Many people dressed in ice cream suits driving around in posh vehicles accomplishing nothing at great expense. The mission was nothing more than a symbol of surrender to the powers of re-emerging nationalism and the aging haters from World War Two. It was a crushing failure for the future of Europe.

* * *

CRJ had grown up in a family with roots in the minor aristocracy of the Austro-Hungarian Empire. The family had bloodlines running back to Alsace Lorraine and was comfortable working in the French and German languages. World War One had been a disaster for them as their lands and titles were lost. The saving grace had been CRJ's great-grandfather. As a minor diplomatic figure, he had seen the war coming as Russia, Serbia, France, Germany, and Britain had all maneuvered for a position after the assassination of the Archduke on the 28th of June 1914. His great-grandfather was a pragmatist who knew that it was not just the Austro-Hungarian Empire that was weak. The Russian Czar was inadequate, and many other leaders were operating under the delusion that the war with Serbia would be a sideshow, over by Christmas.

Thanks to his insights, his great-grandfather had liquidated their property holdings and turned them into gold, which he had discretely sent to Paris. His true brilliance, however, had been in procuring gold of a different sort. His diplomat great-grandfather had learned the location of the archives of the Austro-Hungarian Empire. As the Empire had collapsed in war, his great-grandfather had purloined vast quantities of documents, stealing handfuls of them with every visit.

These documents had proven to be worth more than the physical gold. CRJ's great-grandfather and grandfather used the stolen information to blackmail their way into successful businesses and government positions. The documents had also allowed them to assess what many surviving leaders would do after the war. Again, the insights had been invaluable.

Despite the problems, CRJ had grown up in relative affluence. From his family's history, he had learned the value of having information ahead of time. Blackmail and the promise of wealth were powerful motivators. As a result, his family had not only kept the original documents from the Austro-Hungarian archives, but they had also collected documents and information on everyone they met since then. It was amazing how much could be gained from knowing what the great and the not-so-great did in their private lives.

* * *

CRJ had a problem of his own in his private life. He had a penchant for women.

Brown women.

Powerless, brown women.

CRJ had almost lost his position as the Managing Director of the International Monetary Fund while attending meetings in New York City. The hotel maid he had raped had proven surprisingly strong. A night manager of the hotel had observed the maid as she was leaving at 10:00 PM. The bruises on her face suggested an attack. When the police had figured out who had attacked her, CRJ had been on an airplane headed back to Paris. The US State Department had made representations to the New York City Police Department. They suggested that they should not pursue the case against an influential international figure when the rape complainant was not in the USA legally.

When CRJ met next with Prime Minister Trudeau of Canada, the Canadian leader was sympathetic. But, as he had put it, some women "might have experienced these interactions differently."[14]

* * *

CRJ's planning for the Great Reset was well underway. His plans were ready to take advantage of the moment.

The Great Reset would mutate and become the revolutionary moment Europe needed to leap to greatness.

A victory for the faithful.

A victory for CRJ and the history of his family.

A victory for political violence and success for a clear-minded strategy.

[14] Tyler Dawson, "A Short History of Justin Trudeau's Scandal-Plagued Liberal Government," nationalpost.com (National Post, October 21, 2020), https://nationalpost.com/news/politics/a-short-history-of-justin-trudeaus-scandal-plagued-liberal-government.

Chapter 8: A Meeting With Neptune

LOCATION: Onboard the MS Nordsee Bliss, Bay of Biscay

DATE: 28 July

TIME: 03:15 AM

"Captain!" This from the officer of the deck. "I ordered a crew member to be placed in the Star Observer Pod and had it run-up to full height. He reports flickering orange light ahead."

Captain Jager inwardly recoiled. If the fire was visible from the observation pod at this distance, the fire must be severe. The Captain had thought the Star Observer Pod was a ridiculous piece of equipment for a ship at sea. Passengers bought tickets to sit in a glass-enclosed pod hydraulically hoisted until it was 92 meters above sea level. But now, he silently blessed it. This one bit of information confirmed something he wanted to know. The MS Fulfillment of the Seas was in trouble.

"Good work." Captain Jager looked at one of the rarer aspects of his world – a woman who was the Officer of the Deck for the Nordsee Bliss. When Jager had been offered command of the Nordsee Bliss, he had investigated the backgrounds of all the ship's leading crew members. Wendy Wallace's education and experience appeared solid. A few well-placed phone calls produced no negative information. But now, Staff Captain Wendy Wallace had just gone up one whole notch in his estimation. Her initiative to use the tourist trap as an observation asset had just provided him with a critical piece of information he could act on.

Inwardly, Captain Meyer was concerned. The Nordsee Bliss was a great vessel with the best of equipment and technology. But it was not a warship, and it did not have a warship's crew. If he had been headed towards the MS Fulfillment of the Seas in command of his warship, he would be full of confidence.

His last command in the German Navy had been the lead ship of the Sachsen class. The air defense frigate weighed 5,700 tons and was capable of 29+ knots. It had a turning radius of 570 meters and could maneuver so violently that the crew had to hang on. The ship's twin five-bladed propellers were of variable pitch and could take the vessel from full power ahead to reverse by simply sliding two command levers. The Nordsee Bliss, however, had all the handling characteristics of an overweight water buffalo. Planning to go alongside the MS Fulfillment of the Seas would be tricky. Everything to do with a 168,000-ton ship had to be planned well in advance. There would be one chance to get it right.

Formerly *Kapitän zur See* Meyer had joined the Bundesmarine just before it became the Deutsche Marine. After years at sea, he was now Captain Meyer of a cruise ship. The crew had many strong points, but they were not all blue water sailors. On top of that, he had on this trip some 2500 passengers. The cruise industry had not fully recovered from the pandemic, so the ship was not at its 4000-passenger full load. Most of the passengers would not be an asset in a time of crisis. Instead, they would be a problem. Still, given 2500 of them, valuable skills must exist among them.

He had 1500 crew, but most of them were hotel staff with limited training in emergency procedures. Onboard his warship, he knew every crew member was trained in multiple roles and had the attitude that any new task that came their way was to be met head-on. His cruise ship crew included 20 actors. How, the Captain wondered, does one best employ a stage actor when fighting fires at sea?

With all of that considered, it was now time to act. His ship would be the first arriving on scene, and he was senior in service to the Captain of the MS Fulfillment. Captain Meyer would establish himself as the on-scene commander. After that, the priorities would be firefighting and the possible evacuation of the passengers of the MS Fulfillment – itself a staggering thought.

Captain Meyer turned to his steward, Andre. "Be quiet about it, but I need all three department heads and the senior personnel from both the hotel and ships staff on the bridge now. No announcements."

Five minutes later, they were gathered on the port side of the bridge. Some were in varying degrees of dress after having received urgent calls in their cabins.

Captain Meyer moved towards them, and they fell silent.

"My beloved crew. As you probably already know, the MS Fulfillment has a serious onboard fire. We will be the first major ship on scene, and we will be going alongside to render assistance. The situation is fluid, but we will likely be providing firefighting assistance, and we may be receiving passengers who are injured or suffering from smoke inhalation. In the worst-case scenario, we may have to evacuate the passengers and crew of the MS Fulfillment. The total amount would be some 6,500 people."

He paused while his ship's officers considered the enormity of the situation.

"Officer of the Deck. We will be going alongside - port side. Have your hands ready to secure cables. Also, prepare to run gangplanks across multiple decks. Keep two of them for crew only on the lowest deck possible. Be prepared to launch boats from our starboard side. We may also need the life rafts and boats in the water if this gets worse. Have your deck hands ready to run out fire hoses immediately as we come alongside. Additionally, we may have to run both fresh and saltwater lines across. They may need electrical power as well."

"Engines." This is to the Chief Engineering Officer, whom the Captain always addressed as "Engines" in formal and informal settings. Captain Meyer knew that everything on the ship ran on some form of power or another. All power came from the engines. Meyer had trusted only a few persons in his time at sea, but the current engineer was one of them. "Stand by for multiple demands. We will need water pressure for firefighting, and electrical power may be required for the Fulfillment. We may need to improvise rapidly, so get as much of your gear strung out and ready to go. Our approach alongside may require maximum power in reverse. All four bow thrusters may be required as we run alongside and as we try to remain in close contact with the Fulfillment."

"Hotel Director. All table service dining is canceled. At your discretion, arrange to have the passengers fed in cafeterias and take out only—cabin service for the sick or infirm. We will need at least two of the main dining rooms cleared for the possible reception of the injured. Inform your waiters, stewards, and bartenders to consider the ship at emergency stations, and they will man their posts accordingly."

"Ship's Doctor. We may be receiving injured passengers and crew from the Fulfillment. Arrange for triage as they come aboard. Speak with the Hotel Director and pressgang[15] any staff you need for stretcher-bearers. The Hotel Director should also know who among the passengers might be doctors, or God willing, ER nurses or emergency medical

---

[15] Unknown Editors, "Impressment," Wikipedia (Wikimedia Foundation, May 12, 2021), https://en.wikipedia.org/wiki/Impressment.

technicians. I will arrange an announcement shortly as to where trained volunteers should report.

"Dismissed." The officers gave no verbal responses as they left. None were needed.

"Communications." This from the Captain to his junior communicator. "Get a signal out to that collective gaggle of shore-based bureaucrats that try to run this cruise line company. Tell them the ship will be going to emergency stations as we go alongside the MS Fulfillment. We will be the on-scene command vessel until such time we are properly relieved by competent authorities or until I decide otherwise. Contact the Spanish and French coastguards with a SITREP as fast as possible. Inform them that I assess that the MS Fulfillment is in serious distress."

A nod of the head was the response, just the way the Captain liked it.

"Officer of the Watch - report."

"Captain, we have the course laid out for going alongside the Fulfillment. Expect to be alongside in thirty-four minutes."

The Captain paused to consider an option. On the one hand, he, as Captain, could take control and give orders to the helm for the upcoming maneuvers. On the other hand, the Officer of the Watch was trained to be competent, and this was when the Captain could demonstrate that he trusted his crew. Was this also not the perfect moment to test the Officer of the Watch to see if he was cut out for future command?

So be it. The Officer of the Watch would give the orders to the helm.

"Very good, Mr. Larsen - make it so."

Once again, electricity ran through the crew on the bridge. At this most critical moment, the Captain would depend directly on the crew to do their jobs.

* * *

The approach to the MS Fulfillment occurred without incident. The MS Nordsee Bliss engines went to full power on the final approach, causing the entire vessel to vibrate as the Azipods churned the waters to slow the giant vessel.

The emergency alarms on the Nordsee Bliss sounded. Most of the passengers had already gathered on the vessel's port side, fascinated by the clouds of smoke still emanating from the Fulfillment. Even with the passengers aware of the urgent nature of the situation, the jarring audio blast caused them to jump. As the two ships brushed against each other, the faces of many of the passengers turned to alarm. This was no longer an exciting distraction from an otherwise routine transit. The rescue was a real-life emergency at sea.

However tenuously, the two vessels were secured together tenuously, and lines were run across to the stricken ship. The Azipods and bow thrusters of the Nordsee Bliss kept a slight pressure, allowing the two vessels to stay in constant contact.

Fire teams moved quickly across the gangplanks to the Fulfillment. At the same time, passengers and crew from the Fulfillment who were suffering from smoke inhalation began their evacuation to the Nordsee Bliss.

Captain Meyer watched from the port side of his bridge. His crew was functioning as planned. As tempted as he was to involve himself directly, his officers were managing everything that was required.

"Communications." This to the junior communicator on the bridge. "Contact Captain Martindale on the Fulfillment. Inform him I am requesting permission to board his vessel. I will meet him on his bridge so as not to distract him from his operations."

Captain Meyer looked at the Officer of the Deck as he left the bridge. "You are in command until I return. Contact me by radio if any changes occur." He did not wait for a response.

* * *

Upon ascending to the bridge of the Fulfillment, Captain Meyer stood silently to observe the activity. Captain Martindale was on the port side of the bridge, looking aft towards the fire scene. The few crew members on the bridge appeared active. Chatter was kept to a minimum. Meyer saw this as a good sign. The ship may have been in distress, but discipline was holding, and order was being maintained.

The helmsman on the Fulfillment noticed Captain Jager and called out to alert Captain Martindale.

"Captain Jager. Please join me. I was just heading towards the scene of the fire."

The two Captains left the bridge and headed down the stairwell.

Captain Warren Martindale looked pale. "My crew had mostly stopped the spread of the fire when you arrived. With help from your crew, we should have it contained in less than 15 minutes. We have fire damage to the hull both at and below the waterline. The watertight bulkheads have been closed where prudent, and we are at present in no danger of losing the ship. At least, I do not think so...." The last line was left hanging.

"What has you worried?"

"There are a few things that do not add up. My engineers tell me the fire seems to have started in two places at once. One of the fires started in a machinery compartment just below the waterline. The other fire started in a flammable storage compartment directly above the first. Both the heat and smoke detectors failed to alert. When the fires were discovered, the first two fire teams found that the nozzles on the fire hoses were sealed shut with some sort of epoxy or glue. The crew had inspected them less than six weeks ago. The fire was no accident – it was sabotage. I now have other crew members searching every compartment at or below the waterline. A second fire or explosion could take us to a meeting with Neptune."

"Any indications of trouble in your crew?"

"Nothing to suggest this sort of response. But there are other things."

"What else concerns you?"

"One of the first fire teams that responded to the fire below the waterline told my security officer that they saw a large red 'A' surrounded by a circle. It was not there last night, according to the crew. As the crew members described it, it sounded like an anarchist symbol. Not only that, but the crew also said they had seen a couple of passengers wandering around in crew-only areas. The passengers said they were lost, and the crew showed them back to the passenger area. Nothing unusual. We get a few who are lost and a few who are just looking around. The crew did not mention it at the time as it did not seem that unusual."

"Can they identify them?"

"We asked. The crew said the stray passengers looked like white male persons in their early thirties. Nothing specific. I am not holding out hope to find two white passengers among a few thousand passengers with nothing else to go on."

"Can we see the painted symbol?"

"No. My security officer tells me the fire destroyed evidence as it progressed. But we can go to see where it was when we get aft."

Captain Meyer remained silent when they got to the scene of the first fire. Captain Martindale spoke to a few of the crew, one of whom was the senior engineer. After that, they went up one deck to the scene of the other fire. Captain Meyer recognized a few of his crew members and nodded to them. It was his most junior engineer who had just joined the ship. He approached and indicated the Captain should move off to the side to talk to him.

"Captain Mayer," said the engineer. "Something is wrong here. The Fulfillment crew seem to have approached the fires correctly once they overcame the initial setbacks with the failed equipment. But they believe the fires spread too far and too fast. The Fulfillment crew is not happy. They think their ship was attacked, and the intent may have been to sink it. If the fire on the deck below had burned any longer, the ship may have lost its hull integrity. Given the watertight integrity doors, it is unlikely the ship would have been lost, but it would have been serious."

"Very good. Carry on and help however you can. Keep your views to yourself, and then report back to me when you get back on board. Carry on."

Captain Martindale approached and signaled. It was time to move back to the bridge.

Martindale looked at Meyer. "Your crew member also told you the fire was deliberate?"

"He did."

"My engineer tells me our propulsion systems are intact, and full power is available. But they believe that the hull has been fire damaged below the waterline. We still have watertight integrity, but we do not want to put stress on the hull. The seas are calm, and the forecast is good. We will set a course for the port of Santander, but we must keep the speed low to reduce stress on the hull. I was hoping you could take all the injured passengers and crew ashore as quickly as possible. Unfortunately, your own schedule would be disrupted. Can you request permission from your company for the diversion?"

Meyer nodded his head. "Consider it done. I will inform our headquarters that we will be taking on board your injured passengers and crew and moving them to shore. They were not happy to hear we were on scene, and they will be more upset about our little side trip. We will do the right thing and worry about the consequences later. Your ship has suffered an attack, and we will offer all possible assistance. If the shore-bound bureaucrats are not happy, they can fire me."

"Excellent. I was told you were a traditional naval officer of the old school."

Chapter 9: Taking the Sting Out of a Skorpion

LOCATION: Boeing 777 - East of Iceland

DATE: 28 July

TIME: 4:00 AM

Captain Davies waited until the hijacker with the Skorpion machine pistol walked back into the economy section. The gunman randomly waved his weapon in the air with his right hand, consistently above his shoulder. He seemed to yell at no one in particular. He kept the same pace for each of his forays into the economy class cabin. He turned around at the same point and turned on his right heel each time.

He then briefed Skiffington and Crosby. "Right then. We wait until he comes back, and we let him pass. He appears to be a creature of habit, so he will walk back about four or six rows behind us, yell some more and then turn to his right and head forward again. When he is one row behind us, I will lean out and hit him in the crotch as hard as I can. Skiffington, you have the toughest bit. Jump up and over me and get that weapon. He should have it over his shoulder as I hit him, but it will come down quick. You twist it out of his hand and pass it to me. I will be running forward, so it may be a bit of a long pass. Crosby, you wait until Skiffington jumps, and then you are right behind him.

You are to hold off the terrorist at whatever cost. He must remain down because Skiffington needs a clear throw to me. Got it?"

Both men sat motionless without responding, taking in the plan and making their calculations. They had trained for a hundred different situations, but never one quite like this.

Almost on schedule, Hossein headed back down the aisle. He waved the wicked-looking Skorpion in the air while yelling at random passengers. Then, Hossein stopped, pivoted to his right, and headed forward. Captain Davies turned his head slightly so his peripheral vision would get the man with the gun in his sight as he was about a row and a half back. Perfect.

Hossein began to yell and wave his weapon just as Captain Davies turned in his seat, lowered his right arm, and drove his fist upwards into the gunman's testicles. As he felt the impact, a shadow was created, indicating that Skiffington was in the air over the top of him. Without looking back, Davies sprinted up the aisle towards Ali, who was somewhat startled to see Hossein on the deck and some unarmed fool rushing towards him. Ali raised his knife, ready to slash the approaching passenger. Skiffington, having rotated the Skorpion more than three-quarters of a turn to the left, pulled it free as he heard cracking bones. He turned forward, ducking as Crosby flew by him and collided with the gunman. He yelled "Gun," causing the Captain to look back, and he threw the weapon forward with an overhand pass. Davies caught the

Skorpion with a two-handed catch, rotated the barrel forward while thumbing the safety one position with his right thumb. As the barrel came up, he fired one shot that hit Ali inside his right-side hip bone. As the weapon came up a bit more, the second round fired hit Ali to the right of his breastbone, shattering the fourth rib before it passed through his heart.

Double-tap and assess.

The Captain watched Ali as he imitated a bag of rocks.

Major Berikoff had heard Skiffington yell "Gun" and surmised they were making a move on the two hijackers behind him. He stood up, walked back to the galley, and picked up a coffee pot. The smell of burning coffee told him a pot had been left on a burner in the chaotic attack. It would be rather hot. As he heard the first shot, he walked in a controlled manner towards the cockpit door rather than running. He pushed it in quickly with his left foot as the bomb had destroyed the latch. Qassem had heard the shot and had begun screaming something in Farsi just as the door opened. Major Berikoff tipped the pot over and poured its contents onto the face of Qassem, who could do little while tied in the pilot's seat. Having emptied most of the coffee, Berikoff pulled the pot back and then swung it down as hard as he could on Qassem's head. The terrorist quit yelling and slumped forward. Berikoff grabbed him by the hair and pulled him back.

Captain Davies had sprinted over the body of Ali while yelling back at Skiffington. He ran to the cockpit and saw the Major looking at the now unconscious hijacker pilot.

"Hello, Andrew. I seem to have made a bit of mess here."

For the first time in his career, Captain Andrew Davies was shocked into silence. The Major was not referring to the blood spray patterns, the dripping coffee, or even the terrorist slumped in the seat. Instead, he had a white handkerchief out and was trying to dab some coffee stains on the sleeve of his jacket.

"Blast it all. I picked this jacket up last time I was out in Singapore, about a fortnight back. This trip is the first time I have worn it. Bloody terrorists."

Davies was gobsmacked. They had just killed one terrorist, captured another alive, and a third was *hors de combat.* Perhaps just a small point, but they had just taken over the flight deck of a Boeing 777 in the middle of the Atlantic Ocean, and none of them had a clue on how to fly a Piper Cub, let alone a massive airliner. And no plan existed beyond retaking control of the 777.

Now the Major was fussing over coffee stains on his jacket.

"Horrifying situation, Andrew, but nothing can be done now." The Major tucked his handkerchief back into his inner breast pocket. "Give us a hand, would you? Methinks we should drag this fellow out of here and tie him up, lest he awakens and becomes difficult again."

With over 330 years of Royal Welsh tradition behind him and the rigid discipline of the SAS resting on his shoulders, Captain Davies turned his eyes from the terrorist to the Major and simply stated: "Yes Sir."

Trooper Skiffington had not been idle. Following the overhand pass, he had continued forward behind the Captain. Upon arriving at Ali, he quickly checked his carotid artery pulse. Nothing. He turned back and saw Sergeant Crosby had flipped the gunman face down and had his arms pinned behind him. Somewhat surprisingly, a flight attendant was walking forward from the rear galley with a few oversized plastic wire ties in her hand. She and Skiffington arrived at Crosby's position at the same time. She politely asked if they would like to use the wire ties in her hand. Crosby nodded to Skiffington to grab them. Skiffington took one and began to tie the terrorist's feet together. The flight attendant reached in and quickly used another to secure the wrists of the gunman. With that, Crosby flipped the terrorist onto his back. He then stood up and told Skiffington to take the terrorist to the back of the plane and secure him. "Keep an eye out as well, Skiffers. We might still have a fourth hijacker, although he should have shown his hand when we whacked his friend here."

He then nodded to the flight attendant and suggested that they move forward and find out what was going on up at the pointy end of the 777.

Before either soldier could say anything, the flight attendant placed her heel on the chest of the now face up but still prone terrorist. She forced her weight down on him hard, just over his heart. Next, she twisted her left heel while stepping forward. Hossein howled as she then stomped on his right shin and carried on ahead.

Skiffington allowed himself a few seconds to take his mind off the mission, and he had two thoughts. First, that was a real woman. Second, he may have just met the future Mrs. Skiffington.

Sergeant Crosby arrived in the first-class section and nodded to the Captain and the Major in a close huddle with the Cabin Director and the remaining first-class cabin attendants.

The Major motioned him to step forward and join their impromptu meeting. "Good show, Sergeant, but we were just discussing a couple of problems. We have no one who knows how to operate this magnificent flying tin can. Both pilots are dead, and our hijacker is indisposed. Our Cabin Director tells us that no spare pilots were deadheading. Most passengers in the first class and business cabins must know the pilots are dead, but I am not too sure that the folks in economy fully understand the whole situation."

With that, the Major turned to Cabin Director Kim Bornhym. "Could I ask you to get on the Tannoy and tell folks we have had a bit of an upset? Tell them all is now well. And then ask if anyone would like to volunteer to help fly the plane. And oh yes, I am authorizing your crew to distribute free drinks for all. A few of them look like a shot of gin might do them good. First two rounds free, then no more."

Sergeant Crosby turned to look at the two men who had just entered the business class area and headed forward. "Oi! Who are you two?" All heads turned to see two men in their early twenties with short hair heading towards them. They had a military look about them.

The first man held up his hands. "Your man Skiffington says you might want our help."

"Please tell me you are pilots."

"Well, sort of….". This from the first one.

The Major looked momentarily frustrated with the answer and responded, "Well, you are bloody pilots, or you are not. Which is it?

The second one, rather fair-faced and speaking in his best junior officer tone, looked at the Major and said, "We are mostly 'rotor heads.' Not sure we are the best fit for the current job, although my colleague here did one tour flying Hercules transport aircraft."

"But you are now helicopter pilots?" This from Sergeant Crosby.

"Afraid so." This from the fair-faced pilot. "Better still, zoomies. We normally fly helicopters off frigates and destroyers."

"Well," said the Major. "I am not sure I see any problems. If one of you has flown a C-130 Hercules, then flying this magnificent tin can should not be that hard."

"Canadians?" This from Sergeant Crosby.

The first one smiled slightly and nodded towards the Major. "Captain David Bampton and Lieutenant Al Goldsmith at your service."

"Great to have you. We were visiting your vast land and had some entertaining moments with a few of your Joint Task Force fellows."

"You are snake-eaters?" asked the fair-faced lieutenant again.

The Major suddenly looked quite wounded. "Snake-eaters, dear boy? Nonsense. We are Her Majesty's Special Air Service."

Sergeant Crosby and Captain Davies smiled broadly at the inferred compliment from the Canadian pilots but thought it best to remain silent.

"Cabin Director Kim Bornhym, please cancel the announcement about needing a pilot. But carry on with the drinks." With that, the Major turned. "Crosby. Go aft and see Skiffington. Make sure our terrorist is well secured and leave him with two of the cabin attendants. Tell them to sing out if the terrorist even tries to move. Then you and Skiffington get everything off the three terrorists. Also, check their seats and their hand luggage. Phones. Electronics. Passports. Keys. Money. Wallets. Pocket litter. Check their belts for concealed weapons or information. Check the seams of their clothes for anything sewn into them. Make an inventory of it all and get it to me fast. Tell me what I need to know about them. Then, Davies, go forward with our two Canadians, get into the cockpit, and see what, if anything, the terrorist had with him in the cockpit. Notes. Maps. Anything. It would help to know where they were going. I noticed no course change after they took over. We must still be on autopilot."

Both moved without comment.

The Major then turned to the Cabin Director. "Sorry about taking over like that. Not our airplane, but old habits die hard. Can you remain in charge of the cabin while these lads drive the bus, and we assess what the bad guys were trying to do?"

Kim Bornhym forced a smile. "Not exactly by the book, but yes. The cabin crew will get a few drinks out as you suggested and try to make it look like all is normal. I have the passenger manifest on my tablet. We have two cabin crew deadheading, so I will put them to work. I had checked the manifest before taking off—no known civilian airline pilots. We have the usual collection of rather wealthy passengers in first class and a couple of well-known frequent flyers executive types in business class who think highly of themselves. But no one famous or political. So the hijacking does not seem to be aimed at a VIP, at least not one on board."

The Major's internal optimism meter just went up one more notch. Atlantic Airways did not hire its Cabin Directors off park benches. This one seemed squared away, and she could think on her feet when things were going off course: an asset and one less reason to worry. The cabin and passengers, at least, were in good hands. Now for the airplane.

Captain Bampton and Lieutenant Goldsmith had headed directly for the cockpit.

Once seated, Bampton turned to Goldsmith. "If we can land a Cyclone on a heaving ship's deck in the dark with 40 knots of wind in a sea state five, we must be able to land this thing in broad daylight on a massive flat runway that sits still. Put your headset on. You start with comms and start talking to folks. Squawk 7500 for a hijacking on the transponder. That should get us some attention. Get a 'Pan'[16] out fast and see who answers. I will try to assess if the flight systems are working and then figure out the autopilot. No blinking red lights that I can see, and temperatures and pressures are all in the green. Hull integrity has not been compromised. So that is good news."

Lieutenant Goldsmith turned his eyes from his crew commander and located the transponder. He and Dave Bampton had flown together for two years now. They were often called the 'odd couple' by other

---

[16] Unknown Editors, "Pan-Pan," Wikipedia (Wikimedia Foundation, June 8, 2021),
https://en.wikipedia.org/wiki/Pan-pan.

aircrews. Bampton's personal call sign was 'Bam-Bam.' Goldsmith had never personally seen it, but Bampton was known to launch unsecured objects at human targets who displeased him. Especially other pilots. He had once punched a co-pilot in the head while he was still in the helicopter. The miscreant co-pilot had refused a wave-off from a ship's Landing Safety Officer. As a result, the co-pilot had endangered both the helicopter and the ship. His aircrew helmet had protected him from the worst of the damage, but the point had been made.

Bampton had also amused other aircrew by saying, "I may not be too bright, but I have golden hands." Bampton was old-school and believed that seat of the pants flying was more important than all the fancy electronics. On the other hand, Goldsmith was five years his junior and had grown up with computer flight simulators. He was a tech geek. They worked well together, with each one smart enough to know that the other had some skills that could be useful when things went wrong.

Goldsmith punched the code 7500 into the transponder and spoke calmly into the intercom. "Hijack code 7500 set on the transponder. Sending 'Pan' now."

Goldsmith dialed in 121.5 MHz on the radio and took a breath. In all his years of training and flying, this would be his first distress call. It would be memorable.

"Pan. Pan. Pan. Any station. Any station. This is Atlantic Airways flight 406 en route to Frankfurt from Toronto. We are reporting a hijacking attempt. Pilot and co-pilot killed. Aircraft now under the command of Royal Canadian Air Force[17] pilot Captain David Bampton. Flight 406 requires immediate guidance towards the nearest military airfield, preferably with advanced emergency response and security capabilities. Over."

Goldsmith looked over at Bampton. "I think that will rattle a few teacups. Any bets on how long before we get bounced by fighters from Kef or Lossie? I hope they do not get too excited and shoot us down. I gave them your name in the Pan call. Maybe that will give them something to look up and confirm the good guys are in control."

Their headsets sprang to life with an incoming call. "Atlantic Airways 406, this is Shanwick Oceanic Control. Confirm your last transmission. Are you being hijacked? Over."

"Shanwick Oceanic, this is Atlantic Airways 406. We confirm the hijacking attempt. Three hijackers affected explosive entry into the cockpit and killed both pilots. Passengers onboard retook control of aircraft under the command of Captain David Bampton and Lieutenant Allan Goldsmith, Royal

---

[17] The Royal Canadian Navy no longer has its own fleet air arm. The pilots who fly helicopters from Royal Canadian Navy warships are members of and trained by the Royal Canadian Air Force.

Canadian Air Force. The aircraft hull is maintaining integrity, and we assess no damage to flight systems at this point. You are to provide us with immediate assistance and directional headings for the nearest capable airfield. Over."

"Atlantic Airways Flight 406, this is Shanwick. Wait. Out."

Goldsmith looked stunned. "What does he mean wait, out? What is that? We are in it up to our eyebrows, and he says, wait?"

Bampton smiled. "Think about it for a second. You just told Shanwick that three terrorists blew the cockpit door off and killed the pilots. Then you told him some passengers killed the terrorists. All they know for sure is that a 777 transponder is squawking a hijacking code, and some guy they have never heard of is now in control of an airplane that would make a fine missile. They do not believe what they are hearing. I have a hard time believing it myself, and I am sitting here. They are nearing panic, and many folks are being kicked out of bed as we speak. I would love to hear his phone call to his supervisor."

"Atlantic Flight 406. This is Shanwick Oceanic over." This was a different voice.

"Shanwick, this is Flight 406. Over."

"Flight 406, please identify yourself and confirm your rank, squadron, and service number."

"Shanwick, this is Lieutenant Allan Goldsmith, pilot, 423 Squadron, Maritime Air Group Atlantic. Service number VVG 857 548. Over."

"Flight 406, this is Shanwick. Wait. Out."

Goldsmith took the intervening time to start familiarizing himself with the airplane controls and communications systems. Having been an avid flight simulator fan since he was five years old, he was familiar with the layout of the flight deck of most modern airliners.

While the two pilots remained silent, other folks were communicating rapidly. Two ready-alert USAF-15 Eagles from the 493rd Expeditionary Fighter Squadron rolled onto the runway at Keflavik Air Base in Iceland. Flash message traffic had gone out to NATO as well as NORAD. Calls were being placed to the Canadian National Defence Headquarters to confirm the names of the two Canadian pilots. Atlantic Airways was asked to verify if the pilots had been passengers on board. The Royal Air Force was alerted and told to standby for a possible intercept and shoot down of an airliner flown by unknown persons.

Just then, Major Berikoff knocked on the door while walking into the cockpit. "Gentlemen, status report." Bampton nodded at Goldsmith. Goldsmith looked back and began, trying to remember he was addressing a superior officer of a foreign power who also seemed to be a snake-eater. "Sir. Hull integrity appears good. Flight systems intact, and all temperatures and pressures appear normal. We have informed Shanwick Oceanic of our situation, and they want to confirm our identities. Frankly, Shanwick does not seem to believe our story yet, or at least they have grave doubts. We should expect to see fighters coming alongside us before long. The fighter jocks will be plenty suspicious when they get here."

"Well, I can see why they have doubts. Many folks would love to have a civilian airliner as a missile or for use as a hostage negotiation tool. They are right to be cautious. When they call back, tell them to contact Air Vice Marshall Watkins of the Royal Air Force and tell him that Roy says he is crap at cricket. He should stick to playing rounders. That will tell them everything they need to know, and it will explain to them who is in control of the situation."

"Do you know the Air Vice Marshall, Sir?'

"Rather well. He is my wife's second cousin or something. Good fellow, but he fancies himself as a cricket player, which is a load of tosh."

The Major left the cockpit. Goldsmith looked at Bampton. "What is rounders?"

"It is the British word for baseball, which they think is a girl's game. Send the message to the AVM."

"Shanwick Oceanic, this is Flight 406. Request you relay message traffic to Royal Air Force. Over."

"406, this is Shanwick, ready to relay message over."

Goldsmith thought about it for a second. If a Lieutenant was going to send a message to an Air Vice Marshall calling him crap, maybe it should be in the proper military format and done with a certain flair. Besides, if the Air Vice Marshall could confirm the identity of the Major, their situation might improve rapidly.

"Shanwick, this is 406. Stand by to copy. Message Precedence Flash Zulu. From Atlantic Airways Flight 406 to Air Vice Marshall Watkins, Royal Air Force. Please inform AVM Watkins that he is crap at cricket, and Roy suggests he play rounders. Message ends. Read back for correction. Over."

The airwaves went silent. Shanwick was having a bit of a time trying to understand the message.

"406, this is Shanwick. I read back for correction. Message Precedence Flash Zulu. From Atlantic Airways flight 406 to Air Vice Marshall Watkins, Royal Air Force. Please inform AVM Watkins that he is crap at cricket, and Roy suggests he play rounders. Do you confirm correct? Over."

"Shanwick, this is 406. Read back correct. Out."

Goldsmith inwardly smiled for a second. A Flash message was for operational combat messages of extreme urgency and would override all other message traffic. He was unsure how Shanwick would handle it, but he knew exactly how the Royal Air Force would handle it.

The AVM would get the message in a hurry, as would some of his staff. The use of the flash message he had just sent was probably justifiable, given that a terrorist hijacking had just been thwarted by snake-eaters in mid-flight over the Atlantic in an airliner. The situation seemed to fit the definition of initial enemy contact. It was also the most fun a junior officer could have on a radio without going to jail.

Further back in the airplane, Trooper Skiffington approached the Major and extended his right hand. In his palm were four tiny bits of plastic. All four were the same size, shape, and color. "I had a bit of a hunch and checked that void space that Captain Davies noted in the head. I pulled the panel out completely and found these four bits of plastic. Unless I miss my guess, these bits are used in new mobiles. They are to block the top of the battery from the contact points in the mobile so the battery does not discharge. You take them out before using the phone. I checked with the mobile from the dead terrorist, and its fits exactly. But here is the kicker. We have four bits of plastic and only three terrorists with one phone each. We are missing a mobile. Either four of them are involved, or they had a spare. But here is the real problem. The void space was large enough to hold the four mobiles, the gun, the knives, and the bomb. No sign of the panel having been removed before. Crosby and I think the weapons and mobiles were built into the airplane at the factory. Hard to say, but you have to wonder if other airplanes have their built-in hijacking kits."

"Follow me." The Major headed forward towards the Cabin Director. "Sorry to bother you again, but might I borrow one of your staff? Preferably one who is steady and diplomatic at the same time. We need to examine the mobiles of all the passengers as we think something might be amiss. Skiffington here will go along with your staff member to encourage passenger compliance if necessary."

The Cabin Director thought for a second. "Take Lucille. She is as steady as they come and has taken on a few rough passengers in the past." Skiffington was all smiles. Lucille was the same attendant who had driven her heel into the terrorist's chest as she walked over him.

The Major whispered to Skiffington. "You are right about the weapons. I will get the word out and see if we can get all other new 777s inspected. Not good if they lose one, given we now know how they did it."

Skiffington headed to the rear of the aircraft, assessing that if a fourth terrorist existed, he (or she) was likely seated in the economy cabin. Meanwhile, the Major headed forward to see the Captain.

Captain Davies signaled the Major. "You asked if the hijacker pilot had any information on him. I gave his passport and other personal stuff to Crosby, but he did have some papers in his jacket's inner pocket. I believe it was written in Farsi, so I cannot read it. But it did have the words 'Bonames Airfield' in English. Not sure what that means, but given the circumstance, it had to be their destination. I never heard of the place. Do you know where it is?

"No idea. Germany, France, or Austria, I suppose, but would it have a large enough airfield to handle this plane? No matter. Follow me. We are off to get our pilots to do some radio work for us. You were right about the weapons in the head. Crosby found four plastic inserts. He seems to think we have four mobiles on board that belong to the terrorists, not three."

The Major knocked on the cockpit as he entered. "Gentlemen, I need you to pass on a message for me to the United Kingdom Civil Aviation Authority. Can that be done?"

"No problem. Anyone in particular?"

"No clue. Just tell the civil authority that the bomb, the gun, the knives, and four mobiles used to hijack Flight 406 were most probably built into the aircraft at the point of manufacture. Request that they inspect all other 777s delivered in the past several months. Weapons were in the economy class cabin washroom, furthest forward, port side."

Goldsmith's jaw dropped slightly on hearing this but said nothing.

"Shanwick Oceanic, this is Atlantic Airways Flight 406. Over."

"406, this is Shanwick Oceanic, over."

"Shanwick, 406 is requesting you send a message to the UK Civil Aviation Authority. From Atlantic Airways Flight 406 to CAA. The bomb, knives, and four mobile phones used to hijack flight 406 were built into aircraft at the point of manufacture. Location is the economy class washroom, port side, furthest forward.

Request you inspect all other 777s recently built at the same facility. Over."

"406, this is Shanwick. Confirm that message will be forwarded to CAA as requested. Additionally, please pass a message to person Roy from Air Vice Marshall. Message understood. Additionally, pilot identities are confirmed. We are currently assessing the situation and will recommend a potential landing field. Request you maintain current heading and altitude. Over."

Goldsmith turned to the Major. "Message passed. The Air Vice Marshall passes his regards, and apparently, we are back on the list of good guys. We owe the AVM a drink, I guess."

"Gentlemen, one more quick question for you. Ever heard of Bonames Airfield?"

Bampton and Goldsmith looked at each other. Both shrugged.

"Do you think your magic computers would be able to find it?

With that, the Major headed out the door.

He could see Crosby heading up the aisle with a passenger in tow. The passenger was a South Asian male. Maybe 50 years old. Impeccably dressed. Hair. Glasses. Watch expensive but not extravagant. Leather shoes. He looked too intelligent to be a politician. Maybe a finance person or engineer?

When they met, Sergeant Crosby took the initiative. "Major Berikoff, may I introduce Judge Kapoor of the Canadian Federal Court. The judge appears to be a remarkably well-informed individual, and he would like to discuss his observations on terrorism with you." Crosby turned and headed aft.

Taking his cue from Crosby, the Major had continued his assessment of this passenger while Crosby was doing the introductions. The eyes stood out. Cold. Gray. Emotionless. These were the eyes of someone who had already seen too much.

"Judge Kapoor. Why don't we step into my office while we have a discussion?"

Once they were in the galley, the Major turned to the Judge. "My man Crosby feels you have some insights into terrorism that might be relevant. Do you mind if I ask how you come to have such knowledge on terrorism?"

"My mother died on Air India Flight 182. The Kanishka Disaster.[18] I now hear terrorist cases in the Canadian Federal Court, particularly those related to national security certificates and deportations."

Major Berikoff felt like he had been gut-punched by an unarmed combat instructor. Air India Flight 182 had been blown out of the sky by a terrorist bomb while approaching Ireland, not that far from where they were now. The briefing they had received at the SAS had said that most passengers survived the explosion but died from drowning when they hit the

---

[18] One person whose mother died on the ill-fated Air India flight 182 went on to be a lawyer and a judge. He now works in an advisory position with the Royal Canadian Mounted Police on terrorism matters.

water. They had survived the drop of 31,00 feet only to drown. How had this man felt when he heard the explosion? Did he think he would die the same death as his mother? How was it that he appeared so calm now? The Major awkwardly cleared his throat to help choke back the sudden unexpected emotion.

"My deepest condolences on the loss of your mother, Sir."

"Thank you, Major. Something struck me as a bit unusual here, beyond the obvious hijacking attempt and your fellows shooting a hijacker. From what I could see, there were three attackers. All Middle Eastern and possibly Iranian. They seemed tactically competent and disciplined. What struck me is not what they did but rather what they did not do. Have you ever read Sherlock Holmes's *The Adventures of Silver Blaze*?"

"It has been years. But, if I recall, the case is broken when Holmes wonders why the dog did not bark in the night when it should have, undoing the false story that had been earlier presented."

"Exactly. These dogs did not bark. Look at me. You can tell I am of Indian origin and most likely a Hindu, but the gunman did not even look at me. A few rows behind me was an older man wearing a kippah. He is Jewish. When I boarded, a woman was seated in the front row of the economy class whose dress style suggests she is Yazidi. A few passengers were wearing crucifixes around their necks, most of them women who self-identify as Christian. One woman in the economy class is wearing a hijab, but the hijackers showed no interest nor any sign of recognition. Consider this. The hijackers said nothing during the entire time they were in control. No 'Death to Israel' or 'Death to the infidels.' No 'Allahu Akbar.' Not even a 'Death to America.' If they thought they were doing Jihad and were seeking Jannah, they gave no sign of it. Major, I cannot tell you who they are or what they wanted, but I can tell you they are not jihadists. The hijacking is not about political Islam. It is about business, money, or some form of distraction for a greater event."

The Major stood silent for a few more seconds, considering what he had just heard. Their focus had been on what was happening in the aircraft. They had missed the obvious about what had not happened. The Judge was correct, and this new information needed to be shared as fast as possible.

The Major then guided the Judge out of the galley and headed him aft towards his seat. "Please do not share those insights. And by the way, Your Honour, if you ever decide to get out of the legal business, give me a call. I have a few intelligence contacts who would be most willing to give you a job which might be, umm, slightly less legalistic and with a greater focus on kinetics."

The Judge smiled for a brief second, turned, and headed back to his seat.

The Major watched the Judge walk back several rows. The Major recognized several types of personalities that expressed themselves in moments of extreme stress. This one was stone-cold hard. Then he sighed—another trip to the cockpit.

"Gentlemen. Status report. And what of this Bonames Airfield? Any idea of what it means."

This time it was Captain Bampton who responded. "Good news. Still no signs of damage. We have had the Cabin Director shut down all entertainment systems and food service to lessen the electrical load if damage exists that we have not detected. The autopilot has us on track to Frankfurt, but Shanwick Oceanic is arranging a new landing field, most likely in Scotland or England. Goldsmith here is quite good at pushing buttons, so we should have no problem in programming in a new destination. This aircraft will do everything except the final flare and landing, so we stand a fair chance of hitting a runway and not some trees. Inquiries on Bonames Airfield came up indecisive. It is close to Frankfurt and a former military airfield with one runway, but it has been closed for years, and the runway is listed as unusable even for emergencies. It is a bit of a dead-end so far, but German authorities are now investigating. We have two new contacts on the radio. Shanwick has us linked in with an experienced 777 pilot familiar with this model. The other is a Boeing engineer. Been good so far. Lots of help."

Major Berikoff was talking with the Cabin Director when he saw Sergeant Crosby signal him. Crosby retreated into the economy class galley, and the

Major followed him in. The flight attendant took the hint and headed aft to check on passengers.

Crosby handed him a piece of paper. "Here are the names and passport numbers of the three hijackers. All show Iran as their birthplace. All three have home addresses in the Toronto area of Canada. I have made a list of other documents, such as driver's licenses and Ontario health cards. Nothing of interest in their wallets beyond a few hundred Euros each. No photos or contacts. Nothing in the pocket litter. All three had the same cell phones, which we think had been hidden in the head. The phones have no calls or texts showing on them. Brand new, I would say. None of them had a personal phone which seems strange. Maybe they dumped them at the airport before boarding? Nothing in the clothes, which were midrange, off-the-rack-stuff. No other electronics at all. Their hand luggage was the same: just some extra clothes and shaving gear. No books. Nothing personal. They had just enough stuff to look normal and pass inspection, but nothing to show personal history or other contacts. No indication of where they were going or what they expected to do next. Nada. Zip. Not a sausage."

Major Berikoff was disappointed but not surprised. The whole hijacking operation had been reasonably well run, although the hijackers seem to lack combat experience. However, having the weapons built into the airplane showed advanced planning and someone with an exceptionally long reach. The implications were frightening.

But most of all, the Major was frustrated. There was no indication as to why the aircraft had been hijacked. Outside of the information about a disused airfield in Germany, they had nothing.

The Major felt that a significant event must be about to happen, but he had nothing. Meanwhile, it seemed like a good time to check in with the cockpit.

The Major noticed that something was different in the cockpit. There was tension in the air, and the off-hand attempts at gallows humor were gone. This time, it was all business.

"What is new, gentlemen?"

Bampton nodded at Goldsmith, who began to report.

"We will be landing at Royal Air Force Base Lossiemouth. It is right on the coast. It is a fast air[19] base and operates mostly Typhoons and F-35s. It also has an Anti-Submarine Warfare squadron that operates P-8A Poseidon aircraft, a modified Boeing 737-800. This is good news as they will have fire and rescue crews trained for large, fixed-wing aircraft. That means us. The main runway is 05/23, which is good, as we will be approaching it from the water and will go straight onto runway 23. The main runway shows 9341 feet usable. Better than most, and it will give us some run-out room. Not to put too fine a point on it, but I think they chose Lossie not just for its long runway. If we land short, we hit the water or the golf course. If we go long, we will be plowing up

---

[19] Fast air is a generic military term for fighter aircraft.

some farmers' fields. In other words, if we screw this one up badly, we will not damage anything expensive or important. An overshoot will also take us over the water, so be ready for a right-hand turnout."

The Major looked to the senior officer and crew commander Bampton, who nodded his approval but said nothing. The Major had not wanted to ask what they thought the chances were of landing a 777 on their first try. But his confidence level was up. These two communicate without talking and read each other's thoughts. They were typical of small unit personnel who had to work together under high stress. Rank was not necessary, and the decision-making process was collective and consensual. Outsiders had a hard time understanding the psychology of multi-crew military aircraft, submarine crews, and firefighters. The Major was able to get it, and these two were good. His unit, the SAS, worked the same way. Rank and discipline were very much on display when in the public eye. But when deployed to the field, rank mostly melted away. Small units lived or died on trust and the ability to work as a unit.[20]

---

[20] Contrary to what many outsides believe, the military chain of command is not always about 'following orders.' In small units such as multi-crew aircraft, submarines and special forces units, decision making, and action are frequently taken on a consensus basis which overlooks the rank structure. For instance, a Sea King (CH-124) helicopter that does anti-submarine warfare and search and rescue work. A normal four-person crew would consist of a pilot crew commander (Lieutenant Colonel/Major/Captain), a co-pilot (Captain/Lieutenant), a Tactical Navigator

Bampton finally spoke. "We should be at Lossie in about twenty minutes. It is about to get busy up here."

The Major took the hint. He was, in effect, being told to leave. The Major almost laughed to himself. Not much a 'snake eater could do now anyway. Best to clear out and let folks do their job.

Goldsmith had called the Cabin Director and told her they were about 20 minutes back and would be 'feet dry'[21] and then landing about 10 seconds apart. He had thought to say to the Flight Director to prepare for a rough landing but figured the Flight Director already knew they were in for an 'interesting' landing.

The descent and approach to Lossiemouth were relatively uneventful. Once the new coordinates had been programmed into the flight computer, the autopilot did all the work. There were a few tense moments when the aircraft appeared to hit turbulence and bounced a bit. Neither pilot could tell

---

(Major/Captain/Lieutenant) and an airborne electronic sensor operator (Warrant Officer/Sergeant/Master Corporal). While the pilot crew commander has absolute final decision-making authority, the reality is that when high risk situations arise, the crew must all agree on the decision. For instance, many Search and Rescue flights occur under high-risk conditions. The Sea King helicopter is rated as going 'out of limits' when the existing wind conditions exceed 50 knots (57 mph). However, multiple SAR flights have occurred when the winds were considerably higher. The greater the risk, the more likely the crew is to fall back on a consensus process.

[21] Feet dry is flying over land. Feet wet is flying over water.

if it was turbulence or if it was the aircraft's flight controls. Both silently wondered if the same guy who designed the MCAS[22] system on the 737-MAX[23] had worked on the 777. Unselected command inputs into the flight control system were a pilot's worst nightmare in an aircraft that was fly-by-wire.

Ten minutes back from Lossie, a Typhoon fighter jet appeared on their port side. Lossie had told them the fighter pilot would be under positive control of Lossie radar and would be making a flight approach that should match a 777 on a standard approach. It was a bit of welcome redundancy. The autopilot should keep the 777 on its proper path. Keeping an eye on the Typhoon would confirm all was well. The pilot gave them a thumbs up. A fighter might have unnerved many civilian pilots flying that close to their airliner, but to Bampton and Goldsmith, it was a comforting sight.

Almost suddenly, the 777 was approaching short final.

"Flaps down." This from Bampton, who had hands-on control and would do the landing.

---

[22] Unknown Editors, "Maneuvering Characteristics Augmentation System," Wikipedia (Wikimedia Foundation, May 24, 2021), https://en.wikipedia.org/wiki/Maneuvering_Characteristics_Augmentation_System.

[23] Unknown Editors, "Boeing 737 MAX MCAS Software Enhancement," Boeing.com (Boeing, 2021), https://www.boeing.com/commercial/737max/737-max-software-updates.page.

Time passed.

"Gear down."

"Travelling... gear down and locked."

The aircraft's flight control surfaces were working themselves, keeping the 777 lined up.

Goldsmith spoke. "We are a bit high and above the Typhoon. He is falling back. We are too fast. Something is not right."

"406, this is Lossie. You are above the glide path, and your approach speed is high."

Goldsmith double-clicked the mic switch in acknowledgment.

"Pull the power back, and I will try and bring the nose up to bleed some speed off."

"Power back."

The aircraft bounced twice. Something was jinky, and it appeared the plane was getting unselected flight control inputs again. The runway was approaching fast, and the Typhoon had gone afterburner and climbed away to the left.

"406, you are 500 feet above the glide path."

Goldsmith spoke again. "We are hot and high."[24]

Bampton: "Overshoot.[25] Full power both."

---

[24] The aircraft is travelling too fast, and too high to attempt a landing.

[25] The landing attempt is being cancelled and the aircraft will now try to regain altitude for a go around and another

"Throttles through the wire."[26]

"Gear up."

"Travelling."[27]

"Overshoot right."[28]

"Gear up and locked."

"Override. Taking manual control."

---

landing attempt.

[26] This is an archaic expression left over from World War Two aircraft engines. Maximum power generated by four cycle piston aircraft engines was normally limited by a mechanical stop. This was often a wire that was in the throttle lever. In an emergency, a strong push on the throttle would break the wire and cause the engine to produce more than the 100% rated power. The problem was that the engine life at 'War Emergency Power' might be limited to five minutes or less before the engine self destructed. Gas turbine engines can also go into overspeed which will increase power but will melt the final stage power turbine(s) in relatively short order. No 'wires' exist in the throttles anymore and the expression now simply means that all possible power will be extracted from the engines and the pilot with his hand on the throttles understands the severity of the situation. In other words, this is shorthand for "givin' her everything she's got."

[27] The landing gear lever has been selected to the up positions and the gear is moving but not fully retracted or locked into the up position.

[28] Once the aircraft has gained sufficient altitude and speed, it will turn right during the climb out as it goes around for another landing attempt. The decision is normally made by the pilot in command ahead of time in the pre-landing brief, but air traffic control may have an input based on other traffic in the pattern.

"Lossie, this is 406. We assess unselected flight control inputs on the final approach. Possible damage to the flight computer from the explosion and associated EMP. Flight 406 will climb out to Angels Five and re-establish stable flight. Once in stable flight, we will re-enter flight computer coordinates for another landing attempt.

"Roger, 406. Lossie will monitor. Contact us when at Angels Five."

Bampton looked at Goldsmith. "I think I have it. We were hot and high, and we were getting unselected flight control inputs. But here is the thing. Even with the input errors, the airplane can probably still make a better approach than we can, at least until we are on short final. My plan is this. We make another approach. Suppose it goes well, then great. If the same thing happens again, I think I can beat it. I will take manual control; you pull the power way back, and I will try to nose up for a sharp flare to bleed off the speed. We drop this thing on the runway and hope the gear does not come up through the wings. You hit reverse thrust and bury the throttles while I will try to manage the brakes. We will see what these General Electric engines can do when forced to the limit. Two hundred thousand pounds of thrust should be something if they do not blow.[29]

---

[29] This is a tangential reference to the General Electric GE9X Turbofan engines which are rated at 105,000 pounds of thrust each. Some earlier 777 aircraft had Pratt and Witney PW4077 engines which have had a distressing tendency to suffer fan blade failures in mid-flight such

The second approach proved almost the same as the first. A different Typhoon had escorted them in, and once again, they were too high and too fast. This time Goldsmith started pulling the throttles back, and Bampton overrode the autopilot. With the nose up and the engines back, the sink rate increased rapidly.

Lossiemouth sent a two-word message, "Sink rate." Goldsmith double-clicked again. Their sudden sink rate had alarmed the air traffic controller.

The aircraft hit the fourth set of hash marks with a mighty bang. Unfortunately, it was not so much a landing as the plane ran out of flying speed and fell out of the air.

"Reverse thrust. Full power both."

"Givin' 'er."[30]

The engines roared, and Bampton was trying to control the aircraft as it first tried to head off the runway to the left and then tried to head for the grass on the right. The anti-lock brakes did not seem to understand what was expected of them, and Bampton felt like he was wrestling with a wounded water buffalo. A 777 was many things, but agile was not one of them. Somewhere in the back, they could hear the screams of the passengers. Finally, the

---

United Airlines Flight 238 on 20 February 2020.
[30] A slang expression common throughout much of the aviation, marine and automotive sector. In essence, the engine(s) will be brought to absolute maximum power regardless of potential damage or the risk of engine detonation.

combined efforts of the brakes and the reverse thrusters brought the aircraft down to a controllable speed. A couple of thousand feet of runway later, it was apparent the plane would stop. Goldsmith pulled the throttles back and deselected the reverser thrusters. The aircraft finally stopped. It was well left of center, and only 1000 feet of the runway was left.

"Lossiemouth, this is 406. We are full stop on 23 and are requesting evacuation assistance. 406 is requesting you break out the good stuff."[31]

"Roger 406. Expect immediate evacuation assistance for passengers. Also, RAF police will have a separate boarding stairway at the rear door port side. Please inform passenger Roy to have his special passengers ready to disembark at that point. AVM sends regards."

The Major appeared in the cockpit as if on cue. "Believe it or not, lads, that was not the worst landing I have ever suffered. We had a helo do something much worse than that in Afghanistan. But that is another story. Meantime, congratulations on keeping us all alive. Good show. I suspect you two should get a gong or something for saving Atlantic Airways from losing their shiny new two hundred-million-dollar aircraft. Not to mention all 329[32] souls on board – well – minus the one fellow we sent to his maker."

---

[31] Expensive single malt scotch.

[32] The number of 329 passengers here was chosen as a reference to Air India Flight 182. On 23 June 1985, this flight was enroute from Toronto, Canada to London, UK

Goldsmith turned in his seat and faced the Major. "Forget the gongs. Any chance you have connections here? We asked the tower to break out the good stuff. Get us a good drink, and we will call it even."

"This is Scotland, lads! They have the best stuff here. If they do not serve us the good stuff, I invite you to join the SAS as honorary members, and we will attack the first bar we see. With me?"

"You lead Major, we follow."

when a terrorist bomb exploded onboard. The aircraft crashed in the ocean off the coast of Ireland, killing all 329 souls on board. The bomb had been placed on board by Khalistani terrorists who were supporters of the International Sikh Youth Federation, Babbar Khalsa and the Khalistan Liberation Force. Canada was a safe haven for Khalistani terrorists in the 1980s and remains that today.
https://en.wikipedia.org/wiki/Air_India_Flight_182

Chapter 10: Who Gets the Money?

LOCATION: Amsterdam

DATE: 28 July

TIME: 4:05 AM

Senior Constable Jonker cursed as he jammed on the brakes. Upon turning right out of the police garage, Jonker had pushed the Porsche's throttle down hard as he headed for the end of the street. To his surprise, especially at this hour of the morning, the street was blocked by a large cargo lorry. Jonker flashed his lights and leaned out the window to yell at the driver. Seeing no response, he got out of his car, ran to the cab of the vehicle, and hammered on it with his fist. No driver was visible. Jonker started to get the feeling that something was wrong. He drew his service weapon and carefully circled the vehicle. When passing the front of the vehicle, he placed his free hand on the grill. The engine was still warm. Someone had parked the truck at the end of the street about an hour earlier. He had been blocked in deliberately.

The Porsche sat with its engine idling. The Dutch police maintained a small fleet of high-speed pursuit cars for emergencies. Jonker had been called to pursue two Audis that were seen leaving the scene of a cash center robbery not three kilometers away.

Jonker returned to his car and sat there for about 15 seconds while he calmed himself. Finally, he picked up his radio to make a somewhat awkward report. His super-fast, shiny, and expensive Porsche was going nowhere.

* * *

Gamal's radio crackled. It was Amin calling from the lead car. "We have a problem. The car is losing gas. We don't have enough fuel left to make it to the rendezvous."

Gamal's driver prodded him and pointed at the dashboard. "He is still making 180 kilometers an hour."

Gamal looked behind him. There was no sign of any police pursuit so far. The fog was thinning a bit, but no helicopter was going to be able to track them. "Keep going until you lose power. Then, click twice on the radio when you start slowing. We will transfer everything into the estate wagon and keep going."

Four minutes later, Gamal heard the radio crackle twice in quick succession. His driver jammed the breaks without being told. When stopped, he closed the distance between the two cars. Gamal turned around, addressing himself to Yassir. "Get all the money out of the other car jam it in the back. You and Amin get in the back with it."

Gamal pointed to his driver. "Help with the money and then get everyone into this car. I will be the last person aboard. Then we carry on to the rendezvous point."

Gamal got out of the car and walked forward to where he could see the last of the fuel leaking out of the sedan. Three bullet holes were visible in the car. The police at the cash center robbery must have fired at least three lucky shots. He reached under the front passenger seat of the disabled sedan and pulled out two one-liter containers of gasoline mixed with dish soap – the poor man's napalm. When he was satisfied that the last of the money was out of the car and his team was clear, he began pouring the fluid. One liter went into the interior, and the second liter was poured on the roof. He left the doors open. Walking away, he pointed to his driver to start backing up. When the estate wagon was about 20 meters back, Gamal took a Zippo lighter out of his pocket. He opened the lighter, spun the flint wheel, and threw it at the car. The team heard a satisfying roar as the vehicle burst into flames.

"Good luck getting any evidence off that car." Gamal pointed ahead and told his driver. "Keep us at 160 for about five minutes and then back off to about 120 for the rest of the trip."

The stolen up-chipped Audi A8 was still capable of 160, even with all the extra weight on board.

* * *

Gamal's driver tapped the GPS on the dashboard. "Less than one kilometer back from the rendezvous point." Gamal pointed ahead. "We have a new rendezvous point. Keeping going straight until I tell you. The next turn will be to the right."

After several turns in another industrial park, Gamal pointed out one building at the end of the block. "That one, with the sign that says used tires for sale." With that, Gamal reached into the glove compartment and pulled out a garage door opener. The oversized garage door opened on command. Once under the door, Gamal clicked the button again and heard the door reverse as he scanned the garage. It was empty, except for two small four-door Toyotas. Both were backed up against the rear wall.

Gamal waited until everyone was out of the car and signaled his men to gather around.

"Take the money out of the cars. Dump it out of the bags and sort it out. Two piles. One for the fifties and one for the hundreds. Put the empty bags in the Audi. Then get back here."

Once done, the men gathered around.

"Yassir, you will take the Audi and dump it in the canal as we discussed. All the weapons and other equipment go with it. You should have no problem walking the four kilometers to the train station and then go to Schiphol Airport. You will be back in Egypt tonight. As for the rest, each one of you will find a bag in one of those two cars. The bags have new passports, train schedules, and air tickets. There is also some money in Euros and US dollars for travel expenses. The rest of you should be back in Egypt or Morocco tonight as well. You will shower in the back in the employee washroom using lots of soap. Both you and your clothes will have traces of gun reside nitrates on them, and we do not want to tip off security at the airport. Then you will ditch the clothes you have on and the burner phones I gave you in the Audi. They go into the canal as well.

Once they were cleaned up and had all the clothes and weapons in the Audi, Gamal gathered them around for one last time.

"Any questions?"

"Yeah," said Amin. "When do we get paid?"

"As agreed," said Gamal, "the money has already been sent to your accounts at home. We used the same accounts where you received your advance and expense money. You can check the amounts at an ATM or call home once at the airport. You will find a slight bonus seeing that you all did everything I expected." Gamal had also been smart enough to give the men a generous advance fee. Even if they had been killed or arrested, their families would still be well compensated.

"Change of plans'" said Amin, stepping away from the others. "I want my money now, in cash. And I want it in the fifties out of that pile."

Gamal looked at the rest of the men. Like him, they had come to dislike Amin Attia. He was adequate at his job, but he was self-centered and all too likely to blame others for his shortcomings.

"There will be no change of plan. You get in the car and leave, or you will be put in the Audi and dropped into the canal. Your choice. Do you want to change the plan, or do you want to go back home today?"

Amin knew he had lost as the others trusted Gamal. But he still wanted his money now. "What about the weapons and the cars? They can be traced back to us."

Gamal was about to lose his temper and simply shoot Amin, but he knew that sticking to the plan was still the best move. "The two Audis were stolen three weeks ago and repainted. All three VINs have were removed from each vehicle. The police will eventually figure that out, but it gets them nothing. The weapons were all Albanian in origin – stolen from Albanian military armories when the country's government collapsed in 1997. There is nothing to track."

Gamal looked at Amin for a few seconds and then addressed the rest. "Amin can make his choice now. He can leave with the rest of you, or you can load him into the Audi after you tape him up."

Defeated, Amin headed towards the two Toyotas. The others followed.

Gamal walked over to the Audi with Yassir. He tossed his pistol into the back and then muttered a few words. He then took the garage door opener off the dashboard of the Audi and opened the garage door.

When all three cars had left the garage, he closed the door, walked to the back wall. He took three tires and set them on top of each other, and sat down. From his inner pocket, he pulled out a battered pack of *Gitanes* cigarettes. Reaching inside the pack, he pulled out one cigarette and some paper matches.

Having lit the cigarette, he sat back and relaxed. He reviewed the entire operation in his head. All had gone well, except for the car being disabled on the highway. Even at that, Gamal reasoned that the fire would destroy any evidence. The police would try and get fingerprints and DNA from the expended casings at the cash center, but the rounds had all been washed with alcohol and then lightly re-oiled before being loaded into the magazines. Gamal knew every round had been cleaned as he had done it himself.

The only real problem had been Amin Attia. Gamal had been tempted to shoot him in the garage, but that would have meant a clean-up job and a delay. Not only that, even if the others did not like him, a shooting might cause them to talk later. Letting him go had been the best plan.

Gamal crushed the cigarette butt between his thumb and forefinger and put the butt into his pocket. There was no point in leaving DNA evidence.

He pulled out another cigarette and lit it up.

"I thought you gave up smoking."

Gamal looked over at the small office door. There stood Wilhelm de Haas.

"You have been here the whole time." It was a statement of fact and was neither a question nor an accusation.

"Yes," said Wilhelm. "All went well? Where is the other car?"

"The other car broke down. We burned it on the side of the road. No worries about it. Everything else went as planned."

"What about the one guy who wanted his money now. Was that Amin Attia?"

"No problem there either. Yassir will have him killed after he gets back to Cairo. It will look like a mugging gone wrong. Never liked him anyway...."

"Good," said Wilhelm. "I have called for my driver. He should be here in less than ten minutes. You can help me load the money, and then we are done."

"Who gets all the money?"

"Wouldn't you like to know?"

Gamal smiled. "I will get a quick shower, change clothes, and then we load up."

Once Wilhelm's driver arrived, it took only a few minutes to pile the money in the trunk.

Wilhelm turned to Gamal and shook his hand. "Your money will be sent to you starting tonight and will be sent in increments to the different accounts you stipulated. Thanks for all of this. Will you be heading back to Egypt now?"

"Not sure. Once I clean up here, I think I will be staying here in the Netherlands and lying low. It is a good time to relax for a bit. Then, maybe I will go for a walk on the beach in Scheveningen. The food on the beach near the Kurhaus is rather good."

Gamal watched as Wilhelm and his driver went out the garage door. Gamal wondered what was up. The money from the cash center was new. The cash center knew the serial numbers, which were traceable. Why would someone want all that traceable money?

Gamal wiped off the garage door opener and left it on the corner of the desk in the office. Next, he gathered up his clothes and did one more quick check around the building to ensure no evidence had been left. He then walked out the back door.

Two hours later, Gamal was walking out of The Hague's Holland Spoor train station. The train trip had not been comforting. He had done several jobs for Wilhelm before. Each one had a certain logic, whether it was threatening a political figure or burning down buildings. But this one made no sense.

Gamal had a strange feeling that something big was coming.

* * *

LOCATION: Amsterdam

DATE: 28 July

TIME: 5:15 PM

Wilhelm watched the white van pull away. The money from the cash center robbery had been opened and mixed into different packages. It was put into tubs full of water with a bit of bleach and dirt and then dried in commercial clothes dryers. It would give the appearance of money that had been circulated.

The money was repackaged into cardboard cartons which identified themselves as printed material. Many of the cartons were full of printed advertising flyers that extolled the virtues of the new 5G phones available from Samsung. It was dull stuff and unlikely to attract police attention, even if the van was stopped for speeding or some other minor infraction.

Sitting in the back of his Mercedes 560, Wilhelm pulled out his mobile and sent a text:

'New printed material picked up today and shipped to your clients in Paris as requested.'

* * *

CRJ had been waiting for the text. The final piece of his plan was now in place. The money needed to finance the Muslim Brotherhood Islamists in Paris to start their campaign of violence was now moving. It was the 28th of June. If all went to schedule, the campaign of political violence should be created in Paris by the 6th of July. The needed European-wide terrorism should be underway by the 10th of July.

CRJ was content for the moment. The Islamists of the Muslim Brotherhood would start the violence in Europe. But ultimately, the police and intelligence services would trace the money back to the cash center robbery. If they did not, CRJ himself would provide them with a few anonymous tips to guide their investigation. The media in the Netherlands was already reporting that the cash center attackers had yelled Islamist slogans during the attack. While the Muslim Brotherhood would provide the violence needed for the Great Reset to start, they would also be later identified as the cash center robbers – fairly or not.

Chapter 11: Walking Towards the Revolution

LOCATION: Brussels, Belgium

DATE: 28 July

TIME: 05:55 AM

After changing his clothes, Tarek left the hotel and turned up Boulevard Charlemagne, away from the traffic circle and the Le Berlaymont European Commission Headquarters. The next Thalys train to Paris would not leave until 06:00. He had more than five hours for what would be a short walk to the Brussels Gare de Midi train station. He would take an indirect route to the station and then find a place in the shadows to watch the station entrance. Tarek did some of his best thinking while walking.

At this point, the facts did not add up. The threat letters about Ilhan Benhaddara at Islamic Assistance Transnational had been foretelling. Someone had collected insightful intelligence about her movements. They knew with whom she met and how she conducted her personal life. This unknown individual or group had done surveillance on her and Islamic Assistance Transnational – but to what end?

If the assassin had known so much, would he not have realized that she was a figurehead?

Ilhan Benhaddara had been hired to be the new face of the IAT after two previous leaders were forced to resign in less than two months. One firing occurred after the media had discovered a series of social media posts where he had called for the killing of apostates. His replacement had lasted two months. The replacements' earlier social media posts had called for financial support for suicide bombers.

Tarek had cursed both leaders in private. They could not contain themselves. Their practice of making one set of statements in English and a different set of messages in Arabic had destroyed them. Once easy to cover up, the duplicity had become a vulnerability as everyone could now read Arabic through Google Translate. Despite being warned, they had continued to brag about their ideology, goals, and objectives.

Ilhan Benhaddara was hired after a deep background check. A few of her earlier statements had called for funding to kill Christians in Nigeria, but she had been smart enough not to mention Boko Haram or the Dawah and Guidance Bureau in her postings.

Killing her would bring the organization a propaganda opportunity. The IAT would spin the assassination as another example of Islamophobia. A female victim would be a more sympathetic public face. It would be a great fund-raising opportunity, and they needed the money.

All told, however, Tarek remained perplexed. Was she the actual target, and if so, why? Had he been the target? Had the assassin missed and hit her by accident? His killing would have been the more significant loss to the organization.

The assassination would now work to his advantage as it could be used to inflame the faithful. Muslim Brotherhood front groups' propaganda would directly incite violence. This would be supported by hundreds of Jihadists who would soon be arriving in Europe from Turkey, thanks to Turkish President Recep Tayyip Erdogan.[33]

The further he walked, the more puzzled he became. He lacked the data to assess the situation. Perhaps someone was trying to hurt him and the IAT, which made sense. It would fit in a certain way.

Or was an individual or force trying to help him? Of course, but if so, who? And why?

An even more disturbing thought hit him. Had the threat letters sent to the IAT served a different purpose? Was he now to understand that someone knew months ahead of time an assassin would kill her?

How was he to interpret that possibility? Was someone trying to help him?

Questions. More questions. And then still more questions.

He continued walking as dawn approached.

---

[33] Unknown Editors, "Muslim Brotherhood in Turkey," Counter Extremism Project, 2021, https://www.counterextremism.com/content/muslim-brotherhood-turkey.

Chapter 12: Launch Time

LOCATION: Brussels - Residence of Enrica Leclercq

DATE: 28 July

TIME: 06:00 AM

Enrica Leclercq stared at herself in the mirror for a moment as she headed down to the gym. The one-hour workout was in advance of preparations for the day. The trip to the office was set for 08:00 AM.

She knew when the violence would start. That was today.

She knew why the violence would start. It was the springboard to put their final plans for their Great Reset into action.

She did not know exactly where and how the violence would start. But that did not concern her. It was not her problem, and it would make it easier for her to look surprised when told about it.

* * *

LOCATION: Brussels - Office of Enrica Leclercq

DATE: 28 July

TIME: 8:00 AM

Enrica briefly glanced at the sign on the outer door of her office: *High Representative for the Union for Foreign Affairs and Security Policy.* Her office was a long way from the street protests of her youth when she was an organizer for the French Communist Party. Her mother was pleased with her activism, even after her first arrest. Her father, on the other hand, had remained silent.

Today would be the first day of the most revolutionary changes Europe had seen since Marie Antoinette had lost her head. She trusted others to produce the violence and create the fear required. Without another wave of fear, they would face too much resistance. If the levels of fear created were high enough, then the masses would demand action. And Enrica was ready to provide the answers to their fear and their demands for safety.

She took a breath, calmed herself, and opened the door.

"People are sheep," she said to herself as she walked through the door.

Chapter 13: The Muslim Brotherhood in Europe

LOCATION: Paris, France

DATE: 28 June

TIME: 8:30 AM

Tarek Raman descended from the train at Paris's Gare du Nord station as a troubled man. The Thalys' train had been uneventful. No one had shown any interest in him while embarking at Brussels' Gare du Midi station. A quick scan of the platform in Paris revealed nothing of suspicion.

But he fretted. As was his usual practice, Tarek walked out of the station and only chose which way to turn when he was outside. While taking the Paris Metro was an option, he would walk instead. Walking was needed for thinking.

Besides that, Tarek, more than many others, understood the dangers of underground travel. No matter how small, any explosive device contained in a concrete tube would have its explosive power greatly magnified. Tarek was not paranoid, but underground travel occurred only when necessary.

Without being aware of the irony, Tarek thought that too many terrorists were looking to make names for themselves by blowing up public transit systems. A taxi was also an option, but they all had cameras now. And drivers talked. Tarek could hide himself to some degree from the ever-present street cameras of the panopticon state, but taxi cameras were harder to avoid.

The walk to his destination in Sevran would be over fifteen kilometers, but this was not a problem for Tarek. He believed that Allah had given him the body of a man, and it was his responsibility to keep that body fit. Therefore, when Allah called you to serve the cause of jihad, you needed to be ready.[34] The three-and-a-half-hour walk would do him good.

Tarek would walk several blocks along Rue La Fayette and then turn again. A few blocks more, and another random turn. Each time, the decision to turn would be made only seconds in advance. He stopped at a café to have a quick espresso, allowing him to check his surrounding to see if anyone was following. Another stop in Patin would be to buy a newspaper, which he would pretend to read with interest. To his horror, a photo of Ilhan Benhaddara's body was on the front page. No mention of him in the story. He stopped to drop the paper in a trash can. It was another chance to see if anyone of interest was around him. At this point, he had not detected any

---

[34] Stewart Bell, "Police Investigating Islamic School over Curriculum Comparing Jews to Nazis," nationalpost.com (National Post, May 7, 2012), https://nationalpost.com/news/canada/toronto-islamic-school-removes-parts-of-curriculum-casting-jews-as-treacherous-akin-to-nazis.

surveillance. Tarek picked up his walking pace and set out for Sevran, the poverty-stricken suburb. There, he would find safety and solace.

His time walking was as frustrating as the time on the train. As much as he focussed on the mission ahead, his mind drifted back to the assassination. His mind did not recall the sound of the shot being fired, but it did record the sound of her body hitting the ground. The vision of blood and brain matter on the glass doors remained.

As he approached Sevran, Tarek decided to accept that Ilhan Benhaddara was dead. Her death would now serve his mission, even if he did not understand it.

Allah, thought Tarek, was the greatest of all plotters.

As he crossed Boulevard Westinghouse, Tarek thought back over everything in his life that had brought him to this momentous point.

* * *

Tarek's grandfather had arrived in Graz, Austria, from Egypt in late 1954. Following the Muslim Brotherhood's attempt to assassinate Gamal Abdel-Nasser, the government of Egypt had launched a series of raids against the members of the Muslim Brotherhood – The Ikhwan. On the 9th of December 1954, Muslim Brotherhood leaders were executed, and the organization was outlawed.

Tarek's grandfather had escaped from Alexandria by boat, crossed to Cyprus, and eventually made his way to Graz, Austria, along with many other Ikhwani. His wife and four children made the perilous journey with him. Tarek's father had been the youngest of the four children.

Over the next year, the Muslim Brotherhood had made a collective decision. Egypt was not going to be safe for the Ikhwan for a considerable period. Therefore, if the vision of the founder of the Muslim Brotherhood were to grow, it would have to put down roots in the West. Austria would be the first new home, followed by Germany, France, the United Kingdom, the Netherlands, Canada, the USA, etc.

The spiritual leader of the Muslim Brotherhood, Youssef al-Qaradawi, had watched developments in Europe and gradually began to approve. From his position as the most influential Islamist scholar in the Muslim Brotherhood, he noted that the Brothers would seek "Conquest through dawah; that is what we hope for … We will conquer Europe, we will conquer America, not through the sword but through dawah." [35,36]

---

[35] John Mintz and Douglas Farah, "In Search Of Friends Among The Foes," The Washington Post (WP Company, September 11, 2004), https://www.washingtonpost.com/archive/politics/2004/09/11/in-search-of-friends-among-the-foes/654a7d58-057b-4965-ab44-4b1045915086/

[36] Kyle Shideler, "Ensconced in Doha: Qatar's Resident Islamists," meforum.org (Middle East Forum, January 30, 2019), https://www.meforum.org/57690/ensconced-doha-

Tarek's father had been one of the planners on how political Islam would take over Europe, just as they had planned since their inception of the Muslim Brotherhood in 1928. The first step was to create a variety of social and political organizations. The more they started, the greater the perception that they were more influential than they were.

The Muslim Brotherhood followed its typical pattern of growth and influence. First, they would have a prayer room, then a 'cultural center' followed by a formal mosque. Then would come their school, which would allow them to indoctrinate their youth. Following that would be a variety of university-based Muslim student associations. Finally, once they had a firm base, there would be political entryism and the focus on having sophisticated, well-educated Muslim Brothers in the bureaucracy, the police boards, law firms, and industry.

Then would come the use of Islamophobia. Whatever incident made it into the press, all their organizations would immediately claim that Muslims were victims of systemic racism. Was an Islamist arrested for a violent crime? It was the fault of the police force and the country for failing to integrate them. A woman got raped by an Islamist? Then it was the fault of the host society for not explaining the law to the newly arrived immigrants. An Islamist blew up a subway train? It was the fault of colonialism and an

islamists.

oppressive migration system. All Muslims had to be victims all the time.

But the most insidious plan of all was the use of terrorism to pressure Western politicians. The Muslim Brotherhood front groups would send a limited number of their weaker-minded youth down the path to violent extremism. First, attacks on their host societies occurred with horrendous violence. Then Muslim Brotherhood members would approach the police and the politicians and tell them they must compromise and give in to the Islamists, or more violence would occur. These self-same Muslim Brotherhood front groups would claim that only they could represent the 'moderate' voices and the government needed to fund them. If the government gave in to the Muslim Brotherhood and allowed them unfettered growth, the attacks would diminish.

The Muslim Brotherhood plan worked. But, first, they would inspire the violence and then tell their host governments that they could only moderate the violence. The host government would then produce more concessions, and the cycle of violence would start again.

Driven by globalism, post-modernism, and cowardice, most Western politicians chose to do nothing other than making vacuous statements.

* * *

Tarek had been singled out from birth for a leadership role. His grandfather and father ensured that he was indoctrinated and set on the path to leadership. However, his upbringing had not been easy. Tarek was expected to excel, so he had to study harder and memorize more passages than the other boys at the weekend Quranic memorization school.

During the week, Tarek attended one of the first schools set up by the Muslim Brotherhood. His father stressed to him for as long as he could remember that an Islamic school was necessary. Muslim children need to be stronger, so they would not get mixed with the moral degeneration of the community around them.[37,38]

Tarek's father believed that Allah had provided you with your body. Still, it was the responsibility of every individual to be ready for jihad when called. Every day, Tarek had to run faster and further than the other children around him.

---

[37] The Canadian Press, "Imams Council Rejects Charge That Extremist Writings Common in Mosque Libraries," globalnews.ca (Global News, August 23, 2016), https://globalnews.ca/news/2899151/imams-council-rejects-charge-that-extremist-writings-common-in-mosque-libraries/

[38] The Canadian Press, "Canadian Muslim Leaders Slam Study on Prevalence of Extremist Writing as 'Attempt to Vilify' Community," nationalpost.com (National Post, September 12, 2016), https://nationalpost.com/news/canadian-muslim-leaders-slam-study-on-prevalence-of-extremist-writing-as-attempt-to-vilify-community.

Those around Tarek Raman had also decided that he would become the public face of their struggle for Islamist supremacy in Europe. He would become educated and sophisticated in the ways of the West. Having excelled in school, he was sent to university with the intent of obtaining a Ph.D.

The process of elevating Tarek Raman had not been without its problems. He was a 'clean skin,' which said he had no run-ins with the police during his teen years. However, the university years had not been so smooth. There had been a nasty business with two female students while Tarek was working as a Teaching Assistant. They were silenced with threats of libel suits, saying that they would be accused of Islamophobia and were exploiting their white privilege to attack Muslims. With no support from the university, the girls had dropped their complaints.

Tarek's Ph.D. supervisor was critical of his thesis on the value and prestige of political Islam. The supervisor believed it was not objective analysis but rather a fluff piece promoting Islam as a political force rather than a religion. Moreover, the supervisor had pointed out that nowhere in the thesis was there any attempt to address the perennial political violence and terrorism that began to occur whenever political Islam began to take root.

Tarek had first tried to modify the thesis slightly, but the supervisor rejected it again. Tarek's father and the Islamist community then started a campaign of harassment against both the university and its staff. Finally, the university, wanting the problem to go away, decided to award the degree on the condition he left the campus.

* * *

Tarek had then been sent to the United Kingdom, complete with his new 'degree.' His father and others in the Islamist community in Austria had decided he could not stay in Austria. Still, a bright future awaited him at Islamist Relief Transnational (IAT). His grandfather's pedigree, combined with his Ph.D., would give him standing in the Islamist community. His role at IAT would consist of three main objectives. First, he would leverage his standing to grow the influence of the IAT by establishing new sub-branches, especially in universities. At the same time, he would become a vocal supporter of human rights for Muslims. As had been done in Austria, he would do in France and the UK. Islamists could never be guilty of any crime, no matter how violent or abusive. They would also portray themselves as the victims of racism or white colonialism. Anyone who suggested the Islamists were in part responsible for their actions would be subjected to a campaign of accusations of Islamophobia.

The third role was to be the least visible but the most critical over the long term. Tarek would set up a series of charities, non-profits, and semi-legitimate businesses. Behind them would be a network of shell companies and bank accounts. Built up slowly over several years, they would become the money laundering network necessary to fund Muslim Brotherhood projects over all of Europe and into North America.

Tarek had learned his lessons in Austria. In the future, any woman he chose to stalk would have to be vulnerable and weak. They must be perceived as unimportant or irrelevant by their peer group. So he would entice them, reward them with signs of affection and shiny baubles, then ensure he could compromise them with videos from hidden cameras. Women, especially infidel slags, had to learn their place. If they did not cover themselves and behave appropriately, they would be used accordingly.

In the early 2000s, Tarek's capabilities began to grow. The Emirate of Qatar had been hospitable to the Muslim Brotherhood since the early 1960s. The relationship evolved to the point where the ideology of the Muslim Brotherhood was the ideology of the ruling al-Thani family. Not only could a leading member of the Muslim Brotherhood live in luxury in Qatar, so too could members of their terrorist front groups such as Hamas and Palestinian Islamic Jihad.

For Tarek, they were heady days. He had worked behind the scenes to build a network of contacts for the Muslim Brotherhood in Western Europe, complete with the underlying financial services. Now, the al-Thani family of Qatar would provide millions in cash to advance the ideology of the Muslim Brotherhood in Europe. As the cash flow from Qatar Charity and the Eid Charity grew, so did Tarek's networks. For many Islamists, Brother Tarek was not only a colleague and mentor. He was their financial benefactor. Better still, Tarek would never ask for credit for any of his work. Local Imams and other Islamists could claim the new growth was from ground-up support in their communities. New mosques, schools, and cultural centers began to grow.

In 2012, Tarek had a close call. The founder of IAT, Dr. al Qazzaz, moved to Egypt in 2011 when the Muslim Brotherhood had taken control of Egypt's government. Once established in Egypt, Dr. al Qazzaz had sent Tarek a series of messages, encouraging him to relocate to Egypt. The IAT could now have a global future with its operations funded in Egypt. In addition, Dr. al Qazzaz wanted Tarek to take over the IAT's new international department, which would oversee a global network of IAT affiliate charities. This network could rival the influence of Saudi Arabi and spread the ideology of the Muslim Brotherhood to new heights.

After resisting for several months, Tarek had decided to explore the idea. But, first, he would need to groom a replacement for himself and then tell his network that better days were ahead.

In early May of 2012, Tarek had made the decision. He would announce his decision to move in mid-June and would move to Egypt by early July.

The decision almost cost Tarek everything. The Muslim Brotherhood's government in Egypt was suffering due to the massive discontent of the people. In less than two days, the rotten regime had imploded and been thrown out by the people. Dr. al Qazzaz, who had so strongly encouraged Tarek to move to Egypt, was in jail. The event rattled Tarek. A couple of more weeks, and he would have been in prison.

Once over the shock, Tarek doubled down on his beliefs. The future of the Muslim Brotherhood lay not in Egypt or Saudi Arabia but the West. It was only in the West, under weak democracies, that the Muslim Brotherhood could build the infrastructure they wanted in Western Europe, the United States, and Canada.

The fall of the Muslim Brotherhood did give Tarek a new role. Many of the Ikhwan would have to flee Egypt to seek sanctuary elsewhere. Using his financial networks and charity connections, Tarek was able to find them employment and housing. One of the most promising destinations was soon to reveal itself. With the election of Justin Trudeau as Prime Minister of Canada, the Ikhwan would quickly arrange a steady flow of its members into Canada. Prime Minister Trudeau was seen as such an ally that he would even allow ISIS fighters into Canada, claiming they would be a powerful voice for deradicalization in Canada.[39]

---

[39] Prime Minister Trudeau withdrew Canada's CF-18 fighter jets from their anti-ISIS mission as soon as he was elected as Prime Minister. Following that, he stated in the Canadian Parliament that ISIS fighters would become a 'powerful voice" for deradicalization in Canada. This despite that the Government of Canada has no formal

In late 2014, Tarek began to have doubts. His belief in the mission of the Muslim Brotherhood and its mission of religious and political supremacy was solid. The question was one of timing. Tarek believed that the Ikhwan were on track to establish their dominance in Europe. But it would take a turn of another generation before they were ready to push for absolute power. The year 2030 had been discussed as a possible early date.

But the United Arab Emirates had begun to upset that program in November of 2014. At that time, they had released a list of more than 80 groups that they described as front groups, fund-raisers, or proxies for terrorist organizations such as the Muslim Brotherhood. Many groups were in Europe and America, such as the Cordoba Foundation of the UK and CAIR USA.[40]   Tarek was worried. Lawfare and

---

deradicalizaiton program and no one was appointed to lead the 'Center for Community Engagement and Prevention of Violence. Approximately 90 to 100 ISIS fighters returned to Canada, of whom less than five have faced sanctions of any sort.

[40] The United Arab Emirates listed 83 entities which it described as terrorist groups or front/proxies or fund raisers for terrorist groups. Most of them were Muslim Brotherhood front groups. Among them were the Islamic Relief Worldwide, Council on American-Islamic Relations USA, the Muslim American Society, the UK Cordoba Foundation, the Muslim Association of Britain, and the League of Muslims in Belgium. For more on this see https://www.thenationalnews.com/uae/government/list-of-groups-designated-terrorist-organisations-by-the-uae-1.270037

Islamophobia could be used to silence the infidels and apostates in the West. But opposition from Middle Eastern countries, especially Sunni Islamic ones, could be a long-term problem. They could draw attention to the Ikhwan that was not helpful.

The problems grew again in 2019. The publishing of a book on the Qatar Papers leak had exposed many of Tarek's networks in Europe. Most of Europe ignored the news, but France and Austria began to react. France, in particular, began to move against what they were calling 'separatism' even though everyone knew they meant political Islam. Tarek was unsure if President Macron of France was serious about going after the Muslim Brotherhood or if he just wanted to appear tougher than the political opposition coming from Marie Le Pen. Either way, it was putting focus in the wrong place.

In 2020 and early 2021, Tarek decided that the strategy of the Muslim Brotherhood needed to change. They were under attack from France, and the Ikhwan were being exposed in scandals in the United Kingdom. Even the Netherlands had decided to cut government funding of Islamic Assistance Transnational. Germany was raising questions, and Sweden had started to react.

If the Ikhwan were to dominate in Europe, they needed to move sooner rather than later.

* * *

Tarek once again heard the sound of Ilhan Benhaddara's body dropping to the ground. Could it have been less than 24 hours since the assassination?

The situation became clearer. The assassination of Ilhan Benhaddara was a sign from Allah. Her death would produce fear and anger. It was time to send a message to the infidel rulers of Europe.

The Muslim Brotherhood would speak with the language that they knew would fill Europe with fear. That voice would start with the 800 neighborhoods that the Ikhwan controlled in France and would spread.

Inshallah.

Chapter 14: Islam is The Solution

LOCATION: The Residence of CRJ

DATE: 29 June

TIME: 8:00 PM

CRJ sat at his desk and poured a glass of his favorite Remy Martin Louis XIII brandy. In one more week, the attacks in Paris would start, unleashing the violence he would need to put his plans into effect. Then, Enrica, the Great Reset, and fear would wash over Europe – the fear he needed to demand their submission.

His first wave of four attacks had done their job, better than he had hoped, even allowing for the partial failure of the aircraft hijacking. The fear and speculation in the media were working their magic.

Now came the period of waiting as events unfolded.

CRJ savored the irony of the situation. The forces he needed to unleash his violent plan were the Islamists, most of whom were followers of the Muslim Brotherhood. It was their upcoming outbreak of violence that was required to generate the needed fear. But the key to his ultimate success was that the Islamists would be wiped out when they attempted to create their caliphates.

CRJ reveled in his role as the man behind the curtain. No one would know what was happening until it was too late.

His eyes turned to the flatscreen TV on his wall. The media was hyping speculation about who was behind the attacks. The foolish theories would increase again tomorrow and the day after. CRJ had written letters to a variety of reputable and not-quite-so-reputable news agencies. The contents of the letters would vary. Two of the letters were claims of responsibility that would point to an extreme right-wing group that had assassinated Ilhan Benhaddara. Another would lead a French TV station to believe that the Iranians were behind the whole series of attacks. Just for amusement, CRJ had sent one letter to an online conspiracy theory group saying the four attacks were a false flag operation run by the CIA and Israel's Mossad, which the Rothchild Bank funded. He had put enough detail into the letter to make it seem credible. The online conspiracy nutters would have a field day.

* * *

Sinking back in his chair, CRJ thought about the one photo in a history book that had changed his life. Revelations from that photo took him down the path to where he believed he could turn Europe into the great power it should be.

The photo was of Bosnians.

Bosnian Muslims.

Bosnian Muslim Nazis. A whole group of them.

The formation of Bosnian Muslim Nazis was wearing a hat known as a fez, a holdover from when Bosnia was a Turkish province. But each of them had a Nazi SS death head symbol on their fez. They were the 13th Waffen Division of the SS Handschar,[41,42] a locally raised military unit designed to support the Nazi occupation of Croatia and Bosnia against Tito and other partisan units.

The photo had stunned CRJ. How could Bosnians, who had converted to Islam as a matter of convenience under the Ottoman Turkish occupation, now find common cause with the Nazis? Even more stunning, hundreds of them wound up in the Middle East after World War II. They would fight in the 1947-48 Civil War in Mandatory Palestine and then fight again in the Arab/Israeli War of 1948.[43]

The search for a comprehensive understanding and evidence had led CRJ to the Muslim Brotherhood, which he soon realized lay at the root of what had become an 'Islamist political ideology' instead of religious beliefs.

---

[41] Unknown Editors, "13th Waffen Mountain Division of the SS Handschar (1st Croatian)," en.wikipedia.org (Wikimedia Foundation, May 21, 2021),
https://en.wikipedia.org/wiki/13th_Waffen_Mountain_Division_of_the_SS_Handschar_(1st_Croatian).

[42] Unknown Editors, "Hitler's Foreign Legions – Nine Non-German Units That Fought for the Nazis in WW2," MilitaryHistoryNow.com (Military History Now, February 8, 2020), https://militaryhistorynow.com/2016/05/04/hitlers-foreign-legions-nine-non-german-regiments-that-fought-for-the-nazis-in-ww2/

[43] For more on the role of the Waffen SS in Mandatory Palestine, see book by Benny Morris, *The Birth of the Palestinian Refugee Problem Revisited*.

Their ideology had been developed since the founding of the Muslim Brotherhood by Hassan al-Banna in Egypt in 1928. However, what had started with an organization supposedly based on ground-up community orientation, had soon mutated into an organization that employed political violence. Within a few years after its creation, the Muslim Brotherhood had units fighting in the Palestinian Governate.

Over the years, CRJ had come to understand the ideology of the Muslim Brotherhood as it had developed. The belief system of the movement now included several key points:

- A belief that Islam is not only a religion but also a holistic sociopolitical system;

- The advocacy of Sharia (Islamic) law as divine state law;

- A belief that a transnational Muslim community, known as the Ummah, should unite as a political bloc;

- Advocacy of an 'Islamic' state, or Caliphate, within which sovereignty belongs to God.

What had caught his attention was that the extremist ideology of the Muslim Brotherhood had much in common with not only the Nazis but also the extreme left and even 'progressives.' All of them were collectivist. They had no interest in respecting individual rights. They were anti-democracy and believed that total submission to a totalitarian belief system run by elites was required. This was when CRJ had learned that Islam did not necessarily translate to 'peace' – it could also be interpreted as 'submission.' All of them were supremacist as well. They believed that only their ideology was acceptable in the end, and all others would have to be suppressed.

CRJ had studied how the supremacist ideology played itself out following the Islamist coup in Iran. The leftists in Iran had helped overthrow the Shah from his Peacock Throne. Once firmly in power, the Islamists slaughtered about 30,000 leftists.[44] The Islamists knew a threat when they saw it and chose to be rid of it. Unfortunately, leftists outside of Iran decided to ignore the message and still cooperated with Islamists.

As a part of his overall research and planning, CRJ had started to study the rise of Islamist terrorism as it became a global threat. Up to the 1970s, the Islamists in the Middle East and Northern Africa (MENA) had limited influence. Many of the leading Islamists, especially from Egypt, had fled to Europe to dig in and stay underground. They were also staying out of trouble.

By the end of the 1970s, he saw that the Islamists were beginning to gain strength. As a result, many of the MENA countries were deteriorating, and social cohesion was failing.

---

[44] Unknown Editors, "Blood Soaked Secrets: Why Iran's 1988 Prison Massacres Are Ongoing Crimes Against Humanity," amnesty.org (Amnesty International, December 4, 2018), https://www.amnesty.org/en/documents/mde13/9421/2018/en/

By the 1980s, CRJ learned that the Islamists were spreading like cancer. The year 1979 had ushered in a decade of explosive growth. Three significant events, taken together, had shaken CRJ as he watched the rise of the Islamists. First, in Iran, the mullahs had seized power and put Ayatollah Khomeini in control. Second, in Saudi Arabia, an extremist sect had held the main mosque in Mecca, much to the embarrassment of the Saudi royal family. It had taken the involvement of French special forces to drive out the heavily armed insurgents. Finally, the Soviet invasion of Afghanistan had spread the fires of radicalization throughout the Islamic world.

CRJ had also learned about how the Muslim Brotherhood mobilized its forces in Syria. The Ikhwani, as the Muslim Brothers were called, had launched an armed struggle against the Syrian Baathist regime from 1980 to 1982. They were able to carry out some 69 terrorist attacks in that period, representing about two-thirds of all Islamist terrorist attacks globally.[45]The Syrian Muslim Brotherhood uprising ended when President Hafez el-Assad launched an all-out attack on their stronghold in Hama in February of 1982. Tens of thousands had died.[46] The Ikhwani had left Syria defeated but with

---

[45] Dominique Reynie, ed., "Islamist Terrorist Attacks in the World 1979-2019," Fondapol.org (Fondation pour l'innovation politique, November 20, 2019), https://www.fondapol.org/en/study/islamist-terrorist-attacks-in-the-world-1979-2019/
[46] John Pike, "Hamah (Hama), Syria, 1982," globalsecurity.org (Global Security), accessed June 12,

their heads held high. Saudi Arabia would take in many Syrian Muslim Brothers, something they would regret in later years.

The damage was done. The Muslim Brotherhood had emerged as a powerful movement in Middle Eastern and global politics. They had lost the battle for Syria, but they had demonstrated their organizational abilities. Not only that, the Ikhwanis had spread their message and their ideology. The Islamic world needed to free itself from the past and Western ideologies such as Marxism, democracy, and capitalism.

As Hassan al-Banna had stated: 'Islam is the solution.'

In 1991, CRJ's view of Europe and the Islamists mutated. In that year, Yugoslavia began to collapse into civil war. By the end of 1991, it was apparent to even the blindest of observers that the succession movements in Slovenia and Croatia would spread to Bosnia – the most diverse and potentially violent of the constituent republics.

Bosnia's Muslims were led by Alijah Izetbegovic – a name known to CRJ from his study of the history of Bosnia. President Tito had jailed Izetbegovic for advocating a fundamentalist form of Sharia in Bosna.[47] He had been part of the Muslim Brotherhood, and Tito recognized him for what he was – an Islamist

---

2021, https://www.globalsecurity.org/military/world/war/hamah.htm.

[47] Unknown Editors, "BBC News | Europe | Obituary: Alija Izetbegovic," http://news.bbc.co.uk/ (BBC, October 19, 2003), http://news.bbc.co.uk/2/hi/europe/3133038.stm

who was a threat due to his supremacist ideology. CRJ had quietly warned a variety of European leaders to beware of Izetbegovic, but they ignored him. The results were catastrophic. The Bosnian Muslims and their Party of Democratic Action or SDA[48] tried a pre-emptive political move to seize political control of Bosnia. The Bosnia Croats and Bosnia Serbs reacted violently. Having suffered under the Ottoman Turkish Caliphate, there was no way they would submit to a Muslim Brotherhood leader who had close connections to the government of Turkey. Izetbegovic had made a play for power based on what he thought was 'permission' from German Foreign Minister Hans-Dietrich Genscher. Izetbegovic was naïve enough to believe that the Europeans or the UN would support him. They did not. The *putsch* failed. Following that, the slaughter began. With a completely corrupt government, no capable security forces, and no plan, the Bosnian Muslims were outclassed politically and militarily.

CRJ had watched Bosnia fall apart and knew that Europe was failing. That had become clear in the last week of June of 1992. The United Nations had re-opened the Sarajevo Airport for what was said to be a humanitarian mission. No sooner had the airport been opened than the Iranian Revolutionary Guard Corps (IRGC) were operating around the airfield and Sarajevo.[49] The IRGC would soon spread out around

---

[48] Marcia Christoff Kurop, "Al Qaeda's Balkan Links," The Wall Street Journal (Dow Jones & Company, November 1, 2001), https://www.wsj.com/articles/SB1004563569751363760
[49] The Iranian Revolutionary Guards were first spotted in

most of Bosnia Muslim controlled territory. The move by Iran had proven educational to CRJ. Despite claims that the Shia of Iran could not work with Sunni groups like the Muslim Brotherhood, they were quite capable of doing just that.

CRJ knew that the Muslim Brotherhood founder, Hassan al-Banna, had stated that they would have to work with the Shia. Upon taking power in Iran during the Islamist Revolution, Ayatollah Khamenei had expressed his admiration for the Muslim Brotherhood. It was a sort of mutual admiration society.

Over the next three years, CRJ watched and learned. While every other country closed their embassies in Sarajevo with the diplomats fleeing, Iran kept its embassy open throughout the entire conflict. The Iranian Islamists, no matter how bad the situation, would support their cause.

The contrast between the Islamists and the flabby leadership of the West was astounding. Europe knew genocide was unfolding in their backyard but could not generate the will to act collectively. NATO, the UN, and the European Commission talked the talk, but they could not walk the walk.

In the immediate aftermath of the war in Yugoslavia, CRJ became even more pessimistic. From July to October 1995, a series of Islamist attacks hit France. On 25 July 1995, an attack in the Parisian metro resulted in the deaths of 7 people and 86 people wounded. While the usual platitudes were rolled out

---

Sarajevo in the last week of June 1992.

about the evils of terrorism, few consequences followed.

In late September of 2001, CRJ had allowed himself to become optimistic. Following the 9/11 strategic surprise attack in the USA, it became clear that Osama bin Laden had no follow-up strategic plan for his successful tactical attack. Now that the Islamists had pulled the lion's tail, maybe the rest of the world would wake up to the Islamist threat. Unfortunately, this did not turn out to be the case. Instead, the Islamists began to portray themselves as the victims - as they always did after carrying out the worst atrocities.

CRJ had been one of the first to pick up on the Islamist response of how they would turn 9/11 around to continue their Islamization of Europe and the West. Not surprisingly, the article that alerted him was in the New York Times, the same newspaper that had dismissed the threat of Adolph Hitler in 1922.[50] The insightful article was titled 'Jihad and Truth,' and it portrayed Muslims who had supported terrorist funding before 9/11 as victims of abuse for their interpretation of 'Jihad.'

The Islamists attacks continued, rather than relenting. In France, CRJ's home, 71 attacks occurred between 1979 and 2019. The deadliest of those happened after the formation of the Islamic State in 2014. By itself, ISIS was responsible for 49.5% of all Islamist

---

[50] Mark Bulik, "1922: Hitler in Bavaria," The New York Times (The New York Times, February 10, 2015), https://www.nytimes.com/times-insider/2015/02/10/1922-hitler-in-bavaria/

attacks in France. Worse still, half of all the ISIS attacks in Europe were in France. The low point for France had been the ISIS attacks of the 13th of November 2015. These attacks had killed 137 people and wounded 413 more.[51] But just like the Charlie Hebdo attacks of just seven months earlier, the best Europe could manage was a few hashtags on Twitter and some candlelight parades.

If doubt existed about the Muslim Brotherhood, this dissipated while they were in power in Egypt in 2011 and 2012. Having eked out an election win following 40 years of President Hosni Mubarak's dictatorship, the Muslim Brotherhood had leaped into action. The press was crushed. The judiciary was destroyed, and women's rights were attacked. Egyptian low-income families, trying to have street parties featuring beer and food to celebrate weddings, were attacked by extremist Imams screaming, "Haram! Haram!" Opposition figures were jailed. The Egyptian people, recognizing a dictatorship when they saw one, drove the Muslim Brotherhood out of power in June 2012. Even with support financial support of President Obama and Secretary of State Hillary Clinton, the Ikhwani were crushed.

CRJ had not known whether to laugh or scream out loud when he had read an article in *The Atlantic* magazine. Showing no sense of irony, the magazine had published a report with the title "How Secular is

---

[51] Dominique Reynie, ed., "Islamist Terrorist Attacks in the World 1979-2019," Fondapol.org (Fondation pour l'innovation politique, November 20, 2019), https://www.fondapol.org/en/study/islamist-terrorist-attacks-in-the-world-1979-2019/

the Muslim Brotherhood?" The article responded to the clueless Director of National Intelligence, James Clapper, who had stated in congressional testimony that the Muslim Brothers were a "mostly secular" organization. *The Atlantic* had found several 'experts' to agree that the Muslim Brotherhood was not all that Islamist.[52]

After 2015, CRJ began to map out a concrete strategy of saving Europe from its progressive and cultural Marxist weaknesses. One thing was sure. It was too late to stop the spread of Islamists in Europe through political means. Their political entryism had been so successful that they controlled the agenda in various layers of government in multiple countries.

Stopping the Islamists in Europe would require a kinetic method. But, most importantly, it would have to be before the Islamists moved ahead with their plans to establish a series of mini caliphates in France, Belgium, and elsewhere.

The thought had finally struck CRJ in 2015 when Patrick Calvar, head of the French General Directorate for Internal Security (DGSI), shocked France. As head of the intelligence service responsible for internal security, he had stated that France was sliding towards civil war due to the growth of the Islamists in France. He said the spark for the civil war in France could be something like the mass sexual assault of

---

[52] Elspeth Reeve, "How Secular Is the Muslim Brotherhood?," theatlantic.com (Atlantic Media Company, October 26, 2013), https://www.theatlantic.com/international/archive/2011/02/how-secular-is-the-muslim-brotherhood/342270/

women, such as Germany in Cologne on New Year's Eve.[53]

CRJ had laughed out loud when it struck him:

Islam is the solution!

Rather than opposing the Islamists, CRJ realized that he should be supporting them in their ambitions. Then, when they moved for control, he would ensure their leaders and plans were exposed.

All that was missing, CRJ believed, was a suitable series of circumstances and a crisis.

CRJ knew that if the circumstances were in place, he could generate the crisis. However, unlike the hapless Gavrilo Princip or the strategically challenged Osama bin Laden, CRJ would organize both the proper amount of political violence and the necessary strategic plan.

With his new strategy in mind, CRJ doubled down on his efforts to understand the extent to which the Muslim Brotherhood had grown like cancer in Europe.

* * *

---

[53] Peter Allen Allen and Sam Tonkin, "France Is on the Verge of 'Civil War', the Country's Head of Intelligence Says," Daily Mail Online (Associated Newspapers, July 13, 2016), https://www.dailymail.co.uk/news/article-3685561/France-verge-civil-war-sparked-mass-sexual-assault-women-migrants-intelligence-chief-warns.html

CRJ soon learned that tracking the Islamist extremists required a multifaceted approach. Most analysts watched for terrorist attacks and then traced the terrorist back. By identifying the path to radicalization and then violence, it was possible to assess extremist networks. But CRJ soon realized that the Islamist footprint in Europe was much larger than it appeared. The key to tracking the Islamist's networks lay in tracking their front group charities, their university student organizations, 'cultural centers,' and mosques that had Imams from the International Union of Muslim Scholars. Based on this methodology, CRJ was able to map out the network of Muslim Brotherhood Islamists in Europe. He was also able to form a good working picture of various Islamist networks, such as those run by the Turkish Directorate of Religious Affairs (Diyanet Islerii Baskanlgi) and the Salafists.

In April of 2019, CRJ was encouraged by the book written by two French authors, Christian Chesnot and Georges Malbrunot. The book, titled *The Qatar Papers: How the Emirate Finances Islam in France and Europe*, resulted from an intelligence leak from the state of Qatar. An anonymous source, probably an employee of the Qatar Charity, had leaked hundreds of documents. The documents show the money trail on Qatar Charity funding Muslim Brotherhood projects in Europe and Canada.[54] The

---

[54] Staff Writer Al Arabiya English, "French Book Reveals How Qatar Funded Muslim Brotherhood Mosques in Europe," english.alarabiya.net (Al Arabiya English, May 20, 2020),
https://english.alarabiya.net/features/2019/04/07/Fr ench-book-reveals-how-Qatar-funded-Muslim-

details were stunning as they exposed individual projects and the money they had received.

The Islamist extremist mapping project CRJ was developing was assisted with money he could send to various students and researchers indirectly. In June of 2019, a researcher working for CRJ found a gold mine. The researcher had been looking for more information on the Qatar Charity and its money trail. Instead of finding more on Qatar Charity, the researcher found a backdoor left open during an IT upgrade at the Eid Charity, also operated by the Royal Family of Qatar. Thinking quickly, the researcher had downloaded two significant sets of files.

The first was the mother lode. While Qatar Charity had been funding Muslim Brotherhood projects in Europe and North America, the Eid Charity had been financing many extremist projects worldwide. The files downloaded were a listing of every project funded by Eid Charity from 2012 to 2019. The 50,000 individual project donations were in 70 countries. It also provided an understanding of Qatar's pathways to funnel money for extremist projects from Eid Charity from one country to another before it wound up in the hands of the final recipient. As a bonus, the researcher also found more information on the '10,000 Imams' project run by the Eid Charity. The project was designed to reach out and 'retrain' some 10,000 Imams who would be guided towards spreading the Islamist ideological message.

Based on the public knowledge available through the Qatar Papers, the Eid Charity files, and his own

Brotherhood-mosques-in-Europe-research, CRJ now had a comprehensive picture of the Muslim Brotherhood in Europe and its presence in about 85 different countries worldwide.

CRJ's research had also revealed that 33,769 Islamist attacks had killed at least 167,096 people between 1979 and 2019 in various countries around the globe.[55]

At the end of 2019, CRJ had made several assessments he shared with only himself. Among them were:

- France was finished as a republic. The Islamists had driven so deep into the heart of France that no government policy could now reverse it. The politicians had been bought off or were too cowardly to speak out. The Senate of France had identified the Muslim Brotherhood as the number one Islamist enemy of France.[56] When talking about the Islamists, President Macron had said " "We are talking about people who, in the name of a religion, pursue a political project," he said. "A political Islam that wants to secede from our Republic."[57]

---

[55] Dominique Reynie, ed., "Islamist Terrorist Attacks in the World 1979-2019," Fondapol.org (Fondation pour l'innovation politique, November 20, 2019), https://www.fondapol.org/en/study/islamist-terrorist-attacks-in-the-world-1979-2019/

[56] Nathalie Delattre and Jacqueline Eustache-Brinio, "Radicalisation Islamiste - Sénat," Commission of Inquiry into Islamist Radicalization and the Means of Combating It (senat.fr, July 9, 2020), http://www.senat.fr/commission/enquete/radicalisation_i slamiste.html

- Belgium was in as bad a condition as France, or perhaps worse.

- London had become a hub for Salafi and Jihadist activism in Europe. The name Londonistan was appropriate.[58]

- The Islamists were moving to another stage of their long-term plan. After more than 65 years of infiltrating into the various political, social, and legal systems of Europe, they were planning to move toward taking control. Their decision was based on their belief that the increased focus on them would outweigh their increasing strength. Therefore, they needed to move in the next few years or abandon the plan.

- If Europe had a future as a civilization, it would have to kill the cancer of the Islamists that the Europeans had allowed to grow, starting from its locations in Austria, Germany, France, the UK, Belgium, and the former Yugoslavia.

- Ironically, many countries in the Middle East, the incubators for the most extreme

---

[57] Michel Rose, "Macron Launches Crackdown on 'Islamist Separatism' in Muslim Communities," Reuters (Thomson Reuters, October 2, 2020), https://www.reuters.com/article/us-france-macron-separatism-idUSKBN26N213
[58] Melanie Phillips, "Londonistan: How Britain Created a Terror State Within," Amazon.com (Gibson Square, May 2, 2007), https://www.amazon.com/Londonistan-Melanie-Phillips/dp/1594031975

Islamists, were now turning on them. Saudi Arabia had declared the Muslim Brotherhood a terrorist group. The United Arab Emirates had published a list of the leading Muslim Brotherhood front groups in the Middle East and Europe.

- While the Muslim Brothers were being weakened in the Middle East in general, they were growing elsewhere. Since the Muslim Brotherhood government had fallen in Egypt, its membership had spread to countries where they were welcome such as Canada, Turkey, the United Kingdom, and Qatar.

* * *

The blindness of the Europeans was fascinating to CRJ. Even when the Islamists openly stated their intentions, the leaders of Europe simply lapsed into mindless babble about inclusivity, diversity, tolerance, and social justice. They continued to allow the (intolerant) Islamist infrastructure to be built in Europe and often paid for it. The EU was consistently giving money to organizations they knew were Muslim Brotherhood front groups. Among the most influential front group was Islamic Assistance Transnational.

CRJ had a collection of 'statements of intent' from the Islamists. He had anonymously circulated the list to a variety of leaders and intelligence agencies in Europe. He had carefully monitored the recipients for several months to see if any reaction occurred. It did not.

Among the statements he had collected were:

- *"It is the nature of Islam to dominate, not to be dominated, to impose its law on all nations and to extend its power to the entire planet."* Hassan al-Banna, founder of the Muslim Brotherhood.

- *"Islam wishes to destroy all states and governments anywhere on the face of the earth which are opposed to the ideology and program of Islam regardless of the country or the Nation which rules it."* Abul A'la Maududi, founder of Jamaat-e-Islami.

- *"Therefore, prepare for jihad and be the lovers of death. Life itself shall come searching after you. You should yearn for an honorable death and you will gain perfect happiness. May Allah grant myself and yours the honour of martyrdom in His way!"* Hassan al-Banna, founder of the Muslim Brotherhood, as quoted by the Islamic Circle of North America (ICNA) Youth Wing of Canada.

- *"Conquest through da'awa, that is what we hope for. We will conquer Europe, we will conquer America. Not through the sword but through da'awa."* Yusuf Qaradawi, Speech to the Muslim Youth of North America Conference, Toledo Ohio, 1995.

- *"The mosques are our barracks, the domes our helmets, the minarets our bayonets and the faithful our soldiers."* President Erdogan of Turkey.

- *"Democracy is like a train. You get off once you have reached your destination."* President Erdogan of Turkey.

- *"The process of settlement is a 'Civilization-Jihadist Process' with all the word means. The Ikhwan Muslim Brotherhood must understand that their work in America is a kind of grand jihad in eliminating and destroying the Western civilization from within and 'sabotaging' its miserable house by their hands and the hands of the believers..."* Muslim Brotherhood, *An Explanatory Memorandum: On the General Strategic Goal for the Group in North America,* 1992.

- *"There is a woman who cannot agree to being beaten, and sees this as humiliation, while some women enjoy the beating and for them, only beating to cause them sorrow is suitable..."* Yousef al Qaradawi.

* * *

Following most Islamist terrorist attacks, CRJ watched the news in fascination. It was always the same. A series of so-called experts, talking heads, and politicians would appear on the screen. The politicians would try to outdo each other in the battle of the adjectives. First, the terrorists would be called 'cowardly,' 'craven' or 'spineless.' Then they would be called 'stupid' or 'insane' or 'crazy.' Following that, words such as 'cruel' or 'heartless' or 'despicable' would be used. In the end, someone would accuse them of being 'subhuman' or 'savages.'

Then the promises would start.

The terrorist would be hunted down and caught. These attacks would not be allowed to happen again.

Then it would happen again because none of the political leaders could admit they had an Islamist problem.

Wash. Rinse. Repeat.

CRJ hated the Islamist terrorists and even more so those who put them on the path to radicalization. But unlike those who denigrated them, CRJ had developed an understanding.

Know your enemy.

The enemy was human. The enemy was determined. The individual terrorist was the low end of the scale of the enemy. Because they were collectivists, the front-line soldier was an individual whose life was expendable. The Islamists were often assessed by looking at the terrorists rather than those who paid for the terrorism.

For CRJ, the path to understanding the Islamists lay through looking at their leaders. The leadership class of the Islamists was superior to that of Western politicians. They were cultured, educated, and sophisticated. The Muslim Brotherhood leaders could assess the political environment around them. They could be murderously violent when it was to their advantage. The next day, they could speak the language of human rights, discrimination, and victimhood.

Most importantly, the leadership of the Muslim Brotherhood was strategically competent, unlike Western leaders. They had an objective – which was the global spread of their form of political Islam. The objective led them to develop strategies that could be adapted to individual political systems. Those strategies were, in turn, used to determine how operations would proceed. Specific tactics supported those operations. The Islamist leadership was not infallible, and it did make mistakes. But it was capable of learning from those mistakes and adapting - unlike Western leaders who failed to stop terrorists every time and then went back to the same strategically bankrupt set of worn-out tactics.

* * *

CRJ had a conclusion by the end of 2019. The future of Europe was at stake, failing due to its own internal incompetence and the skill of a new class of invaders – The Islamists.

Rather than taking a Clausewitzian approach and trying to attack their center of mass, CRJ had studied the enemy and would use their strength against them. He would provide the final push and money necessary to get them to rise– and then destroy them.

Sun Tzu would be proud.

Chapter 15: A Lawyer at Knife Point

LOCATION: Credenhill, Hereford, UK

DATE: 30 June

TIME: 04:00 AM

Captain Davies woke with a start. His instincts said something was wrong. He was in bed, at home. He looked at this wife next to him. Asleep as she should be. The house was silent. The alarm clock said it was 04:00.

He reached for his SIG Sauer P226 pistol, tucked down between the bed and the side table.

"Don't," came the whispered command.

Captain Davies turned towards the bedroom door while continuing to reach for the pistol with his right hand.

Major Berikoff briefly appeared in a silhouette in the doorway, waved, and moved away. Davies jumped to his feet and moved into the hallway.

Without so much as hello, the Major pointed to the street, stating, "My motor is out front. We head for London. Wear something nice." He started to head down the stairs to the front landing and turned his head back for a second. "Don't forget to reset your house alarm."

Captain Davies' training and discipline took over. He grabbed his blue blazer, pants, shirt, and tie. Then off to the loo. He carried out a quick but painful dry shave with a dual blade disposable, and a splash of mouthwash finished the ablutions. Pants on. Shirt. Socks. Jacket and tie in hand, down the stairs.

While heading down the stairs, it hit home. Being tossed out of bed and sent on a mission with no warning was normal enough, but how had the Major entered his house? He had either defeated the alarm system or had the code, which only he and his wife held. For Davies, it was likely to remain one of life's little mysteries. He reset the alarm and headed to the Major's vehicle.

Upon entering the vehicle, the Major immediately moved down the street at an alarming speed. He handed a disposable coffee cup to the Captain. "The coffee is some of that horrid take-out stuff from a drive-thru, but it might be better than nothing." The Major was aware that Captain Davies was an early morning coffee drinker. Drinking coffee was somewhat of a character flaw to the Major, but one that he had decided to indulge, given the early morning entry into the Captain's house.

The Major looked ahead into the darkness and said nothing more. The inference was obvious. The Major wanted silence for the time being and did not explain the break-in or the mission in London. Or wherever it was, they were going.

Once on the A40, Davies could see Gloucester to the south. He was now confident they were headed to London, usually a drive that could take four hours or more. However, Davies figured that they might arrive sooner. The speedometer appeared to be stuck at 160 kilometers per hour. Strangely to him, no wind noise existed, and the car's engine did not indicate that it was straining to maintain the speed.

The Major seemed to have a thing for 'motors' as he described them. The Jaguar F-Type was done entirely in black, which was fitting for their current high-speed night run. The only thing that was not black seemed to be the yellow brake calipers, which Davies had noted walking from the front door to the car. They seemed vaguely out of place.

When they were a few minutes past Gloucester, the Major reached over to the screen in the center of the console. Two quick touches and music filled the car's cabin, seeming to come from nowhere in particular.

Davies saw this as a signal that the Major was now ready to communicate.

Uncertain of where to start, Davies decided to start with the car. "Hard to believe we have been doing over 160 kilometers an hour. The car is quiet and hardly seems to be moving."

"We are hardly moving, Andrew. This coupe is supposed to be able to go twice this speed flat out. Never actually tried it."

Davies decided to try prodding a bit. "Are we in a rush to get to London?"

"Something has come up that needs our attention. A law firm wants to sue Trooper Skiffington for a human rights violation. It seems that Hossein Jafari is going to file a lawsuit claiming that his human rights were violated on Flight 406. He believes we physically abused him during his detention. Something about the broken bones in his hand and bruises on his chest and right knee."

The Captain thought about this for a few seconds. It did not make sense. "How could he file a lawsuit against us? He is a terrorist, and the injuries to his hand were in the fight to get his gun. The bruises were not even from us. That was the flight attendant. On top of that, how could a London law firm know what went on during the flight, let alone have the time to form the intention to file a lawsuit this soon? And if I may ask, how do you know about it?"

"Good points. The law firm involved is the same one trying to sue our boys for war crimes in Ireland back in the days of the troubles. A bunch of lefty progressives who knew full well what went as the war was being fought. Still, it gives them a chance to wear down support for law and order while at the same time charging shameful fees paid by the taxpayer—an outrage all around. A well-placed source in a low-level position at the law firm overheard a few details and passed the information along to MI5. They called the Colonel. The law firm intends to make the lawsuit announcement this morning."

"Should I ask what our role is on all of this?"

"All in good time. I have the makings of an idea of what to do, but we need a bit more yet. We are going to do a little intelligence collection and then make a quick stop at the firm."

With that, the Major refocused his eyes on the road and went silent again.

Just over two hours later, they arrived in the City of Westminster. Captain Davies was silently thankful that the city traffic had forced the Major to slow down. Then, looking up, he saw they were at Thames House, otherwise known as the headquarters of the MI5 – the UK's internal counterintelligence service.

The Major exited the car and looked back at the Captain. "Stay here and keep an eye on the motor. If told to move along, just tell them we are here on official business, and they should check with Deputy Director-General. I will be back in a flash."

Captain Davies almost had to laugh. He had been dragged out of bed and driven through the countryside at racetrack speed on some mission on which he had no details. So now it was his job to sit and mind the car. 'Hurry up and wait' was the lament of every soldier who madly dashed about under orders, only to be told to sit and do nothing.

Davies thought about the contact point. The Deputy Director-General was responsible for operational activity, so this stop might prove interesting.

Forty minutes later, the Major arrived back, looking bright and cheery.

"Wonderful news, Andrew. We are off to the viper's den, otherwise known as the law firm of Chevalier and Tag. You have been extremely patient. Let me tell you about my supper last evening and how I wound up in your house this morning."

The Major now seemed rather animated, especially after remaining silent for most of the drive to London.

"Just as I was sitting down to supper last night, the Colonel rang me up. He had received a call from a contact at MI5 telling him about the possibility of a lawsuit against us. He was not surprised by the lawsuit but rather at the speed of it. On top of that, the lawyers involved seemed to have an incredible amount of detail about an event that had only happened two days prior. When he mentioned that Chevalier and Tag were involved, it came as no surprise as they have created an entire enterprise around bogus lawsuits harassing the military."

"The fellow behind the law firm's efforts is Niles Chevalier. A nasty piece of work. He is not the brightest lawyer ever called to the bar, but he is cunning and well connected to all the right people. I thought last night that he must be the driving force behind this, so we passed this onto MI5. Following that, I met the Colonel in his office. He suggested I follow up on any possible further avenues. When I left the Colonel, I gave a call to a London-based security company. Not too many folks noticed it last year, but Chevalier was rather suddenly divorced from his wife. The whole thing happened overnight, and not even The Mirror picked up on it. A dodgy fellow runs the security company, but he is good at what he does. I explained to him that it would be useful if he cooperated with us, as he might soon need a favor as well. Rumors were that his security company had been working for Chevalier's wife during the divorce, so he had to have some background material that would sully the lawyer's name. As it turns out, our recently divorced lawyer has a few predilections of the unsavory kind. These character flaws have to be why the divorce went through quickly. The wife threatened him, and he agreed."

Captain Davies sat in silence, putting all of this together. Something was afoot.

The Major continued. "The trip to MI5 this morning was quite profitable. After the Colonel told MI5 the lawyer's name, they did a little digging of their own. They asked GCHQ for a bit of help. The good folks at GCHQ[59] could not give much, but it turns out that our lawyer friend, whom we shall soon visit, received a call from a cell phone in Brussels on the same day as the hijacking. The cell phone was a burner, so it

---

[59] Unknown Editors, "Government Communications Headquarters (GCHQ)," en.wikipedia.org (Wikimedia Foundation, May 29, 2021), https://en.wikipedia.org/wiki/GCHQ

cannot be traced, but right after Chevalier was called, he, in turn, called two of his associates. GCHQ says the call outlined the necessary details for the lawsuit, including detailed information on how we grabbed Hossein's gun and shot Ali. But get this, it also told them about the flight attendant and her actions. Whoever it was, had to have been on the plane or was talking to someone who was. And they had to be in the economy cabin."

The information hit the Captain like a battering ram. A fourth hijacker must exist, or at the least someone on board had been working with them. That person must have had the fourth phone. The Major paused for a minute while collecting his thoughts and then continued. "Now that we have all the necessary bits of intelligence, we are going to visit the viper in his lair. He has injected poison into enough people for now. Your job is to play along and back me up. I will do most of the talking."

Upon arriving at the lawyer's office, they took the stairs to the second floor. The Major approached the reception desk with a bright smile. "Good morning. We have an appointment with Niles Chevalier." The receptionist's eyes looked away from the Major, over to the Captain, and back to the Major. "Sorry," she said, "But Mr. Chevalier has no outside appointments booked for today. Perhaps I can make an appointment for another time?"

The Major gave her a bright smile. "That will not be necessary. We will show ourselves in." With that, the

Major headed off down the hallway to the left, with the Captain two paces behind him.

Niles Chevalier looked appropriately startled as his office door flew open unannounced. The look of shock turned to one of horror as he recognized who was in his office.

"Roy. For God's sake. Have you ever heard of knocking? What are you doing here? Who is he?"

A somewhat-less-than-discrete knock sounded from the door. The Major turned to Mr. Chevalier and told him, "Send her away. Tell her all is well."

The Captain opened the door enough to let Chevalier pass the message. She was not convinced, but nothing more could be done. She turned right upon heading off. The Captain nodded to the Major to indicate that she had not returned to her desk. She would most likely be going to tell another staff member that something was amiss.

The Major suddenly pushed Mr. Chevalier back into his chair. Turning to the Captain, he instructed him to knock any other lawyers who entered the room into a state of unconsciousness.

The Major then pulled his Fairbairn–Sykes double-edged fighting knife and pointed it directly at the throat of Niles. He remained silent for about 15 seconds while the lawyer considered his new reality.

"Let me explain this to you in simple terms, Niles. We know all about the press release you sent out this morning stating you are launching a human rights case against Trooper Skiffington. We know all about the phone call you received from Brussels telling you about the hijacking. And we know you immediately called your colleagues to start working on the case that same evening. So here is what you are going to do. You are going to issue another press release as soon as we leave. The press release will say that the whole case is based on misinformation and that you apologize unreservedly for the entire process. On top of that, you will add a couple of lines about how the enlisted soldiers of Her Majesty's forces did an amazing job of stopping a terrorist plot. You will conclude by saying they are the cream of the crop and among the best in the world."

The Major turned and smiled at the Captain. "I think our two lads will like that last bit."

"So, Niles, are we in agreement?"

By now, Niles had recovered some of his composure. "Not only do I not agree, Roy, but I will also file a complaint against you and your thug. My staff knows you are here. By the time I am done, you will not get a job as a security guard at Bluewater Mall. Your regiment will be in tatters, and I will sue the entire chain of command for millions of pounds for this assault. You are done!"

The Major pulled Niles to his feet. "Look out your window. See the Canary Wharf Tower?"

Niles turned without thinking and then collapsed to the floor as the air left his lungs. The Major's right fingers had driven up into Nile's diaphragm, and he quit breathing for a bit.

"Give me a hand, Captain. Pull him around to the front of his desk."

Once he was laid out in front of the desk, the Major sat on his chest. Niles weakly attempted to push him off but then saw the knife back at his throat.

"I am sorry about this awkward situation, Niles. My fault entirely. If I had explained the situation more precisely, we would have departed by now, and you could get back to doing whatever it is you do. Now, let us begin anew. You will agree to issue the press release. It will have a full apology. If you do not, I will walk out of this office and address your colleagues on some of the finer points of your divorce. For instance, they will be told that your ex-wife hired a rather well-known security firm to track you. What they found, of course, was the reason for the divorce. I will also show them a few photos that may not otherwise be in the family album. Photos like this one, for instance."

The Major pulled a photo out of his jacket pocket and physically forced it into the face of Niles.

Niles had the common sense to remain silent.

The Major put the photo back into his pocket. "Just before we head out, Niles, I have a quick question for you. How long have you had this predilection? Even in your rarified social circles, this sort of thing must be seen as a bit off." Niles remained silent.

"One more thing, Niles. You will now apologize to my colleague as well. He is a highly trained killer, to be sure, but he is no thug. He might not wear the right ties to the right clubs, but he miles ahead of you in character."

Niles looked over at the Captain but remained silent. The Major touched the knife to his throat.

"Sorry," was the one-word response.

"We are off." This to the Captain. "Put this well-mannered and cooperative lawyer back into his rather posh Rische Ergonomic chair. We can be back home for tea."

"Ta-ta for now, Niles. Will I be seeing you at Henley for the Royal Regatta in a few days?

No answer was forthcoming from Niles.

As they approached the car, the Major tossed the key fob to Davies. "You are driving. You looked distinctly uncomfortable for most of the trip down, so you can do the honors on the way back. But first, a quick call to report on some of the finer details."

Once back in the car after the call, the Major simply announced. "Been a bit of a long couple of days. Wake me up in two hours. We need to have a bit of a chat before our next meeting with the Colonel."

Two hours later, to the minute, Captain Davies used his left elbow to prod the Major slightly. The Major surveyed the terrain around him. "We are not yet at Gloucester. Did something go wrong?"

"I have been trying to do the speed limit. Unfortunately, this sort of motor does tend to attract police attention."

"Step on it anyway. We have much to do when we get back. Now, Andrew, tell me. What have you learned since this morning?"

"I will skip over the bits where it turns out you are uncommonly well-connected. The first thing is that it is now clear that Skiffington was correct. Four hijackers must have existed, or at the very least, a fourth who was an observer or communicator. Maybe he or she was to have played some sort of role that would have only been important when the plane landed. Given the details, whoever it was had to be in the economy cabin. We can start to look for them in that area of the plane. Second, whoever is behind this has reach. If our lawyer Mr. Chevalier was not in on the hijacking beforehand, someone with influence must be close to him. Why would he go public with the action against Trooper Skiffington so quickly? Someone is leaning on him and hard. Then the call from Brussels. Of all the places in Europe, why is the call coming from Brussels? The city is the center of power for the European Union. Whoever is behind this could be connected to the EU. Maybe someone who is still upset with the whole Brexit mess? An individual, or a group, has put a considerable amount of effort into an aircraft hijacking for reasons that are not clear. But they have incredible reach, and we are being manipulated into some sort of a much larger affair. I fear we have not heard the end of this, and it may not end well. One thing I did not get. What was on the photo you showed the lawyer? The photo scared him more than your knife."

The Major allowed himself to smile for a second. "What the lawyer has been doing is not a violation of anyone's human rights. Rather, it is something that should be reported to the Royal Society for the Prevention of Cruelty to Animals."

Captain Davies sat in silence while he contemplated the implications of that statement.

"Any other thoughts, Andrew?"

"Does a connection exist between that airfield in Germany and the phone call from Brussels? Does this lawsuit have a connection to something else? Lastly, Mr. Chevalier will not be sending you a Christmas card this year, and you might want to watch your back if you go to the Henley Regatta."

"All good points, Andrew. You will come along with me when we meet with the Colonel. It should be an interesting conversation. Have you called your wife yet? It could be a long day. Or week. Or month."

The Major lapsed back into silence, and the Captain stepped on it. A speeding ticket at this point no longer seemed a concern.

Chapter 16: Risks and Rewards

LOCATION: Frankfurt Hauptbahnhof, Germany

DATE: 30 June

TIME: 07:30 AM

Jochen Stenhammar should have been having a good day. He was walking to work with clear skies, and the train had not been crowded. His new girlfriend was planning a four-day getaway to the Greek Islands. His personal car, a two-seater, had just come back from the dealer after maintenance. To his surprise, nothing was seriously wrong, and the cost was minimal.

Yet he had 'that feeling' again. Something was wrong. Seriously wrong.

Jochen was the Vice President of Operational Risk at the Frankfurt-based Hessen Reinsurance Group. It was a massively wealthy reinsurance company whose main line of business was to insure other insurance companies in case of catastrophic losses. One wrong decision, or one bad claim and billions of Euros could be lost. His bosses at Hessen Reinsurance took risk seriously. This was why he was well paid, but also the reason he knew he could be fired and blacklisted in a heartbeat.

As he was walking up Kaiserstrasse, Jochen stopped and waited for traffic as he was crossing Elbestrasse.

Not five meters off the main thoroughfare was a man dressed in worn-out clothing. He was motionless, seated on the sidewalk. The heroin needle was still in his arm, and the rubber hose he had used to tie off his arm lay on the ground beside him. Such was the situation in the new Germany that no one noticed.

When he judged he was about five minutes away from his office, Jochen sent a group text to his staff, telling them to meet with him.

* * *

As he continued walking, Jochen thought back over the events that had led him to be at Hessen Reinsurance.

Some events had happened several years earlier.

He had started his working life as a criminal analyst in Wiesbaden with the Bundeskriminalamt (BKA), Germany's Federal Criminal Police Office. His work on social unrest and violence, mainly concerning economic conditions, caught the attention of several senior officials. His written reports were clear, precise, and – to the surprise of many – consistently accurate. He had been able to define which groups would create violence at otherwise peaceful protests and was generally able to identify the individuals involved.

Not all had been good at the BKA. His work sometimes created discontent with senior officials as his methods of analysis were controversial. His work embarrassed senior officials who had entrenched but frequently wrong views of the changing world. He had quickly learned that being precise in his analysis was not appreciated by those who had made careers out of being conventional, if often wrong. In a bureaucracy, it was essential to stay within proscribed boundaries. Being right but out of the limitations would be punished. Being wrong, but staying within limits, would be rewarded.

Governments, he learned, often reward failure.

Jochen had occasionally laughed to himself while watching his superiors. Robert Michels' book *The Iron Law of Oligarchy* had been correct in many ways. All bureaucracies, when they grow, become oligarchies. All organizations, sooner or later, will come to be led by a 'leadership class.' The leadership class will take over all aspects of the organization and cease to become 'servants of the masses' and instead become the rulers. Michels had also argued that a representative democracy's goal of eliminating the role of the elites was impossible. Sooner or later, the elites would come to control the bureaucracies and corporations. Such was the history of civilization over the two thousand years or more, and he could do little about it.

With some relief, he had left the BKA after ten years and had gone to work for Deutsche Bundesbank – Germany's central bank. A senior official at the BKA had told him to apply and suggested he would be hired, and he was. Jochen had then understood that while he had made a few enemies with his work, he had also made a few well-placed friends.

His time in the operational risk section of the German Central Bank had been outstanding. He was allowed more latitude inside the organization and was able to work with other Central Banks. Travel to meetings in other financial centers had been educational, as were the side trips to the problem areas. Athens. Barcelona. Ankara. Beirut. Cairo. Toronto. New York.

While visiting some of the more problematic areas, he identified himself as Danish rather than German. It was an effective way to avoid some conversations which might not have gone well. Nevertheless, one thing had become apparent. The situation on the ground varied widely from what the official statements said. The so-called danger zone of the Exarcheia District in Athens turned out to be much friendlier and safer than Omonoia Square or Syntagma Square. But that was not something he would mention in a trip report to his superiors. They had been among those who warned that the Exarcheia District was too dangerous for a visit.

Almost five years after being hired at the Central Bank, Jochen was surprised by a short notice to meet a member of the bank's Executive Board for lunch in his private office. It was not so much an invitation as it was a summons.

Now what? Who had he upset this time? It must have been something rather serious to draw the attention of such a senior official, but why a lunch meeting? Was it something good? With trepidation in his heart, he headed up the Executive Board's office area.

Upon arriving at the office, he was greeted by an assistant. Cool. Professional. Friendly in a correct sort of way. But no indication as to whether he was walking into a meeting room or the lion's den.

He was met by Sebastian Koehn, a member of the Executive Board, as the assistant opened the door. "Come and join us. First, please say hello to Aldo Lange. He is the head of Hessen Reinsurance. He will be joining us for lunch and wants to discuss matters of social stability. Your name came up, so here you are. Feel free to share any views with him, and be aware that your views will stay in this room."

Jochen's internal warning systems went into high gear. Mere analysts, even senior ones, did not get invited to lunch with Sebastian Koehn. This was doubly true when the head of an organization that dealt with tens of billions was in the room. Jochen had surveyed Aldo Lange upon entering the office. Italian wool suit. A watch by Jaeger-LeCoultre. German briefcase. Silk tie – probably Japanese. Cufflinks with a single discrete diamond on a 100% cotton shirt with French cuffs. The uniform of the European technocratic class.

Sebastian Koehn seated them and called for lunch, which appeared as if by magic. Once they had started the meeting, Koehn initiated the discussions. "Jochen, you should know that Aldo and I went to university together. He has gone on to a leading position in business while I remain a mere servant of the people." Sebastian Koehn had the decency to smile at his obvious understatement. "Aldo is concerned that the research he is reading about some of our European Union partners. He seems to think that our colleagues in the intelligence services may be too optimistic in some areas and not well informed in others. As such, they may be missing a growing wave of social unrest and discontent in Europe. He tells me that he fears groupthink and stove piping[60] are a problem in these areas. You tend to bang heads with senior folks, which is why your views are worth reading. Explain to him, for example, your contrarian views on our friends in Greece and your little foray into the Exarcheia District."

Jochen took a drink of water (sparkling from France) as a means of delaying his answer for a few seconds. The Exarcheia visit had not been in his trip report.

---

[60] Stove piping is a major problem in the intelligence community. Critical intelligence may move up and down through an intelligence agency, but it may not get shared with other intelligence or law enforcement agencies. One of the key factors, for example, in the intelligence failure around 9/11 was that the FBI and the CIA both had significant intelligence on the potential hijackers. An interagency lack of cooperation, fueled by years of acrimony, ensured that the intelligence did not move horizontally between the agencies. Despite much discussion, considerable evidence suggests that the problems remain in the USA and many other countries.

Instead, a game was being played, and he did not know what it was.

One truth was obvious. If you are at a table and you do not know the rules, you are the mark. At this point, he reasoned only one approach could work. Be direct. Be 100% honest. Listen to the questions and answer what was being asked.

Jochen had turned slightly in his seat to face Aldo Lange. The movement was a body language signal to show he knew to whom he would speak. "Sir, a colleague from another bank and I went to Greece on a three-day visit to assess matters of the economy and social stability. We visited Athens and arranged it so that one day of the visit would fall on the national day parade, so security levels were high. The official view of security agencies in many countries is that Greece had internal stability issues. Most of the problems originated in the Exarcheia District, which is too violent to visit. We were also told that anarchists were controlling the area with threats of violence against the inhabitants. The advice was that the rest of Athens remained relatively safe. To be blunt, we found that most of this information was nonsense."

"You entered the restricted zone despite being warned against doing so?" This from Sebastian Koehn.

"Yes, we did. We visited the Syntagma Square area in front of the Parliament. It had a limited amount of tourist traffic but had been shut off to the residents of Athens unless they could show business in the area. The police were afraid of more riots. Following that, we went to Omonoia Square, the tourist area. It was depressing. The storefronts were mostly occupied with half-empty tourist shops, but a quick look around revealed that most office spaces above them were empty – an economic desert. However, we were offered multiple deals from street vendors on Rolex watches, cocaine, and heroin. Criminals operated in the open with no police in sight. We left that area quickly and decided to enter Exarcheia. If we had met any resistance or hostility, we would have said we were lost and left. Our cover story was that I was a Danish photographer, and my assistant was a Canadian journalist. We entered the zone at about 10:00 AM. Several of the inhabitants looked at us with curiosity but no hostility. We arrived at the former parking lot at Navarinou and Zoodochou Pigis Street, taken over as a gardening zone. That project was highly symbolic for them to show they can organize projects on the ground and not just burn things. Lunch was at a well-run and economical sidewalk café. Following that, we spent about three hours surveying every side street we could find. We assessed several things. First, we were safer in Exarcheia than in downtown Athens. We saw no police and no sign of any type of government officials. No ATMs were visible, and all stores used cash only. No chain restaurants or stores existed. No Costa coffee shops. No McDonalds. The streets were clean and free of litter. However, every square meter of wall space was covered in posters, most of which had revolutionary themes. In the late afternoon, we entered a bar. The bartender was male, but upon seating ourselves, we noted that everyone else was female. Maybe 15 customers in all. Again, we were regarded with curiosity but not hostility. We were tourists to them who had probably wandered off the beaten path. We noticed that all the women were in their twenties or thirties. They wore no make-up or nail polish and only limited jewelry. Their clothes were clean and of good quality, but nothing we could identify by a fashion label. After a few minutes, we concluded that we were in a most unusual bar. It was a gay-feminist-anarchist bar. Most likely, they were anarcho-syndicalists or anarcho-communists. We felt it a good idea not to ask too many questions."

"You did not feel yourself at risk at this point." This time the question was from Aldo Lange.

"No, Sir; quite the opposite."

"Why would you say they were anarcho-syndicalists or communists?"

"Several indicators. Posters on the wall had advertising about upcoming protests. The symbols were anarchist. Some customers had books. I could not read the titles, but one of them had an image of Tasos Theofilou on the cover. Another had a book with the logo of the Conspiracy of Fire[61,62] on it. They

---

[61] Unknown Editors, "Conspiracy of Fire Nuclei," en.wikipedia.org (Wikimedia Foundation, June 7, 2021), https://en.wikipedia.org/wiki/Conspiracy_of_Fire_Nuclei
[62] Unknown Editors, "'Conspiracy of Fire Nuclei' Terrorist Group," europarl.europa.eu (European Parliament,

also lacked any sense of humor. Every one of them looked deadly serious in the discussions, and not one of them smiled the entire time."

Jochen continued. "We noted one security issue. On our first evening, we visited Syntagma Square, directly in front of our hotel. Preparations were being made for a national day parade. On the reviewing dais, chairs were placed for the dignitaries the next day. Each one had a piece of paper on it showing who was to sit in that position. If someone wanted to attack a certain minister or foreign guest, you would know their position ahead of time. One other thought, this one on economics. On our last morning in Athens, we visited the Acropolis. A rather large sign says that the European Union has paid millions of Euros to restore the sight. But I was at the Acropolis five years ago. I can assure you that not one *sou* of the money was spent on restoration."

Jochen took another drink of water to create a pause in the discussion. The next few minutes would determine his future.

"All told, Sir, the governance model for Greece has effectively collapsed. The government-controlled areas are in decay. By contrast, the anarchist area appeared to be stable. The government and the anarchists appear to have reached an understanding. The police stay out of Exarcheia while the

February 25, 2020),
https://www.europarl.europa.eu/doceo/document/E-9-2019-004044_EN.html

government continues to provide water and electricity. The anarchist zone runs entirely in cash, and no one collects or pays taxes. It is becoming an autonomous zone outside of the control of the government."

Jochen paused again for a moment. "It is not clear to me, but this arrangement may become the new normal for cities in southern Europe where the economy is failing and weak governments cannot respond. The 700 Euro generation[63] will become a catalyst for discontent. Movements such as OCCUPY and Los Indignados should be seen as Indicators and Warnings[64] of future social unrest. The European Union and its constituent governments are failing. Badly. They are blinded by their vision of a united Europe and suffer from delusions of their competency. They are missing the not-so-faint signals that show the failures."

---

[63] Hannah Mercedes, "700 Euro Generation," https://utsglobalstudio.wordpress.com/ (UTS Global Studio, June 10, 2016), https://utsglobalstudio.wordpress.com/2016/06/10/700-euro-generation/

[64] Indicators and Warnings (I&W) is an intelligence discipline. Analysis is done to see if activities by a potential adversary or source of unrest indicate an attack or upcoming crisis. For instance, if a country suddenly experiences a widespread shortage of vehicle batteries, this might be an indicator that their military is suddenly putting their forces on a high rate of readiness. Unusual shortages can be seen in the same way. For social unrest, a combination of high youth unemployment and a sudden spike in food prices is an indicator of potential unrest.

With that, Jochen readjusted his chair back to a more neutral angle between the two and picked up a sandwich. This was his signal that he was done, at least for the moment.

It was now the turn of a member of the Executive Board to speak. Whatever game was being played, Jochen sensed the outcome was at hand.

"Aldo, have you learned what you need to know?

"Indeed, I have. My visit here has been time well spent."

"Good." Sebastian Koehn turned to Jochen.

"It is almost 2:00 PM. Your employment here is finished, and you have the rest of the afternoon to clear out your desk. Let my assistant know if you need a car to move anything."

Jochen sat in stunned silence. Had he just been unceremoniously fired? And in front of one of the most influential persons in the financial community of Europe? He had suspected issues were at hand, but nothing this drastic.

Sebastian Koehn stood up and signaled to Jochen to stand as well. He pushed himself to his feet, wondering if he would remain standing or if his legs would collapse under him.

Aldo Lange smiled as he faced Jochen. "This is awkward. It seems Sebastian has fired you because of me. Perhaps this could help."

Jochen took the single sheet of paper and unfolded it. Across the top was the logo of Hessen Reinsurance. The following line stated it was an employment offer. Jochen struggled to read the short paragraph that was followed by a few lines with some rather large numbers. An annual salary that was well into six figures. A car allowance in five figures. A travel allowance in five figures. A long list of other benefits. An option to hire up to three staff of his choosing with their salaries to be determined.

Aldo Lange took up the conversation again. "I told Sebastian last week that I was in desperate need of an analyst who was grounded in risk analysis and social stability, especially in the economic context. We are heading into rough waters, and you might be just what I need. By the way, your former employer here is an extortionist. He insisted that I pay you a rather generous salary, or he would obstruct my attempt to steal you away from his clutches. You will be at our offices just before eight on Monday morning. Announce yourself to the front desk guards, and they will know how to direct you to our office. Don't be late."

A broad smile accompanied the last line.

With that, Sebastian Koehn reached over to shake Jochen's hand. "Thanks for all you have done for us. I predict great things for you. You best move along. You have much to do this afternoon, and Aldo here wants to spend another hour trying to tell me how to do my job. He is telling me that Central Bank policies are creating even further social unrest and political instability."

Shortly after that, Jochen found himself standing alone outside the office, the assistant being absent for the moment. After thinking for a bit, he opted for the stairs instead of the elevator. He walked down half a flight and then sat on a stair, staring at the concrete wall. He had just lost a job with no warning. One minute later, he had another job where he would – what? He had no idea what the job entailed, although the salary was enticing. No one had asked him if he would even take a new position. The option, he reasoned, was to either show up at Hessen Reinsurance on Monday morning – or be unemployed. Upon further reflection, he wondered if he should be flattered. The decision to have him moved had been taken at a relatively high level, and his input would not have affected the outcome.

Jochen stood up and headed down the stairs. It would take him less than an hour to remove his personal effects and get them stored in a locker. After that, it would be time for a glass of apple wine, or "Stöffche," as it was known. His favorite came from Schneider's Obsthof Am Steinberg, just north of Frankfurt. Jochen was happy to note that even in turbulent times, local apple wine producers kept up the traditions of providing excellent local versions of this cider-like drink, used by so many to kick-off a new adventure.

Chapter 17: Finding the Unknown Unknowns

LOCATION: Hessen Reinsurance, Frankfurt Office, Taunusturm Building

DATE: 30 July

TIME: 8:00 AM

Jochen smiled as he walked past the security guard at the Taunusturm Building, which housed the offices of the Hessen Reinsurance company. A quick trip up the dedicated company elevator and the swipe card reader allowed him into the double-doored office area. The team would be along shortly.

His first few months at Hessen Reinsurance had flown by quickly, and now, two years later, he was well into the pattern of working at Hessen.

While Hessen had the latest computers and technology, Jochen had startled a few people with his installation of a two-meter by three-meter whiteboard in the common area between their four glass-walled offices.

Now he stood and stared at the whiteboard. He considered the existing facts, the 'known unknowns, and the most troubling of all. The 'unknown unknowns.'[65]

He drew three circles with solid lines with a black marker. One for the assassination of Ilhan Benhaddara. Another for the aircraft hijacking of Atlantic Airways. The third was for the Amsterdam cash center robbery. A fourth circle was drawn off to the side with a dotted line – this for the MS Fulfillment of the Seas cruise ship fire.

Jochen sat back in a reclining office chair and stared some more. Were the three events connected? Was it possible to have three violent incidents in Europe in one day and seriously believe they were not related? But how were they linked?

A wild card existed. All reports suggested that the cruise ship fire in the Bay of Biscay was nothing more than an accident at sea compounded by failed electronics and inadequate firefighting gear.

Jochen considered the assassination first. Ilhan Benhaddara of Islamic Assistance Transnational had been killed in a public area with multiple witnesses, none of whom reported any helpful information beyond the obvious. Whoever planned the killing wanted to send a message with a public execution. Why kill her in Brussels and not in the United Kingdom, where IAT had its headquarters? The press release from IAT inferred that the dark forces of

[65] Unknown Editors, "There Are Known Knowns," en.wikipedia.org (Wikimedia Foundation, May 23, 2021), https://en.wikipedia.org/wiki/There_are_known_knowns

'Islamophobia had threatened her life.' By late afternoon on the 29th of June, the IAT suggested that Tarek Raman was 'unlocated.' According to police reports, Benhaddara attended meetings in Brussels with Tarek Raman. Where was he? Did he fear he would be assassinated next and go into hiding? And what was the message of her assassination? Islamic Assistance Transnational was a Sunni Muslim organization with multiple ties to the Muslim Brotherhood. Was it a right-wing group that killed her, as IAT had inferred? Or was this a power play within the ranks of extremist Islamists? Iran? Hezbollah? ISIS? More than 48 hours after the assassination, Jochen and his staff had more questions than answers.

Then there was the cash center robbery in Amsterdam. What stood out above everything else was that dozens of shots had been fired, a limited number from a .50 caliber sniping rifle and the rest from a 7.62mm PKM. Yet, no one had been injured. Whoever carried out the attack and robbery had demonstrated fire discipline.[66] On top of that, the attackers were either lucky or good. They had attacked the cash center just as the central vaults were being opened and the cash moved to the

---

[66] Fire discipline, in military terms, is the habit of direct control over a weapon which enables the soldier to obtain a high rate of hits per round fired and to ensure the weapon is only fired for effect when desired. When you see terrorist groups such as HAMAS firing off hundreds of rounds into the air, this is a sign of poor fire discipline and an indication of a unit which will not be effective in battle.

distribution area. Maybe they had done surveillance ahead of time to know when the vaults were opened? The attackers had taken nothing but 50- and 100-Euro banknotes. Following the escape, the one police car that might have been able to give chase had been mysteriously blocked in by a stolen truck. One last detail hit him—the weather. The early morning fog had ensured that a police helicopter would not have been practical, even if it could have been launched in time. The press had focussed heavily on reports that the attacker had yelled 'Allahu Akbar' during the attack. According to the talking heads and TV experts, this meant it was a jihadist attack. But this was no gang of ISIS terrorists or local jihadist wannabes. This was an attack force with incredible fire discipline that seemed more like a special forces attack than a gang of thugs. Once again, an event recorded on cameras with multiple witnesses had produced more questions than answers. Who put this kind of long-term surveillance and effort into a cash robbery? Was this funding for the Muslim Brotherhood? It was possible, but Qatar funded the Brothers generously. Why carry out this attack?

The aircraft hijacking was the worst. Over three hundred witnesses and no one could provide insightful information. The UK government press releases were useless. The three hijackers had been named, and witness reports suggested they were Iranians. Were they Iranian Revolutionary Guards? Was this an attempt at revenge for the killing of General Qasem Soleiman?[67] The press reports from

187

passengers said that the aircraft had been landed by two Canadian pilots who had been flying to Europe for a meeting at NATO School in Oberammergau.[68] The pilot scenario at least seemed plausible. But press reports that passengers had overpowered the hijackers seemed unlikely. Beyond rampant speculation, no indication existed as to why the aircraft was hijacked. It has been on its way to Frankfurt, but this meant nothing. Where did the hijackers want to go? And why? Again, a highly public event with 'politics' written all over it, but all that existed were questions.

Finally, there was the fire on the MS Fulfillment of the Seas. Was this connected? Cruise ship fires were rare, but this one seemed severe. Press reports indicated that the situation could have been worse if not for the presence of the MS Nordsee Bliss. The press quoted passengers who said the fire had spread rapidly. The passengers reported that preparations had been made for them to abandon ship. Nothing about the event seemed political. Multiple passengers had minor injuries and suffered smoke inhalation, but none had died. The only fatalities were the first two firefighting crew members who had perished attempting to fight the fire.

---

[67] Unknown Editors, "Qasem Soleimani," en.wikipedia.org (Wikimedia Foundation, May 23, 2021), https://en.wikipedia.org/wiki/Qasem_Soleimani
[68] Unknown Editors, "NATO School Oberammergau (NSO)," NATO School Oberammergau (NSO) - Home (North Atlantic Treaty Organization (NATO), 2021), https://www.natoschool.nato.int/

Jochen looked up as he heard the electronic lock on the outer door click. The inner door opened, and his three staff members entered, each carrying a stainless-steel thermos bearing the company logo. The team had a routine of meeting in the cafeteria before moving up to the office.

Jochen pointed at the whiteboard. "As we discussed yesterday, these events seem separate, yet three of them are highly political and raise more questions than answers. The fourth is a wild card. You are to work separately in your offices from now until 10:30. Then I want you to work together in front of the whiteboard until 11:30. At that point, you will tell me what you know. Feel free to order whatever food or drink you want from the cafeteria and have it delivered. Charge it to my account. I will be leaving the office shortly but should be back before 11:30. I have to go see a man about a dog."

Jochen wanted them to work in isolation from each other at the start. An arrangement like this tended to prevent groupthink[69] from setting in early, which would often weaken intelligence analysis.

Jochen then headed back to his own office, grabbed his small soft-sided briefcase, and headed out the door.

---

[69] Unknown Editors, "Groupthink," en.wikipedia.org (Wikimedia Foundation, May 5, 2021), https://en.wikipedia.org/wiki/Groupthink

* * *

Jochen sat outdoors at the Frankfurter Hof Hotel. The shade from the large red umbrellas and the immaculately trimmed hedges provided a tranquil atmosphere. He had received a rather cryptic text suggesting a meeting at the 'usual place.' The text number did not trace back to anyone he knew, but the reference to the usual place suggested his former boss at the BKA was the sender. At 09:30, Burnard arrived, looking as he always did. A policeman wearing a suit. It had been more than two years since Jochen had met with him. Waving at the waiter for the same espresso Jochen had on the table, Burnard sat down. "You are looking good, Jochen. How is life working among the rich and powerful? What is it like, coming down from the silver tower in the clouds to meet with us mere mortals?"

Burnard laughed at his own statement, and then his face lost all expression. "I have a problem, and you are going to help." Jochen noted the nature of the request; this was not quite an old friend asking for a favor. This was a member of the BKA stipulating his cooperation. Such requests were not to be ignored, and Jochen owed favors in this case.

Burnard went silent as the waiter approached. As the waiter retreated, he started again. "You have heard about the aircraft hijacking and how the hijackers were overpowered, and the aircraft landed at a Royal Air Force base?"

190

Jochen nodded, thinking it might be better to remain silent at this point.

"Did you know the destination of the hijackers might have been the Bonames Airfield, located just south of here?"

The name of the airfield was news. Nothing had identified an alternative landing field in Germany.

Jochen paused for a moment, gathering his thoughts and wondering why he was being informed. Something was coming. "The Bonames Airfield. Was it not some sort of military airbase? I heard about it years ago as it was closing and have heard nothing since then. Are you sure the hijackers were headed there?

Burnard nodded his affirmation. "Not completely sure, but the British MI6 is asking questions. You won't believe it. A private company with serious money had bought the whole airfield. The story seems to be that they want to turn it into a private airfield for executive jets. They were planning to have a repair and overhaul facility built along with some sort of training facility. There was to be a kitchen and supply system to keep the jets full of food and drink. We sent our people to the airfield yesterday. No one there. The only construction work done was to clear and expand the runway and install some electronics—nothing else. Even stranger, no one from the company can be found, and the company itself has already been dissolved. They were a front company, nothing but a shell corporation. When you trace the records, they lead nowhere. What do you think of that?"

Jochen felt a sense of intellectual calm for the first time in more than 24 hours. Now it was clear. The events had to be connected. Someone, or something, had to be pulling strings. His feelings had once again been correct. Now he could move ahead with the analysis with a greater level of confidence.

He looked at Burnard and smiled. "Why are you telling me this?"

Burnard remained expressionless. "You are going to help us. Your boss is Aldo Lange. He has contacts with whom we cannot talk. We are aware of how much money he spends seeking information. If anyone in the private sector can track these companies, it is his company. He hears things. You will impress him with your insider knowledge of the investigation. Then you will impress us by telling us who is behind the money."

The world's second-oldest profession[70] was playing the same game it had played for a few thousand

---

[70] A common joke in the intelligence community states that: "Intelligence is the world's second oldest profession, and it is every bit as honourable as the first. (A reference to prostitution.) The expression may have derived from the Book of Joshua in the Bible where it is stated that "*And Joshua the son of Nun sent out of Shittin two men to spy secretly, saying; Go view the land, even Jericho. And they went, and came into a harlot's house named Rahab and lodged there.*" (Joshua 2:1.)

years. Information is given, but more information is expected in return.

Jochen looked around and surveyed the Steigenberger Frankfurter Hof hotel area for a few seconds and then looked back at Burnard.

"Done."

"By the way, Jochen. How is that new company car – the 535i? And say hello to your girlfriend for me. Tell her I hope you enjoy your trip to Greece."

Jochen did not answer, but the point was made clear. He might have left the BKA, but the BKA had not forgotten him. For better or for worse.

Chapter 18: Fuzzy Thinking and Hard Data

LOCATION:	Frankfurt, Germany
DATE:	30 July
TIME:	10:30 AM

Having left the Frankfurter Hof sidewalk café meeting with his former superior at the BKA, Jochen had intended to head directly back to the offices of Hessen Reinsurance. Instead, he walked to the train station, bought another coffee and a newspaper. He sat, staring at the open pages of the paper. To the casual observer, he was just another bored commuter waiting for a train. The train station was a great place to sit. No one bothered you.

He was having another one of those moments. On the one hand, he was distraught. It was now clear that the terrorist attacks were not what they had seemed. A larger game was being played out, and he did not know what was behind it. On the other hand, the meeting with the BKA had confirmed his suspicions. Others were also raising questions.

Finally, after half an hour of sitting and thinking, he came to a decision. The path ahead was at least a bit clearer. He would have to put all the information together into a report and do what he had not previously done at Hessen Reinsurance - request a direct meeting with Aldo Lange. At the meeting, he would present his information and then ask for his help tracking down the front companies who had owned Bonames Airfield and then disappeared.

The meeting with BKA would not be in the report. Nor would he mention that the company information, if found, would be shared outside of Hessen.

Along the way back to his office, he looked down Weserstrasse. To his surprise, several police officers in riot gear were standing in a casual group. They were holding rather than wearing their helmets. But they had an armored vehicle, and all of them had 'NRW' in white letters on the back of their uniforms. The letters stood for North Rhine-Westphalia. They were probably from Koln, but what were they doing in Frankfurt? Outside police forces mean either some sort of training operation or problems were anticipated. He had heard of neither.

While he walked, Jochen wondered how to tell his staff about Bonames Airfield. This was a significant detail. But he wanted to hear the views they had developed before sharing this.

His staff was waiting as he entered the common area. The whiteboard was now a mass of lines and arrows: some red, some green. Bits of papers with names of individuals and group names were taped around the edges. Much had been discussed in his absence.

Jochen looked at his three team members. The first to be hired had been Horst. He was young and a hard-core numbers analyst who lived in a world of Big

Data, spreadsheets, multi-user gaming, and searching the Dark Web. Hiring him had been easy. All it took was a wheelbarrow of Hessen's money and the promise he could buy lots of 'toys.' Keeping him had been somewhat more complicated. A few problems emerged, especially after Aldo Lange had received a visit from the Bundesamt fur Verfassungsschutz, the Office for the Protection of the Constitution[71], or the BfV. Some of Horst's earlier efforts online had attracted the attention of the federal-level intelligence agency. They were not pleased to know Horst was now working for Hessen.

The second person hired had been Karl. Jochen had first heard of him when working for the BKA and met him through the European Experts Network on Terrorism.[72] Karl had worked for the Militarischer Abschirmdienst (MAD) or Military Counterintelligence. He had developed a stellar reputation for turning up information when no one else could. It was not just that he was brilliant, but

---

[71] Unknown Editors, "Federal Office for the Protection of the Constitution," en.wikipedia.org (Wikimedia Foundation, May 26, 2021), https://en.wikipedia.org/wiki/Federal_Office_for_the_Protection_of_the_Constitution
[72] Unknown Editors, "European Expert Network on Terrorism Issues (EENeT)," https://www.european-enet.org/ (European Expert Network on Terrorism Issues (EENeT), 2021), https://www.firstlinepractitioners.com/cve-infrastructure/european-expert-network-on-terrorism-issues-eenet

that he had a network of contacts in police, military, and security services through the West and much of South Asia. In the intelligence business, it was not what you know but who you know. Hiring him had been a bit more complicated. Attempts to lure him with money and opportunity had initially shown progress until the MAD found out about it. Jochen had been told to back off by an army colonel who appeared to have no personality or sense of humor. Jochen then resorted to asking Aldo Lange for assistance to see if strings could be pulled. They were, and Karl was now at Hessen. Lange had suggested that he not cross swords with the military for a while. They had not been impressed at having one of their star analysts taken through political pressures.

The third staff member hired had been Bettina. Unlike the other staff, she had no military, security, intelligence, or police experience. She had never worked for the government and had spent most of her life in universities. She was the daughter of an academic mother who studied linguistics and an engineering father who worked with systems integration. She had grown up with books, languages, and maths. As a child, she had traveled extensively with her parents. The trips had taken her from the highlights of Parisian art museums to the old spice market of Delhi. Hiring her had been the idea of Jochen's sister, who had met her at Heidelberg University.

On first meeting her, Jochen had wondered if his sister had been pulling a prank on him. She seemed a bit scattered and would speak in rapid bursts and then go silent. As the interview progressed, however, Jochen felt something unusual was happening. She could move effortlessly from discussing the tactical to the operational and the strategic without skipping a beat. She could integrate knowledge across disciplinary boundaries. She described complex analytical theories of analysis and did it in precise, straightforward language.

Most bizarre, when presented with a written exam aimed at testing her analytical skills in network analysis, she had read the two pages of information and put them aside. She described the premises of the test as weak. To his amazement, she had then provided examples of two illicit weapons trafficking networks in southern Europe and how they were organized. She identified that conducting a social network analysis of such organizations was a practical approach to breaking them up. But to her, the key players or 'cutpoints' identifiable by their 'betweenness' were information brokers. They were not the heads of a cell or the mafia chief that ran them. If you want to disrupt such a network, take out the brokers first, not the kingpins. She then said the test was interesting but had asked the wrong questions.

While listening to her, Jochen came to realize that she had that rarest of all abilities. She could take in a thousand points of data and see the organizational patterns in her mind.

Jochen had hired her on the spot. Convincing Karl that she was a good addition was not hard. Karl had been around and knew such people existed and, on occasion, could be helpful. Making a believer out of Horst had been difficult. He demanded hard points of data for everything and had little use for 'fuzzy thinking.' Over time, however, he realized that Bettina could fill in the intelligence gaps and do it with minimal time and effort.

With this in mind, Jochen decided to start with Karl. "Have the three of you come to any conclusions?"

Karl moved to the front of the whiteboard. "The good news is we all agree on several points. The three violent attacks are connected. The fourth event is reported as an accident, but we are less confident. The fire on the MS Fulfillment was severe, and a variety of reports suggest the Fulfillment could have been lost without the assistance of the Nordsee Bliss. We raise the possibility it was not an accident and may have been sabotage.

Additionally, we all agree that each of the three violent attacks raises more questions than they answer. The violence was managed and directed, but the intended outcome of the violence is not clear. Two of the violent attacks were designed to appear as terrorism, but terrorism is political violence. We know the Where, When, and How of these attacks, but not the Who or Why? Why these targets? The assassination has a terrorist attack feel about it, especially given that all three attacks happened on the same day. But what was the intent of the assassination? Ilhan Benhaddara was killed, but Tarek Raman has disappeared. Is he hiding out of fear? Was he the target? Or was the organization itself the target?"

Karl paused and looked at the other two. They nodded to him to continue.

"Now, this is where we begin to disagree. Horst thinks we lack sufficient data to conclude the fourth event is involved. I think that we can assess that the attacks are coordinated and have a common goal. That includes the fire at sea. We will find out that it was no accident. The intent of the attacks is not clear, and we cannot assess them at this point. But there is another possibility."

Karl looked at Bettina. She remained unmoving; her eyes focussed on a far distant point. She had spaced out again, which seemed to happen just before something profound came out.

She suddenly rejoined the other three as though embarrassed at having arrived late for a meeting. Her jaw moved up and down a bit, but nothing came out.

Finally, she pointed at the whiteboard. "Each event has no obvious political objective. Therefore, they are not, technically speaking, terrorist attacks despite what the media and security services report. The four events are coordinated. This analysis is based on temporal probability, geographic proximity, and logic. Three attacks and one 'accident' in one day, each with no objective, defies reason. The attacks are a diversion. They were designed to have an indirect effect. Each one may provide the opportunity for one or more groups to call for violence in their way. The question is not what the attacks were intended to do. The question is not even who organized them. These attacks are provocative but highly likely intended to act as cover for an even greater event. The assessment is simple. We need to do some horizon scanning[73],[74] and find a way of searching for the 'faint signals' that will tell us what events are about to occur."

With that, Bettina sat down again and went back into silent mode.

Horst looked skeptical, but Karl shrugged his shoulders, suggesting he could not disagree with her.

In his heart, Jochen knew Bettina was correct. "Well, good work, everyone, but now onto greater things. Would it help if I told you that the destination for the hijacked aircraft was Bonames Airfield, located just north of here?"

Horst and Bettina gave only blank stares. Karl looked over with interest. "The airfield was closed, and the runway was unserviceable. Or at least it was. Did I miss something?"

---

[73] Unknown Editors, "Horizon Scanning," en.wikipedia.org (Wikimedia Foundation, June 3, 2021), https://en.wikipedia.org/wiki/Horizon_scanning
[74] Peter Padbury, ed., "Introduction to Foresight," horizons.gc.ca (Policy Horizons Canada, 2021), https://horizons.gc.ca/en/our-work/learning-materials/foresight-training-manual-module-1-introduction-to-foresight/

Jochen picked up a black marker and wrote 'Brunel Industries' on the whiteboard. "This is the name of the company that bought the airfield. The plan, allegedly, was to create an executive jet airfield for the rich and famous. The company staff has disappeared, and initial investigations suggest it was a front company for an offshore company which – guess what – was another front company. The only work that was done was to clear the runway and extend it enough to make it useable for a one-time landing. Tell me why someone would want to land a hijacked 777 at Bonames Airfield. Then tell me who provides the money for the front companies. Then we get somewhere."

Karl almost laughed. "You said you were going to see a man about a dog. Did the dog tell you the name of the company?"

"Yes. Now we need to find out everything about that company. I am back to having a bad feeling again. And contact the Deutsche Marine[75] and see what they know about the ship fire. The Captain of the Nordsee Bliss was previously their man. They must have more information if this was more than an accident."

* * *

---

[75] Unknown Editors, "Deutsche Marine (German Navy)," en.wikipedia.org (Wikimedia Foundation, May 23, 2021), https://en.wikipedia.org/wiki/German_Navy

LOCATION: Office of Hessen Reinsurance

DATE: 30 July

TIME: 11:00 PM

Jochen looked up when he heard the electronic lock disengage on the outer office door. Karl walked in and waved at Jochen.

Jochen waved back and waited for Karl to arrive in his office and drop himself unceremoniously into the chair across from his desk. "How did you know I would be here at this hour of the night? I sent you all home at 18:00 hours."

"The same way I know the sun will rise tomorrow morning. Some things in life are predictable, and you are one of them."

"You have been drinking." It was a statement and not an accusation. If Karl had been drinking, a reason existed.

"Yes, I have." Karl's face was suddenly alight with a smile. "And you can tell our beloved 'Lords and Masters' that I was using the company credit card to buy copious amounts of alcohol. You will be pleased to know that the single malts were the most expensive on the menu at the Burbank Restaurant in the Roomers Hotel. Did you know that one shot of Port Ellen 8th Islay was one hundred and thirty Euros? But remember, it would not be good to have our beloved Hessen company accused of buying the cheap stuff. The US Prime beef was not bad either, especially given a few bottles of a good dry red. And the dessert wine. Did you know that the Burbank Bar keeps a few bottles of Canadian ice wine hidden away that are not on the menu? A bottle of outstanding ice wine is a great way to finish a meal, even if the price is a bit high."

"Do I want to know who you were with and how much you spent?"

"Would it help if I told you the number at the bottom of the bill had four digits?"

Jochen groaned. Four digits meant that Karl had spent at least a thousand Euros. "Please tell me that the first digit was a one?"

Karl laughed out loud and swayed in his seat. Jochen realized that Karl was quite drunk.

"I would love to tell you that the first number was a one. But it was not. I recollect that the first number was a two. After that, I am afraid, it gets a bit blurry."

More than two thousand Euros on a restaurant bill!

"Karl. Who were you with?"

"Some of the best minds in the army's counter intelligence service and a couple of disreputable-looking types from Deutsche Marine."

"Did these fine warriors tell us anything?"

"Plenty."

Chapter 19: Fear is the Ultimate Weapon

LOCATION:	Office of Enrica Leclercq, Brussels
DATE:	1 July
TIME:	8:00 AM

Enrica sat at her desk, waiting for the call. CRJ had told her a week ago that he would send a car to pick her up for an important meeting, precisely at eight in the morning. He had been unusually vague about why he would need to see her, but he had been insistent that she kept this time clear of other meetings.

Now the reason was becoming apparent. CRJ had indicated that he would set up the political circumstances necessary for the final push towards the Great Reset. His discussions on this had made it clear that constructive political violence might be required, but his intents remained elusive even then.

Enrica was now confident that today was the day. Her assistant called on the intra-office phone. "Were you expecting a car?"

"Yes. I will be out for about an hour."

Enrica walked out to the street to see a limousine with a driver standing by the rear door. The driver waved her over and reached for the car door handle. She was surprised when the driver opened the door enough for her to enter while moving behind her. It had the effect of blocking the view of anyone looking into the limo.

CRJ put his hand to his mouth as she entered the car, indicating that she should remain silent. The hum of a motor could be heard as the soundproof glass shield rose. At the same time, CRJ took out his phone and placed it in a small black pouch. He then pulled a small device out and put it on the seat between them. Another black pouch appeared, and CRJ indicated she place her phone in it.

CRJ then gave her a brief smile. "Sorry for the precautions. The black pouch is a Faraday Cage.[76] It will block any signals to or from your phone. If someone has hacked your phone to use it as a microphone, that will be stopped. If anyone is monitoring your location through the GPS, that also will stop. This other device is a white noise generator that interferes with bugging attempts. The car is mine, not the IMF's. It belongs to my family's holding company. I have it swept once a week to ensure no bugs have been planted. Also, the car will be in motion, so even if there is an attempt to monitor our conversation by hitting the window with a laser, it will be impossible for them if we keep moving.[77] You can

---

[76] Unknown Editors, "Faraday Cage," en.wikipedia.org (Wikimedia Foundation, May 10, 2021), https://en.wikipedia.org/wiki/Faraday_cage

[77] A laser beam can be used to transmit and received audio. A laser beam can monitor sound in a room or vehicle. The vibration of the window, caused by the sound, can be

keep the Faraday Cage and the white noise generator. Use them any time you want added privacy. By the way, the driver also works for my family and can be trusted. He has served us well for many years, and we take good care of him and his family. Treating your staff well is an important part of your own security."

Enrica was taken aback by the security precautions. The magnitude of what they were about to do hit her. People had died. Institutions were about to collapse. Lives were about to be devasted while others would be uplifted.

CRJ momentarily stared at her while she put her phone in the Faraday Cage – much the way a wolf stares at a lamb. His face became neutral again when she looked up.

CRJ decided to start the conversation by making it clear that she was as responsible for the terrorist attacks as he was. "We have dipped our hands in the blood, and now we are committed. Will the attacks give you what you need?"

"More than what was necessary. Were all four attacks yours? Was the cruise ship fire part of the plan or just a coincidence?"

CRJ held up four fingers to indicate the affirmative.

Enrica continued. "The four attacks put us exactly where we need to be. The press is already filling the airwaves with fear, and social media is running amok with rumors and conspiracy theories. The idea of

---

detected, and 'decoded' by the laser.

having four different attacks, with each one seemingly carried out by different ideological factions, was brilliant. It is multiplying the fear factor. I have already reviewed formal intelligence assessments blaming all these attacks on ISIS. Others are saying Iran and the Revolutionary Guards are behind this. Social media has millions of hits already blaming right-wing extremists and neo-Nazis. The assassination of Ilhan Benhaddara was particularly interesting. Everyone from the CIA to Mossad and British White Power groups is being blamed. Starting this afternoon, I will be putting out a series of messages to the EU Parliament, the EU Commission, NATO, the OECD, the UN Security Council, and every head of state in the EU. The message will be clear. My title as the *High Representative for the European Union for Foreign Affairs and Security Policy* means that I am the primary national security advisor for Europe. The message will be clear. Given this new wave of terrorist attacks, we have much to fear. Our leaders have been weak from fear. Now is the time for action to stop the fear. Now is the time to drive away the fear and secure the future."

CRJ smiled for the first time since Enrica had entered the car. "Exactly. And you are right about the killing of Ilhan Benhaddara. Her death will give the Islamists all over Europe a perfect opportunity to claim they are again the victims of violence. They will love it as it plays into the cult of victimization they have worked so hard to create. By the way, you might see some flare-ups of violence starting in a few days. Most of it will be in the areas around Paris and Vienna. The Muslim Brotherhood will use this as an excuse to burn some more cars and stage demonstrations. You can use the attacks to stir up more fear but do not worry about them. They will just be noise and distraction."

"What about the aircraft hijackers? That was not good. I have heard that one was killed, but at least two of them are being held. Are they a loose end? What if they talk?"

"No worries there," said CRJ. The plan had called for them to demand cash for the passengers and then say they were to land at Frankfurt International. They would then switch course at the last minute to land the aircraft at the Bonames Airfield. The intent had been for them to stop the plane at the far end of the airfield, deploy the escape chutes and tell the passengers to make a run for it while they placed a small bomb under the right wing to start a good fuel fire. The hijackers would run into a field where they would be picked up and escape. It would have caused no end of panic and confusion. But seeing how the Brits decided to interfere and stop them, it works out just as well. Their story is that the Izz ad-Din al-Qassam Brigade hired them.[78] Given that the Iranian Revolutionary Guard has taken over Hamas, it will make sense to those who closely follow the security situation. Frankly, I hope they tell them everything

[78] Unknown Editors, "Izz Ad-Din Al-Qassam Brigades," en.wikipedia.org (Wikimedia Foundation, May 25, 2021), https://en.wikipedia.org/wiki/Izz_ad-Din_al-Qassam_Brigades

they know because they believe it was Iranian money and influence behind their contract for this attack. The truth will cause more confusion and raise more fears about Iran."

Enrica nodded her head and paused for a moment to absorb all of this. "Is the IMF ready to move as well? Are your plans in place?

"Yes. All is good. I have just confirmed with Thierry at the World Economic Forum. They will put out a few *White Papers* on how they believe that now is the time to combine the central banks with the respective treasuries and leave Europe with only one central bank. They will also propose that a new European Economic Institute be created. The new organization will apply Artificial Intelligence with economic statistics to determine the appropriate production levels and where that production should occur. We will respond in minimal time, given that we have already mapped out most of what is required. There are many other details to be discussed soon, but we will assess that private property is the greatest obstacle to efficiency and stability. This follows the belief that most small and medium-sized enterprises are obstacles to the future. When the timing is right, we will plant enough stories to create a stock market crash. Do you get the reason why we need to do that?"

"I understand it," said Enrica. "We need the economic crash to cause a financial crisis. That, in turn, will cause a sovereign debt crisis, and most countries will hit a wall on borrowing. That will cause a significant austerity crisis which will cause social unrest at a massive level. That is when we make the final push to get rid of national sovereignty and private property. I can declare an emergency for three months to control social media and the press long enough to put the plans into effect. This can work."

"Absolutely." CRJ now wanted to close this meeting off in a positive manner. "Everything is going well. All your plans and dreams are coming together. Everything you have envisaged is now in play, and the results will surprise even you. Your name will be remembered forever for how you responded to what happened on the 28th of June. History will record you."

The car slowed and stopped immediately after turning right onto a side street about 200 meters from Enrica's office. "You will get out here. No one will notice you. It is best if this car is not seen twice in front of your office in one day. CRJ pointed at two men on the opposite side of the street. Those two men work for me, and they will discretely follow you back to your office. You cannot be too careful in Brussels these days. If our fine citizens are willing to attack the Belgian King and stone his car,[79] no one is safe. Be careful. Before you know it, the Great Reset will be well underway, and Europe will never be the same."

---

[79] Staff Writer, "Belgian King's Car Hit during Riots over Death in Police Custody," bbc.com (BBC, January 13, 2021), https://www.bbc.com/news/world-europe-55656138

Enrica simply nodded and left the car. She did not look back.

CRJ watched as Enrica walked away. He then reached into his shirt pocket and pulled out his miniature digital voice-activated recorder. The indicator light was glowing green. To outward appearances, it looked like a USB stick, but it could record up to 48 hours of audio. Its noise reduction feature assured a clear recording. CRJ would have the recording edited so that only her voice would be heard. When it was necessary to have Enrica destroyed, he would have enough evidence to leak to the press.

Chapter 20: Four Attacks and a Revolution

LOCATION:	Hessen Reinsurance, Frankfurt
DATE:	1 July
TIME:	08:55 AM

Jochen sat in his office alone, staring at the clock. It would take him two minutes to leave his office, climb the stairs and present himself to the receptionist of Aldo Lange. That should put him in place about one minute before the meeting he had asked for late yesterday afternoon. To his surprise, the receptionist had told him that she would move meetings to accommodate him. He would have 15 minutes.

One of the conditions of his being hired was that he would have direct access to Aldo if he deemed it necessary. The door, he was told, would always be open. The agreement had been known to others who were not happy at such direct access. Skipping links in the chain of reporting would always cause jealousy. Consequently, he had never asked for direct access, preferring to depend on written reports, secure emails, and the infrequent discussions with Aldo at conferences or company receptions.

Jochen looked down at the two-page intelligence summary. Writing intelligence reports for senior readers was the most demanding intelligence writing function. Any fool could write an excellent ten-page paper but writing a 'cover plus one' intelligence report was the most difficult of all writing assignments.

The report was laid out in a standard format developed for this type of event by intelligence agencies. There was a title at the top, centered in large font bold upper-case letters. Underneath in a smaller font was a subtitle, lower case but with each word capitalized. Underneath was an image, also centered – in this case, a slightly blurry photo taken from a French newspaper website that showed the body of Ilhan Benhaddara covered by a sheet. The purpose of the image was to set the tone of the report for the reader before they had read one word. Most senior readers were highly visual people.

Under the image, left adjusted, was the "Key Judgements." Following that were three single lines of text, each one indented with an asterisk at the start of each line. The format required that the key judgment lines be one line only – short and to the point. If the senior reader were only to read the cover, that person would have the basic knowledge required to understand the report. At the bottom left of the page, in the footer area, was the date of the report. At the bottom right of the page was the ICOD[80] date. Nowhere on the page was any reference to who the report was addressed or who had written it. The

---

[80] ICOD = Information Cut Off Date

company name Hessen did not appear anywhere on the document.

The second page had three sections. The first was the 'Subject' which could be a maximum of one line long. The following section was 'Context,' which could be two lines long. The final section, 'Assessment,' could take up the rest of the page.

Jochen stood up and looked around at his office. Take-out food wrappers and drink containers were strewn on desks and the floor. He had sent the staff home just before midnight. They had explored every possible source of intelligence and called in favors.

Their assessment was by no means complete, but Jochen was convinced they had broken down the main factors.

As he entered the outer office of Aldo Lange at 08:59, the receptionist waved him in and pointed to the open office door.

"Jochen, please join me for coffee. To what do I owe the pleasure of this unexpected visit?" Aldo rose from his desk and indicated a separate table set with coffee and mineral water.

"Sir, here is our two-page assessment of the recent series of alleged terrorist attacks that occurred on the 28th of June. Our view is that these terrorist attacks are not what they seem."

Aldo took the two pages and set them on the table as he poured himself a coffee – black – and began reading in silence.

Jochen checked his watch and timed him as he read the document. A total of 10 seconds on the first page and 60 seconds on the second page. Aldo was a fast reader and a quick study.

Aldo stared out the window for another 30 seconds in silent contemplation.

He finally turned to Jochen and said, "Walk me through this. How did you come to the conclusions?"

"Each of the four attacks…"

Aldo cut him off with a wave of the hand. "You say four. The press and my government contacts are not certain that the ship fire was an attack, as you indicate here. Are you certain of this?"

"We are certain. The initial distress call from the ship suggested that the fire was an accident. But whoever set the fire left some markings suggesting it was set by an anarchist group. This seemed logical enough in a certain way until a crew member sent aboard the MS Freedom of the Seas from the Nordsee Bliss observed an individual who was showing too much curiosity near the fire scene after the fire was out. This individual had a 1488 tattoo that suggests he is or was connected to an extreme right-wing group. It is hard to believe that someone with a neo-Nazi background would be working with anarchists. We believe that the fire on the ship was deliberately set, and it has nothing to do with anarchists, jihadists, or right-wing extremists. Hard to say, but it is probably a contract job."

"How do we know this?"

Jochen hesitated for a second. "We have a new source close to the military. He was quite helpful. Perhaps now might be a good time to tell you that an expense account might be brought to your attention. It was for more than two thousand euros."

Aldo flashed a momentary smile. "Apparently, my money was well spent. Explain the rest to me, and I will not interrupt again."

"Each of the four attacks was staged to appear as a terrorist attack. The cash center robbery is of particular interest. The attacking crew fired dozens of rounds but hit no one. The machine gun fire appears to have been aimed deliberately high. The shots into the police car hit the engine only. At least two of the attackers were yelling 'Allahu Akbar,' but nothing else suggests a jihadist attack. They could have killed all the staff and the responding police officers, but they willfully chose not to. They exhibited a type of fire discipline and control typical of Swat teams or special forces. The aircraft hijacking is also strange. The hijackers intended to take the 777 to Bonames airfield, just north of here. Their hijacking likely would have been successful if it were not for three or four British special forces who were en route from a training mission in Canada to an unknown function here in Germany. The UK government, the passengers, and the press suggest the hijackers were Iranian — possibly from the Iranian Revolutionary Guard. But again, at least one well-informed passenger believes that they were not behaving in a manner consistent with those holding an Islamist ideology. They made no demands, and the airfield they were to have landed was abandoned. The same goes for the cruise ship fire. As we already discussed, the evidence from the fire scene suggests an attempt to mislead. The fire came close to be a major disaster, and the MS Fulfillment of the Seas was heavily damaged. But it almost appears as though there was no attempt to kill the passengers."

Jochen paused for a few moments. Silence filled the room.

"That brings us to the first attack, the assassination. It is the only attack where we do not have information on who carried it out. As far as information from newspaper reports and videos on social media, Ilhan Benhaddara was the likely target. She was the head of the Islamic Assistance Transnational and was accompanied by Tarek Raman. An overview of the organization suggests that she was recently promoted into the position but lacks the background and experience. She replaced two other former senior leaders who were removed one after the other due to their online glorification of terrorism. She was put there to be a positive public face as a public relations exercise. The most powerful figure in the organization is Tarek Raman. He has a family history in the Muslim Brotherhood that goes right back to the movement's founding. The strange thing is that he has disappeared. It makes no sense. He should have stayed at the scene for several reasons. Perhaps he ran out of fear of being shot next which would be reasonable, but he should have resurfaced. Like so many other aspects of these events, his current disposition does not make sense."

Aldo picked up the two-page assessment and turned it to the second page. "Do you believe that these attacks are the first step in a larger plan?"

"We believe it. It is the only possible explanation. There is an unseen hand at work. An individual, or more likely a movement or an organization, is behind these attacks. From the company's point of view, we are telling you that the risk to the company's holdings and properties could be significantly increased in a short period of time. If these attacks intended to create an atmosphere of fear and instability, then they might work. As you already know, social unrest has been building for years. The recession that started in late 2019, the pandemic, and now the new financial crisis is raising the temperature. Trouble has been building for years."

Aldo stood up and walked over to the window. After more than two minutes, he finally turned around and faced Jochen.

"Your assessment is reasonable, and the background information that has gone into this is remarkable. Some day you will explain to me the source of this information. But that is for another day. Right now, I believe you have something to add that is not in the assessment. What is it? What are you holding back?"

"It is nothing I can prove, but it is not that there is a risk of increased violence, instability, and property damage. I believe that these attacks intend to cause exactly that. You and the company should be prepared for a period of increased attacks and significant property damage. Further to that, the final purpose of these attacks may be to create enough political instability to effect a change of government."

"You mean a revolution?"

"Yes."

Aldo turned to the window again, staring at some unseen object in the far distance. "Throughout this meeting, you have constantly spoken in the plural by saying 'we believe' or 'we are telling you.' But for this last assessment, you used the singular 'I.' Why?"

"The assessment work in the paper is a team effort. It exists because of the experience and work of all of us. Not to mention we spent a fair bit of your money doing it. But the last part about the potential social unrest and violence is my assessment alone. It is based on intuition. It is, as they say, a bit of an analytical leap."

"How many people are aware of this assessment?"

"Just the four of us. Horst, Karl, Bettina and I."

"Good. Keep it that way. Meanwhile, keep digging."

Jochen turned to leave but then decided to take a leap of faith. "There is something you could do in all of this. A source told us the name of the company that owns the Bonames Airfield. It is a shell company. We tried to trace it, but all we turned up was a series of other shell companies. At the end of it, we got nothing. If we provide you the list of companies and the charts, can you identify who is behind them?"

"You think that I have better hacking skills than Horst?"

"I will not answer that one, but I do believe that you have a better set of business contacts than anyone I know. Whoever did this must have significant money, superior business skills, a massive list of contacts in both the business and criminal world, and a creative mind. He is likely a sociopath as well."

"You think a sociopath is among my contacts?"

Jochen simply nodded and headed out the door.

Chapter 21: The SAS and Swivel Serpents

LOCATION: Colonel's Office, SAS HQ

DATE: 1 July

TIME: 09:59 AM

Major Berikoff was facing his most nerve-wracking situation yet since joining the SAS – a meeting with the Colonel of the Regiment. The Colonel was going to ask questions about the aircraft hijacking, and Major Berikoff did not have all the answers. The Colonel was not known for his empathy or understanding. Having checked his watch one more time, Berikoff noted it was 09:59 hours.

Major Berikoff momentarily smiled as his mind drifted back a bit. He thought about the most recent lecture the Colonel had given to the regiment. It had occurred when the UK Ministry of Defence had ordered that all commanders update their units on the government's new policies on inclusivity, diversity, and climate change. Having gathered most of the 22nd SAS regiment together for a training day, the Colonel stepped up to the podium after a presentation from Whitehall's uncomfortable-looking senior civil servant.

"I thank their Lordships at Whitehall and the Parliament for their interest in the well-being of our unit. As for the regiment, I will continue to have inclusivity for success, and I will generate a diversity of methods for removing those who fail to meet the standard. If we have enemies who are creating a climate of fear, I intend to change that climate. Any questions?"

Not surprisingly, no questions were forthcoming. Instead, the Colonel had turned to the civil servant with a polite smile. "Will you please tell those pencil-necked, paper-pushing, swivel serpents at Whitehall that the SAS is now up to the standard on political correctness and identity politics?"

The Colonel's voice broke Major Berikoff's moment of reverie.

"Berikoff! Enter!" The Major checked his watch as he entered the office. 10:00.

The Colonel did not cut an impressive figure. He was about 5'7'' and appeared to be of average build. His hair was longish, and a comb would not have hurt it. His suit was a bit rumpled. The Colonel could have passed for greengrocer or perhaps a mid-level functionary from a quango or a government ministry on the street.

The Colonel indicated a chair. "Berikoff. Welcome back. Tell me about the Canadians. How were the briefings? Did you hit the hijack pilot with a coffee pot?"

"Yes, Sir. The mission with the Canadians went well. Our exchange of weapons-handling information and tactical intelligence is on track. In addition, we have agreed to a joint training mission next February in the high Arctic. With the increasing focus from Russia and China on the Arctic, building cold-weather skills will be important."

"Excellent. Now, tell me what I need to know about this hijacking that you and the lads interrupted. I am getting a few questions that I cannot answer. You are going to solve that problem for me. What do we know?"

Major Berikoff took a deep breath and began. "You already know the basics. Three men tried to hijack the aircraft. Along with Skiffington and Crosby, Captain Davies dispatched two of them in the back of the aircraft. I removed the pilot from the equation with a coffee pot, as you noted. Two Canadian military pilots landed the aircraft at Lossie, and here we are. A Canadian terrorism judge who was a passenger observed that the hijackers did not seem politically motivated. We agreed with him."

The Major continued. "The human rights complaint against Skiffington came from a London-based law firm which was in turn influenced by information flowing directly to them from an unknown party in Brussels. Someone has significant money and was well informed about details of the hijacking that only a few would know. We believe that at least one other passenger knew that the hijacking would occur and informed the unknown party in Brussels. The unknown party in Brussels must play a key role in the overall conduct of this hijacking, and we believe that he or she must also be involved in the three other incidents of 28 June."

The Colonel looked concerned for a moment. "You are certain the four events are linked?"

"Yes, Sir. We are reaching out to a few friends on this, and the vibrations suggest these events are coordinated. The intended destination of the hijackers was not Frankfurt, as is being suggested in the news. The real destination was Bonames, a disused military airfield that had been recently purchased by an unknown shell company. It had been a military airfield and then a sort of nature reserve and a skater park. Big money and planning were involved in buying the field and doing enough work to make it serviceable for one landing. The work included a runway extension. Discrete inquires suggest that there are similar unusual aspects to the other attacks. The cash center robbery is being blamed on jihadists, but the robbery seems out of context for them. The assassination of Ilhan Benhaddara also seems off. Whoever took her out did so without leaving a trace. The assassination suggests insider info on knowing where she would be ahead of time and great field skills. We are waiting on more info from the cruise ship's owners, but that also seems a bit strange. Four attacks in one day, and each one seems a bit off? They are connected, and it was not jihadists that are behind this."

"An excellent bit of work," said the Colonel, "in retaking control of the aircraft. The trip to London was also profitable as it got Skiffington and the regiment out of a jam. But I am of two minds here. Your involvement on the plane was luck, even though the conspiracy theorists feel we had advanced knowledge. We were also fortunate to get the necessary intelligence on the law firm to move them out of the picture. What do we do next? This sort of skullduggery is not our role. Properly speaking, we should give what we know to MI6 and Whitehall and then step back. But someone attempted to take out Skiffington with that horrid law firm, and that makes it personal. That cannot stand. Where do you think we should go next?"

Major Berikoff considered his answers. The Colonel was not asking to appear polite. When he asked a question, he was looking for honest input.

"Sir. At this point, we have more questions than we have answers, but it is clear to me that these four attacks represent the first shots fired in a larger operation aimed at Europe. As you noted, our involvement was an accident, but we may be a jump ahead of many others. Given the whole Brexit mess, I suppose we should be careful of any involvement on the continent. The politics of this could go pear-shaped quickly. Let us appear to be standing down on the outside, but we should push every possible source of information we have to figure out what is happening. If that means going for a bit of an informal trip to the continent, then so be it. Once we reach a better understanding of what is going on, then we push that intel up the food chain."

"Agreed," said the Colonel. "Take Davies, Skiffington, Crosby, and a couple more of the lads if you want and get moving on this. If you find out anything, you call me directly on the satellite phone, no matter what time of day or night. Off you go. I have others to meet with who are, alas, much less interesting."

Major Berikoff left the office. Standing in the hallway was a man in his late fifties wearing a bespoke suit. He looked vaguely academic, minus the fuzzy aura. Suit. Shoes. Clear eyes. Briefcase. He had to be MI6. Their movements had been attracting attention already.

Chapter 22: Small Teams Win

LOCATION: Jochen's Office, Frankfurt, Germany

DATE: 1 July

TIME: 10:00 AM

Jochen entered the team office area to see all three of his staff staring at him. The leftover food wrappers and drink containers were gone. The whiteboard had been wiped clean.

Karl followed Jochen's eye to the board. "Don't worry. We took photos of the board and stored them. We are ready to start working on wherever you think we should be going next. What did Herr Lange have to say about the assessment?"

"He said little. It was clear that he understood the paper. He also seemed to accept where we were going with the analysis that was not in the assessment. His reaction was normal, I think, for such a situation. Senior leaders often resist hearing new information that falls outside their previous experience and understanding. It can take several attempts to get them to overcome their cognitive biases.[81] But, I believe he accepts the premise of the

---

[81] Charlotte Ruhl, "What Is Cognitive Bias?" What Is Cognitive Bias? | Simply Psychology (Simply Psychology, May 4, 2021), https://www.simplypsychology.org/cognitive-bias.html

briefing inasmuch as he cannot provide an alternative explanation by himself. We have done well. At least so far. Now it gets interesting."

Bettina walked over the whiteboard and drew a single black circle on the board. "This is where we need to go next. If we figure out who is behind the money at the Bonames Airfield, that will lead us to who is behind this. If that organization is identified, then we should know what is happening. The same can be said for the other three attacks, but this seems to be the one with the most hope of finding a trail. It is the only attack that had planning work done on the ground ahead of time."

Horst nodded in agreement. "Bettina is right. Any idea if Herr Lange will help with tracking down the money trail? Did you ask him?"

"I asked him at the end of the meeting. He did not answer the question. Nor did I think he would. That was a lot to take in, and it indirectly suggests that when we find out who did this, he might know them or know of them. It will take him time to take all of this in."

Jochen walked up to the board. "Spend the next few hours working on the airfield and the money behind it. Do not make any plans for tomorrow and the day after. Stay flexible and bring a suitcase tomorrow for at least one night."

"Where are we going?" asked Horst.

"Away," said Jochen.

* * *

Jochen sat in his office staring out the window. He had 'that feeling' again in a way he never felt. Nothing made sense. Yet it had to. One of the worst aspects of intelligence analysts was their willingness to assess that a situation 'did not make sense' and that you were missing 'pieces of the puzzle.' If it did not make sense to you, perhaps it was because you did not understand the context. Everything had to make sense if you were able to let it. But try as he could, there was no scenario which would explain what had happened.

Jochen had learned several lessons over the years. One lesson was that large intelligence agencies with massive resources regularly failed to make accurate assessments. How could the CIA have missed the collapse of the Soviet Union? The CIA had over one thousand analysts. But the CIA had its problems. One fault was that they had hired the best and the brightest of American society. But in so doing, they hired an entire class of people who mostly thought and worked the same way. The CIA did not have one thousand analysts. It had one form of analytical thought that was replicated one thousand times. Not only that, the CIA and many other Western intelligence agencies had become cult-like in their behavior. There was only one acceptable way to think about a problem, like the Soviet Union or the jihadists who made up al Qaeda and the Islamist groups. Anyone who suggested thinking about the problem in another manner was regarded with suspicion. Any form of analysis that suggested the enemy might have weak spots was unacceptable. Any attempt to understand the grievance narrative of the enemy was a sign that you favored them. For some so-called analysts, reading the major works of the terrorists such as Ayman al Zawahiri was an act of heresy worthy of expulsion. As such, groupthink and mindsets ruled the analysis, much like it had at Pearl Harbor and 9/11.

The lesson was clear. Jochen believed that a small team of dedicated analysts, working with even limited resources, could provide better analytical insights than large government agencies. That assumed, of course, that the small group of analysts came from different backgrounds, had different experiences, and saw the world differently.

It was time to reach out. And besides, why have an extraordinary budget if not to spend it?

Jochen knew what was needed. He would call five people and invite them to Frankfurt for two days. These were people whom he had worked with in the past on global problems. He had kept contact with them for the precise reason that they were different. They challenged authority. Thought differently. Saw the world on their own terms. But most importantly, they were people who had intense curiosity and imagination. Without those two qualities, analysts were nothing.

Jochen would gather them together, and they would spend the time in an off-site conference site owned by the company. A call to Aldo Lange's receptionist would have it cleared of other company personnel.

He looked at the clock. It was 9:45 AM which meant it was 3:45 AM in central Canada. He would get Daniel Godson out of bed. This would be good fun. Twice in the past, Daniel had called him out of bed on business matters. This time, it would go the other way.

Jochen flipped through the contact list on his phone and pushed on 'Daniel.' The phone rang twice before a clear voice answered. "Jochen! What is it? Why the call at this hour? Did somebody we know get arrested?"

"Not this time. You are coming to Frankfurt. Book a flight and get yourself to Toronto's Pearson Airport this afternoon. You will be picked up at the airport here and brought to a two-day long meeting. Book a business class seat. We need you awake when you arrive, and it is going to be a busy two days. We are paying. Can you get to the airport by 14:00?"

"Uhh, OK. What is the rush? Who will pick me up?"

"Learn everything you can about the four so-called terrorist attacks. Don't worry about the pickup. The folks driving you will know who you are."

"So-called terrorist attacks? Something funny behind the attacks, eh? They did seem a bit strange."

"Just get here. See you tomorrow."

* * *

Jochen spent the next two hours calling the Netherlands, Norway, and Italy. Each call was the same. Dr. Isabel Hooft of the Netherlands would be at the meeting. She had written extensively on modern military and security strategy – or its lack - in Europe. Berndt van der Schalk of the Royal Dutch Marines would participate. His views on how a crisis of leadership was destroying society would be potentially valuable. Berndt believed careerist politicians and technocrats were the problems. Rather conveniently, Berndt and Isabel were married.

Carsten Berg from Norway would bring another dimension. His area of interest was the relationship between money, social unrest, and terrorism. But, like many of his fellow Norwegians, his erudite manner, calm voice, and expensive suits hid the reality that he was a descendant of Norse Raiders – the Vikings.

Finally, there would be Sergio Capelli of Italy. Typical of many Italians, he arrived at every meeting or meal dressed as he had just stepped out of a Milan fashion shoot. His family, however, had suffered under both the boots of fascism and communism. During the war in the former Yugoslavia, his time on the ground had taught him again what he already knew. When the forces of fascism, communism re-emerged, it was in the form of blood-filled violence. On top of that, he had seen firsthand how the Islamists of the Muslim

Brotherhood had been supported by, ironically enough, the Iranian Revolutionary Guard to produce one of the most violent Bosnian factions. To Sergio, fascists, communists, and Islamists were different faces of the same problem – a totalitarian ideology.

* * *

At 11:30, Jochen gathered his local team in the common area. He could feel a bit of tension in the air as they all stared at him in silence, rather than being greeted with the usual banter and jokes.

"The next two days will be quite interesting," said Jochen. "We are going to the off-site conference center owned by the company, and we will be staying there overnight as well. An outside catering company will provide food and everything. No one else will be in the building except for the four of us and the five guests I have invited from Canada, the Netherlands, Norway, and Italy. Our mission is to create one working hypothesis as to who is behind the attacks and what they are trying to accomplish. If we create two or three, that is good as well. The five persons coming were invited today and will be here tomorrow. They are all long-term friends and colleagues of mine, and they represent a selection of the most interesting minds in the analytical and financial business. Based on this, I have two immediate plans. The first one is we are leaving now and going for lunch. You will pick the restaurant, and the company is buying. Pick a good place. The second plan is that the three of you return after your no-drinking-allowed-past-one-glass-of-wine lunch, and you will prepare a one-hour briefing. This briefing will be given to our five guests tomorrow morning when we start the meeting at 9:00. You can choose among yourselves who will do what part of the briefing. I will give the introduction and objectives only. By the way, be at the office door tomorrow morning at 6:50. We will be driven out to the conference site at 7:00. Any questions?"

"You have changed," said Karl. "Normally you are careful with money, spend nothing that is not necessary, and you count every *pfennig*. You have never gone to see Aldo Lange directly in person before. Now you walk into the boss's office with no notice, have the conference center rebooked, and advocate that we spend more for lunch than necessary. What has happened to you? Why the change?"

Bettina poked her finger into Karl's ribs. "That was rude," she said. "You should not ask questions like that while all of us are standing here."

"These are good questions," said Jochen. "I normally try to run a frugal operation even given the obscene amounts of money this company spends. It is a matter of being responsible as well as appearing credible. Right now, however, I feel that major events are about to overtake all of us. If we produce a solid analytical report at the end of the next two days, then I believe that we could spend 100,000 Euros on lunch, and no one would question it. On the other hand, if we get the analysis wrong and miss the problem, the company could lose billions, and we will be unemployed. Enjoy lunch together, but you must work hard this afternoon. I have to go see a man about a dog again."

* * *

As they parted ways after lunch, Jochen headed off to see Burnard from the BKA. He would share the two-page briefing with the BKA that he had given to Aldo Lange, but he would not go past that unless the BKA were willing to give more. He also would not tell them about the two-day off-site meeting.

Checking his watch, Jochen realized he would be about 10 minutes early getting to the café meeting. The timing was good, and he wanted to arrive either exactly on time or about one minute late, just to see if there was any surveillance around the meeting.

As he sat down on a public bench, his mind drifted back to the meeting with Aldo Lange and the one problem it produced. Lange was wealthy, powerful, and well-connected. He attended all the right charitable fundraisers and political events. He was a keynote speaker in financial circles and rubbed elbows with major organizations such as the IMF, the World Bank, the German Central Bank, and the Bank for International Settlements. Lange was cautious about appearing neutral on matters of political partisanship and was never pinned down during interviews as to his personal views on ideology. Jochen had been asked, discretely, several times as to what political views were held by the company or by Aldo Lange. He had been able to respond to the questions by saying, "I do not know." Even the BKA had pushed – and got nothing.

A few clues existed. The family was essential to Lange. The bookcase on the sidewall of his office has the requisite photos of his wife and three children who appeared to be in their late teens and early twenties. Jochen had noticed them while in the office that morning. In one photo, the family was all dressed in high-quality ski gear. In another, the family appeared to be in shallow water surrounded by dolphins at an aquatic animal rescue center. They all seemed genuinely happy, and Lange himself was photographed with a broad smile – something rarely seen in business circles. Other pictures showed his wife at charitable functions and his children receiving academic degrees. There was only one picture of Lange by himself. The photo showed him in the doorway of a church. Lange looked much younger in the photo. The word *Schlosskirche* – castle church – was at the bottom of the picture. Jochen had looked it up and compared some Internet images to what he remembered of the photo. The photo was the Wittenberg church where in 1517, Martin Luther had nailed his list of 95 grievances to the door. Intended or otherwise, Martin Luther had sparked the historic split in the Christian church and began what was known as the Great Reformation or the Protestant Reformation. Jochen thought this was curious. Lange had only one photo of himself. Absent were the usual photos of him meeting with the great, the near-great, or those who were merely celebrities.

He chose to show the one photo of himself where the foundations of modern Europe and the Westphalian state system were formed. Was Lange a believer in the values of the Reformation? Or was he a believer in the money and the power of modern-day Frankfurt?

The question vexed Jochen greatly. If their investigation and analysis showed that significant organizational money was involved, then where was Aldo Lange? Would he want to know who was behind this wave of violence, or would he know the players involved? Jochen decided to ignore the question for the next two days. First, they would do their best work and pass it onto Lange. Then would come the question.

Whose side would Aldo Lange be on if there was a political fallout?

Chapter 23: Sex, Pizza, and an Assassination

LOCATION: Tofino, Vancouver Island, British Columbia, Canada

DATE: 3 July

TIME: 5:45 AM (Pacific Time)

Cabinet Minister Rory Newson fumbled through the Keurig coffee capsules, looking for his favorite Tim Horton's coffee, unaware that the body of Prime Minister Justin Trudeau was gradually cooling in his bed just 10 meters away.

Minister Newson was a lifelong alcoholic, the aftereffects of college partying followed by years on the campaign trail with drinking and other questionable behaviors. As the Prime Minister himself had said about his political campaigns, "There's pizza, sex, and all sorts of fun things."[82]

The last few rounds of rehab had not helped. Rory was sober enough if he was in recovery or back home. But as soon as he was in the whirlwind activities of

---

[82] Jeff Green, "Sex, Pizza and Politics with Justin Trudeau," thespec.com (The Hamilton Spectator, October 13, 2011), https://www.thespec.com/news/hamilton-region/2011/10/13/sex-pizza-and-politics-with-justin-trudeau.html

politics, his alcoholism and debauchery returned. He was once again at the bottom of a bottle of dark rum. The demons returned nightly and howled at him in his dreams about past depravities.

He thought back over the last few days. Prime Minister Justin Trudeau had been in Ottawa for the national day celebrations on the 1st of July. Although the scope of the celebrations had been toned down, even though the pandemic was officially declared over, it was standard stuff.

The press was told that the Prime Minister would be spending a few days of personal time at his Harrington Lake summer retreat. In reality, he had jumped aboard his Royal Canadian Air Force-operated Challenger private jet for the flight to British Columbia. Tofino had great surfing and – perhaps more importantly – a luxurious estate owned by a discrete friend.

Trudeau, Newson, and another college buddy had planned their two-day getaway. The time alone would be filled with in-depth strategy discussions. It would also have 'pizza, sex, and other fun things.'

Minister Newson may have been an alcoholic, but he maintained a disciplined routine. His feet had been on the floor at 5:45 AM, despite the hangover. Into the shower, a quick shave, and he was down to the kitchen. Now, at 6:00 AM, he had his coffee in one hand and his iPad in the other. It was time to peruse the domestic news and international events. He also needed to check out a few blogs and forums to see what kind of political rumors were being floated.

After reading for a while, Minster Newson looked at the microwave's clock and noted the time.

6:45 AM.

What he did not know was that by 6:46, his life would be upended.

The scream came from upstairs. It was Frank Arsenberg. Seconds later, he appeared at the top railing of the stairs and stared down at Rory. Nothing came out, even as his jaw moved up and down. Finally, he blurted out, "Justin looks like he's dead."

Rory sprinted up the stairs and ran into Justin's room. He was lying in his bed, and everything looked normal. Well, almost normal. The sock used to strangle him was still around his neck. Rory froze for a few seconds, and then the lizard part of his brain – the political survival part – kicked in and took control.

He forced himself to walk to the head of the bed, and he pushed his index finger into the Prime Minister's throat. No pulse and the body felt decidedly cool. He tried to push his chin to the left, but the body felt partially stiff. He must have been dead for a few hours if rigor was already setting in.

The Minister then turned to Frank, who stood blubbering in the doorway. "Go downstairs. Gather up any signs of the drugs and anything else like that. Leave the booze bottles, glasses, and pizza. Put all the drug stuff in a baggie and bring it up here. I will check out this room and the rest of the upstairs. Go! Now!"

Frank gathered himself together and set off to do as he was told. The Minister worked hard to suppress the panic that wanted to rise within him. A sitting Prime Minister of a G7 country had just been murdered. He and Frank were in the house at the time. Frank, who was downstairs cleaning up the drug paraphernalia, had one of the greatest minds in strategy and politics. His obsession with politics had kept him single and often isolated. He knew how to manipulate everything and everyone around him to get things done. But in a physical crisis, he was almost useless. Minister Newson knew what only a few others did not. Frank was a physical coward.

The Minister considered what to do. Not only was the Prime Minister dead, but he also now saw that it was two socks that had been knotted together that were used for the strangulation. The socks looked familiar. The Minister's heart skipped a beat. They were the red, blue, purple, and yellow Halal socks presented to the Prime Minister by one of his Cabinet Ministers, Omar Alghabra.[83]   While he still did not have an overall plan in his mind on what to do, one thing was clear. Justin Trudeau would not be found by the police and photographed with Halal socks around his neck. He removed the socks as delicately as he could

[83] Joe Castaldo, "Justin Trudeau Wore Our Muslim Hipster Socks," Macleans.ca (Maclean's Magazine, June 27, 2017), https://www.macleans.ca/news/canada/justin-trudeau-wore-our-muslim-hipster-socks/

and shoved them in his pocket. He would wash them in his ensuite bathroom sink and hang them in the shower.

By now, Frank had ascended the stairs with a plastic baggie in his shaking hands. "Is he dead?"

"Yes, you idiot. He is dead. Now, shut up and listen. I am going to my room for a couple of minutes. You are going to flush that bag down the toilet in your room. Then we are going downstairs to the living room. When I get there, you will call the head of the Prime Minister's protective detail in the guest house. We are going to tell him everything and tell them exactly what happened. You will lie about nothing because if you do, it will get found out sooner or later. Remember, we did nothing wrong, and we are guilty of nothing. The only subject neither of us will EVER talk about again is that you cleaned up the drugs, and I removed the socks. Got it?"

Frank meekly nodded and headed off to his room with the baggie.

Once they were both in the living room, the Minister turned to Frank and told him, "Call the police now. Tell them something horrible has happened and they need to come now. When they get here, remember what I told you - tell them the truth. You found the Prime Minster dead when you went to wake him up. You left the room, saw me in the living room, and the two of us checked to see if he was dead. Then we called them and met them at the front door. Can you remember this?"

Frank pulled out his cell home looked for "RCMP PMPD[84]" in his contact list. He punched it, and the phone was answered before the second ring. "Sergeant, this is Frank Arsenberg. Come to the main house now. Something horrible has happened."

Sergeant McMullin of the Royal Canadian Mounted Police Prime Minister's Protective Detail stared at his phone. Then, as he headed over to the main house, he called the Inspector in charge of the unit. Any day that started with that sort of call would be a long day.

* * *

LOCATION: Ottawa, Canada

DATE: 3 July

TIME: 10:30 AM Eastern Time (ET)

Deputy Prime Minister Brenda Elishchuk willed herself to be calm, waiting for the phone call she knew was coming. She rechecked her phone, only to discover it had been two minutes since the last time she had checked it.

Even at that, she jumped when the phone rang. RCMP PMPD appeared on the screen. She let it ring twice more and then answered, "Elishchuk here."

---

[84] Royal Canadian Mounted Police – Prime Minister's Protective Detail

"Deputy Prime Minister, this is Inspector Doshen of the PMPD. You should be aware that we received a call this morning at about 7:00 AM local time from Frank Arsenberg. He told us that an event had occurred in the estate's main residence where the Prime Minister was staying. We entered the house and found Arsenberg and Minister Newson in the main entryway. They seemed to be in a state of shock."

"Inspector, skip the details. Why are you calling me?"

"The Prime Minister was found dead, Ma'am. He died during the night but was found at about 6:45 AM. You should be aware that unusual details may emerge."

"Unusual details?"

"It is too early to say, Ma'am. But it appears the Prime Minister may have been strangled in his bed."

The phone line was silent for more than 15 seconds when the Inspector asked, "Are you still on the line Ma'am?"

"Yes, Inspector. Still here. This is too much. Are you suggesting someone killed him? What happened? Where was your team? What were they doing? The investigation into this will not go well for you, allowing the Prime Minister to be murdered right under your nose. You absolutely must keep me informed of every detail, no matter how small. Call this number at any time of the day or night. Understood?"

"Yes, Ma'am."

Deputy Prime Minister Elishchuk surveyed her office. The first bit of the plan was already put in place. She would make sure the Prime Minister's Protective Detail was blamed for the murder, distracting at least some attention away from the actual killer or killers.

Elishchuk had learned the political system. As soon as something goes wrong, throw a subordinate official under the bus to distract attention from the issues.

More needed to be done. Canada's constitution did not have a chain of political succession as many others did. Her own position as Deputy Prime Minister was not in the constitution either. But most of the citizenry simply assumed the Deputy Prime Minister would take over in the event of the prime minister's death. She would seize the initiative to ensure that it would happen that way.

She allowed herself a moment to smile. Today was the start of a whole new chapter in her life and of that in world politics.

Picking up the desk phone, she called her executive assistant. Without any formality or introduction, she told the assistant to reach all the Cabinet Ministers. They were to be in the Langevin Block at 2:00 PM for an emergency meeting. Attendance was compulsory. She then added that the Prime Minister had died during the night. The EA had pretty much choked and then said, "Please confirm you said 2:00 PM for the meeting?"

Elishchuk was pleased. With Parliament out of session and the short Canadian summer just getting started, only a few Cabinet Ministers would be in Ottawa. The rest would be spread over Canada's vast landmass. The fewer, the better. She would be able to establish herself as Prime Minister, and the fewer questions asked at the first meeting, the better. Of course, a new Liberal Party leadership race would be required, but that was weeks or months down the road.

She picked up the phone again. "Call the White House. Tell them I am on the line and need to tell them that Prime Minister Trudeau has died, and I am filling the Prime Ministerial position. Then call the Ambassador to the EU. I need to talk to him directly."

* * *

LOCATION: Brussels, Residence of Enrica Leclercq

DATE: 3 July

TIME: Evening hours

Enrica Leclercq, the High Representative for the Union for Foreign Affairs and Security Policy, was also waiting for a message. This one came in the form of a call from one of her security detail who was posted at her residence. "Sorry to bother you, Ma'am, but the Ambassador of Canada to the EU has just arrived unannounced and insists on seeing you. We have checked his ID, and we can confirm a personal identification as we have met him before.

Unfortunately, he will give us no information on the purpose of the visit, but he says it is a major security matter."

"Send him to my office on the main floor."

Enrica Leclercq prepared herself upon entering the office. She positioned several papers on her desk and turned on the desk lamp. She wanted to give the appearance of a dedicated servant of the European Union who works in the evening, even at home.

She rose and turned towards the door when she heard two sets of footsteps approaching. She had left the door open, so her guard had stopped in the doorway, awaiting permission to enter. She nodded to him while looking into the eyes of the Canadian Ambassador. He was a man under some stress.

The guard, well versed in how the High Representative ran her office and household, announced, "Madam. The Ambassador of Canada to the European Union." He pivoted on his right heel and quickly exited the room.

"Mr. Ambassador, what a surprise. Please call me Enrica in these surroundings. To what do I owe the pleasure of this rather unexpected visit?"

The Ambassador was a bit taken aback. Enrica Leclercq had a reputation for being strict on protocols and was ruthless when she perceived a slight.

"Enrica, my apologies for the unusual circumstances. We have an impending crisis in Canada, and our

Deputy Prime Minister felt I should inform you immediately."

Enrica noticed the use of the term Deputy Prime Minister and allowed herself to raise one eyebrow in response. The Ambassador continued as if he had rehearsed the lines on his way over, which he had.

"Prime Minister Justin Trudeau is deceased. It will be in the news shortly. But our Deputy Prime Minister wants you to know that his death was not natural or accidental. It is possible that he was murdered and that the murder may have been an assassination."

"My God, Mr. Ambassador, how could this have happened? And in Canada? Who could have done this? Why would anyone want to kill Prime Minister Trudeau?"

"We have only the most limited information at this point. It seems, however, that he was murdered in his sleep, and no immediate suspects are apparent. But our Deputy Prime Minister did make it clear that the death of the Prime Minister changes nothing, and Canada's relations with the EU will not be affected."

"Please pass my condolences to your Deputy Prime Minister. You can assure her that we can offer any possible assistance in this matter should the need arise. Let me walk you to the door, Mr. Ambassador. I am sure you have a busy time ahead with many matters to attend."

The Ambassador felt that he had just been given the rush. A very polite rush, but a firm push out the door now that the message had been passed. That was the Enrica Leclercq about whom he had been warned. A rather imperial manner of doing business.

For her part, Enrica went back to her desk and sat down. She was not overly surprised by the possible assassination of the Canadian Prime Minister.

It was, after all, she who had first suggested it.

* * *

The plan to remove the Prime Minister of Canada had begun in January at the Swiss meeting of the World Economic Forum. The annual meeting was a gathering of national leadership figures and the leaders in the globalist movement. The theme at the conference had been creating stakeholder capitalism' which was little more than a front for more ways to have government and multinational corporations become more integrated. Modern Monetary Theory[85] had been the backdrop for many of the financial and monetary system meetings.

Following an evening session, the Canadian Deputy Prime Minister had signaled to Enrica Leclercq that they needed to meet. Enrica had arranged for a private booth in an out-of-the-way Italian restaurant.

---

[85] Deborah D'Souza, "Modern Monetary Theory (MMT)," Investopedia.com (DotDash Publishing, June 3, 2021), https://www.investopedia.com/modern-monetary-theory-mmt-4588060

She had a member of her staff hand carry an envelope with the time and place.

They settled in with wine and two small servings of *Arancini di Riso.* The small rice balls were a weakness for Enrica.

Brenda began to unload her fears. The two women had earlier discussed Prime Minister Trudeau on at least three occasions. Both had agreed he was a genuine misogynist with deeply rooted narcissistic problems. Moreover, they believed him to be intellectually lazy and uninformed about world events, unlike his father, Pierre.[86] He was, however, a firm believer in globalism, progressivism and had good relations with the Islamists[87] and China.[88] But all things told, they regarded him as a mascot for the globalist movement rather than a leader. His prancing about in fancy-colored socks was amusing for the press, but he was an embarrassment.[89]

---

[86] Shahid Mahmood, "Opinion: Justin Trudeau Needs to Get Real," theglobeandmail.com (The Globe and Mail, September 27, 2019), https://www.theglobeandmail.com/opinion/article-justin-trudeau-needs-to-get-real/

[87] Unknown Editor, "Watch: Trudeau Calls Question on Returning ISIS Fighter Divisive," YouTube.com (YouTube, May 11, 2018), https://www.youtube.com/watch?v=mhzWYELrJhU

[88] CTVNews.ca Staff, "Trudeau under Fire for Expressing Admiration for China's 'Basic Dictatorship'," CTVNews.ca (CTV News, November 9, 2013), https://www.ctvnews.ca/politics/trudeau-under-fire-for-expressing-admiration-for-china-s-basic-dictatorship-1.1535116

Trudeau's weeklong formal visit to India had embarrassed Canada, India, and himself, all at the same time. The results were so stunning that Enrica had her intelligence contacts find out more about the undisciplined Prime Minister. Not only had he taken a convicted terrorist who had attempted to murder an Indian cabinet minister on the trip as a guest,[90] but several other members of his entourage had connections to terrorism as well, including two cabinet ministers. Moreover, on an earlier trip, the Chief Minister of the State of Punjab had refused to speak with the Canadian Defence Minister, stating he did not deal with those who supported terrorism.[91]

Then there was the situation with Iran. Brenda was worried about Justin Trudeau's brother Sasha and his relationship with the Iranian government. Sasha had

---

[89] Brian Lilley, "LILLEY: Trudeau's Socks Being an Embarrassment Would Be Least of Our Worries," torontosun.com (Toronto Sun, April 23, 2020), https://torontosun.com/opinion/columnists/lilley-trudeaus-socks-being-an-embarrassment-would-be-least-of-our-worries

[90] Candice Malcolm, "Terrorist in Trudeau's India Entourage Arrested Again in Surrey," tnc.news (True North Canada, February 14, 2020), https://tnc.news/2020/02/12/terrorist-in-trudeaus-india-entourage-arrested-again-in-surrey/

[91] Suhasini Haidar and Vikas Vasudeva, "Amarinder Remarks on Canadian Ministers Sparks Row," thehindu.com (The Hindu, April 14, 2017), https://www.thehindu.com/news/national/amarinder-remarks-on-canadian-ministers-sparks-row/article17991450.ece

earlier worked for the state-controlled Iranian media[92] and millions of Iranian government money was flowing into Canada. Now Alexandre 'Sasha' Trudeau was an official advisor to the Prime Minister. Brenda had tried to find out what they were discussing, but Justin had silenced any discussions before anything could be determined. Worse yet, Justin had been taking meetings with a Member of Parliament from Toronto who had close ties to Iran. The same Member of Parliament was connected to a financial scandal that revealed Iran had been moving millions of dollars into Canada.[93] Brenda worried that the Iranians might gain enough influence to distract Justin away from what they needed him to do. At this stage of the game, Justin Trudeau was becoming more of a liability than an asset.

The final political issue had been Canada's botched vaccine program during the pandemic. Despite Canada's close working relationship with both the United States and the United Kingdom, Justin Trudeau had decided to enter into an 'all in' deal with China to get all of Canada's vaccines. However, once

---

[92] Mike Fegelman, "When It Comes to Israel, Alexandre Trudeau's Got It Wrong," huffingtonpost.ca (HuffPost Canada, December 25, 2012), https://www.huffingtonpost.ca/mike-fegelman/alexandre-trudeau_b_2018038.html

[93] Stewart Bell and Sam Cooper, "MP Says He Was Unaware of CSIS Allegations against Iranian Businessman When They Met," globalnews.ca (Global News, November 25, 2020), https://globalnews.ca/news/7483597/liberal-mp-csis-allegations-iranian-businessman/

they had an agreement signed, China reneged on the contract, and Trudeau had 'forgotten' to tell the Canadian public about this failure for three months.[94]

But for Enrica, the most stunning part was his history with women. She was not put off by the long list of ski bunnies and glitterati. On the contrary, he craved attention and was just like his mother in that sense. But it appeared that the Prime Minister had a least two past situations where violence and coercion in a sexual context were of concern. On top of that, his own Parliamentary Secretary, a black female Member of Parliament, had quit in anger when the Prime Minister would not meet with her for even 15 minutes a month.[95] And then he had thrown two female cabinet ministers under the bus and blamed them for his scandals.[96]

---

[94] Charlie Pinkerton, "Days after Announcing Deal, Ottawa Learned China Blocked CanSino's Vaccine Shipment," iPolitics.ca (iPOLITICS, January 27, 2021), https://ipolitics.ca/2021/01/26/days-after-announcing-deal-ottawa-learned-china-blocked-cansino-vaccine-shipment/

[95] The Canadian Press, "Celina Caesar-Chavannes Quits Liberal Caucus, Will Sit as an Independent MP," nationalpost.com (National Post, March 20, 2019), https://nationalpost.com/news/canada/celina-caesar-chavannes-quits-liberal-caucus-sits-as-independent-mp-2

[96] Rahul Kalvapalle and Amanda Connolly, "Jody Wilson-Raybould and Jane Philpott Kicked out of Liberal Party Caucus," globalnews.ca (Global News, April 3, 2019), https://globalnews.ca/news/5123526/liberal-caucus-wilson-raybould-jane-philpott/

But now, Brenda had brought more bad news. Another woman might be coming forward with two claims. First, Trudeau had been abusive to a current reporter with the CBC, the state media corporation. Worse still, this same female reporter was prepared to say that the Prime Minister was involved in a long-term sexual relationship with another cabinet minister, a male. While all of that was perhaps a survivable scandal, the reporter was also willing to state she knew that the same cabinet minister had been the chief procurer of drugs for the Prime Minister and his inner circle for years.

Brenda had told Enrica that she was at the end of her rope. Trudeau's fluffy hair, silly socks, and boyish charm had been an asset, even during the pandemic. But this might be enough to derail him, even with Canada's press that had been bought off with a few hundred million dollars of taxpayer money.[97]

Enrica had grave concerns. Trudeau was of little value to her, but Brenda Elishchuk's position as Deputy Prime Minister was a crucial part of her plans. Enrica needed someone who had influence with the White House and could be counted on to convince the Americans to help, or at least not interfere with their

---

[97] Spencer Fernando, "WATCH: Arrogant Trudeau Brags About Bribing The Media With Your Money," spencerfernando.com (Spencer Fernando, September 1, 2019), https://spencerfernando.com/2019/09/01/watch-arrogant-trudeau-brags-about-bribing-the-media-with-your-money/

upcoming reset plans. Brenda's personal relationship with President Harris of the United States was critical.

Enrica had closed off the meeting with a smile and words of encouragement. She told Brenda that a plan would soon be available, and this miscreant mascot would not damage their larger ambitions.

* * *

A month later, Brenda and Enrica would meet again in New York under the auspices of a UN conference on the environment. Enrica had dreaded sitting through the formal session, being lectured to by some well-meaning, chin drooling, climate alarmist armed with more baseless computer models. This time, the UN meeting was about how the pandemic had been caused by the environmental damage of the white Christian nations exploiting it.

Enrica had managed to sit through the first presentation without having her head explode. She even managed a few well-placed diplomatic comments about how the environment was tied to security, such as was befitting the High Representative for the European Union for Foreign Affairs and Security Policy.

Late in the afternoon, Enrica had a personal staff member carry an envelope to the Canadian Deputy Prime Minister. The directions were to meet her at her hotel and to ask the front desk staff for the meeting room.

Brenda arrived at the hotel and was directed to a small conference room on the mezzanine level. She was alone, but the room was laid out with coffee, sparkling water, and a few pastries. Several minutes later, Enrica arrived. She seemed pleased with herself.

She handed Brenda a small black pouch and indicated that Brenda should put her phone in it.

Enrica took the pouch and folded it shut with its Velcro fasteners.

"Sorry for the late arrival. I had the hotel staff change the room at the last minute just before you arrived. This fancy little bag is a Faraday cage. It blocks all electronic signals, and no one can monitor your phone now."

She then pulled a small device and placed it on the table between them. "This is a white noise machine. If the room is bugged, what they will hear will be electronic noise." She then poured herself a coffee and sat down across from Brenda.

"We have a plan in place to solve our problem. The brilliant part is that you have only a limited role. Are you ready for this?"

Brenda nodded in affirmation. She had been involved in a few dirty deals involving money, lies, and fake software in voting machines, but this was moving into another league. The idea of killing a sitting Prime Minister was sobering, to say the least.

"You will remember that a Khalistan terrorist group blew up an Air India flight in 1984. The bomb was built and placed on an airplane in Canada. In so doing, they committed the largest mass murder in your country's history and the largest loss of life in an attack against a single airplane. They killed 268 Canadians and 331 people overall.[98] You also know that none of the major leaders in the terrorist campaign were ever caught in Canada, and a few of them are still living free. One of them was even involved in a multi-million-dollar major tax scam a few years later and beat those charges as well. Now, all these years later, they are at it again. Another breakaway faction exists, which calls itself the Global Khalistan Society. They are still trying to create their own Khalistan homeland, and they still think blowing up buildings and killing police will help them. Their political arm has offices in Canada, the UK, and Brussels as well. They have been consistently trying to lobby for EU support, and we have consistently ignored them."

Enrica smiled again. "Does this all make sense so far?"

Brenda once again nodded her head yes.

"Great. Here is the good news. I had an off-the-record meeting with Kulwant Singh Kaur, their head of office

---

[98] A total of 329 people died in the Air India 182 crash. Two baggage handlers were killed in Tokyo when another bombing attempt on the same day went wrong.

in Brussels. It was clear to him that the EU might be interested in officially meeting with him soon. I also told him that significant policy changes were coming and that his Khalistan movement might benefit, especially as India and the EU are moving into a rough patch. But here is where you come in. During the discussion, I suggested to Mr. Kaur that the EU would be more likely to respond to him if they could show they were a capable and robust organization. Many observers still think they are just malcontents with a Facebook page and a Twitter account. What you need to do is to talk to one of the leading Khalistani figures in Canada. Your defense minister is well-connected, and so is your new Minister of Economic Recovery. Either one of them can be the messenger boy. All you need to do is tell them you want Trudeau removed. I guess that they are already waiting for you to talk to them, although they have no idea of what is required.

Brenda sat in silence while she considered the elegance and simplicity of the plan. But she could also see the pitfalls. What about the Khalistani members of her cabinet? Would they go along with it? What would she have to promise them?

"Enrica, this is an amazing idea, but I am not sure they will go for it in Canada."

"They will. Carrots and sticks. People will do something when they are given the incentive to do it. In this case, you can tell them the carrot is greater recognition for their cause, EU financial contributions to their NGO, and pressure on the Indian government. You can promise a few of them some high-paying government positions that require no work on their part. The stick will be India. If they do not cooperate, we will tell India and the world that his colleagues are building bombs and training more terrorists in Canada and Europe. That will finish them for a few years. But do not worry. They are serious, and they will cooperate because they want the outcome. Besides that, they have already murdered a few journalists, including one in Canada,[99] without being caught. Such an action is not a leap for them. After you murder over 300 people in one terrorist attack, the rest comes easily."

With that, Enrica rose and headed to the door, asking Brenda to remain for 10 minutes so they would be less likely to be seen together. Then, she undid her Faraday cage pouch, handed the phone to Brenda, and was gone.

LOCATION: Vancouver International Airport

DATE: 5 July

TIME: 8:00 AM

---

[99] Kim Bolan, "Journalist Tara Singh Hayer's Assassination Still Unsolved 20 Years after Fatal Shooting," vancouversun.com (Postmedia News, November 16, 2018), https://vancouversun.com/news/crime/journalist-tara-singh-hayers-assassination-still-unsolved-20-years-after-fatal-shooting/

Bhupender Valtoha was patiently waiting for his flight to New Delhi. His brief trip to Canada had been, for the most part, both enjoyable and profitable. He had flown into Toronto (legally) a week earlier on a 'one-time' visitor visa, which allowed him to attend his cousin's wedding in Mississauga. He had not gone to any wedding, but he did stay at the house of one of his uncles for two days. After that, he had flown to Vancouver on a domestic flight.

His visit to Vancouver Island had gone according to plan. His rented car had been booked in the name of another distant uncle. The walk into the private estate had been a bit of a chore given the distance, as had his time spent waiting in its safe room. He had watched the occupants of the house with the internal security cameras. Once the three occupants had gone to bed, he left the safe room, fulfilled the requirements of his contract, and left the house. The walk to his rented car seemed longer than the walk to the isolated house. Maybe that was because the adrenalin flow and the anticipation were now gone.

Chapter 24: Washington – A Revolution?

LOCATION: Brookings Institute, Washington DC

DATE: 5 July

TIME: 10:00 AM

Acting Prime Minister Brenda Elishchuk looked down at her notes one last time. Then she looked out over the podium at the Brookings Institute. A larger than normal number of attendees were in the room. Unfortunately, many were attending out of curiosity rather than genuine interest for this first international presentation from the 'new' Canadian Prime Minister.

Of morbid interest, no one seemed to know who had killed the last Canadian Prime Minister, although rumors were rife. ISIS agents in Canada? A sex scandal gone wrong?   Right-wing anti-globalist terrorists? Would someone try and kill the new Prime Minister?

Brenda Elishchuk had far-reaching plans for this speech. The purpose of this meeting, called on short notice, was to discuss American foreign policy objectives in the global recovery and 'building back better.' For Elishchuk, three objectives existed. The first was to establish in the eyes of the world that she was the Prime Minister and that the 'acting' title would be soon dropped. The second was to leave no doubt that the Government of Canada believed that right-wing extremists were behind the assassination. The third, and most important, was to indirectly use the speech to advance the agenda of the Great Reset and to infer that the American Administration of President Kamal Harris was supportive of Europe taking the lead for this great leap forward.

Following the usual introductory statement, Elishchuk dove straight into the message she needed to deliver.

"Neo-Nazis, white supremacists, incels, nativists, and radical anti-globalists who resort to violent acts are a threat to the stability of my country and countries around the world. [100] My country cannot tolerate any more assaults from them, and soon, it will not have to worry about such issues. The world's future lies not in the bitter right-wing history of the past and sovereign borders but in the shining future of globalism and a world without boundaries. Borders cause wars. Free movement builds diversity. Those who resist are trapped in Judeo-Christian values, which covers the white supremacy that has dominated the globe for almost four centuries. The Treaty of Westphalia ushered in the age of national sovereignty, which begat war and colonialism. We need to decolonize our national structures. We need to 'build back' a

---

[100] Global Affairs Canada, "Address by Foreign Affairs Minister at UNSC Debate on Terrorism Financing," Canada.ca (Government of Canada, March 30, 2019), https://www.canada.ca/en/global-affairs/news/2019/03/address-by-foreign-affairs-minister-at-unsc-debate-on-terrorism-financing.html

better world. The pandemic caused disruptions in the political, social, and economic arenas of the entire world. The inadequacies that have been exposed are in our health, energy, financial and educational sectors. We are at a historical crossroads. We are entering a unique window of opportunity to shape the recovery and reset the entire system of systems. We can determine the future of national economies; we can set the national priorities and manage the global commons. Canada will be a leader in implementing the post national society[101] , and it will be a city on a hill with shining lights to inspire those who are yearning for equity. These shining lights will not be powered by dirty hydrocarbons but by clean green energy technology. By the year 2030, and following the UN's agenda, we foresee a world where private property is no longer an obstacle to equity and social justice for all."

Elishchuk deliberately paused for a few seconds and looked down at the journalists. Most of them were busy scribbling notes, much to her satisfaction.

Now was the time to deliver the *Schwerpunkt,* the main message.

"Earlier this morning, U.S. President Kamala Harris and I were discussing how the world will be shaped in

---

[101] Charles Foran, "The Canada Experiment: Is This the World's First 'Postnational' Country?" The Guardian (Guardian News and Media, January 4, 2017), https://www.theguardian.com/world/2017/jan/04/the-canada-experiment-is-this-the-worlds-first-postnational-country

the post-pandemic era. She is a leader. A leader with vision. A leader who can scan the future and see beyond current horizons. A leader who knows that those with experience in supra-national organizations are best prepared for the future. She has assured me that she will watch with admiration those who have the zeal and the courage to make great leaps into a bold future."

With a hand flourish, Prime Minister Elishchuk pointed over the assembly as though pointing to the future. She leaned forward with her eyes focussed well beyond the confines of the room. The pose had an almost Stalinesque feel about it. The great leader was pointing towards the glorious time yet to come.

"We need to draw from the vision and vast experience of the leaders who have been involved in global forums to build a new social contract that honors the dignity of every human being. Imagine a more inclusive world. Imagine a more diverse world. Imagine a more equitable global common. But most important, imagine it all starting now."

The meeting hall had gone quiet. However, an unusual event was occurring. The assembled gathering of global political leaders and ambassadors was listening attentively to a Canadian Prime Minister. It was not that they were interested in Canada, but rather the message.

One of those listening to every word was the Assistant Secretary of State for Europe. The Canadian Prime Minister had just made a speech that essentially declared war on capitalism, national sovereignty, Christianity, and the Jews. Further to that, the message seemed to indicate that a physical revolution may be about to start in Europe in which the Great Reset would no longer be a buzz phrase but a political reality.

But for the Assistant Secretary, the American President's stunning message indirectly indicated that the USA would not interfere in Europe should some revolutionary changes occur. Either the USA was sending a message through an untested voice, or the Canadian Prime Minister had just massively overstepped her bounds and spoke out of turn.

The Assistant Secretary had been briefed about the new Canadian Prime Minister. She had been close to Kamala Harris back in her high school days. Harris had lived in Montreal, Canada, and had graduated high school after four years in the Canadian system.[102] Brenda Elishchuk had attended the same high school, and yearbook pictures showed them together in two different high school clubs. They had not kept in close contact, but they had followed each other careers to some degree. Both were progressives, and both had close ties to Europe.

---

[102] Nicole Bogart, "Kamala Harris' Canadian Roots: Montreal Classmates Reflect on Historic Win," CTV News | America Votes (CTV News, November 7, 2020), https://www.ctvnews.ca/world/america-votes/kamala-harris-canadian-roots-montreal-classmates-reflect-on-historic-win-1.5179442

This left the Assistant Secretary with the view that President Harris had approved the message sent today.

The Ambassador wondered about his future. If President Harris had approved these comments, then he was most likely out of a job. To have this announcement made at Brookings without informing him ahead of time was a severe breach of internal protocol.

Another thought had struck him as well. Was the Canadian Prime Minister signaling that it was a right-wing or neo-Nazi group that had murdered the Prime Minister? Or was this a distraction campaign to draw attention from the perpetrators while preparing to move against the right?

Either way, the Ambassador was heading back to his office. Phone calls had to be made, and a report filed. Fast.

In the view of the usually jaded Assistant Secretary, something big was about to happen.

* * *

Following a few brief courtesy statements, Brenda Elishchuk quickly left and headed to her waiting car. A short drive to Reagan National Airport and her Challenger jet would make the one-hour hop back to Ottawa. After that speech, it was better to leave everyone guessing as to its meaning.

The opening bit about neo-Nazis and white supremacists being a threat to Canada was a deliberate fabrication. Still, it would be sufficient to generate rumors that it was right-wing nutters that had killed Prime Minister 'Black Face McGropy Hands' as he was often known in Canada. Elishchuk had tried to get the Canadian Department of Public Safety to put out a statement about the threat from right-wing terrorism in Canada, but they had dragged their feet. Canada had officially listed some 57 entities as terrorist groups. Of the 57 in total, 40 of them were Islamist. That was almost 70%. Of the remaining 17, nine of them were nationalist in their orientation. That included groups such as the Basque Homeland and Liberty Front. One group was listed as communist in orientation. And one was a Jewish group that had never been active in Canada.

The Prime Minister was disappointed to find out that only two terror-listed entities had right-wing or white supremacist views. Moreover, neither of them had attacked Canada, and neither was known to have any members left in Canada.

But none of this mattered. The truth was not the issue. Anyone with views that opposed the Great Reset had to be slandered, silenced, and canceled. Canada's press would likely go along with the story, being too docile and submissive to raise any questions or do any research. Elishchuk allowed herself to think positively about Trudeau for a moment. He had accepted her idea to buy off most of the mainstream press in Canada by giving them 600 million dollars in funding, supposedly to assist them in making the transition from the analog age to the digital future. Only the most naive had tried to maintain the position that this was not money aimed at buying the press's silence.[103]

As the Challenger jet began its descent into Ottawa, Brenda was content. The various obstacles put up in her path were being knocked down one by one. Those who had not cooperated could be removed later once she was firmly in her new position.

---

[103] Stuart Thomson, "$600M In Federal Funding for Media 'a Turning Point in the Plight of Newspapers in Canada'," nationalpost.com (National Post, November 22, 2018), https://nationalpost.com/news/politics/600m-in-federal-funding-for-media-a-turning-point-in-the-plight-of-newspapers-in-canada

Chapter 25: The Islamist Attacks Start

LOCATION: Paris, France

DATE: 6 July

TIME: Just after Midnight

Ground zero for the new war in Europe had been chosen.

The Parisian suburb of Sevran was amongst the most radicalized areas in all of France. With a population of 50,000, the tiny suburb had 15 of its youth killed while fighting for ISIS. Over half the residents were born outside of France, most of them from North Africa. Poverty was rampant, and the Islamists had exploited the situation to spread their ideology.

The anger, instilled by the ideology, was just below the surface. The youth, especially the males, were perpetually frowning. There was never a public display of joy or happiness, except when the most radicalized residents celebrated after a successful terrorist attack by sharing sweets on the street.

Many dressed in the clothing they thought made them look more 'Muslim.' Beards were common, with many shaving their upper lip, which they believed demonstrated their Salafist orientation. Girls as young as six were forced to wear hijab, and burqas were common. No Muslim women were allowed in the cafés[104] or working in the stores. Long since it was identified as a 'no go' zone, the police avoided the area and only entered it in force when responding to emergency calls. Domestic violence and femicide were common, especially among women in their late teens. Their deaths were explained away as suicides, rather than drawing attention to the fact they were 'forced suicides' – killed or forced to swallow poison by their male relatives to cover up honor crimes.

Sevran was trapped in a spiral, perhaps as bad as Molenbeek in Belgium. The education of the youth was focused on memorizing the Qur'an and studying Hadith. Their education would never result in employment. Even the few who had developed real-world skills were refused employment when perspective bosses found out they lived in Sevran. The ideology of the Islamists and their refusal to allow integration ensured a continuing supply of angry young men who were never allowed to develop hope.

Following the assassination of Ilhan Benhaddara, the Imams in Sevran followed a familiar pattern. The daily prayers raised the level of anger. The youth were told that Muslims were once again victims. They were

---

[104] David Chazan, "'This Isn't Paris. It's Only Men Here' - Inside the French Muslim No-Go Zones Where Women Aren't Welcome," The Telegraph (Telegraph Media Group, December 17, 2016), https://www.telegraph.co.uk/news/2016/12/17/french-bar-tells-women-isnt-paris-men/

forced to believe that they could only be safe once France and Europe were under Sharia's protection.

Within a few days, however, the message began to change. The Imams now began to suggest that only the language of strength would be heard. Years of oppression must end. The dreams of Hassan al-Banna must be realized, and Sayyid Qutb's message of political violence must be heard.

It was normal to yearn for a caliphate.

Sharia was the will of Allah.

Martyrdom would be rewarded.

A caliphate was their goal.

Envelopes with small amounts of money began to appear. Looks were exchanged. The money was spent on small cans filled with jellied alcohol fuel, customarily used for warming food trays. The tiny fuel cans would become the basis for incendiary devices to start fires under cars. More money was spent on buying liquid dish detergent, helpful in turning gasoline into a poor man's form of napalm. Metal bars and sledgehammers appeared, and bricks were quietly stacked in back alleys.

It was July, and the sun would set just before 10:00 PM. By 10:30 PM, it would be dark.

By 11:00 PM, the light would return. Sevran and its surrounding areas would be glowing red and orange as cars would be set alight. Shops owned by infidels would be smashed and burned. Electrical substations would be attacked and set on fire to extinguish the

272

streetlights. Tires and other garbage, carefully accumulated, would block intersections until the police arrived – and suddenly, they would be burning as well.

By the following day, the word would be spread to Clichy-sous-Bois and hundreds of neighborhoods controlled by the Muslim Brotherhood. Then, over the next four nights, the fires would spread from Paris to Nice, Lyon, and many other cities.

The time for the caliphate had arrived.

Chapter 26: Erdogan's Tidal Wave

LOCATION: Ankara, Turkey: Office of President Recep Tayyip Erdogan

DATE: 7 July

TIME: 11:00 AM

President Erdogan sat reading the latest financial reports sent to him by the Governor of Turkey's Central Bank. He was weary of discussions about endless debts, interest rates, foreign reserves, quantitative easing, lira devaluation, synthetic derivatives, and plans to ban stocks' shorting.

He sighed in frustration. Did Suleiman the Magnificent[105] have to deal with such fools? Did Mehmed the Conqueror,[106] one of the greatest of all the Ottoman leaders, spend his days crushed by such details? Or did the great leaders make the significant decisions and let the underlings deal with the problems?

---

[105] V.J. Parry, "Süleyman the Magnificent," britannica.com (Encyclopædia Britannica, inc., 2021), https://www.britannica.com/biography/Suleyman-the-Magnificent.
[106] Halil Inalcik, "Mehmed II," britannica.com (Encyclopædia Britannica, inc., April 29, 2021), https://www.britannica.com/biography/Mehmed-II-Ottoman-sultan

After reading through the financial reports, Erdogan turned his attention to intelligence reports. These were interesting. The assessments on Europe continued to indicate that social unrest was increasing as the pandemic recovery was failing and the recession was moving towards depression.

The ground in Europe was shifting.

But what fired his imagination was the reporting from his international network of Islamist cleric spies known to the world as the Diyanet.[107] Their reports indicated that unrest was building rapidly among a variety of Islamist factions in Europe, especially in France, Germany, and Belgium. The assassination of Ilhan Benhaddara had caused deep resentment and anger. As a result, many Islamists, and even secular Muslims, believed that the four attacks on the 28th of June were designed to create more trouble for them.

The date of 28 June was not lost on Erdogan. The 1914 terrorist attack in Sarajevo, formerly controlled by the Ottoman Empire, had been the spark that lit the fires of the Great War – which in turn had brought about the final collapse of the exhausted Ottoman caliphate. Thus, to Erdogan, the attackers were sending a historical message as well as a political one.

---

[107] Unknown Editors, "T.C. Diyanet İşleri Başkanlığı: İman: İbadet: Namaz: Ahlak (Republic of Turkey Presidency of Religious Affairs)," T.C. Diyanet İşleri Başkanlığı | İman | İbadet | Namaz | Ahlak (Republic of Turkey, 2021), https://www.diyanet.gov.tr/tr-TR

Erdogan had called the President of the Diyanet the day after the terrorist attacks. Rather than an overview of the intelligence reports from the Diyanet mosques, he wanted each mosque to send an individual account of how the attacks had affected them. With over 900 mosques in Germany, 150 in the Netherlands, 270 in France, a dozen in Sweden, and a handful in the United Kingdom, it was an enormous pile of paper.

For Erdogan, this was time and effort well spent as he randomly selected several dozen reports and read them in detail. The attacks had caused a rise in resentment among the faithful. Anger was building. Speculation over the origins of the attacks was increasing. Among the youth, calls for violence were increasing. Among the more senior Imams, a growing number believed that it was time for a more aggressive approach.

Erdogan hated the Europeans with a passion. Turkey had done everything it could to meet the entry requirements for the European Union, only for the goalposts to be moved. While Europe looked down on Turkey, he could see daily how the whole EU project was wilting, consumed by delusions of its own grandeur.

Of course, Turkey, like Europe, had its own migration problems. Turkey had over three million refugees, most of them Syrians driven out by the war. Others were from Iraq, Iran, and Afghanistan.

Erdogan had been able to extort billions of dollars from the European Union by threatening to unleash even more waves of migrants into Europe.[108]   More money had come from the United Nations. The Turkish intelligence services were aware of the number of violent Islamists among the refugees – largely because they were often training and recruiting them. Many of them had been hard-core ISIS fighters who had committed rape and genocide.

Erdogan decided it was time to act.

It was time for Islam to return to fulfill its proper role. Islam must rule over Sarajevo, Athens, Cordoba, Madrid, Zagreb, Lisbon, and Belgrade. On top of everything else, Paris, Nice and Vienna had to fall to Islam.

The plans were already in place. Erdogan would give the orders to start tomorrow. The first part of the plan would be to flood the Aegean Sea with refugees. They would be told that the European Union had changed plans, and they would be moved to France, Italy, Germany, and the United Kingdom after they landed on the Greek Islands. The first wave would consist of more than 250,000 refugees in the first two days. The Greeks would be overrun by refugees and

---

[108] In 2016 alone, the European Union agreed to pay Turkey up to six billion Euros ($US 7.6 billion) to aid Syrian refugees in Turkey. Additionally, the EU agreed to fast track Turkish ascension to the EU and allow for visa free travel for Turkish citizen travelling in Europe. In exchange, Turkey agreed to stop the flow of migrants from Turkey to Europe and the numbers dropped significantly.

would be clamoring for the EU or NATO to step in. Erdogan would tell the EU that he had tried to stop them, but the refugees wanted to go to Europe now that Turkey had run out of money to pay for the costs of hosting them.

The second wave would be different. It would consist of the most violent and motivated Islamists. A few of the old fighters would be inserted with the refugees on small boats. Their job would be to organize the refugees to be as destructive and challenging as possible. They would demand halal food, accuse the Greek authorities of Islamophobic behavior and start fires to destroy camp facilities. They would give interviews to the press on how abusive the Greeks were and how they needed to be moved to Europe.

The most skilled of the younger fighters, especially the clean skins, would be flown into the heart of Europe through a variety of indirect routes. Each would have new passports, cover stories, and money. The most violent, if not the most skilled fighters, would be sent to Libya and then given boats and told to go to Italy. Others would cross from Morocco and Algeria into France. Once on the ground in Europe, their mission would be to strike out and commit terrorist attacks starting on the 10th or 11th of July. The quality of the attacks was not that important. The quantity was – Europe needed to be overloaded with violent problems so the Islamists could take the initiative.

Erdogan recognized the risks. His information sources in the Diyanet were extensive, but they were not perfect. Their hopes and ambitions shaped their views. There was also the question of how much the reports were written to please their paymasters in Ankara. But the consistency of these new reports was encouraging. The patterns of reporting were remarkably consistent across a wide range of reporting mosques.

Separately, Erdogan's diplomatic service had told him that senior members of the EU and many of its institutions were troubled. They believed that the economic and social dislocation from the pandemic had unnerved the technocratic and political classes. Their confidence had been weakened by the inability of the European Union to act collectively when it was most needed.

It was time for Islam to retake its place in Europe.

* * *

LOCATION: Querini Castle, Astypalaia Island, Greece

DATE: 8 July

TIME: 5:45 AM

Tasso felt his heart pounding as he neared the peak of the hill. The blue dome of the Cycladic Church in the Querini Castle stood out against the black and grey stones of the castle walls.

As with every morning, he was out the door at 5:00 AM for the start of his 45-minute ride. His circular route included a climb towards the castle every morning. He would be rewarded with a stunning view of the sunrise over the Aegean Sea for his efforts. After his bike ride, it would be time to head to the market to buy the fresh food needed for his restaurant. Today would be a good day as the Olympiacos would be playing AEK Athens in the Greek Super League. The cost of the satellite feed for the games was high, but the customers would be many, and they would be spending freely.

As he crested the hill, Tasso suddenly stopped peddling. His bike rolled to a stop. The western horizon had a series of growing dots that did not belong. For a few moments, he struggled to understand what he was seeing before it hit him.

Several dozen small boats were moving towards the island. An invasion? It was possible as the Island of Astypalaia had been invaded several times in the past. One such invasion had been the arrival of the Ottoman Turks, who had arrived in 1522 and stayed until 1912. By why invade Astypalaia now? The island was of no significance beyond its proximity to the Turkish coast.

After staring for several more minutes, the purpose of the boats became clearer. It was not an invasion of the Turkish Army or Navy. It was a wave of refugees. Given the large number of them, the island was about to be overrun by them. Tasso turned his bike around and headed down the hill as fast as he dared.

His next stop would be the police station to raise the alarm.

Chapter 27: Joining the Caravan of Martyrs

LOCATION: Paris, France

DATE: 10 July

TIME: 10:15 AM

Tarek Raman was elated. It had been 65 years since the Muslim Brotherhood had arrived in Austria following the attempted assassination of Egyptian President Nassar. Mistakes had been made. Losses had been taken, and lives had been lost. But today, all the pain, suffering, and blood would be worth it.

Today would see a meaningful move towards a renewed European caliphate. Within days, territories in France, Belgium, the Netherlands, and Germany would be declared as caliphates. From those first secured areas, the soldiers of Allah would fight to link up their neighborhoods, thus forming contiguous zones of control.

Tarek was under no illusions. Not all their attacks would be successful, and some territory would be lost again. But with Europe about to be consumed by a revolution of its own, the caliphates would have time to dig in and build defenses for their new territories.

Once the European revolution was settled, the largest of the new caliphates would be defensible. They would be able to negotiate with the new leaders of Europe. They would control the territory they had taken. They would control taxation, education, localized immigration, and social policy on their territory. They would, however, tell the new governments they would not attempt to interfere with matters of foreign policy, defense, or international trade.

Tarek had reasoned that it was not the perfect solution. Others had argued that the goal should be to take over the national governments in a coup and declare them all caliphates. However, Tarek knew that the idea of taking over a European government was, to use a European term, a bridge too far.

But taking effective control of several hundred neighborhoods would give them a base from which to build. Once solidified, each independent district would then grow outwards. A campaign of low-level terror and harassment would be unleashed on those living close to the caliphates. It would not be long before they would be willing to sell their properties cheap or abandon them altogether.

Tarek thought back to Osama bin Laden and the events of 9/11. While the blessed Osama had stirred the hearts of hundreds of millions of Muslims, his attacks had been fatally flawed. Bin Laden had pushed America to the edge, and then at the moment of his most significant victory, failed to follow up. With only a few dedicated men, al Qaeda would have been able to turn America on its head. A train station shooting here. A small bomb there. Fires set in underground parking lots in government office buildings. Phone calls warning of bomb threats causing the evacuation of airports—white powder attacks with homemade ricin in massive shopping malls. A few shootings and America could have been closed, just as the DC sniper with one car and one rifle had terrorized the capital city for months in 2002.

The blessed attacks of 9/11 had opened the door for the deployment of the greatest weapon of all – fear. But there had been no one to walk through it. As a result, the attacks were a publicity success but a strategic failure.

This time would be different. With most of the Islamist neighborhoods in France and Belgium already alight, the next phase would be unleashed.

Severe attacks in the daylight hours would now start in Europe. Not only did the small teams necessary for such attacks already exist, but the new arrivals from Turkey would also support them. These were experienced ISIS fighters. Skill and subtly were not their strengths. Violence of the most blatant variety was their role.

After several days of attacks, Europe would be destabilized and ready for conquest.

* * *

LOCATION: Vienna, Austria

DATE: 10 July

TIME: 12:15 PM Local Time

The early shoppers in the 'Golden Quarter' of Vienna were unaware that they were to become the first victims of another protracted political struggle. The Golden Quarter shopping area attracted those with high disposable income levels with a taste for the finer possessions in life, especially jewelry.

The two gunmen had been given clear instructions. When dropped off by car on Wallnerstrasse, they were to run northwest towards the pedestrian area at the heart of the Golden Quarter. Once there, they were to turn right and begin firing their weapons on the semi-automatic setting. Their AK-47 rifles were equipped with 30 round magazines, and each man had two extra magazines. When the rounds were expended, they were to drop the rifles on the ground and head down Jungferngassee towards St Peter's Church. At that point, they were to shed their outer jackets, gloves and backpacks and leave the area on foot at a walking speed, slipping away in confusion. But, rather unusually, they had been told that what was most important was that all the rounds were fired. They were to kill as many shoppers as possible, but all the rounds had to be fired before they could flee.

* * *

LOCATION: Berlin, Germany

DATE: 10 July

TIME: 1:15 PM Local Time

Hassan finished loading the petrol cans into the back of the vehicle. The containers were chosen because they were plastic and would melt in a fire. Each container weighed about 16 kilograms when it was filled with a mixture of 90% gasoline and 10% waste motor oil. The total weight of the 15 fuel containers was about 240 kilograms, less than the weight of four adult passengers. Thus, the vehicle would not appear overloaded.

The Volkswagen 'Transporter' van had been stolen one week earlier from a bakery in a small town about 50 kilometers east of Berlin. The police had put little investigative effort into the theft of a five-year-old commercial vehicle, seemingly stolen at random, especially given that the driver had left the key in the vehicle as he always did.

Once stolen, it had been painted and stored out of sight. The license plate was modified. The plate would be traced to a legitimate van owned by another small company in Berlin in the unlikely event that the police were to check.

Once the cans were loaded, Hassan placed cardboard boxes over them. The bottom of the boxes had been cut out so they could be placed over the cans. To the outside observer, the van was loaded with baked goods.

Hassan would approach the target from the east. The Parkhaus Mall of Berlin had been chosen as the target. With 981 parking spaces, he would find a parking spot even at a busy time of the day. Traveling down Leipziger Strasse, he would turn left and then enter the parkade at Wilhelmstasse 95. With a height of 1.948 meters, the van would fit under the two-meter bar at the entrance. Once inside the parkade, Hassan would look for a parking space midway between the driving entrance and the pedestrian entrance to the mall.

Once parked, he would partially lower the driver's and passenger's side windows and descend from the vehicle. After one last check to see if there was anyone close to him, he would open the sliding cargo door on the side. Next, he would reach under the cardboard box nearest the door and unscrew the caps off two of the petrol cans. A small cardboard box next to them contained a tiny kerosene camp stove intended for use by campers. It was already fueled, and the wick was set on a low flame. Hassan would then take the plastic top off a tin can that was about half-full of petrol. It would be placed on the camp stove. Hassan would then take three ice cubes from a small, insulated bag and put them in the fuel can on top of the stove. He would pull the Bic lighter from his pocket and light the camp stove. With the camp stove burning, Hassan would gently close the cargo door and walk to the rear of the vehicle, where he would partially open the rear cargo door. Taking the small wooden block inside, he would then allow the door to descend. The wooden block would stop the door from closing entirely and would allow air to enter the vehicle from the rear.

Hassan would then walk out of the mall and head south and east to the McDonald's restaurant. Once there, Hassan would 'accidentally' spot a friend driving by and then leave the area together in his car.

The kerosene camp stove, set on low, would take several minutes to boil the petrol in the can. The ice cubes would extend the time required, acting as a delay mechanism. Once the petrol and water were boiling, the can would overflow and would set itself on fire. That fire would spread to the cardboard boxes and would, in turn, start another fire at the mouth of the petrol cans which Hassan had opened. Made out of plastic, they would soon melt. The first two 20-liter cans would provide a raging fire in the vehicle, which would then cause the other 13 petrol containers to explode or melt. With almost 300 liters of fuel in the containers and another 65 in the vehicle's tank, the fire would spread rapidly as the fuel leaked and burned. Other cars would be engulfed.

The Feuerwehr (fire department) would have difficulty fighting the fire in a parkade, especially given the black smoke given off by the waste oil mixture. The entire mall would have to be evacuated, and the news media would be treated to scenes of smoke pouring out of the mall and concerned shoppers running out of the building.

* * *

LOCATION: Paris, France

DATE: 10 July

TIME: 3:15 PM Local Time

Ricin was chosen as it is one of the deadliest poisons known. As a toxic protein, it can infect cells in the human body and destroy them. Death from inhalation of the powder usually occurs three to five days as the body's organs slowly dissolve. Unfortunately, despite being a known threat, no antidote has been discovered.

Momin was disassembling his lab and destroying any evidence of his homemade ricin. The equipment involved was not extensive. All that had been needed was a few coffee pot filters, some bottles of nail polish remover from a local pharmacy, some glass jars, and a few pots. The packages for the castor bean seeds had already been burned.

Momin was under no illusions. The ricin powder he had created was unlikely to be highly effective, especially given his method of weaponization. His internet research, done on a second-hand laptop using Wi-Fi at a local coffee shop, had indicated that homemade ricin was likely to be weak. It would only be effective if the intended victims were to ingest it rather than breathe it in. He also had no proper means of weaponizing the ricin powder. But this did not concern him.

The target was to be the 'Westfield Les 4 Temps' shopping mall in Paris. With 270 stores, 40 restaurants, and a 16-screen cinema, it was a Paris landmark. He planned to simply drop a small bag with the powder off the side of the escalator when he reached the upper level of the mall. The bag would be open when he tossed it, and the contents should at least partially scatter. With any luck, no one would notice the fall of the bag.

Once the bag was tossed, Momin would leave the mall. When clear of the mall, he would call the emergency 112 emergency number and tell them that the Westfield Les 4 Temps mall had just suffered an attack from a biological weapon. Momin would say to them it was ricin powder and where it could be found. He would then dispose of the burner phone by taking the battery out and throwing it in a garbage can.

Momin's plan was diabolically simple. While it was unlikely anyone would be poisoned, the mall's security measures would ensure the evacuation of the mall. The police would arrive, as would a hazardous materials team. Having been told they were facing a possible biological threat, they would approach the location of the powder dressed in their full protective gear.

Once at the scene, the hazard materials team would run a field test on the powder. Although it was relatively weak, Momin was confident it would test positive for the presence of ricin. The mall, having already been evacuated, would now be sealed off. Specialized cleaning teams would be called, scrubbing the entire mall and its air systems.

Two hours after he left the mall, Momin would make another phone call. This call would go to *Le Figaro* and tell them the police were investigating the mall attack, and they had already determined it was ricin.

It would take at least 24 hours for the police to determine the ricin was not that powerful. By then, however, the damage would be done. All of Europe and most of the world would have heard that a ricin attack had occurred.

Paris may have previously shocked by burning cars and shops, but this was a biological attack on an upscale mall.

The attacks would be followed tomorrow across much of Europe.

Momin would make 20 phone calls to a variety of malls across Europe. Each one would be told they were the target of a ricin attack. The police and hazardous material teams would arrive at the malls as they had done in Paris the day before. The media would have a field day, and social media would be filled with photos and videos of panicked shoppers and hazmat teams.

The attacks would be successful despite the mostly harmless powder.

Fear, driven by the first ricin attack, would do the work. Malls would be empty, and retail sales figures would plunge to levels much like they did when the pandemic started in March 2020.

The weapon of terrorism was not the bomb, the gun, or biological weapons.

It was fear.

* * *

LOCATION: Brussels, Belgium

DATE: 10 July

TIME: 4:15 PM

Qasim al-Qazzaz stepped back from the van and admired his work. He thought of it as a truck bomb. The police and the media would call it a VBIED when it exploded – a vehicle-borne improvised explosive device.

The bomb weighed only 100 kilograms, but that would be sufficient to do its work. Qasim had positioned the ANFO[109] bomb under the backseat of

---

[109] Unknown Editor, "ANFO Explosives: Dynamite: Dyno Nobel," dynonobel.com (Dyno Nobel, 2020), https://www.dynonobel.com/practical-

the van. He had ensured the bomb would not slide out from under the seat by placing two L-shaped brackets on each side, securing them by bolting them to the floor of the van.

The bomb was complete – ready to explode. All that was missing was the two cell phones installed in the brackets on top of the container. One cell phone would be attached to the connector on the top of the bomb and then held in place with heavy packing tape. The other would sit in the small container designed for it on top of the bomb. When the van departed from the garage for its target location, both cell phones would be turned on. One would be the detonator. The other had been converted to an electronic jammer so no accidental signal or wrong number would set the bomb off at an inappropriate time. When Qasim left the van, he would reach into the back and turn off the jammer phone. All that was missing was for someone to call the detonator phone. The detonator's number has been programmed into Qasim's third phone, a burner he had someone else buy a week earlier for cash at a small store with no cameras.

Qasim was experienced with the technology needed to have the cell phone become a detonator. When called, the cell phone would send a charge to the detonator that would, in turn, set off the stick of gelignite which had been stolen from a construction

innovations/popular-products/anfo/

site more than a year ago. The gelignite, in turn, would set off the main charge of ammonium nitrate.

Qasim's knowledge of electronics, built up during two years of technical school, had focused on microcircuitry. But his interest in bomb-making had taken him in new directions. He had studied how the Irish Republican Army had used radio-controlled bombs to attack the British Army. But he had also learned how the British Army had killed several IRA bombers by driving around their suspected bomb-building sites with specialized radio transmitters, setting off the occasional bomb and killing the bomb-makers.

Qasim's reading had also taught him about electronic warfare – the process of how to maintain control of the electromagnet spectrum when others were trying to control it. The phone he had modified as a jammer would send out a signal which would block any incoming calls to the bomb. An unintentional premature explosion was not going to turn Qasim into a martyr for the cause. Instead, he intended to lead a long, if somewhat violent, life for many years to come.

The smell of an overheated electric motor filled his workshop. The cheap Chinese-made coffee grinders had not lasted long. Each coffee grinder had only been able to work its way through about 20 kilograms of fertilizer before the motor burned out. Nevertheless, Qasim was pleased with the outcome, though he had burnt out the motors of five coffee grinders. The ammonium nitrate fertilizer had gone from being coarsely granular to be a relatively fine powder. It was not a nano- explosive, but the fine powder would oxidize much faster now, creating a more powerful explosion.

The five coffee grinders had been broken apart. Each one was smashed into small pieces, and the fragments were washed with bleach and water. Qasim would go for a walk later this evening and drop the parts into public garbage cans. No one would find them, and even if they did, no DNA or fingerprints would exist. He would burn the packaging material from the fertilizer, the phones, and the aluminum powder in an old wood stove at the back of the shop.

While grinding the fertilizer, Qasim had also added small amounts of aluminum powder. The addition would increase the power of the bomb. The powder, frequently used to make silver paint out of white paint, had been bought at a hardware store by the wife of a friend of Qasim. It would be hard to trace it back to him. The woman had bought several liters of white paint at the same time. She had used cash and worn her hijab pulled low over her face, so it was unlikely that anyone would remember her or be able to trace the purchase.

The final ingredient for the bomb was diesel fuel. Qasim had considered using nitromethane which would have helped create a larger explosion as well. But buying such a fuel would attract attention, so Qasim decided to go with diesel fuel. Mixing the correct percentage of fuel by weight with the powder was a laborious process. But getting the amounts right and doing it promptly was critical to the success of the bomb. During his time at a training camp in Kashmir, he and the rest of the brothers had studied how the 1993 World Trade Center bombing had failed to bring down the buildings. The bomb had fizzled and only killed six people instead of tens of thousands. The reason for the bomb's failure had been bad chemistry – the bomb makers had not used the right amount of diesel fuel and had done a poor job mixing it. Qasim would not make the same mistake.

This project had taken Qasim several days to finish. Much of the work had been in collecting the ammonium nitrate fertilizer needed. The bomb was going to weigh over a hundred kilos. The police and intelligence services were tracking the sales of fertilizer, especially the 34-0-0 ammonium nitrate. Because of that, Qasim had asked several contacts to buy single bags of fertilizer. He had suggested that they drive out of the city to pick up the fertilizer to attract less attention. If the police were tracking individual sales, they would not see a sudden upsurge in purchases in one area.

Qasim's family would be proud of his work. His mother had been a Kashmiri refugee living in Molenbeek, Belgium, when she met Walied al-Qazzaz, his father. His father had been studying to be a water engineer while his mother was studying history and politics. She had drawn him into the world of politics and violence. Within a year, Walied al-Qazzaz had been thoroughly radicalized through his mother's work and the university's student association of Muslims. The mixed marriage was unusual, to say the least, but Qasim had grown up speaking French, Walloon, Arabic, and English. He had the ability to move in several cultures at once without drawing notice.

The time had come.

Qasim had charged up the three phones one at a time during the day. His usual cell phone was still in his flat. He carried it all the time, except when he was doing his 'special work,' in which case the phone stayed in his flat. He even left the GPS feature on. If anyone should ever check the phone, all they would find was his flat, work, mosque, and a few restaurants.

The burner phone was turned on and placed in his left pant pocket. The jammer phone was positioned into its container. The detonator phone was located in its slot on top of the bomb. Qasim then taped it into position. All was ready.

With that, Qasim opened the garage door and moved the van onto the street. It had been bought, for cash, from an old shopkeeper who was retiring and selling off his property and vehicles. The VIN numbers had been carefully removed, and the plates had been stolen more than a year ago, along with several others. The police would have a difficult time tracing the origin of the vehicle, and if they did, all they would get was the last legitimate owner.

Closing the garage door behind him, Qasim headed off to the flea market at the Place du Jeu de Balle. It would be a relatively short drive from Molenbeek. The market would be crowded, so the number of dead and wounded should be reasonably high. The worn old van would fit in with the other vehicles in the area. Qasim had walked around the market to pick out the best approach for driving in and had scouted out three likely places to leave the van.

Allah had been with Qasim. His chosen place to park the van was available. He drove into the area slowly, put the van in 'Park,' and turned off the engine. Turning around in the seat, he reached for the detonator phone, turned it on. With his head down, he walked away from the van in a carefree manner. When he had counted off three hundred paces, he stepped into an alcove entrance to a building and reached into his left pant pocket to pull out the last of the three burner phones. He called up the denotator phone number on the screen and placed his thumb gently on the 'call button.' Holding his thumb carefully in place on the phone, he then put it back in his pocket. Once he had gone another fifty paces, he pushed the call button. Less than 10 seconds later, he was rewarded by hearing the van explode. Like everyone else, he turned and looked at the smoke already rising into the sky. He then turned down a side street and began the walk back home.

* * *

LOCATION: Cordoba, Spain

DATE: 10 July

TIME: 3:15 PM Local Time

No one paid any attention to the two young men who had descended from a taxicab in front of Cordoba's train station. Having remained silent throughout the trip, one of the men had paid the driver in cash and briefly thanked him for the ride. They walked a few feet together until one man headed into the train station, and the other turned towards the bus depot. Both were modestly dressed, and each carried non-descript backpacks.

Each man had the same mission and the same plan. Once in their respective stations, they would head into a pre-selected men's washroom. Once in a washroom stall, they would take off the backpack, remove the folded-up cardboard and place it to support the pack on the toilet seat. Next, they would remove the sign from the pack that had the words "Closed for Maintenance" on it. Then they would peel off the tape that would secure the sign to the outer side of the stall door when they left.

The timers were already placed on top of 10 carefully packed Balactan UHT one-liter milk containers. The milk containers had been drained and refilled. Eight contained gasoline, and two had waste motor oil. The top three containers would have their lids unscrewed and the timer set between them.

Finally, they would reach into the top of the backpack and set the timers for five minutes. The timers were simple affairs made from old-style rotary kitchen timers, a couple of wooden matches taped to the dial handle, and a friction pad made of fine-grain sandpaper. As the matches rotated with the dial, they would light as they scraped over the sandpaper.

The men would leave the washroom stall, place the "Closed for Maintenance" sign on the door, and walk away. Each would take their own taxi away from the stations.

With the top three milk containers open for five minutes, even the slightest spark from the matches would start a fire. The fire would heat quickly and spread to all 10 of the containers as they melted. The gasoline fire would spread quickly across the washroom floor. The waste fuel oil would ensure that large clouds of billowing black smoke would fill the washroom and pour out quickly.

With both fires starting simultaneously in the train and bus stations, the word would spread quickly that these were coordinated attacks and not accidents. In addition, the billowing smoke would make for great images on social media, given that seemingly everyone in the world now had a cell phone with a video camera along with a Facebook account.

Having already been exposed to terror in the 2004 train bombings by an al Qaeda-inspired terrorist group, Spaniards would react with fear.

LOCATION: Central Station, Amsterdam

DATE: 10 July

TIME: 4:15 PM Local Time

Hashim had his thumb pushing down on the plunger of the suicide switch in his pocket. When his thumb was released, the high explosive bomb in his backpack would explode.

He was at peace with himself. The Mother of Satan[110] was about to speak to the infidels. If a few slags[111]died, this too would serve the will of Allah. His name would be held up in his home neighborhood as a martyr. His mother would have status as the mother of a shaheed. His father, beaten down by time and hard labor, would be able to hold his head up at the mosque during Friday prayers. His neighbors would step aside as a mark of respect as his parents walked down the street. Not only that, but his family would

---

[110] Unknown Editors, "Acetone Peroxide," en.wikipedia.org (Wikimedia Foundation, June 6, 2021), https://en.wikipedia.org/wiki/Acetone_peroxide
[111] Islamists frequently refer to women who are not Muslim and wear 'inappropriate" clothing as slags. They believe the death or rape of such women is not a problem as they were not following proper Islamist rules in the first place.

also get a reward, a martyr's pension, for having given up a son to serve as a martyr in the cause of Allah.

He had been guided at every step on the path from Gaza to Amsterdam. Following the covert trip out of Gaza, his handlers had provided everything. The trip took them across the Sinai Desert to Alexandria. After that, they had boarded a small freighter just as the ship was leaving the dock. The mainly Syrian crew had initially treated them as unwanted baggage and cursed them when they had first sat down to eat in the freighter's cafeteria. But by the following day, the crew had changed entirely. The crew remained silent but bowed their heads as Hashim walked by. He was given the best of food. The cook insisted on serving Hashim himself.

Once the ship had docked, the three remained on board the vessel until it was dark. After that, they walked to a run-down warehouse. As the handlers had been told, they were met inside the warehouse. Their contact had provided them with a six-year-old Toyota SUV. The contact told them it was low profile so as not to draw attention, but it was in good enough mechanical shape to make the drive to The Hague. There was food and water in the truck, which would reduce the amount of interaction they would require. The gas tank was filled, and cash was provided to pay for the fuel.

Once in the Schilderswijk district of The Hague, overnight accommodation was provided along with training. The suicide backpack was simple enough. One handler would accompany Hashim on his final trip to Amsterdam's Central Station. Once the train had reached the station on track four, the handler would arm the suicide bomb in the backpack after Hashim had pushed down on the dead man switch in his pocket. Arming the bomb was simple enough. The handler only had to unzip a side pocket on the backpack, flip a switch up and watch for the power light to come on. At that point, the handler would walk with Hashim down the stairs from the train platform to the lower concourse. The handler would point him to the front of the station. He would bless Hashim and tell him that he was about to achieve martyrdom. "Paradise awaits," he would say to Hashim as he walked away.

Hashim would walk alone to the most crowded part of the concourse. Once there, he would release the plunger on the suicide switch, and the bomb would explode.

Hashim would join the Caravan of Martyrs.[112]

---

[112] One of the most (in)famous books on jihad was *Join the Caravan of Martyrs* by Sheik Abdullah Azzam. The author was a leading clerical figure in the war against the Soviet invasion of Afghanistan. Despite his commitment to jihad, he was murdered by either Osama bin Laden or Ayman al-Zawahiri. Azzam had wanted to use the experience of the Afghan War to turn Afghanistan into the ideal caliphate. Bid Laden and Zawahiri had global jihadist ambitions, so it was necessary to kill Azzam.

Chapter 28: Analytic Deliberations Off-Site

LOCATION: Hessen's Off-site Conference Center, near Frankfurt, Germany

DATE: 11 July

TIME: 8:00 AM

At 7:55 AM, Jochen entered the conference room. Karl had organized the room as requested. One large round table for everyone. Four large whiteboards, each with its own set of four different colored markers. Behind the round table were two other small tables, each with two chairs and a laptop connected by wire to a color printer. A good supply of coffee, tea, sparkling mineral water, and flat water was at the back.

Despite the travel challenges, everyone was present. His team of Karl, Horst, and Bettina were gathered at the coffee pot. Berndt van der Schalk of the Royal Dutch Marines and his wife, Dr. Isabel Hooft, stood with Carsten Berg of Norway and Sergio Capelli of Italy. Daniel Godson of Canada, who had arrived in-country in the early morning hours, was standing at the window alone, staring off into the distance. Jochen suspected that Daniel was slightly down the spectrum a bit, sometimes gregarious, sometimes withdrawn. Daniel was also a born cynic. He could accept no idea, information, or process without first trying to disassemble it intellectually.

Jochen called out and asked everyone to take a seat.

"My dear friends. We are here today due to the generosity of Aldo Lange, the head of Hessen Reinsurance. Our task is simple. We need to produce a working hypothesis as to who was behind the four recent terrorist attacks, why these attacks were conducted, and how the political situation will evolve. Our plan for doing this is also simple. This meeting will begin with a briefing by my colleagues. We will share everything we have to date. After that, we will have a free-flowing discussion."

"We have two workstations for additional research, and Horst has set up these workstations with VPNs. Between the VPNs and an anonymizer, we should be able to do web searching without being traced back to this building, at least for the next two days. In addition, we have access to Hessen's database of business and finance material. The financial aspects of the Hessen database are significant, perhaps superior to that of some government agencies. Any questions so far?"

The room was silent, so Jochen carried on. "As you have heard me say before, I believe a small group of diverse thinking analysts with access to open-source information can do a better job as political analysts rather than large agencies with huge staffs and classified information. They suffer from a cult-like necessity for groupthink, and their mindsets are often fixed. Worse still, despite a long history of strategic failure, the agencies still suffer from the silo effect[113] and will not share information, even at times of critical stress."

Jochen then pointed at the back of the room. "Everyone get a coffee, sit down, and my colleagues will brief you on what we know and what we think we know so far.

Karl walked to the whiteboard and pointed at the first slide. "We assess all four of these attacks were not terrorist attacks but were staged to appear as so. We also assess that they were coordinated and planned out ahead of time. All four attacks were carried out by skilled individuals, especially the cash center robbery, which displayed remarkable planning and fire discipline. Some of the planning for the attacks seems to be more than three years old and possibly more. Three of the attacks went as planned, and one was interrupted – that being the hijacking. It appears the hijackers planned to continue the flight to Frankfurt and then divert at the last minute and land at the abandoned airbase of Bonames instead. The minimum amount of guidance electronics had been installed at the field, and the runway is in reasonable condition after a cleanup and extension. Beyond that, we have information that suggests the attack was not

---

[113] As a general rule, intelligence information frequently moves well up and down a chain of command inside an intelligence agency, but it does not move well between agencies. This lack of movement laterally is called the silo effect.

an Islamist attack, despite the press reporting and various government statements. The attackers were semi-professional Iranians with violent and criminal backgrounds. The planning for the hijacking, especially the weapons on board, suggests an operation that goes well beyond their capabilities. In other words, they were the hired muscle for the attack only. Someone else did the planning. All told, the attacks have a common source - someone who is patient, well organized, well connected, and has access to large amounts of money. All the evidence trails lead back to Europe even though some of the attackers were from outside the continent. Nothing says Russia, Ukraine, Turkey, or Syria were involved."

With that, Karl turned the briefing over to Bettina. "We heard that the weapons used in the hijacking were built into the Boeing 777 at manufacture. Checking for the weapons should be a simple task that can be done during routine maintenance and cleaning at an airport. Our working assumption is that if any weapons or signs of tampering were to be discovered, the aircraft would be pulled from service at that point. Since hearing this, we have gone through every airport flight schedule and news report concerning a Boeing 777-9 series. To date, we have seen no evidence of a 777-9 being pulled from service on short notice. There have been several delays, but each appears to have been related to more mundane maintenance issues. One flight was delayed for several hours after two women got into a fist fight over which one of them would be allowed to leave the aircraft first. Slightly off-topic, but if I were a flight attendant these days, I would insist on having a Taser with me at all times. Bad enough having to deal with terrorists but have to referee fights with idiots is way beyond the call of duty."

Bettina handed the presentation remote back to Karl. "The assassination provides us with more questions than answers. Ilhan Benhaddara appears to have been the assassination target, even though she is more of a figurehead. It remains a possibility that Tariq Raman was the target, given that he is the real power behind Islamic Assistance Transnational and much of the Muslim Brotherhood in Europe and Canada. But everything else in the assassination seems to have gone perfectly. There are no witnesses who say they saw a shooter. No weapon was seen, and no shell casing was found. The ballistics provide nothing of use beyond the caliber of the round and the probable make of the weapon. The most interesting part of this attack is the disappearance of Tariq Raman. He is originally from Austria, but there is no trace of him there or in the UK. His family had a long history of being involved in Islamist extremism and the Muslim Brotherhood. He could be anywhere by now. Our working assumption is that he is in Paris and is behind the Islamist violence, but he could be in Vienna or London, or Manchester. Altogether, we have a few well-founded assumptions, a few suspicions, and an increasing number of questions."

Karl then passed the remote to Jochen, who walked up to the whiteboard. "Beyond the attacks themselves, much has happened since then, including the widespread outbreak of reactionary violence. The greatest single question that remains is to figure out what group or organization is behind the attacks. So, we will start there."

"Carsten and Isabel. Can I ask you to use the three whiteboards to outline what views and hypotheses emerge? Berndt and Sergio, we have many pads of paper. Using the Analysis of Competing Hypothesis, can you begin developing an ACH matrix and be prepared to answer questions and provide challenges? Karl and Horst will provide ongoing research such as names, places, or groups that come up. They can find sources for the information you have, or they can search for new material. Bettina, take one whiteboard and list our 'Key Assumptions' that emerge that we need to think about and review as we go. Daniel, you will be our devil's advocate for our deliberations. Each of you can jump in at any time and play any role you want, but it might be helpful to at least start with some structured tasks."

Carsten pointed at the board and stated. "There is no group or organization involved. You are looking for one person."

The group all turned to Carsten at once.

"Wow," said Jochen. "Tell us how you came to this assessment."

Carsten appeared calm, but Jochen could see emotion below the surface as Carsten began to explain his assessment.

"Many people may have been involved in planning the various individual attacks. But only one person can have a complete picture of what is happening. The planning of these attacks took years, yet we have no evidentiary trail that shows the four attacks were planned together. Many of you will recall the horrific Norwegian terrorist attacks committed by Anders Breivik[114] on the 22nd of July in 2011. He set off a bomb in Oslo, which killed eight people and wounded 209. He followed that with a gun attack at a vacation camp on an island that killed 69 people and injured 110. The question had to arise? How did he buy so much explosive material and so many guns and not leave a single shred of evidence as he planned this over several years? The answer is simple. He told no one what he was doing. Not a soul. On the final page of his manifesto, he pointed out that a single person carrying out an illegal task such as building a bomb ran a 30% risk of being caught over a given time. But he also said that having two people involved would double that risk to about 60%. His chart further showed that having three people would increase the risk of being caught up to 85%, and have five people involved would have a risk of being detected at 90 to 95%.[115] As Breivik himself put it, *more than one chef*

---

[114] Unknown Editors, "Anders Behring Breivik," en.wikipedia.org (Wikimedia Foundation, June 12, 2021), https://en.wikipedia.org/wiki/Anders_Behring_Breivik
[115] The numbers used here are taken directly from Anders Breivik's manifesto. His "Risk vs Labour" chart appeared at the end of the document which was more than 1,000 pages long. After years of investigation, it appears clear that one

does not mean you will do the tasks twice as fast. In many cases, you could do it all yourself, and it will just take a little more time and without taking unacceptable risks. The conclusion is undeniable."

The room remained silent. It was clear from his face that the terrorist attacks in Norway had been a deeply personal event for Carsten. Norway, with a population of only five million, was more like a city than a country. The circles of influence were small, and many of Norway's government workers knew someone who has killed or injured in the attacks.

Carsten continued. "The first four attacks are staggering in their nature, the impact, the cost, and the amount of time involved. The concept and strategic planning stage may have taken years, as did the tactical planning. But nothing leaked, and no one heard anything? It is my belief one person is behind all these attacks. Only one person would have known ahead of time how the attacks unfolded. Given the costs and coordination, you are looking at a single person who is highly placed with access to money ranging the millions."

Karl rose from his seat and walked around the table until he was behind Carsten. He put his hands on Carsten's shoulders for a few seconds. He then began to walk again and circled the table while speaking, forcing the others to move their heads to follow him. "Carsten could be correct. I cannot prove or disprove

---

reason for Breivik's ability to carry out these attacks is that he told no one of his intents or actions ahead of time.

his beliefs. But I do know this. Each of the four attacks had many factors in common. Each attack was carried out with considerable precision and discipline. For example, the cash center robbery stands out as an example of excellent fire discipline on the part of the attackers. No injuries occurred, despite the number of rounds fired. The assassination appears to have been the same. Ilhan Benhaddara was killed with one shot. No one else was injured, and no evidence of the assassin has been found. This sort of discipline and coordination is rare. The hijack was interrupted, but in fairness to the skills of the hijackers, the SAS were there. Otherwise, they might have been successful. To me, this suggests that one hand had designed each attack. This means one person or one organization. The question arises, based on Carsten's assessment, who in Europe would have this kind of patience and planning?"

Horst had remained mostly silent as he often felt out of place with the others. They had traveled internationally and worked in the physical world. He had traveled little and lacked international experience. Despite working together, he felt little in common with Karl. The latter came from a world that was often filled with physicality and violence, unlike Horst's digital world of the Dark Web and faceless interactions.

"Karl is right," said Horst to no one in particular.

Karl turned suddenly to stare at him, as did Bettina.

"Karl believes the planner had precision and discipline. My view is that an absolute uniformity exists in the financing behind these attacks. Take the aircraft hijacking attempt. We can trace the new owners of the airfield who ordered the work done to accommodate the 777. But it is a shell company in the British Virgin Islands. The shell company traces back to another shell company in Liberia, and it traces back to a series of bank accounts in the Cayman Islands and the Isle of Man. Finally, the trail ends because these banks tend to air gap[116] their records, making it impossible to hack them. Of note, some of these accounts are more than four years old. The same goes for the airline tickets for the hijackers. They were paid for by separate credit cards, each one of them legitimate and each one of them about a year old with a series of purchases that raise no questions – other than the airline tickets. But each credit card was being paid off by a common bank account in Toronto. Once again, that bank account traces back to an offshore shell company that traces back to another shell company with an account in the Caymans and the BVI. There is a certain elegance and simplicity to the patterns here that suggest one person was behind all of it."

Jochen stood up and pointed to the coffee table. "With those insights from Karl and Horst, now would be a good time to take a bit of a break before we

---

[116] Unknown Editors, "Air Gap (Networking)," en.wikipedia.org (Wikimedia Foundation, May 27, 2021), https://en.wikipedia.org/wiki/Air_gap_(networking)

consider the larger ramifications of what has just been said."

Horst saw that Karl was standing by himself at the end of one of the coffee tables. Karl had seemed impressed with his work on the hijackers, so he thought this was an excellent chance to talk with his colleague, who seemed a bit distant on occasion. But for once, he suddenly felt completely in tune with his older and somewhat fearsome colleague. Karl saw him coming and smiled. "A fine piece of work on the hijacker's tickets and the credit cards. This type of information helps us put the larger picture together. I would ask you how you did all of this, but I would not understand it anyway. Further to that, maybe it is best if none of us knows. When did you figure all of this out?"

Horst felt an inward feeling that was alien to him. All his life, he had been a loner. His work on the Dark Web and other related activities had driven him into an ever-smaller subset of people who could even understand what he did. But now, for the first time, Horst had a sense of belonging to a group, even if they were so divergent from his world.

"I got up about three o'clock this morning after having made some initial progress late last night. Once I found one thread of information, everything else seemed to follow. Well, at least most of it followed."

Karl suddenly felt distinctly uneasy. "What do you mean, at least most of it followed?"

Horst gave one of his crooked grins, typical when he could not figure out how to behave in a social situation. "Well, all of the hijackers are tied together through the payment scheme, but one of the other passengers also had a credit card that traced back to the same Cayman Island account."

For one fleeting second, Karl could envisage his hand around Horst's neck while he strangled him. The blood was distilling through his hands as Horst gurgled his last breath. *He knew there might have been a fourth hijacker but had not thought to tell anyone?*

Fortunately for all concerned, Karl's self-discipline took control. As much as his composure would allow, he asked Horst: "Did this fourth credit card trace back to a name? Do you know who he is?"

"She," said Horst, realizing that Karl looked like he was about to pop a vein.

"Did you think it a good idea to share this rather staggering bit of information?"

"I thought that was why we were all here today. I would have mentioned it had anyone asked the right questions."

Bettina, who had been standing with Isabel and Berndt, suddenly pointed across the room. "Oh, oh. It looks like Karl is being Karl again. And Horst does not look happy."

Karl had grabbed Horst by his upper arm and was marching him towards Jochen. By the time he got there, the whole room was watching. Karl leaned over and whispered something in Jochen's ear. Jochen simply stared at Karl while all the blood drained from his face.

"Could we all gather around the table? It seems that Horst has further information to share with us." Jochen guided Horst towards the table.

Horst smiled awkwardly. "As I said, the hijackers were all connected by a common bank account that was paying for their credit cards. One other passenger also had her ticket paid for by the same account. But there is no information that she played any role in the hijacking. For that matter, she seems to be some sort of public relations person who used to work for the International Monetary Fund and now runs some sort of crisis reaction PR firm called Waveview Strategies."

Karl looked directly at Jochen. "We could be in water over our heads here. We need to tell at least the BKA about this fourth potential hijacker and tell the Brits. Maybe MI6 at their embassy?"

Karl then turned to Berndt. "I suspect you may wish to make a few calls to your Korps Mariniers, the AIVD,[117] and SHAPE?" Berndt simply nodded in agreement, having already come to the same conclusion.

---

[117] Ministerie van Binnenlandse Zaken en Koninkrijksrelaties, "About AIVD," AIVD (Ministerie van Binnenlandse Zaken en Koninkrijksrelaties, October 14, 2019), https://english.aivd.nl/about-aivd

Karl looked back at Jochen and smiled. "You might want to call Aldo Lange and tell him what we are doing. He is going to start getting a lot of phone calls."

* * *

Following a twenty-minute break, everyone gathered around the table again.

Isabel led off the discussions. "We need to contextualize the problems here. Over the last generation, it has become evident what we call 'The West' or the G20 or the Organisation for Economic Co-operation and Development have been in decay. Our leaders have become vacuous and seemed more captured by polling or self-preservation rather than being driven by a sense of goals or direction. Consider the last few years. The whole leadership class has been adrift. Closer to home, look at the response of the European Union to the pandemic. Even when faced with a pandemic threat, they could not work collectively to develop a common approach. Back in mid-2021, both the United Kingdom and Serbia were doing a better job of producing and obtaining vaccines than the EU. How can that be? Cannot we work collectively?"

Karl spoke up. "You are saying our leaders are clueless?"

Isabel smiled at the interjection. "It is not so much that they are clueless. On the contrary, as individuals, a few of them are rather bright. But here is the issue. We cannot come to any conclusion other than that we are quite good at the tactical disruption of our enemy, but we cannot generate a strategic effect. As a class, our leaders are aimless."

Sergio, who had been quiet, stepped into the conversation. "Isabel is correct. All too often, I have seen this. Our leaders are asked a question about some problem in the headlines, so they throw money at the problem and think something will happen. But it is useless. The proper way to think about problems is to have a belief system in place first. Then you have to create realistic objectives. Following the objective, then you develop a strategy. Out of the strategy comes the tactics. We are failing as we have no effective guiding light and no objectives. Every day is just another example of organizations 'muddling through.' It is a good thing the general population does not realize how vacant are the minds of our leaders."

Sergio paused for a moment. "Let me also take us in another direction for a moment. All bureaucracies, when they grow, become oligarchies. All bureaucracies, sooner or later, will come to be led by a 'leadership class.' The leadership class will take over all aspects of the organization and cease to become 'servants of the masses' and instead become the rulers. Michels had also argued that a representative democracy's goal of eliminating the role of the elites was impossible. Sooner or later, the elites would come to control the bureaucracies and corporations. Such was the history of civilization over the two thousand years or more. We know of this in Italy well, as we saw this in the rise and fall of the Roman Empire. It is, perhaps, possible that the leadership class of the supra-national organizations is working on expanding their powers."

Jochen was silently nodding his head in agreement. Michels had nailed the problems in his book.

At that point, Daniel stood up. Slowly walking around the table, he reiterated the points of Isabel and Sergio. "I believe they are right. However, the terrifying part is that whoever is behind these terrorist attacks may be doing exactly what Isabel and Sergio were talking about. Perhaps they have an objective, even if we cannot see it, and then have a strategy. What we are seeing are the tactics beginning to generate the strategic effect that they desire. The first four terrorist attacks have generated low-level responses and now more pointed actions. Whoever is behind this has a playbook laid out, and they are running it. We, on the other hand, are caught reacting."

"An observation at this point," said Karl. "But the force that is on the offensive has a limited need for intelligence assessment at the strategic level, as their offensive means everyone else has to react rather than plan. By contrast, those on the defensive have the highest need for effective intelligence at the tactical, operational, and strategic levels. If anyone is missing my point, the bad guys are on the offensive, and we are losing. We need to come up with answers quickly, or we become part of the problem rather than part of the solution."

"This does fit in well with part of the military assessment as well," said Berndt. "The Islamists are carrying out most of the violent activities. That much is true, and it is no surprise. They have been laying the groundwork for years. They will seize control of several hundred neighborhoods ranging in size from one block up to several square blocks. But something is wrong. Rather than leading the events, they are following them. Or perhaps it might be better to say the events are driving the Islamists rather than the Islamists driving the events.

"You are saying that they are reacting rather than acting?" This from Daniel.

"Exactly. The current events were put into motion by the attacks of 28 June. We strongly believe that Islamists did not carry out most or all the four attacks. At least two of them were carried out by cradle Muslims – at least nominally so. That was the aircraft hijacking and the cash center robbery. But it is a long way from being born a Muslim to becoming an Islamist. Anyone could have done the assassination of Ilhan Benhaddara. From everything we have learned so far, not a single shred of physical evidence had been found to determine who shot her. Ironically, her assassination has cost the Islamists little and has given them a propaganda coup, at least within their community. The fire on the ship appears to have been done by a small number of individuals, at least one of whom may have had ties to a neo-Nazi group. This fits the theory that the attacks are orchestrated as part of a larger plan. Given the variety of incongruities common to each of the attacks, my view goes back to that of Carsten's earlier ideas. One person, or a small group, is behind this."

The discussions continued while Carsten and Isabel were charting out the ideas, with some being developed and advanced while others were rejected and erased. Finally, a list of possible individuals or organizations responsible was created.

At 18:30, just as they were finally preparing to break for supper, Jochen had gathered everyone around the board.

"We should break now for supper. Take a bit of time and enjoy. There is beer and wine. A bit of alcohol may add another dimension to our analysis." Everyone smiled at that one. True enough, alcohol did tend to loosen the tongue and change the way the brain worked. Then, just as he was about to continue speaking, his phone pinged. It was a text message arriving on his Signal app. He did not recognize the number, but the message was clear enough:

Meet me at the front door. Now.

It could only be Aldo Lange, but Jochen was at a loss to understand why he would be arriving at this time of day. Whatever the reason, Lange did not suffer fools gladly and did not enjoy being kept waiting. Jochen headed at a fast pace for the conference door and, as an afterthought, turned and faced his friends.

He said, "I'll be back."

Daniel laughed loud. Bettina giggled. Berndt had a smile that went from ear to ear. Even Isabel Hooft, the most intellectual and reserved of them, could not suppress her laughter.

Jochen stood in stunned silence. "What is so funny?"

Daniel waved him off, directing him to keep going. "We will tell you what is so funny when you get back, Arrrnnnold."

Jochen groaned as he walked to the front door. The unintentional use of a line from the movie *Terminator* had caused a momentary break in the day's tension. The laughter had been good, but it showed the degree to which there was underlying stress in the room.

When he arrived at the front door, Jochen could see a 7-series BMW parked about 25 meters short of the front door. The same black BMW served as Lange's official company car, usually driven by a chauffeur who seemed overly protective of his primary passenger. When he was within 10 meters of the vehicle, the rear door opened. Aldo Lange stepped out and stared at Jochen.

Jochen's internal threat radar went to its highest setting. Lange's face was rigid, tense, maybe even hostile. Lange turned and began to walk away. "Give your phone to my driver and walk with me."

Jochen heard another door on the car open. It was the chauffeur who walked to the rear of the car.

Jochen handed him his phone, and his blood ran cold. The chauffeur was glaring at him and was in a fighter's stance, looking like he might spring into action. Jochen wondered whether you would feel any pain if your neck was snapped from behind. Would you even know something had gone wrong?

Aldo Lange was still walking away, and Jochen quickened his pace to catch up to him. But just as he caught up, Lange turned towards him and stopped.

"Why am I getting strange phone calls from Brussels? Why am I getting visitors to my office whom I do not know?"

Lacking any context on the calls or the visitors, Jochen decided to remain silent and waited for the next question.

Lange's face and posture changed. His face relaxed a bit, and he shrugged his shoulders. "Keep walking. At 13:30 this afternoon, I received a phone call from an Undersecretary of Political Affairs at NATO. He wanted to know why General van der Schalk was in Frankfurt and why he was in our building. I may have slightly misled the Undersecretary by telling him that I did not believe the General was in Frankfurt – which is technically true, given that he is out here. An hour later, I get a phone call from the Bundeskriminalamt. The BKA! They wanted to know what you had told me about your current investigation – as they called it. I told them I had not talked to you recently – which again was true if again somewhat misleading. Then – to make my afternoon perfect – security called at

16:00 from the front desk. A senior official from the Bundesamt fur Verfassungsschutz was on his way, accompanied by an unknown individual. Spies, Jochen. You have got spies coming to my office! Oh, and wait for it. After they left, security called back and said they had tailed my last two visitors after leaving the building. One got into a car with local plates. But the other man, who never said a word the whole time he was in my office, was picked up by a driver in a Land Rover with British diplomatic plates. The plates traced back to their Berlin Embassy, not the Frankfurt Consulate. Not only German spies but British spies with them. The official from the BfV wanted direct information on what you were doing. I told him you were unavailable. When he left, he threatened me. He said that you and I had best be available to explain ourselves tomorrow morning. And one final thing, on the way out the door, he made a series of disparaging remarks about Horst, his parents' marriage, and even his species into question. Our spies seem to have a particular dislike for Horst. What do I tell them? Or should I just have my chauffeur carve you up now and serve you on a platter to the BfV tomorrow morning?"

Jochen decided to stall for a bit of time to think about how to answer the questions. He started with the easiest one. "The Bundesamt fur Verfassungsschutz have a reason for their hatred of Horst. When he was 18, he might have, umm, stumbled over some information on the Dark Web, which revealed the BfV had made some significant mistakes during an investigation involving an alleged right-wing terrorist group. Not only did Horst post some of the errors on a hacker forum, but he also revealed in detail the security weaknesses of the BfV and how they had messed up their investigation. That was bad enough, but he later placed a meme on the same forum that suggested that the head of the BfV may have been related to a farm animal from Bavaria. I believe that beating the BfV at their own game was bad but mocking them pushed them over the edge. Like many influential organizations, they can withstand criticism, but they will not be mocked."

Aldo Lange laughed out loud. "A farm animal from Bavaria? No wonder they hate him."

With Lange now in a slightly better state of mind, Jochen turned back to the serious questions. "We were going to call you tomorrow morning and suggest a meeting with you later in the day. But given the folks visiting your office, maybe the best plan would be to suggest that all of them meet out here tomorrow at 13:00? At that point, we should have enough put together to tell them what we believe."

"What do we believe?"

"If you have 15 minutes, maybe you could come inside and meet everyone who is here. The information is fragmented, but it shows who is behind the attacks of the 28th of June. You may not be pleased with the situation, as you may know, a few of the players whom we think are involved with the problems."

Aldo Lange looked at his watch. He turned to his chauffeur and said, "Stay here. If I am not out in 15 minutes, call me. And give Jochen back his phone."

Jochen swiped his card on the door and held in for Aldo Lange. He smiled at Lange and said, "Paradise awaits."

Lange got the joke but did not smile.

Chapter 29: The Islamists are Winning the Battle

LOCATION:	Hessen Reinsurance conference center
DATE:	12 July
TIME:	1:00 PM

At 12:50 PM, Jochen had sent Karl to watch for the arrival of Aldo Lange and the others. A small convoy of four vehicles had arrived at 12:55. The first vehicle was a 7-Series BMW. This would be Aldo Lange. The second car was an Opel, likely belonging to the BKA. The third was a 5-Series BMW, most likely the BfV. The final vehicle was a Land Rover with British diplomatic plates. Karl was a bit surprised. This was not the vehicle you should be driving unless you want to attract attention to yourself.

The only unusual issue was that there were three passengers in the Land Rover in addition to the driver. The first passenger in the front was likely the MI6 man. An expensive suit – tailor-made. A thin black leather portfolio rather than a briefcase. Expensive shoes. The watch. One passenger from the back seat looked similar. Posh suit and the shoes to go with it. A Rolex – a real one. He had that air of sophistication that suggested he was comfortable around the hallways of power. Still, he moved with a certain fluidity and economy of purpose. A trained fighter? Military?

The second passenger was different. He was wearing a suit that was off the rack. It was OK, but not expensive. The shoes were leather but looked more practical than posh. Not only that, but he also did an almost involuntary 360 degree look around when he descended from the vehicle. He was assessing his environment. When he started to walk towards the building, Karl could see that he led off with his left foot and tended to dig his heels in a bit more than the average person would have done. This man had to be military, or perhaps ex-military. Stranger still, the MI6 man was speaking to them as they moved towards the front entrance. The body posture and hand motions suggested that the MI6 man saw the other two men as equals. Karl had observed frequently that intelligence personnel often thought of themselves as superior purely by being in the intelligence world, even though they often had only basic field skills and limited combat experience. Perhaps the two men with their military bearing were former military and now in the intelligence world? Or maybe they were British Special Forces? SBS? SAS?

Karl headed back to the conference room. He signaled Jochen to approach him. "Pretty much what we expected. Mr. Lange. A BKA person. One from the BfV. But something is a bit strange about the Brits. One passenger looks to be MI6, but there are two other men with him. They look military – I would guess they are Special Forces. They could be SAS or

SBS. Hard to say. Four drivers, all of whom are staying outside. All four of the drivers look relatively young and fit. They are not chauffeurs but rather bodyguards who are also drivers. They spread out a bit and took up positions to give them a good visual of the approaches to the building. All things told this is a pretty high-powered delegation. We have attracted the attention of some serious people. The good news is that all of them looked serious, but none of them looked overtly hostile. My best guess is that they are here to listen and learn, not to silence us. At least, I hope so." Karl shrugged and headed back to his seat.

Once the guests were in the conference room, Aldo Lange took over as the host. He did a quick round of introductions of Jochen and his team. As for the guests, Lange had only introduced them as 'German government officials' or 'British officials.' They were introduced by first names only. The only exception was the two Brits. They were not introduced, although neither seemed offended by the oversight.

Jochen looked at the BKA agent when he was introduced as a 'government official.' It was Burnard, the same BKA man he had met with just days earlier.

With the introductions finished, Lange suggested they all sit. He motioned Jochen to join him in front of the whiteboards.

"Jochen, let us skip over the formalities. Instead, tell us why we are here."

Jochen had a temporary vision of himself standing in front of the room with a circular target painted on his chest. The imaginary target had several red dots moving around. This was one of life's moments. What happened in the next hour would cement his future or see him buried – perhaps literally.

"This briefing will take part in two phases. The first will be assessing the facts of the situation and what we can prove with evidence. All of us support these first views, each of whom is willing to testify to them in any forum. The second part will be what we believe but cannot yet meet the standard of evidence necessary for a criminal investigation or a parliamentary hearing. Let me go through the solid points first:

1. The four attacks of 28 June were coordinated and centrally planned.

2. Some of the attacks required at least six months of prior tactical planning. We have evidence on another that traces back three years.

3. The attacks required the equivalent of millions of Euros of funding. The financial trails are, however, limited.

4. None of three of the attacks were carried out by groups or individuals who are Islamist in nature. The fourth event, the assassination, still has no known perpetrator.

5. The wave of violence across Europe is mainly driven by Islamists, especially those connected to the Muslim Brotherhood or the Turks. A portion of the violence is of a grassroots nature – that

being the initial violence in Paris. That was in response to the assassination of Ilhan Benhaddara. The rest of the violence is planned and orchestrated.

6. The coordination and planning for the attacks and outbreak of violence suggest an institutional capability.

7. There are many public discussions about a possible 'Great Reset' and what it may involve. These discussions are an integral part of the overall plan.

8. The pre-planned violence on the ground is causing further social unrest among a population that has been disillusioned for more than 15 years. More spontaneous riots should be anticipated from both the extreme right, the extreme left, and a whole variety of others who are neither left nor right but just angry. This is violence caused by the immature rage of the disenfranchised middle class.

9. The Islamists are winning the battle on the ground and will continue to do so. They are better prepared, better organized, and have both tactical and strategic objectives. Regardless of whether they chose the timing for this violence, they have the momentum. Within a few days, they will control some 800 or more neighborhoods in France and several hundred more spread across the United Kingdom, Germany, and elsewhere.

10. Finally, the Islamists doing the fighting are overwhelmingly Sunni to date. We have not seen any large-scale intervention from the Shia at this point."

Jochen had positioned the room ahead of time so that Karl was sitting slightly off to the side with the best view of all the participants. When Jochen had stated that the announcement of the Great Reset was part of a larger plan, Karl thought he could see the surprise on the faces of the BfV man and perhaps Aldo Lange as well. The British military men seemed to nod their heads in agreement.

Jochen paused long enough to reach out for a glass of water and took a small drink. He did this for several reasons. The first was to check his nerves. To his surprise, his hand was still steady. The second reason was to give the audience a momentary pause to assess what he had just said. The third reason was that his mouth was going dry.

With that, he put the glass down and looked around the room. Isabel looked at him and nodded her head. The slight smile suggested all was going well. However, Bettina seemed to have drifted off again to another dimension. Jochen wondered where she went on these 'Amazing Journeys,' as Karl called them. He turned and faced Aldo Lange and began again.

"The first 10 points should not have been a significant surprise. The following five are a bit more challenging. However, we believe them to be accurate, based on the information to date. We do not agree on the finer details, but we all agree on the general assessment.

1. The individual or small group behind the four first attacks and the ensuing political violence is institutional. We believe the institution involved could be the International Monetary Fund, the World Bank, or the European Central Bank. The IMF is most likely, given the relatively long tenure of its leader, his background, and the hierarchical nature of the organization's structure. But we have no strong evidence one way or the other.

2. Enrica Leclercq and the office of the High Representative for Foreign Affairs and Security Policy for the European Union are involved. However, it would appear that she is the figurehead and not the actual leader.

3. The initial Islamist violence was a grassroots response to the assassination of the 28th of June and the other attacks. For the rest, however, the Islamists are reacting to the overall situation and not driving it. They appear to be working for whoever is behind this crisis and not driving it.

4. The Islamist violence will accelerate out of control. The police have neither the skills nor the staffing to face this sort of violence. At some point, either military forces such as Special Forces or mechanized infantry will be required, or the fighting will continue to spread in the Islamist's favor."

Jochen took one final look at Aldo Lange, pausing long enough to leave a silence hanging in the room.

"Our fifth and final point is this. What you now see in Europe is a coup in progress."

The result of Jochen's briefing was near-absolute silence. The only noise was the soft background hum of the air ventilation system.

Chapter 30: The Great Reset & Climate Lockdown

LOCATION:	Residence of Enrica Leclercq
DATE:	13 July
TIME:	8:30 AM

The hand-delivered message arrived at 10:00 PM the previous night by an anonymous courier. "Be out front tomorrow morning at 8:30." The message had to be from CRJ.

Enrica was standing at the entrance at 8:30 AM when the car arrived. It was a different vehicle from their last meeting but the same driver.

CRJ smiled as she entered the car. "Are you prepared for today?"

"Everything is in place," said Enrica. "Has the press been primed?"

"The press conference is set. Plenty of reporters will be there because we have put out a few leaks telling them to expect big news. The network bosses were told major changes are coming. Most of them will be expecting news about the security situation or NATO."

"Announcing the Great Reset and a state of emergency at the same time without telling any of the other leading figures is a risk. Do you think the population will accept such massive changes so quickly, especially with all the violence in the streets?" Enrica looked uncertain as she said this.

CRJ nodded. "The masses will gladly exchange their freedom for security at this point. The level of fear is high in the population. The four attacks of 28 June worked even better than we thought. The triple promises of today will work, especially for the youth. You will promise them financial security, physical security, and a green, prosperous future all in one day. Against the current backdrop of deprivation, violence, and lost hope, the combination is unbeatable. The EU has made a mess of everything for the last 30 years. The war in Yugoslavia. 9/11. The financial crisis. The pandemic and the vaccine mess. On top of that, even the dumbest technocrats in Brussels and Strasbourg know we are headed into a sovereign debt crisis, depression, and possible civil war if something does not happen fast. The 700 Euro Generation and the Gen Z crowd have been dumbed down so badly they cannot think for themselves on anything other than their entitlements. Promise them everything, and they will buy it. This is one of the problems with a low IQ population. They can only focus on their immediate wants and needs. But this works to our advantage now."

"The idea of offering a Universal Basic Income and student loan forgiveness at the same time will be brilliant. Combined with rent and mortgage buyouts, we should create so much hope and confusion the press and those who oppose this will not be able to focus."

"Indeed," intoned CRJ. "My only regret is that I cannot be in the office of the EU President when all of this happens. I would love to see the looks on their faces when they realize their time is up. When they figure out how to respond, the momentum will be ours, and they will have become irrelevant. You will become the effective head of government, and the EU Presidency will be reduced to little more than a ceremonial head of state. As for Strasbourg, that hopeless gaggle of fools we loosely call a Parliament will either vote in favor of all the legislation we send them or face the rioters. The EU Parliament will not enjoy its new role as the one body between the enraged masses and all their new free money, but that is too bad for them. They played a role in the pandemic by voting for bailouts and free money, so they can suffer the results of their actions now. If they even try to oppose the student loan forgiveness and the Universal Basic Income, the mob will eat them alive."

"Tomorrow is Bastille Day. I wonder if the mobs will shift some of their violence towards government institutions after we announce the state of emergency?"

"I am counting on it," said CRJ. "If a few politicians and bureaucrats lose their heads tomorrow, so much the better. Most of the EU has been so tied up in creating their narrative about a 'right wing' resurgence that they are blind to the threat from the

Islamists. They are so occupied in trying to understand the current violence that they do not understand their time is over."

Enrica pushed CRJ for the details. "Are you certain everyone else outside of the EU is on board? Will we receive the support we need?"

CRJ nodded. "Everything is in place for you. The International Monetary Fund will issue a series of statements immediately. I have personally written them. The first one will express the unconditional support of the IMF for these actions. The follow-on statements will address technical areas, especially regarding the Universal Basic Income Program and how this will be financed. The World Bank will be immediately behind them. Then, within 24 hours, statements of support will come from the World Economic Forum and the Organization for Economic Coordination and Development. Once that is in place, the Secretary-General of the United Nations will make a statement, suggesting that the new European Union should be considered for a permanent position on the Security Council while France and the United Kingdom are removed."

"The United Kingdom will not be pleased, but I do not think they can interfere in the post-Brexit period. France will probably just cave in. They are in the worst mess of all."

"Remember," said CRJ. "You need to repeat the messages over and over and over again. The Great Reset is here. Guaranteed incomes are here. Debt will soon be gone. So, keep repeating that message until the press and the people have no choice but to believe it. You know how that works."

"We will. It should be good enough to get us through the first few weeks. After that, my sources tell me the White House will issue an ambiguous statement. President Harris wants to wait a week to make sure we have events under control before she pushes Congress to support us. But most importantly, she will not oppose us directly. Prime Minister Brenda Elishchuk of Canada has also assured me that she will either remain silent or make a vague statement of support at the outset."

"The USA not opposing us is the most important issue. The two biggest wild cards will be NATO and the Russians. NATO will be too busy dealing with the security situation on the ground, and they will follow whatever lead comes from President Harris. We have sent some early signals to the Russians and told them that a new negotiation position would be forthcoming, especially on the Nord Stream Two pipeline and other energy concerns. You will have to follow up quickly with the Kremlin. We do not need to give them anything, but make it clear we will be leaning towards issues they want to be resolved."

Enrica opened her briefcase and pulled out a file. "Here are my speaking notes. Everything we have discussed is covered. Have one final look."

The Great Reset

To my beloved European Citizens and our global friends. It is time to end the fear.

Today we officially launch the Great Reset.

We will move together and guide Europe into a glorious peaceful future while leading a new global order. We move towards a new reality of diversity, equity, and social justice. The struggle to save the planet will be won as we complete the transition to a carbon-free economy in less than 10 years. Much will be required to save the earth, but it must be done.

These are all issues of security. If we do not save the planet, then nothing else matters. This is the most significant security challenge of our times. Suppose we do not achieve diversity and equity. In that case, we are doomed to continue the wars foist upon us by outdated concepts such as national sovereignty, borders, and their resulting wars. If we cannot achieve social justice, then nothing else matters as the streets will be uninhabitable. To achieve social justice, we must rid ourselves of the so-called Enlightenment and Renaissance values. Judeo-Christian values are the shackles of ancient history about our necks. We will free ourselves from the burdens of such supremacist belief systems as we achieve equity and security.

We have suffered from the fearful pandemic, the terrifying depression, and the sovereign debt crisis. Your everyday fears and pains are known and felt. Now, we see the explosion of violence on the streets. Fear is growing everywhere, and you should be afraid. Unfortunately, the current leadership has failed and left you subject to the killings and violence that can only increase if we do not act.

Action is needed. Results are needed.

We cannot continue to live through the pain, the fear, and the threat to the planet from climate change.

The fear must be stopped.

All of these matters are security matters. Public safety. The economy. Social Justice. The climate.

Starting today, the Office of the High Representative for the European Union for Foreign Affairs and Security Policy will be taking up a new mission to focus on the failures and the fears. Henceforth, it will be known simply as the Office of the High Representative for the European Union. In order to build the future, a cultural revolution is required as well. Part of this revolution in cultural affairs will be the new European Union Civil Monitoring Agency that reports directly to the High Representative's Office.

Let me now inform you as to the decisions reached to ensure your security and address the fear that is spreading.

1. The International Monetary Fund, the World Bank, and the European Central Bank will coordinate the new policy directions of the national central banks to ensure seamless policy directions under central control. National treasury departments and finance ministries will now be able to have coordinated recommendations to guide their work. This will provide economic and financial stability. Artificial Intelligence programs will guide their work.

2. To ensure an orderly economic and financial system in the European Union, the official cryptocurrency of the EU will be the European Central Bank Crypto Currency or ECBCC. Other cryptocurrencies will not be banned, but they cannot be used for transactions within the EU. Citizens will have a year to convert other cryptocurrencies into the ECBCC if they wish.

3. Within 60 days, the European Central Bank will initiate a Universal Basic Income Program for all European Union citizens. The 700 Euros a month payment will be made electronically in the new ECBCC, which will be equal in value to the Euro. All businesses in the Euro Zone will be required to accept the new cryptocurrency.

4. Citizens with mortgages in arrears due to the pandemic and depression will have the option of selling the remaining equity in their apartments, condos, or houses to the European Central Bank. They will have the option of renting the premises at a rate equal to or lower than the previous mortgage payments. The citizens will receive compensation for the equity in the ECBCC. The financing will be provided through the Special Drawing Rights of the International Monetary Fund. Those citizens with personal debt will have the option of having that debt relieved through the Global Debt Reset Program. The details of that program will be released from the IMF within the next two weeks.

5. Small businesses with 100 employees or less who have outstanding loans or rental payments in arrears will have the option of selling their businesses to the European Central Bank and then renting the company back if they chose. Those choosing to lease the business will be required to meet European standards for minimum wages, unionization, and workers' rights. This will assist small businesses in finding their correct position in the modern economy as we build back better for the future.

6. A new directorate in the European Central Bank will assign quotas at the national level in major industrial sectors to ensure effective production and avoid waste and overlap.

7. All university and technical school tuition rates will be reduced to zero. The new Directorate of Education at the ECB will assign funding to quota approved positions at selected universities that agree to cooperate in the new program. This will ensure the correct level of education to meet the needs of the emerging equitable society. In addition, the educational requirements will be broadly redrawn to support stability, diversity, equity, and climate justice.

8. All student loans to European Citizens will be eligible for forgiveness. Current and former students will be able to apply for relief if they take up volunteer monitoring positions with the new European Union Civil Monitoring Agency (EUCMA). The EUCMA will be responsible for monitoring citizen compliance with climate directives and social equity goals. The monitors will also be able to report and track social deviations from citizens who do not conform to new European policy standards of social behavior.

9. To ensure social cohesion and economic stability, monitors from the European Union Civil Monitoring Agency will observe behavior on social media. Student volunteer monitors will counsel those who use social media to undermine the credibility of the government or criticize public institutions. Upon a second offense, violators will be encouraged to relearn social cohesion skills at European Union Civil Monitoring Agency camp facilities.

10. Europol will assume policy and operational responsibility for European Union national and sub-national police forces. They will set quotas for arrests and enforcement actions in coordination with the European Union Civil Monitoring Agency.

11. The new Office of the High Representative will assume responsibility for negotiating security and trade agreements with the European Union. Rather than the past confusion, the European Union will have synchronized policies as our economy rotates towards the Great Reset.

12. The North Atlantic Treaty Organization will be renamed EUROFOR. It will be Europeanized and enter into new security arrangements to focus on European goals.

13. In order to provide for human security at the global level, the Office of the High Representative will establish definitive goals for saving the planet from climate change. We will begin a series of rotating climate lockdowns in the immediate future. As the pandemic lockdowns have proven, both individual lifestyles and the environment benefited during the pandemic lockdowns.[118] The lessons have been learned and will be adapted so that we can gain the social and environmental benefits of the lockdowns without the economic damage. The methodology for this will be developed in conjunction with the Executive Secretary of the United Nations Framework Convention on Climate Change and the newly

---

[118] James Macpherson, "The World Economic Forum: 'Lockdowns Are Improving Cities around the World'," spectator.com.au (Spectator Australia, February 28, 2021), https://www.spectator.com.au/2021/02/the-world-economic-forum-lockdowns-are-improving-cities-around-the-world/

formed Greta Thunberg Academy for Climate Science. This new climate agency will provide us with the outlines of science-driven legislation needed for a carbon-free lifestyle. It can be achieved by 2030. When we achieve climate justice, we will also achieve social justice and equity.

14. The youth of Europe are the key to the future. With this in mind, the new Climate Youth program will be implemented immediately. Children from the age of six upwards will be encouraged to join the league of Climate Youth workers division as helpers to the climate change agenda. Those who enroll, avoid religious organizations, and live correctly will be granted privileges based on their years of enrollment and activity. Those youth who grow to maturity in the Climate Youth program will be well suited for future leadership roles, having been experienced in self-criticism and expunging unwanted ideological views. Thank you for your attention.

Once he had finished reading, CRJ handed the file back to Enrica. "You need to deliver this speech as though these plans are the only alternatives available. Do not worry if parts are repeated. We need that. Also, present this as though they are not just ideas or options. These must be the only available alternatives. By the way, leaving the climate lockdown issue to the last point is probably the best approach. By offering everyone a guaranteed income, student loan cancellations, and debt relief, they will buy into the program even if it means giving up their freedoms. The press has been preparing everyone for this anyway, so it will not be that shocking for most.[119]

Enrica agreed. "It will work. It is the only way ahead, and we have been working on it for years."

"Good," said CRJ. That is the attitude you need. We will do the same as last time. The car will stop just short of your office. Two of my men will follow you just to be sure nothing goes wrong. I will be watching your press conference on TV. As it is happening, we will put everything else into action. The press releases will be coming out so fast from so many agencies that no one will be certain of what is happening for the first 24 hours. Speed is of the essence. Remember. *Viribus Unitis* – With United Force. This is how we will win."

CRJ watched Enrica as she walked away. They were by no means united on this. He had his plans, and she had hers. The difference was that she was about to be jammed up for creating the most significant upheaval in modern European politics, not him. He laughed to himself for a few seconds.

"Old age and treachery will overcome youth and skill. Every time," he said to himself.

---

[119] Fiona Harvey, "Equivalent of Covid Emissions Drop Needed Every Two Years - Study," theguardian.com (Guardian News and Media, March 3, 2021), https://www.theguardian.com/environment/2021/mar/03/global-lockdown-every-two-years-needed-to-meet-paris-co2-goals-study.

* * *

The press had been somewhat surprised that the High Representative for the European Union for Foreign Affairs and Security Policy briefing had been scheduled for 5:00 PM. This was late in the day, and much of what was said would probably not make it into the evening news. This conflicted with what they were told was intended to be a significant announcement. Even more surprising was that the conference started at 5:00 PM. Nothing started on time in the EU.

The press officer had started the briefing by stating that it would be a briefing only, and due to time constraints, no questions would be taken. The assembled journalists were also told that a briefing transcript was available but would only be given in hard copy to the reporters once the verbal briefing was done. Again, this was unusual by EU standards.

With all the terrorist attacks and violence going on in Europe, the reporters had expected the briefing to contain matters of substance.

Several of the older reporters started looking at each other. They were sitting up in their chairs and were alert. Maybe something was going on. Several noted that no teleprompter was on the podium, nor were there any of the IT staff that usually present for such briefings.

A couple of reporters even texted their producers and editors, telling them to keep a few extra staff on hand as they may be needed.

At 5:03 PM, Enrica stepped on the platform in the press hall. The atmosphere was tense. With none of the usual greetings or statements of welcome, she began to read the prepared text.

> To my beloved European Citizens and our global friends. It is time to end the fear.
>
> Today we officially launch the Great Reset.

By the time Enrica had read out the first three points, the reporters were in a state of shock. Many simply stared, trying to understand what they were hearing. Others were scribbling madly in their notebooks. A few were texting notes to their producers. The texts, as short as they were, began to get the message out.

Arthur Jones of the Guardian texted his editor, "Pathway to climate justice now open through Great Reset. This is big."

Laila Hullinger, of Deutsche Welle sent, *"Great Reset is no longer a conspiracy theory. It is a conspiracy fact. Recall all staff. Long night ahead."*

Huw Derbyshire of the BBC sent *"Biggest news since the invasion of Poland on 1 September 1939."*

Alison Smith of Reuters had waited to hear the full announcement before sending a message to her editor. She had covered wars in Iraq, Afghanistan, and Tigray in Ethiopia. Her first degree had been reading Shakespeare at Cambridge before moving onto journalism. To her, this was not an announcement. It was a declaration. She considered several possible lines but then sent: *"Casca has just stabbed Julius Caesar.*[120] *They aim to bury the EU, not to praise it. A coup is in progress."*

---

[120] Publius Servilus Casca was the first person to stab Julius Caesar in Shakespeare's play (Act Three, Scene One).

Chapter 31: Bastille Day and Offensive Jihad

LOCATION:	Parisian suburb of Sevran
DATE:	14 July – Bastille Day
TIME:	6:00 AM

Tarek screamed at his laptop, a rare moment for him as he lost control of his emotions. He had not watched the live version of the announcements from the High Representative for the European Union for Foreign Affairs and Security Policy. His working belief was that the press conference would be another example of mindless platitudes and virtue signaling dressed as news. The so-called 'strategies' and 'goals' they spoke about were little more than weak ideas which were – at best – capable of becoming feeble tactics. No European Union leader had demonstrated a 'strategy' for years.

Upon watching the press conference on YouTube, the following day, Tarek had become incensed. The Great Reset should have been called the Great Betrayal. The Muslim Brotherhood had done everything it could to cooperate with the progressive left and position against their enemies. Islam and the Muslim Brotherhood were not even mentioned in the announcement. But clearly, the Jews and Christians would be targets of the Great Reset and the 'new'

European Union and its security-led agenda. If they could go after the Jews and Christians, they would go after the Muslims next. The 'climate lockdown' proclamation was not lost on Tarek either. The outer borders of the EU would be closed again, and internal travel would be greatly restricted.

Just as he was finished watching the video, Ishaan had knocked on his office door frame and entered. "Brother Tarek, here is a copy of the speech of that slag from the EU. They have posted it everywhere on the Internet. This does not bode well for us."

Tarek took the two-page printout and set it on his desk. He handed Ishaan 10 Euros. Go get us two coffees and something to eat. Then come back and see me. There is much to discuss."

* * *

Fifteen minutes later, Ishaan returned. "Sorry for the delay, but I was stopped three times on the way to the café. Everyone was asking about the announcement from yesterday, and they want to know what will happen to us. There is a great fear building among the ummah."[121]

"Fear not, Brother Ishaan," said Tarek. "Allah is the greatest of all plotters, and we serve Allah. First, you

---

[121] Unknown Editors, "Ummah," en.wikipedia.org (Wikimedia Foundation, May 16, 2021), https://en.wikipedia.org/wiki/Ummah

and I will sit down for a few minutes and discuss what is happening. Then, I will explain what we must do next and how we will triumph because of it. Are you with me?"

Ishaan did not understand what was going on, but he knew that Tarek had built the largest Islamist operatives' network in Europe. He had brought in vast amounts of money to grow the cultural centers and the schools. Ishaan had soon realized that Tarek's networks had their roots in the strength of the Muslim Brotherhood in Egypt, the money of Qatar, and the organizational capabilities of the expanding network of Brotherhood sympathizers in Turkey, sanctioned by no lesser a soul than President Erdogan. Though they never communicated directly, Ishaan knew that Tarek had developed personal contacts with the General Guide of the Muslim Brotherhood, the Emir of Qatar, and the President of Turkey. Whatever he was talking about, Tarek was well connected and was comfortable in the politics of Europe, North America, and the Middle East

"Brother Tarek, I am with you always. What do I need to do?"

"Ishaan, listen carefully to me. Once I am done speaking, you need to take everything I say and write it down. Keep the terms simple and straightforward. Then ensure this message goes out to every Imam. Every mosque. Every school and cultural center we control. Post it in Arabic, English, French, German and Turkish. It also goes to all the websites we maintain. Do you understand?

Ishaan nodded. "Let me get my iPad, so I can make an audio recording of everything."

Once he was ready to start, Tarek prayed silently for a moment and then began: "In the name of Allah the Most Compassionate, the Most Merciful. All praise and thanks be to Allah, the only owner of the day of recompense. You have bestowed your grace upon us and will guide us to the well-trodden path."

Tarek paused and looked at Ishaan before starting again.

"To the faithful. The announcement of the Great Reset by the infidel Enrica Leclercq will not affect us. It was intended to create fear and doubt in your hearts.

Remember only this:

Allah is our objective.

The Prophet is our leader.

The Quran is our constitution.

Jihad is our way.

Martyrdom and dying in the way of Allah is our highest hope.

This is the call we serve. Many of the faithful have already achieved the wish of martyrdom. We are here for Dawah."

Ishaan, for the first time in many hours, felt relieved and hopeful. Hearing the creed of the Muslim

Brotherhood repeated by Tarek gave him great comfort. It gave him hope.

Tarek continued. "Our goal will not change because of the Great Reset. Our strategy will not change because of the Great Reset. The outcome of our Dawah will not change. The infidels are weak, and this announcement has only proven their desperation to act before their entire house collapses. They have never recognized Allah as their one true God, and they have even lost their faith. They do not even believe in their own hateful and secular values. They worship only sin. They have put the most horrific of beliefs at the forefront of their society and worship only the most decadent. The only change is that of timing. Our goal had been to create the first of the caliphates in Europe in 2030. This was the result of decades of planning and work. The pandemic and the economic crisis had accelerated the timetable for us as the weaknesses of Europe became obvious. The violence of the last two weeks has advanced our cause. We have already taken control of territory in France, Belgium, and Germany. Shariah is in effect in those blessed areas, and those areas will grow more today, tomorrow, and the day after. The longing for a Caliphate for the Sunni and our Shia brethren will soon be a reality."

Tarek paused again; his eyes focussed on the floor in front of him. Ishaan remained silent. Having known Tarek for years and having seen him in various situations, Ishaan instinctively knew that what was coming next would be the critical part of the message.

"As Sayyid Qutb informed us, offensive jihad is necessary to reform societies so the word of Islam can be spread. All societies must be liberated. It is the destiny of every Muslim to perform jihad wherever he is and wherever he lands. When the final hour comes, there is no escape from destiny. The struggle by the sword is not just for defense but for societal reformation, which can enable the implementation of Islamic values, morals, and laws. Modern society is ill at the global level, and a cure for that illness exists. The greatest of all jihads is to rid the earth of tyranny and those who falsely worship."

Tarek paused one more time and looked at Ishaan, and he smiled in return. They were on the same wavelength. Tarek took a deep breath and started again.

"The final hour has come. Victory is within our grasp, and we will seize it. When you carry a sword into battle, you must be prepared to swing it both to the left and the right. The greatest enemy now is not the Christians or the Jews, or other believers. They can be brought into Islam or forced into submission. The first enemy is the leftist – a plague of non-believers who have no conscience and no belief in anything other than their arrogance. Attack them first. Kill them first. If you are seeking martyrdom, seek them out, and you will be rewarded in Jannah.[122] Let the fires alight. Islam is the solution."

Ishaan smiled. "Brother Tarek. My soul is at peace. This message will be spread to all our neighborhoods in France within an hour. It will be across all of Europe in less than four hours. By noon today, Europe will be on fire."

* * *

LOCATION: Office of CRJ, Brussels

DATE: 14 July – Bastille Day

TIME: 1:00 PM

CRJ was having a difficult time constraining himself. Outwardly, he had to present the image of the senior international civil servant, carrying the weight of the economic world on his shoulders. But, inwardly, he wanted to dance around his office like a four-year-old around a Christmas tree.

Enrica's press conference had been a brilliant show. She was composed. Calm. Cool. Her presentation had focussed on building up the fear in Europe. Following that, it had provided the answers to all the security, economic and social fears. The climate lockdown, held to the last, was hardly noticed considering the shocking news of the Universal Basic Income and all of the debt forgiveness.

True to his word, CRJ had waited for an hour after the late afternoon press conference and then began

---

[122] Paradise.

releasing statements. He managed to confuse his staff and make it appear that the statements were only being written after the conference was over. He would give one staffer a draft and tell him, "I was just given this draft. Have a look and see if you can clean it up a bit. Then go ahead and release it if you think it looks good." The same would happen to another staffer and then another. Each one thought that the drafts were being created in a crisis mode without realizing that CRJ had written all of them ahead of time.

The late afternoon had turned into the evening. CRJ had finally ordered his staff home around midnight, telling them to go while he would stay and continue to work. When the staff began to return about 7:30 AM, they were not surprised to find more draft statements for distribution on their desks. They assumed that CRJ had worked all night, when in fact, he had distributed the papers shortly after they had left. Following that, he had slept on his couch for a few hours. He thought that the slightly wrinkled suit in the morning was a good touch.

Just before noon, one of CRJ's staffers had breathlessly called him out of a meeting. Reports of violence were flaring across Europe, and the reason could not be more apparent. The staffer told CRJ that the Islamists had declared a Holy War on the Great Reset. Their message was being broadcast to every member of the faithful in Europe. CRJ tried to look appropriately surprised and concerned. He thanked the staffer for the interruption and told him to intensify their monitoring of the violence.

At that point, CRJ returned to the meeting. The room was full of senior officials from various economic and financial institutions who had been summoned last night. CRJ had told them that the announcement of the Great Reset was a surprise to him as well. He had known, of course, that massive changes were needed to the European Union. Now, they had no choice. They had to act as though they had known about the announcement ahead of time. If they did not, CRJ told them the Great Depression of the 1930s would look like a spring picnic.

As the assembled officials began to leave, CRJ carefully pulled a few of them aside, one at a time. He asked them if they had known the announcement was coming. Each one professed shock. CRJ had not offered his view, but each official walked away thinking that CRJ had not known about the Great Reset announcement either. CRJ had already begun to undermine Enrica, and she had no idea that the whole Great Reset announcement was a setup.

Following the meeting in the conference room, CRJ had returned to his inner office. He flipped through multiple TV channels in French, English, and German. Each one had the same story. Europe was on fire as violence was unfolding in every major city. A few of the talking heads were still using words like 'violence from disaffected youth' or 'social unrest in sensitive quarters.' Others were blunter and called it a Muslim uprising. CRJ was quick to note that only one of them had identified the violence as having come from 'Islamists' instead of Muslims. This was fascinating. Almost 25 years after 9/11, the press still had not bothered to educate themselves on the issues. CRJ was pleased, however, as an intelligent and functioning press would have made his life difficult.

CRJ silently thanked the Islamists for being so predictable. He hated them and their 6th-century ideology with every fiber in his being, though he admired their dedication and adherence to their cause of political Islam. Their greatest weakness was now CRJ's greatest strength. Because of their rigid commitment to their strategy, they were also predictable. Not only could CRJ see their uprising coming, but he had also counted on it.

Taking one last quick look at the TV screens, CRJ laughed to himself again. It was unlikely that the Islamists had used the term 'Holy War' in their declaration. Not their style. But the use of the term helped inflame the masses in Europe, so CRJ had seen no reason to correct the message.

Heading off to his next meeting, CRJ was rather pleased with himself. Enrica had performed excellently, and the Islamists were rising violently, precisely as needed. All told, it had been a great day, and it was still only lunchtime.

* * *

LOCATION: Office of Enrica Leclercq

DATE: 14 July – Bastille Day

TIME: 2:00 PM

Enrica was not having a great day.

The problems had started in the morning. Her usually enthusiastic and outgoing staff had taken to staring as she walked by. A few of the looks were openly hostile. Finally, one of her assistants had asked her if it was safe to walk home. The question was asked with accusing eyes. They were telling Enrica that they blamed her for the violence.

Since the announcement of the Great Reset, divisions were growing in her organization. Most of the younger staff appeared nervous but were in favor of the climate lockdowns. They were especially thrilled with the student loan forgiveness and the universal basic income programs. But the longer-term staff who were over 40 had become sullen. Depressed. Disrespectful. Surly.

Just before noon, her head of human resources had sent her a text message. Employee absenteeism had soared to over 30%, up from its average level of less than 10%. At a time when the organization most needed its staff, they were not showing up. And that was in just one day.

For the first time, Enrica was feeling doubtful about the Great Reset. The level of violence had soared well past anything she had been warned about. Her incoming text messages and email were flooded with questions and statements. All of them held fear and concern. Yet, few had actually questioned the idea of the Great Reset. Most supported it.

But there was one overwhelming question that rose again and again.

Why?

Why had she made such an announcement?

Why had she made such an announcement without warning everyone first?

She realized it was not just a doubt building up as to how the Great Reset might go. If the Great Reset plan went south, it would be her left holding the ball.

She needed to contact CRJ. And soon.

Chapter 32: Violence on the Continent

LOCATION:	SAS HQ
DATE:	15 July
TIME:	9:00 AM

Major Berikoff arrived at the Colonel's office to find Captain Davies and his two NCOs already seated in the waiting area. All three begin to rise as the Major approached, but he greeted them by saying, "Be seated. It has been two weeks since I have seen you in person, but I have been reading all your reports. Your minor invasion, or perhaps I should say incursion, of the continent was productive by all accounts. The Colonel says he is under pressure to provide more intelligence on the four initial terrorist attacks and what has followed. It strikes me personally that the pressure is coming directly from Number 10. Because it was us that gave some of the first insights into what was happening, the Prime Minister somehow feels we are an intelligence agency and not special forces.

Nonetheless, here we are. Keep in mind, the Colonel has already read most of your reports, but he wants to hear it directly from you. With this Colonel, you should also state what you have learned with certainty and feel free to add what you think about it.

He does not want just facts; he wants your opinions and thoughts."

Three heads nodded in agreement.

At precisely nine o'clock, the Colonel's voice rang out. "Enter."

The Colonel greeted them as they entered. "Skiffington, Crosby! How was the vacation on the continent? I trust you enjoyed your two weeks of idle pleasure at Her Majesty's expense?"

"Excellent, Sir," replied Sergeant Crosby. "Best bit of fun we had since that little incident in the South China Sea."

With that, the Colonel's face changed from 'munificent leader mode' to 'business mode.' "Tell me what you have learned."

Sergeant Crosby unfolded his 1:500,000 scale map of Western Europe and attached it to the Colonel's whiteboard with magnets. "We went through the Chunnel on the night of the fourth of July and headed directly to Paris. We traveled and slept in an old Bedford van with enough gear to make us look like a couple of mates out on a rugby match tour. Most days, we left the van in public parking on the outskirts and would go into the various city centers on foot or by the local tube. On the fifth of July, we started in central Paris and worked out to the suburbs in the northwest. Nothing seemed amiss, although there was a lot of police presence on foot and many police vehicles on the move. On the sixth of July, we decided to go to Sevran and the areas around it. You could feel the tension in the air. We dressed down, wore hoodies, and had not shaved in a bit, but even at that, we could sense hostility if someone looked directly at us. They know who does and who does not belong. That night was when the media first started reporting a rise in car burnings and vandalism. We decided to stay in Paris for another night. On the seventh, it was pretty clear, at least to us, that the street violence was concentrated in the Islamist held areas, and it was coordinated."

With that, Crosby turned to Skiffington. "That sounds about right. Did I miss anything?"

"Sergeant Crosby covered that part well, Colonel. I have walked through a souk in Jordan, a hawker center in Singapore, and Tahrir Square in Cairo. Each time, it was done without drawing attention. But as the Sergeant said, the locals in Sevran have an uncanny sense of who belongs on their turf. Worse than parts of Glasgow in that sense."

Sergeant Crosby continued. "After Paris, we moved on to the Brussels area, especially Molenbeek, then moved further north to Antwerp. Belgium is a mess, Colonel. Parts of it are as bad as Paris. After that, we went to Rotterdam, The Hague, and then over to Amsterdam. On our way out of the Netherlands, we quickly drove by to pay our respects in Arnhem[123] and

---

[123] The Battle of Arnhem was a heroic, yet ill-fated and disastrous campaign undertaken by Allied Forces in World War II from 17 to 26 September 1944. It was part of

then headed into Germany. We saw some of the street violence first-hand. It was dreadful. In addition to the usual Molotov cocktails and burning rubbish bins, we heard plenty of semi-automatic and full-auto rifle fire. Mostly AKs. We also heard the rattle of a couple of PKMs, which makes this pretty serious stuff. Difficult to tell, but we did see some of the rioters moving in what appeared to be small unit tactical formations. We could see two groups of guys dressed in black with AKs shooting their way up a street in one case. They had two others providing supporting fire for them with a PKM. Not brilliant stuff, but not thugs with guns either."

"Anything else, Skiffers?"

"Just one thing. On two separate occasions in Islamist areas, we saw kids between eight and twelve years old out in the early morning hours. If I did not know better, I would say they were out policing the brass[124] and taking it all back to one shop. If that is correct, we see an urban fighting force with support and training throughout the community. There were also lots of kids running around on bicycles and skateboards with cell phones. So again, best guess, but they have a

---

Operation Market-Garden. One excellent book on this military failure is *A Bridge Too Far* by Cornelius Ryan.
[124] The military uses the terms 'policing the brass' or 'policing the battlefield' to describe clearing a weapons range of empty brass casings after target practice. The term has no inference or reference to police forces of any sort.

spotter network in their neighborhoods run by young teens."

With that, Crosby started again. "We were getting ready to leave Germany and head back here. After that wave of terrorist attacks started on the tenth of July, you could see and feel the increased tension in the cities and even remote villages. We decided to extend Germany a bit and made our way to Frankfurt. When we heard that announcement about the Great Reset on the thirteenth, we decided it was time to head for home 'toot sweet,' but we went a long way around to the south of Paris and thought we should honor our French colleagues by being in Paris for Bastille Day. The suburbs we saw are a complete mess. No services. The police only move in convoys. The power is out in many areas, and the only folks on the street looked like Islamists or armed drug dealers. So we decided to bug out of the Paris area in the early afternoon and drove straight back here."

"Do you think you were compromised at any point?" This from the Colonel. "Given all that is going on, having it come out that that SAS is doing tactical recce in Europe might not go well."

The two NCOs looked at each other. Skiffington took the lead. "No way we were made as SAS or even soldiers, even though we stood out a couple of times. We slept in the van and only bought food in small village gas stations with stores. I paid cash for everything. We talked to many folks, but mainly we let on we were Brit rugby fans traveling and worried about the violence spreading. We would usually engage the locals by asking them what they thought was the best way to get to the next town or city, given the violence. That got us lots of interesting views on what the locals think. But no worries on having been compromised, Sir."

"Fine work," said the Colonel. Turning to Major Berikoff and Captain Davies, he said, "While these two were going walkabout in Europe, tell me about your time. I have read your reports but give me your versions directly."

Major Berikoff took the lead. "As you remember, Sir, we had some initial success in determining that the terrorist attacks were a setup and that they seemed to have some faint traces back to Brussels. After that, the trail ran cold for a few days. There were a few tidbits, but nothing substantial. However, GCHQ told us they were tracking some intermittent traffic about the Bonames Airfield landing site. Someone appeared to be tracking the money trail. We could do nothing with it as all we could tell was that it was in Frankfurt. However, some discreet face-to-face inquiries with the Germans at their embassy here in London produced a surprise result. They told us they knew nothing about it, yet GCHQ tracked their communications after that. It seems they were genuinely surprised by the news. After that, we approached the BKA in Frankfurt and promised them we would share a few things if they would. Their earlier work had produced nothing, but once we tipped them, they said it was a private company in Frankfurt doing the digging. We thought this was them trying to mislead us. That, of course, was when we contacted you on the seventh of July."

"Right," replied the Colonel. "You rang a few bells with that because I had MI6 here again, asking about your activities. I told them that you believed a private company in Frankfurt seemed to be tracking the money behind the attacks. You should have seen the look on his face. He was not at all pleased. I think by that point that the BKA and the BfV were now involved with what turned out to be the Hessen Reinsurance Company. It took more than a few calls, but our embassy in Berlin was able to get you invited to the Hessen meeting on the twelfth of July."

The Colonel paused for a drink of water. "Tell me more about the meeting at the Hessen off-site conference center. I already know the details but tell me about those in attendance. Who are they really, and who put them up to this?"

Major Berikoff exhaled deeply. "This is going to sound strange, Colonel, but it appears that that group is almost exactly what they said they were. The core group of four is from Hessen Reinsurance in their risk analysis section. The larger group was made up of a series of contacts who have worked together in the past. It is a rather eclectic group of ex-military, ex-police, ex-finance, and at least one hacker who seems to have a dodgy history. They seem to have some academic experience, with two of them being mostly eggheads. From what I could see, they are loosely held together by a common belief that open-source intelligence, loosely defined, is what works best. They also can use information and knowledge across institutional boundaries, so they are perhaps better at strategic intelligence than their budget and size indicated. As for who is behind this, our best assessment is the most obvious one. Aldo Lange of Hessen pays directly for his four core analysts. He then seems to allow his unit to call in others when they want to, for which Hessen is paying. Weirdly enough, it seems to work for them."

"What do we know about this Lange fellow? What is he on about in all of this?" asked the Colonel.

Captain Davies took the lead on this question. "What is interesting about him is what we cannot find. All the usual stuff is there. He went to the right schools. Top marks. Student athlete. Married well, but to a wife who stays deeply in the background. He is much sought after as a financial and economic speaker, something he regularly does. Well thought of in almost every circle, and he has navigated Hessen Reinsurance through some rough water but has come out on top every time. He also appears well connected, not surprising given the size of the company and his speaking tours, where he appears alongside everyone in government and finance. But here is the weird bit. We have been able to find almost nothing on his political views. He was not in student politics. He is not a party member that we can see. He makes no personal donations to politicians, and Hessen as a company has donated only modest money to politics and all parties. The company appears to be socially responsible, but most of the charity events it supports are non-political. The last big public donations were to a children's hospital and a series of food banks during the pandemic. Everything is apolitical. By the standards of his peer group, he is an unusual character."

"So, what do I take from all of that, Captain?"

"Bluntly put, Sir, we have no idea which way he will turn in the event of a crisis. It is hard to tell if he is pro-EU, pro-Germany, or pro-anything. His record, at least that which we can find, is silent. He must plan it that way as he has had the same pattern since school days."

Major Berikoff interjected. "Whatever is going on over there at Hessen, their hypothesis cannot be dismissed, and it seems to fit what is happening. There is a crisis within a crisis within a crisis. The most obvious is the violence on the ground, especially in France, Belgium, Germany, and the United Kingdom. If that violence is not stopped in the next few days, little else will matter as we will be facing both an Islamist insurrection and reactive violence that will destabilize much of Western Europe. The second crisis is this coup attempt by Enrica Leclercq. Her attempt at a takeover has a limited chance of success, especially with the widespread violence. The view that Enrica Leclercq is the main driving force behind this is unlikely. She is the face of this coup attempt, but she is not the brains. The third crisis is one of leadership. No one has a solid assessment of which way the various national leaders and institutional leaders in the European Union, or any other organization will go when the going gets tough."

The Colonel was staring at Trooper Skiffington. "You look like you have something on your mind. What is it?"

"Just my view, Sir, but in times of trouble, folks tend to follow their tribe. When push comes to shove, the leaders who lead their tribes might survive. Those leaders who sit on the fence or try to serve many tribes will be devoured by the pitchfork and rope brigades."

The Colonel turned to Captain Davies. "Do folks tend to follow their tribe? Is that where we are at?"

Captain Davies looked at the Major, who simply shrugged his shoulders. "Trooper Skiffington is probably right, Sir."

The Colonel stood up and walked over to the map. "Not that any of those buffoons at Whitehall or Number 10 ever listen to us, but I think my report up the food chain today will be short. Europe will return to tribalism, and we best be prepared for the worst."

With that, the Colonel waved his hand, indicating that the meeting was over.

Chapter 33: Europe Marches or Europe Dies

LOCATION: NATO Headquarters, Brussels

DATE: 16 July

TIME: 9:45 AM

General Berndt van der Schalk of the Royal Dutch Marines (Korps Mariniers) stared at his office bookshelf. *That book* stared back at him in silence. He was staring at his copy of the famous 1926 publication by Basil Mathews: *Young Islam on Trek: A Study in the Clash of Civilizations*.

It seemed to Berndt that Europe was fast falling into civil war. It was not that surprising. Various voices had made it clear that the violence was coming for years. Among them had been Patrick Calvar, the head of France's internal security service, who warned that France was headed for a civil war. [125]

The Great Reset announcement on the 13th of July had guaranteed more violence in the mind of Berndt.

---

[125] Peter Allen Allen and Sam Tonkin, "France Is on the Verge of 'Civil War', the Country's Head of Intelligence Says," Daily Mail Online (Associated Newspapers, July 13, 2016), https://www.dailymail.co.uk/news/article-3685561/France-verge-civil-war-sparked-mass-sexual-assault-women-migrants-intelligence-chief-warns.html

Were the technocrats who ran the EU removed from reality?

Rumors had been reaching Berndt since late yesterday afternoon. Officials from multiple organizations had privately been asking if anyone had foreknowledge of the announcement. The answers were always the same. Everyone was expecting something – but nobody had expected such a shock. A few of Berndt's NCOs were quietly saying what others were thinking. The coup known as the Great Reset was starting to look more like 'The Great Mess' rather than 'The Great Reset.'

As he sat in his chair for a few moments, Berndt wondered if it mattered. Europe was on fire. If the political fires were not brought under control, then nothing else would matter. Europe would be fragmented into a series of Caliphates fighting against a series of nationalist and ethnic enclaves.

The meeting had been set for 10:00 AM. At 9:40, Berndt rose from his office chair and walked with outward calmness through the maze of corridors to the main briefing room at NATO headquarters. The new building in Brussels had cost over a billion Euros in 2018[126] when NATO could not put an armored division into the field.

---

[126] Robin Emmott, "New Home, but Same Worries, as NATO Moves into Glass and Steel HQ," Reuters.com (Thomson Reuters, April 20, 2018),
https://www.reuters.com/article/uk-nato-headquarters-idUKKBN1HR1H8

Most NATO meetings Berndt had attended were so dull that staying awake was a struggle. But this one would be a meeting for the ages. The remaking of the political order in Europe was underway now that political control was being lost. So the question for today was whether NATO would finally play a role in Europe or just remain an expensive club where soldiers dressed up as players in a Gilbert and Sullivan operetta.

Berndt arrived 15 minutes early for the 10:00 AM meeting. This was part military habit and part leadership skill. He was interested in seeing who arrived and with whom. What were they saying as they arrived? The initial few that entered after him were low-grade political lackeys who had come to stake out their boss's turf. They were subdued. The swagger, which helped hide an absence of any life experience, besides being party hacks, was gone. The big dogs would arrive soon.

Berndt looked over at the five-meter wall screen. CNN International was again showing the video of Tim Gantry's head stuck on an iron spike. The spike was part of the gate under the archway entrance to the famous Parisienne *Cimetière des Chiens* – the Dog's Cemetery. The cemetery had a lovely view of the River Seine, which continued to flow at its undisturbed pace despite the violence.

Tim Gantry was an international financial guru and a close confidante of Rahm Emanuel, the former White House Chief of Staff. Gantry had been the chief spokesman and leader of the NGO *Queers*

Undermining the Oppression of Muslims. When the earlier widespread rioting in France had turned to insurrection, Gantry had arrived from New York in a flare of publicity. His group declared that they would negotiate an end to the conflict. Further, he and his followers had announced with great enthusiasm that the fascist simpletons attempting to run Europe's governments would follow his example. Next, they would learn to build a society based on climate justice with social equity. Only then, he said, could Europe give a voice to its most oppressed members. Then they could build a diverse society that would blossom in a tolerant and multicultural future.

His head was cut off at the first meeting with the Islamists.

The notoriously violent group Jamaat al-Bekkari had executed him during the opening moments of their first meeting on the 14th of July. Apparently, the Islamists were not great believers in the Great Reset, Tim Gantry, or his ridiculous NGO.

Nader Mohammed al-Hasan, the urbane and sophisticated spokesman for the group, calmly stated that homosexuality was a crime against Islam and the punishment was death. Apparently, Nader's classes on criminal trial procedures had not impacted him while he was reading law at Cambridge and later at the Sorbonne. But, on the other hand, Tim Gantry and his group had not believed the threat briefings given to them by the Directorate-General for Internal Security (DGSI).

Gantry and his followers had died, destroyed by the mythology of their intellectual capabilities.

To Berndt, the grand experiment between the left and radical Islam was a dog's breakfast befitting a death at a Dog's Cemetery.

Not that he would question it out loud today, but Berndt wondered what sort of ideological indoctrination the late Tim Gantry had undergone on his secretive 'Common Purpose'[127] Matrix course. According to Gantry, it was a life-changing experience that caused him to create and fund his ill-fated NGO. Did these courses include behavioral modification techniques? Why did the UK, the USA, Canada, and so many other countries support them or give them charitable status? 'Common Purpose,' Berndt thought, lacked any common sense.

The map on the opposing wall showed that the Jamaat al-Bekkari group now controlled much of Paris's northern and eastern suburbs, including the infamous Clichy-sous-Bois. Their span of control was extending rapidly to the north and west as well. A swath of land running from Paris to Saint Quentin and then up to the border with Belgium showed a newly expanding level of violence. The fighting was heading block by block towards the heart of Paris, and cameras on the Eiffel Tower could see the smoke rising from the looting, burning, and fighting

---

[127] Unknown Editors, "About Us - Common Purpose," commonpurpose.org (Common Purpose, 2021), https://commonpurpose.org/about-us/common-purpose/

engagements. With several other French cities partially under their control, the newly declared series of caliphates were a force-in-being. Jamaat al-Bekkari was just one group claiming to be a part of the "Islamic Cordoba Immemorial State" (ICIS) as the newly proclaimed caliphate liked to call itself collectively. It had declared its allegiance to ISIS, which remerged after being beaten so severely in 2014 and 2015.

Much of Belgium was now experiencing violence from forces claiming to be allied to ISIS and the new ICIS. The same was happening in Austria, especially Vienna. The Netherlands was consumed with a battle for control of parts of The Hague, Rotterdam, and Amsterdam.

Manchester was starting to burn in the UK, while in East London, a caliphate had been declared. As Berndt's intelligence briefing NCOs would say, 'the situation was fluid but violent.' Germany had seen extensive rioting up to the 13th of July, but even with the Great Reset announcement, political control seemed to remain in the Reich Chancellery and with the Chancellor. Berndt wondered which way the Turkish population in Germany would turn. Caliphate or Chancellery? Most likely, their leadership would do whatever President Erdogan of Turkey told them – and that had already been made clear. Erdogan was pushing for more unrest and violence.

Berndt took a seat against the wall, under the video screen, and looked directly at the opposing wall's situation map. Little was to be learned by watching

TV. With its colorful array of unit symbols, confrontation lines, and constantly updated ground events, the map spoke volumes of hard truths. This map, as Berndt knew, was the real reason for the meeting.

Berndt had earlier gained a brief bit of international attention, perhaps notoriety, when a young sympathizer of the Dutch *Politieke Partij Radikalen* (Political Party of Radicals) had secretly taped some of his off-hand comments made following an academic conference. Berndt's views that a crisis of leadership had been created by careerist politicians who had never had a real job caused a minor press flare-up. His further comments on bureaucrats who placed process over goals and outcomes were deemed unhelpful by the Chief Spokesperson of the EU Parliament.

Fortunately for Berndt, a major corruption scandal in the EU Parliament concerning the overcharging of expenses by Members of the European Parliament had emerged only two days later. The press, with the attention span of a gnat, had utterly forgotten him. Squirrel!

Checking the digital clock above the map, Berndt noticed that the higher-priced help was arriving with four or five minutes to the start time. They were looking for the spaces already secured for them.

After that, the following figure entering the room at 09:58 was SACEUR: The Supreme Allied Commander Europe. Behind his back, he was often referred to, only half-jokingly, as the Supreme Allied Being. It was not known to others, but his role would be clear. SACEUR's conversation with the US President late the night before had been short and sharp. American combat forces were not to be involved. Behind him sat an unidentified colonel wearing a United States Marine Corps uniform. The General knew that the US Marines deliberately under-ranked their officers. This meant that he was the equivalent of a one-star general in the other American services. The Colonel seemed to shadow SACEUR but was not openly submissive to him. He must be SACEUR's own staffer. An unknown factor – but a possible player in real terms. And no name tag – strange for an American.

Next to SACEUR was the 'G3' or the Assistant Chief of Staff, Operations and Plans. He was a Brit and a former paratrooper. His public biography seemed to have a few gaps in it, at least to the professional eye. His service in his younger days was not noted, suggesting that he had served in covert military operations. Berndt had noticed in earlier meetings that SACEUR would look in his direction when speaking on a point. SACEUR valued his experience.

Berndt noted the lawyers were present as well – primarily military and with only one civilian. Their job would be to sufficiently mangle the English language to explain how NATO's Article Five would apply and how an attack against 'one' would justify a response by all. Then troops could be used to begin the actual fighting, even if the threat was internal rather than external to NATO's member states. Unless, of course, you were one of those who believed that the fighting was part of a foreign invasion that had occurred in slow motion over the years.

The political staff arrived, sitting against the wall and away from the table – a sign of what was coming. A few sharp minds existed in the political teams. Still, a depressing number of them were little more than party hacks with wonky degrees in social justice and gender studies from obscure universities. Thankfully, most of them would remain silent today. Empty politics, virtue signaling, and diplomacy were coming to an end. Instead, kinetic force would be at the forefront.

Then there were the Public Relations folks. For a moment, Berndt felt sorry for them. Good luck trying to put lipstick on this pig known as the Great Reset! All possible outcomes were going to be ugly.

At 10:02, the Head of the European Commission arrived and sat in his chair, accompanied by Enrica Leclercq, formerly known as High Representative for the European Union for Foreign Affairs and Security Policy. Her new title as the High Representative for the European Union was – politely put – ambiguous. Berndt knew that she was closely tied to the head of the World Economic Forum and the head of the IMF.

Once again, Berndt had the same thought. Were people who arrived late at meetings so lacking in grace and self-confidence that they believed a late arrival was a way of showing authority? Did forcing the others to wait to give them an ego kick?

Narcissists, he wondered? Berndt thought that such people suffered from delusions of adequacy.

Without really noticing it, Berndt's right hand reached down and checked to see if his stainless-steel water bottle was positioned 5 centimeters to the right of the forward leg of his chair. The water bottle might be needed as Berndt had a habit of throwing up in the back of his throat whenever senior political figures lied through their teeth and made stupid statements. The water bottle could wash through the bile, stopping the burning sensation and relieving the vile taste.

Berndt stared at the President of the European Commission for few moments. This position, and indeed this person, was seen to be more powerful and influential but with less profile than the confusingly named President of the Council of the European Union, or the equally confusing President of the European Parliament. Somewhat bizarrely, the President of the European Commission was not elected but was the appointed holder of a position resulting from a secretive process. The European Council (not the Commission) would put forth a consensus candidate who was then approved by the European Parliament (not the Council). The whole situation made the election of a Pope look like an exercise in utopian parliamentary transparency.

Now, after the Great Reset, they had a 'High Representative for the European Union.' How many chefs did it take to run one kitchen?

SACEUR rose and waved one hand in the air. The meeting was about to get underway. It was an American General who would moderate a forum of the future of Europe. How ironic. The General called the meeting to order.

Somewhat out of his usual character, SACEUR did not begin to speak from his chair. Instead, he stood up and walked the short distance to the speaker's podium. Interesting, Berndt thought to himself. His movement forces the audience to follow him, and now all the attention will be on him and not split with his co-chair and the others—another small sign about who might be calling the shots – literally in this case.

"Why are we here?" SACEUR posed the rhetorical question and left it hanging for several seconds.

"The purpose of this meeting is to decide the future of Europe, the Great Reset, and with it the direction of Western civil society. Do we want to continue to have our values, ethics, and freedoms? What of the gains of the Renaissance, the Reformation, and the Enlightenment? Do we stand on these, or do we submit to the other values and allow them to determine the future?"

"Do we call upon NATO and determine that sufficient conditions have been reached for Article Five[128] to be

---

[128] Article Five in NATO reference to collective defence. This article of the Washington Treaty (NATO Treaty) is considered as the cornerstone of the whole organization. Collective defence means that an attack against one Ally is considered as an attack against all Allies.

invoked? Alternatively, do we allow each country to try and deal with the problems on their own, knowing that some might lack the will or stable leadership to endure?"

"If we are going to answer in the positive, then you must fight in the streets with physical force as well as redefine our political, economic, and social institutions. This will not be easy. We should have reacted to the voices of extremism in the 1980s when they first began to spread. We should have responded in the 1990s when the voices of extremism shifted from subversion to open defiance. We should have reacted in the early 2000s when extremists were expanding their financial operations through taxpayer-funded charities and had thoroughly infiltrated government, school systems, and the universities. But this did not happen as the voices of political correctness and appeasement crushed the voices of reason and knowledge. We should have reacted again in 2014 when the news of mass rapes and sexual abuse in Rotherham in the UK focused on a much larger extremism issue.[129] But even then, we chose to remain silent. As it had in the past, the politicians failed to act when non-violent change could have been put in place."

---

[129] Alexis Jay, ed., "Independent Inquiry into Child Sexual Exploitation in Rotherham (1997 - 2013)," rotherham.gov.uk (Rotherham Metropolitan Borough Council, August 21, 2014), https://www.rotherham.gov.uk/downloads/download/31/independent-inquiry-into-child-sexual-exploitation-in-rotherham-1997-2013-

"Now, the announcement of the Great Reset may force our hands."

SACEUR paused and looked down at the podium as though reading some imaginary notes in front of him. Instead, he was just giving his audience a few seconds to absorb what he had said. He gave his hands an unnecessary dry wash to occupy a few more seconds and then looked up.

"If we do not get this done, then the Islamist uprising may succeed. We can look forward to a future where women return to a position barely above slavery; free thought and free speech are destroyed; pluralism is crushed, and education will be reduced to memorizing cherry-picked radicalized quotations from the Quran. Everything we have worked for since the Treaty of Westphalia will be cast away, and we will enter a new dark age that will last for hundreds of years."

"When done, either we will have shaped our future towards freedom, or allowed four hundred years of hard-won progress to simply slide away because we lack the will and the ability to think in practical and reasonable terms."

"Before we go any further, the G2 (senior intelligence staff officer) will bring us up to date. General Berndt van der Schalk will outline the current situation for us and explain how we got to this point. Without a clear view of the past and present, we cannot look forward to a future."

Following the lead of SACEUR, Berndt decided to speak from the podium rather than the map.

Just as he was about to speak, Berndt looked over at Dr. Isabel Hooft. They stared silently at each other for less than a second, but the message passed clearly. Almost imperceptibly, she nodded her head. Berndt would go ahead with the version of the brief that laid out the facts. No big words. No academic bafflegab. No nausea-inducing bureaucratic terms. Above all, no politically correct crap.

She was the real intellectual power in the room and one of the few in Europe who could think about the current situation at the strategic level with rational knowledge. If history should record one person as having played a pivotal role, this was the person. The decision of the Dutch government to completely fund advanced graduate degrees, which allowed the brightest to advance regardless of family wealth, had proved itself in this case.

Among many other things, Dr. Hooft was an adviser on strategy to NATO with a job description that was sufficiently vague to allow her the broadest range of access to senior military and civilian leaders. She was also Berndt's wife, having met in graduate school. Several years ago, Berndt had a dinner discussion with his wife and another couple about an upcoming election and the future of internal security matters in the Netherlands. As was her habit, she deconstructed their views and refocused the discussion. Updating was needed, she stated, and it would happen soon.

The next day four of them had met again for an extended evening meal outdoors at the Het Plein — the central plaza of the Dutch city of The Hague. While they ate and talked, the statue of "William the Silent" stared down at them. At that point, Berndt's education began to take a new turn. His degree had been in history and economics, and his military education had focused on strategy, operations, and tactics in joint and combined arms environments. Now, he would be pulled into the fascinating world of insurrectional movements and the dynamics of social unrest as it translated into civil strife, confrontation, conflict, and then war. He realized how little was known about the contemporary forms of struggle, conflict, and warfare in civil society, especially in an age of technology. And what of the youth who were distant from the political process, especially that of the European Union? How did they view the future? What were their views on climate change and social justice? When would their high unemployment rates translate into social unrest? Much of what he knew may have been helpful in conventional conflicts. Still, his skills were akin to that of the dodo bird when dealing with the emerging problems of Europe framed by the unchallenged spread of foreign extremist influences.

The political and military minds that ran NATO and the EU had a weak grasp of tactical matters in security. This may have allowed them to make minor disruptions to the spread of extremism. But not one in a position of power knew how to have a strategic effect on the forces destroying the nations of the European Union. Even the current Chancellor of Germany seemed to sense the issues were threatening but was captured by the past and could not make the final leap.

Two days after the dinner in the plaza, Berndt had an extended afternoon meeting that had later drifted into the Pub Aran in Amsterdam. Berndt's cousin was the head of a little-known intelligence organization that operated on the Stadhoudrskade. To the casual observer, the sign on the building said Heineken. It did contain offices and a processing plant for the Heineken Brewery. However, Heineken had one of the world's most exemplary intelligence networks that could reach as far up into government as it wished and as far down onto the streets as was necessary. This was for two reasons, the first of which was the marketing of beer. The second reason was a bit more exceptional. Freddie Heineken, the patriarch of the company and one of the richest men in the Netherlands, was kidnapped in 1983.[130] After a 35-million-guilder ransom payment, Freddie ordered that such a thing would never happen to him, his family, or his company again.

---

[130] Iain Martin, "Kidnapping Freddy Heineken: The Story of Europe's Largest Ransom," Forbes.com (Forbes Magazine, September 28, 2019), https://www.forbes.com/sites/iainmartin/2019/09/27/kidnapping-freddy-heineken-the-story-of-europes-largest-ransom/?sh=2982e3c331d0

Additionally, Freddie Heineken had worked to meet everyone in the elite circles from the inner sanctums of the security and intelligence circles in countries where they did business. From his truck drivers up to the boardroom, everyone was an information source. The result was a security and operational risk operation with serious resources, fantastic access, and few limitations. Wealth and rank, Berndt noted, have their privileges.

Meeting in his cousin's office, Berndt had posed a series of questions about youth unemployment, social unrest, Los Indignados, OCCUPY, Islamist extremism, BLM, no-go zones for the police in the Netherlands, and a myriad of other questions. Much to his surprise, his cousin answered calmly and without hesitation. His cousin agreed that the social and economic situation in Europe was as bleak as Isabel had suggested. But, in his view, discussions of the Great Reset were little more than pseudo-intellectuals playing socialists after having done their graduate studies in sociology.

Turning back to the present, Berndt was fully aware that the Article Five question was about political cover, even at this late date as the Great Reset was being launched. Each state might be able to use its military to attempt to crush the insurrection. Still, it was not clear if they had the political will to do so or if they had the necessary stability and loyalty of the population to make it happen. Having NATO's Article Five invoked would provide the needed political cover and give an appearance that the decision had been made somewhere else. But, even as the noose was being slipped around their necks, the careerist politicians remained true to their primary electoral methodology: Make sure you can blame someone else ahead of time and take the credit afterward.

It was clear many of the political leaders had been supporters of the Great Reset in the past. They were part of the overall circle of modern-day technocrats, nurtured by the World Economic Forum and indoctrinated by them, Common Purpose, and other political entryist organizations.

Berndt began. "As SACEUR noted, we will bring you up to date on what ground has been lost and which ground we expect to lose soon. A brief description will follow on how we arrived at the current situation as well as a view of the future."

Berndt was speaking in the plural form, using 'we' rather than 'I.' This was not just his opinion, but rather the combined views of many of his analysts and advisers. As always, he thought of himself as a leader within a larger group, not an entity unto himself.

"Look at the map on the briefing wall. It shows Paris and an approximately fifty-kilometer radius around the city. The circle is Ground Zero, and it is where the first major riots broke out on 06 July. The dark green areas show the terrain under the total control of Jamaat al-Bekkari. Those areas in light green show contested territory, and this also represents territory which we expect to lose in the next twenty-four hours to forty-eight hours, regardless of what decisions are reached today."

Berndt paused for a few seconds to allow the audience to take in the scope of the map. He had them focused not so much on what was lost but what would be lost in the following days.

He continued.

"As you can see, most of the northern and eastern suburbs of Paris have been captured. To the western side, the Seine River from Saint-Denis down to Boulogne-Billancourt may form a defense line to stop an advance, but this is by no means a given. The status of the French capital from twenty-four to forty-eight hours from now is not clear, although Central Paris will likely hold."

"This next map shows the French territory from Paris to the English Channel and over to the border with Belgium. You will notice again that there is a significant amount of green shading, which represents contested territory. This is a minimalist interpretation as we have only shown those areas confirmed as being in the throes of fighting. Additionally, we predict with a high level of confidence that the territory which is shaded in light green will also be lost."

"To date, we assess that most of the weapons being used are AK-47s, medium machine-guns such as the PKM, and rocket-propelled grenades such as the RPG-7 and RPG-9. Handguns are common, as well as a mixed variety of shotguns and hunting rifles. A variety of IEDs have been used, many of which appear to have been command-detonated. This capability is worrisome, as it suggests an advanced level of skill and organization. The police, however, are reporting that petrol bombs are the single biggest threat, with numerous police vehicles and buildings having been destroyed. We have had reports of missiles fired at civil aviation aircraft, and most major civilian airports near the conflict areas have closed."

"Since the announcement of the Great Reset, the reports suggest that there may be a limited number of man-portable surface-to-air missiles employed, but some of those reports also suggest that it is RPGs being fired at aircraft on the ground. Unfortunately, those doing the on-the-ground reporting are operating under some pressure, reports are fragmented, and the ability to identify different weapon types is often weak."

At that point, the G3 (Assistant Chief of Staff, Operations and Plans) stuck out his forefinger and pointed at the map. "General van der Schalk, you state you do not have solid information on what has been lost, yet you have high confidence in what will be lost. How can you have a high level of confidence on what territory will be lost in the next 24 hours when you are still working to form a stable picture of what has already happened?"

"Good question, Sir. How can we have such confidence about the future when the present and immediate past are a bit confused?" Berndt was falling back on an intelligence briefer's trick. Repeat

392

the question back to ensure clarity while allowing yourself several seconds to think.

"In late 2014, one of our rather long-in-the-tooth Warrant Officers designed a methodology for determining just this very scenario. When the Warrant Office, as a soldier with one year's service, had been sent to Bosnia as a private in 1992 and had seen how the intelligence staff had made some SWAGs (sophisticated wild-assed guesses) about where the next confrontation lines would emerge. They could see what ethnic/religious group would seize control of any given ground. Their work was based on census data that was more than 10 years out of date combined with individual reports of violence. It was not perfect, but it worked most of the time. Remembering this and his other experience in Afghanistan, he set about mapping out Europe with a series of relevant factors. He used census data to determine population concentrations by nationality, religion, and/or ethnicity. Added to that, he layered income levels and employment figures. On top of that, he again overlaid mapping data as to which suburbs and neighborhoods were no-go zones for the police and those that had high concentrations of returning ISIS fighters. In France, for instance, in 2014, there were 1,100 *"Zones Urbaine Sensibles"* or "no-go zones" where French police could not go without permission and protection. Similar no-go zones based on Muslim populations have existed for more than 15 years in the Netherlands, Denmark, Germany, Sweden, Belgium, etc. Then he and his team took crime data and overlaid that as well. Minor crimes such as assaults and theft were not used, but major crimes where a large amount of cash or explosives were taken were used. On top of that, he layered immigration data from conflict zones such as ISIS or Algeria, Morocco, Egypt, Iran, Pakistan, and Saudi Arabia. A layer of extremist mosques was added together with institutions and organizations associated with the Federation of Islamic Organizations in Europe and funding data from Qatar. The final layer was areas where widespread, systematic, and long-term sexual exploitation of children was known to have existed over some time. Rotherham was the first example used at that time back in 2014. All told, it gives us a good predictive tool and has so far worked better than it did in Bosnia, Iraq, Afghanistan, or ISIS."

"In short, this is an advanced form of pattern-based predictive analysis."

Berndt paused at that point and thought about adding that the Warrant Officer and his team had done most of the work on their own time and used all open-source data. Once senior authorities understood their efforts, their work was stopped, and all the material and products produced were ordered destroyed. The team was promptly broken up, and the members were returned to their home units with letters of disreputable conduct. Some senior civilian bureaucrats had felt that such work was 'culturally insensitive' and could be determined to be Islamophobic and, therefore, must be stopped.

Finally, the military authorities had relented. Fortunately, someone in the military chain of command had 'overlooked' the destruction of at least one complete set of the data and methods. It was tempting to comment about the stupidity of large bureaucratic systems, but for once, Berndt stifled himself and carried on.

"Looking at a larger map of the Atlantic to the Urals (ATTU), we can see similar situations developing. Our data is strong for France, Belgium, Germany, Luxembourg, the Netherlands, and the UK, but significantly weaker in other areas such as Norway, Sweden, and Denmark."

"Although it is no longer in the EU, I will start with the UK. We can see that the entire contiguous territory defined by the cities of Liverpool, Manchester, and Leeds is in conflict with only isolated islands of control left. Most of those are military bases. Much the same can be said of the territory from Leeds down to Sheffield. Refugees, or perhaps more correctly internally displaced persons, are fleeing the area in hundreds of thousands in response to the random violence, arson, and the beheading of figures identified with authority or religion. East London is in flames, and we are struggling to provide a stable picture. Lutfur Rahman is alleged to have declared a caliphate in the Tower Hamlet's council area through his spokesperson Rabina Khan, but no reliable source can confirm this."

"As with France and the larger cities, UK-based police, firefighters, and paramedics are withdrawing from conflict areas and consolidating elsewhere, based on their own initiative and local knowledge. However, confrontation lines have not yet firmed up, and we expect the period of uncertainty to remain for at least another twenty-four to forty-eight hours. Other areas where the rioting appears to be turning into insurrection and civil war are marked with the flame symbols."

"Moving to Belgium, you can see the light and dark green zones. We can consider Antwerp, Brussels, and Charleroi to be the main areas of conflict. As with the rest, the confrontation lines are fluid, and the situation will take some time to stabilize."

"In Germany, we can see that Munich and Koln are probably the worst-hit areas, but the violence there was slower to start. Nevertheless, German authorities have acted quickly. It appears that the Turkish areas of Germany are problematic, but those areas with Syrian, Moroccan, Algerian, Saudi, and Tunisian populations are the worst. Whether the open fighting for the control of territory spreads to Turkish areas is not yet clear."

"In Austria, we can see that a similar situation to Germany is developing."

"In most areas in Europe, Sunni areas are worse than Shia, but perhaps the Shia are simply slower off the mark. The Shia may be awaiting directions from Tehran before committing themselves to the fight. On the other hand, known Hezbollah personnel are moving continuously, and their level of chatter is up, suggesting that they are collecting battlefield intelligence for future operations if President Rouhani and his Ayatollah master give the word."

"As for the rest, you can see that we have limited information to date."

Berndt paused for a moment and took a quick drink from his water bottle. He intended to allow a momentary pause before moving onto an assessment of what the actions meant in military and political terms. Instead, much to his surprise, Enrica Leclercq rose to speak. As the new High Representative for the European Union, she had been the national security advisor for the European Union. Her latest role was not clear. Her announcement on the Great Reset had been one of the leading causes of the violence now tearing Europe apart. Berndt had been surprised to see her name on the list for the meeting. Her position entitled her to attend, but the mess she had made was descending into a catastrophe. Berndt was surprised she dared show her face in public, let alone at a meeting like this one.

"General," she intoned, "You stated that police and fire services are withdrawing from areas where there is fighting and then regrouping in other areas. Is that correct?"

"Yes." Berndt was madly trying to figure out where this line of questioning was going.

"Well," she said accusingly, "Could we then say that the police did not function properly at the moment because of their inability to adapt to the required modern standards of working in a diverse and tolerant multicultural environment? Can we say that their failure and withdrawal have led to social unrest? Is it not fair to say that the fault for this fighting lies with their inability over the years to address issues of social justice which have been aggravated by global warming?"

Everyone in the room froze.

For Berndt, the shock was complete. For years, police and intelligence services had warned about social unrest, economic disparity, uncontrolled migration, and the failures of multiculturalism. In 2021, a long list of retired French generals had openly warned of civil war.[131] The very existence of no-go zones in every country that had a large Islamist migrant population spoke to that failure. On top of that, the middle class had been beaten down, and the 700 Euro generation agitated for social unrest. Now, as years of warnings had failed again and the violence was about to explode to levels not seen since WWII, Enrica Leclercq was trying to find a way to blame the individuals who had made the warnings.

He stared back at her.

Mute.

Frozen.

Uncomprehending.

---

[131] Unknown, "Anger as Ex-Generals Warn of 'Deadly Civil War' in France," BBC News (BBC, April 27, 2021), https://www.bbc.com/news/world-europe-56899765

Slowly, the circuits started to come back on in his brain. His head turned slightly and noted the G3. The British General was looking directly at Enrica - with his hatred and anger on open display. SACEUR's jaw was moving, but no sound came out. In the back of his mind, Berndt began to have fantasies of violence that would later shock him.

The mind of Dr. Isabel Hooft was still working. First, she coughed loudly, the sudden noise distracting everyone in the silent room. Then she looked directly at SACEUR and mumbled an unnecessary word of apology. SACEUR snapped back to reality and took the cue offered to him. He and Dr. Hooft both looked back to Berndt, indicating that he should not answer the question and continue the brief.

At that point, one fact became clear. Enrica Leclercq was now irrelevant to the rest of the meeting. Strangely enough, she was one of the few who did not get it. She wondered why the briefer was so disrespectful as to ignore her question. To her, it was filled with insights.

Berndt was sorely tempted to ask Enrica Leclercq if she was part of the plan, which had seen four seemingly unconnected terrorist attacks cause the fighting. But that was a fight for another day.

Berndt turned back to his audience and asked, "How should we think about this conflict?"

"For those of you who study history, you will know that history does not repeat itself, but it does rhyme. In living memory, we have the conflict in Bosnia and

Kosovo for a slight comparison. Regarding the nature of the violence and its intensity, we might think about the Bosnian civil war when it was at its lowest in 1993. For the number of people who the fighting will displace, we might think about the magnitude of Kosovo in 1999, although this is a weak comparison. In terms of the scope and meaning of the war, nothing in the former Yugoslavia compares. Perhaps we should think more about the 30 Years' War from 1618 to 1648. From the ashes of the 30 Years' War came the Treaty of Westphalia and the unfolding of a new order. Likewise, from the ashes of this current war will come a new order. It may look like Lebanon for a while, or maybe worse. Maybe it will look better in the future. But whatever it looks like, the old order is gone."

"Now, let us look at how we found ourselves where we are today."

"The immediate cause of this violence – or civil war if you prefer - is the four terrorist attacks that occurred on the 28th of June. They were the spark that lit the fire. The announcement of the Great Reset has spread the flames. But the reasons go deeper."

"It had been known for years that following the 2008 economic crash that a series of doubtful measures had been undertaken to prop up the debt-ridden economies of the West. Long-term debt, a problem since the mid-1980s, was dealt with by long-term, low-interest rates. Quantitative Easing, known better as money printing, tried to re-ignite the economy but resulted in even more debt. The result was a hollowed-out economy, long-term structural youth unemployment, and the largest transfer of wealth ever seen in history, which went from the middle-class pension and saving systems to the financial sector. In short, the economy was financialized, and the middle and lower classes had their futures damaged. Many believed that a form of inverted totalitarianism had evolved whereby the politicians had allowed the financial class to take over both the economy and the government. Faith in government was further eroded, and capitalism, that great creator of wealth, had become cronyism which stole it."

"The immediate result of that economic crisis and more unemployment was seen in a variety of areas. Among those were the race riots in the United Kingdom that began in the Rotherham and Bradford areas and spread rapidly. Years of frustration at the mismanagement of the economy and unchecked EU migration led to the anger being turned against 'the other.' This time it was migrants who were largely unemployed as they had not integrated. As a result, their populations had proliferated, frequently while receiving long-term welfare support. Similar riots were seen elsewhere in Europe and North America."

By late 2019, the world was sitting on the edge of recession, at least in the OECD countries. Massive debts, incompetent leadership, and a brainwashed youth full of entitlement had driven the system to the edge.

"The pandemic undermined the European Union again as it demonstrated it was incapable of taking collective action even on something as straightforward as a vaccine program."

"At this point, let us look at the groups who are doing the fighting. We have a series of reports of fighting teams of 6 to 10 men who are highly trained and employ good tactical skills with a mix of small arms and explosives. They appear to be mobile, and their coordinated attacks are nasty, brutish, and short. While they have killed numerous civilians, we assess that they target mainly police forces and any other individuals, groups, or infrastructure that represents state authority. This has been seen particularly in Paris, Brussels, London, Rotterdam, and Manchester. In all of those cities, the no-go zones or sharia zones were hit first. They also appear to have high levels of fire discipline, engage rapidly, and then withdraw quickly. This brings to mind the types of individuals that the police have seen doing high-value cash centers and diamond robberies since 2011. The coordinated nature of the attacks also suggests a practical level of command and control. Casualties on their side are minimal at this point, with no reported deaths of these fighters. We assess that most of the leaders and fighters have had military or paramilitary experience outside of Europe but have lived in Europe for extended periods, giving them an excellent knowledge of their surroundings."

"At the same time, we have also had reports of larger groups of usually 15 to 20 fighters who demonstrate some tactical skill but not to the same level of the smaller groups. They also attack authority figures and

402

infrastructure, but they follow up their brief firefights with extended periods of random violence and destruction. They are burning police stations, fire stations, banks, municipal offices, churches, synagogues, media outlets, and similar targets. Petrol bombs appear to be the main weapons for infrastructure attacks, but we also have limited reporting on the use of explosives. They have killed a larger number of civilians and appear to lack the fire discipline of the smaller groups. We assess that at least the leaders of these small groups are returning figures from ISIS, AQIM, or similar groups."

"The third group that we have observed in several cities are mobs. They can range from a few dozen to several thousand. They are extremely violent and destructive but appear to lack specific targets. Some rioting mobs are spontaneous or simply riots of opportunity, but other riots appear to have been staged or organized through social media. As with the other forms of violence, an ethnic/religious cleansing occurs, much as it did in Bosnia. Widespread rapes. Random killings. Looting and destruction. The non-Muslim civilians in these sectors either flee, die, or are forced into servitude. Those who suffer the worst come from families or marriages that were mixed in ethnic or religious terms. They are attacked by all sides and are suddenly forced to declare themselves one way or another."

"When several countries passed laws from 2015 to 2020 forbidding police from monitoring social media without warrants, the skills, and abilities needed to track these groups withered away quickly. We are rebuilding this now, but it will take several days or weeks – if at all – before we can develop a more effective assessment of what is happening. Moreover, with communications networks being shut down, this tool will lose effectiveness as time goes by."

"Overall, we believe that the chaos caused by the pandemic, lockdown protests, the new economic downturn, and the terrorist attacks have created a period of gross instability. Almost all civil society sectors have lost faith in their central governments, and everyone is suspicious of the relationship of Big Tech with the government. Groups such as Los Indignados, M31, and OCCUPY were clear indicators and warnings about the extent of social unrest. Now we have the Reddit Rebels and the Wall Street Bets. Yet, youth unemployment rates of over 50% were explained away as non-structural temporary aberrations when they were the precursors of future trouble. The fact that youth in France, Austria, and Germany was turning to *"soupe identitaires"*[132] as a means of social discourse was lost or ignored by the authorities of the day."

"Several radical Muslim leaders, especially those in the Muslim Brotherhood, were inspired by the ongoing survival of ISIS throughout 2015 and 2016.

---

[132] Unknown, "French Court Bans Right Wing Soup," english.aljazeera.net (Al Jazeera English, January 6, 2007), http://web.archive.org/web/20080203185028/http://engli sh.aljazeera.net/NR/exeres/AA79DF82-6E88-4927-AD4B-726832EC22FF.htm

Their hopes for a global caliphate soared. The economic crash enhanced their own beliefs that Western society was corrupt. This belief was further elevated by the social unrest they saw around them. Thus, it was easier to believe they could attempt an ISIS-style takeover of territory. The model used now is much the same as the June and July 2014 ISIS situation in Iraq. Rapid attacks are employed with extreme violence that spreads terror quickly. Fear is the real weapon, and we believe that the initial attacks were more a matter of opportunism than a well-developed strategic plan. While the individuals concerned were intent on destroying the political institutions of Europe, they probably did not perceive the possibility of a takeover this soon."

"At the same time, the situation inside the radical Muslim community was also in a state of rapid change. For instance, Yousef Qaradawi, one of the leading inspirational thinkers of radical Islam, was suddenly displaced. Qaradawi was a gradualist and believed in taking control over some time. He was not afraid of violence, but he did not focus primarily on it. His voice and method were trusted in many of the most radical circles until ISIS demonstrated in 2014 that an explosion of violence could produce a caliphate."

To himself, Berndt had another thought which he did not present to his current audience. What was the term English speaking bureaucrats used when they did not have accurate answers to criticism? Ah yes, the comments made against them were judged to be *unhelpful*.

"When the systematic rape of 1,400 young girls in Rotherham was publicly disclosed in 2014, nothing happened. While much hand wringing had occurred, all of the old arguments about cultures being equal and the need for more outreach came to the forefront. The class struggle was the issue, said some Fabian types, and it had to be addressed. To various groups of people, having 1,400 girls and women raped in one place is typically the type of action you associate with a conquering army."

The UK had already been conquered in 2014, but saying so would be judged to be unhelpful.

He continued.

"Many of you probably did not notice that Yousef Qaradawi, the former ideological leader of the Muslim Brotherhood, had made it clear that the conquest of Europe was an ongoing goal. His earlier statements in the 1990s were made even more evident in 2007 when he said:

> The peaceful conquest has foundations in this religion, and therefore, I expect that Islam will conquer Europe without resorting to the sword or fighting. It will do so by means of dawah and ideology. Europe is miserable with materialism, with the philosophy of promiscuity, and with the immoral considerations that rule the world "considerations of self-interest and self-indulgence.

"Many of you also did not notice that the works of al-Maududi were being circulated as required reading in mosques, cultural centers, and universities throughout most of Europe and North America. His works are to radical Islam what *Mein Kampf* was to Nazism, or *Das Capital* was to Marxism. Al-Maududi was quite clear on his views. He wrote that:

> *Islam wishes to destroy all states and governments anywhere on the face of the earth which are opposed to the ideology and program of Islam regardless of the country or the Nation which rules it. (...) Islam does not intend to confine this revolution to a single State or a few countries; the aim of Islam is to bring about a universal revolution."*

"Many of what we loosely call the *intelligentsia* were also informed by postmodernism, critical race theory, and deconstructionism. Their thinking skills were further corroded by cultural relativism and the crushing weight of political correctness that was enforced in universities and government."

"That combination did what Orwell had feared. If you can take control of the language, you can take control of the discourse. Intelligent thought has been virtually wiped from public discussions, and anyone who has a differing opinion is removed from the process by being labeled racist or regressive. The so-called progressives have been trapped on their moral high ground by their views on Fabian socialism and their Common Purpose method of organization and ideology. Even now, as their cities are being burned and their children raped, the so-called progressives cannot climb down off their own self-described moral high ground to descend into reality. To admit that there truly is a difference in cultures and that these differences can be described as better or worse would shatter their artificial paradigm. Reality is now shattering that perception for them."

"In conclusion, we can see that four things have happened which will now have a critical impact on how we react."

"First, the economy has been undermined by a high level of long-term debt at all layers of government. The so-called austerity program never started as most governments continued to spend more than they could extract from their populations and tax base. Too much centralization of the economy meant the long-term survival of banks and corporations that should have gone bankrupt were instead rewarded. This was done with huge taxpayer-funded bailouts, which meant fewer resources for the new companies, which might have been productive. The unchecked program of allowing non-qualified migrants rather than a program that sought useful skills furthered this problem as welfare costs soared while debts increased. Fixing this will be the work of a generation, assuming we survive this war."

"Second, the masses, especially those below 50 years of age, have lost faith in the institutions of society. This includes the EU, the IMF, the World Bank, and the UN. These institutions are relics of another age and were designed to maintain the status quo of 1945 to 1948. They are part of the problem, not part of the solution."

"Third, intelligent discourse in society has been virtually destroyed. Many did not see the problems coming because we were not allowed to talk about them. This was like failing to see the fall of the Shah in Iran or the collapse of the Soviet Union. A few people saw the problems, but they were crushed if they spoke out."

"Perhaps most importantly, as a result of the collapse of civil discourse, we were not able to discern the critical threat that was posed by both violent and non-violent extremism. Non-violent extremism was much more dangerous as it undermined the institutions of our state rather than attacking them head-on. We could not discuss extremist Islam in public because we were told we had to be tolerant and could not be Islamophobic. The fact that the Islamists are more intolerant of differences than even fascism or communism was lost."

"The media may be the most to blame. The leading figures were afraid of lawsuits or being responsible for the results of their work. So they chose to remain silent on critical issues even as they were loudly protesting even the most minor of other perceived offenses against political correctness elsewhere."

"Finally, we have allowed the problems to become so far advanced that the normal solutions of policy change, new laws, and fine economic tuning are irrelevant."

"The question is actually rather simple in one sense. If NATO is engaged with the declaration of Article Five, then we will launch into an extended period of killing, which will eclipse the horrors of Bosnia or Kosovo. It may be that most of Europe will look like Lebanon in the 1980s. If we do not, then we can watch the nation-state system in Europe fragment into a series of minor caliphates and principalities as we descend into a new dark age."

"The Great Reset has accelerated this."

"This is the choice you face."

"Europe marches or Europe dies."

Following his brief, the true measure of reality began to sink in. Then the questions started. Berndt knew that most of the questions were simply a way of delaying the inevitable decision that would have to be made.

- What will the Shia groups in Europe do? Will Tehran involve itself in Europe, or will it look to exploit the situation and move in the Middle East instead?
- How many refugees and internally displaced persons are involved? Can it exceed the 20 million being reported in the press? Could it go even higher?
- What of the Russians? Which do they fear more? Will they stand for a series of caliphates in Europe? Are they afraid of radical Islamic uprisings to their south in the 'stan' republics? Would the Russians use tactical nukes in their south to create a

radioactive buffer zone as their radical right is demanding?

- Will the Turkish military mutiny and overthrow their Muslim Brotherhood-inspired leader? If not, will Turkey continue to funnel more arms, money, and personnel into Europe? What does it mean when the press says that Turkey is currently not participating in NATO meetings?
- Will this spread to North America? Are the USA and Canada in the same situation?

Berndt answered each question to the best of his ability, but he knew the answers were hollow and that any single event could suddenly throw off all the calculations.

Berndt noticed that no one had asked who he thought was behind the four terrorist attacks of the 28th of June. It was the question that he dreaded the most, yet no one had asked it. Unfortunately, such was the state of thinking at the strategic level in Europe.

The room eventually relapsed into silence as the various individuals attempted to process and understand what they faced. It was tough to decide what had hit them harder, the nearly casual observation that they were entering a period of civil war or the not-too-discrete implied threat that came from the analysis of failing police morale and capabilities. The police withdrawal and regrouping also suggested their unwillingness to protect civic leaders at nearly every level.

The Head of the European Commission and Enrica Leclercq remained silent.

SACEUR and his G3 sat without moving for what seemed an eternity.

Finally, SACEUR broke the silence. Quietly and lacking any emotion in his voice, he stated that NATO would be called upon to enforce Article Five if the decision were reached. This would create a legal fig leaf, and the various states would begin military action to retake the territory declared to be caliphates. The foreign invasion would then be fought.

He asked, "Are there other views that we need to hear?"

Chapter 34: Riding the Fear

LOCATION: Residence of CRJ, Brussels, Belgium

DATE: 17 July

TIME: 7:00 PM

CRJ was preparing to stick a knife in Enrica Leclercq. His long-term plan to seize power was unfolding as planned. The next major step was to discredit Enrica and blame the violence on her and her Great Reset program.

The violence needed by CRJ for his plan was accelerating. The levels of fear in Europe were building everywhere, from street-corner cafes to the headquarters of NATO. Better still, social media discussions were awash with fear and angry rhetoric. The targets of the anger discussions were wide-ranging. Among them were the European Union, the Islamists, NATO, and the economy. More importantly, from CRJ's point of view, most of the angriest comments on news articles and social media sites were aimed at Enrica and her Great Reset launch.

The knife, such as it was, was ready.

CRJ had spent five years anonymously leaking information to various journalists, podcasters, and social media influencers. His approach had been to send insider information to the recipients, typically on financial announcements about to occur in a week to ten days. The cleverest recipient might be able to use the information to profit from insider trading, but nothing huge. CRJ also sent occasional tidbits of hot gossip about the most senior leadership figures from around the world. The gossip leaks intended to show the recipients that their anonymous source was an insider with access to financial data and connected at the senior political level.

Now, after five years of grooming, CRJ had a cadre of media contacts who would inherently trust whatever he sent them. Better still, this time, he would send audio recordings with the leaks to back up his stories. Enrica had provided the material when they had met in his car on the first of July without knowing it. A bit of creative editing would show that the Grand Reset was Enrica's project from the start and that she was the driving force behind it.

CRJ was cheerfully working away on his computer. He had chosen five journalists, two social media influencers, two podcasters, and one individual he knew to be little more than a conspiracy theorist. Each would get a small package consisting of two sheets of paper and one USB stick. One sheet of paper would make a coherent argument that Enrica Leclercq, while acting as the *High Representative of the Union for Foreign Affairs and Security Policy*, put into motion a series of actions that set Europe on fire.

Even with a history of accurate anonymous leaks to his contacts, CRJ recognized they would have a hard time believing this story. It was for this moment that

CRJ had recorded his conversation with Erica on the first of July. Could that have been only 16 days ago? He was now making a transcript with two selected extracts. CRJ had deliberately guided their conversation in the car, hoping to lead Enrica into making incriminating statements. Instead, he had deliberately remained silent and let her speak.

CRJ looked down at the first transcript and reread it. It was what he needed. He could imagine the recipients reading the first page and wondering whether they should even believe what they were reading. Then they would read the transcripts and shake their heads in wonderment and disbelief. Then they would put the USB sticks into their computer and listen to the MP4 files named Enrica1.mra and Enrica2.mra.

The voice of Enrica Leclercq describing how a financial crisis was needed to create a political crisis and how the assassination of Ilhan Benhaddara had been 'particularly good' would send them over the edge. CRJ laughed to himself as he pictured the various contacts calling their editors and producers, telling them they had the story of the century.

CRJ printed off his transcripts and held them up. It was, he decided, time for another drink of Remy Martin Louis XIII brandy.

> Enrica1.mra *"We need the economic crash to cause a financial crisis. That in turn will cause a sovereign debt crisis and most countries will hit a wall on borrowing. That in turn will cause a*

significant austerity crisis which will cause social unrest at a massive level. That is when we make the final push to get rid of national sovereignty and private property. I can declare an emergency for three months to control social media and the press long enough to put the plans into effect."

Enrica2.mra *"The assassination of Ilhan Benhaddara was particularly good. Everyone from the CIA to Mossad and British White Power groups are being blamed. Starting this afternoon, I will be putting out a series of messages to the EU Parliament, the EU Commission, NATO, the OECD, the UN Security Council, and every head of state in the EU. The message will be clear. My title as the High Representative for the European Union for Foreign Affairs and Security Policy means that I am the primary national security advisor for Europe. The message will be clear. Given this new wave of terrorist attacks, we have much to fear. Our leaders have been weak from fear. Now is the time for action to stop the fear. Now is the time to drive away the fear and secure the future."*

After the drink, CRJ set back to work, this time wearing surgical-style gloves. He would open a new package of paper and envelopes and new stamps. He would touch none of them. As each sheet of paper came out of the printer, he would take his scissors, carefully wiped them down with bleach, and cut a small section of paper out of each page. If the police were to investigate, they would not even be able to determine the type of printer used.[133] The audio recorder that had recorded the conversation with Erica had been bought for cash in a small shop in downtown Brussels. There was no metadata or other information that would track back to CRJ himself.

Once the letters were sealed and stamped, his driver would be directed to drive around Brussels and drop off the envelopes in widely separated public mailboxes. Of course, the driver would have no idea of the contents, just as he had no idea of the contents of the other mail drops that he had been making for five years.

The pen, CRJ thought to himself, is sometimes mightier than the sword.

A few pieces of paper would now change the course of history, God willing.

---

[133] Chris Baraniuk, "Why Printers Add Secret Tracking Dots," BBC.com (BBC, June 3, 2020), https://www.bbc.com/future/article/20170607-why-printers-add-secret-tracking-dots

Chapter 35: That Which We Once Feared

LOCATION: Hessen Reinsurance

DATE: 18 July

TIME: 05:57 AM

Jochen was sitting outside Aldo Lange's office. The clock on the wall said it was 05:57 AM. The head of security for Hessen Reinsurance had arrived at Jochen's apartment just after midnight. The message had been short. "Mr. Lange requests your presence in his office at six in the morning. You will come alone and will tell no one about this. You will turn off your phone now and will not turn it on again until after the meeting."

When Jochen had attempted to ask the purpose of the meeting, the head of security had simply turned his back and walked away.

Message delivered.

Looking out the windows, Jochen could still see smoke rising from buildings that had been set afire last night. Each night, more fires occurred, and they were spread out over a wider area. It was not just the Islamists causing the violence. Since the 'Great Reset' announcement from Enrica Leclercq, it looked like every extremist group, from the anarcho-syndicalists to the neo-Nazis, were on the streets. The Frankfurt police were overwhelmed, and no help could be expected from neighboring police departments as they were equally overstretched.

The night had been sleepless.

Jochen had sat in front of his laptop all night, trying to keep up with the news of the expanding violence and reading several reports on extremist websites.

His mind was not on the news. Instead, it was on Aldo Lange. The request for an early morning meeting had been unprecedented but perhaps not a surprise given the events of the last 20 days.

In his heart, Jochen was uncertain about Aldo Lange's views. On the one hand, Aldo had provided Jochen with nearly endless resources and information. Even more so, Lange had run interference to protect Jochen and his team from both the federal police and intelligence services when their work had implicated government authorities or strayed into gray areas of the law. Jochen and his team had provided Aldo the first assessment of how the violence in Europe had been planned. However, the critical point was that Aldo Lange, even though he was in private industry and not government, was well connected to the elites of Europe, including the IMF, the European Central Bank, the European Union, and a multitude of others.

Now, with one minute left to the meeting, Jochen still did not know if he could fully understand or trust Aldo Lange. It was clear that the entire European economic, financial, social, and political landscape of Europe was about to change. Violently.

At precisely six o'clock, Aldo Lange opened his office door. Despite the early morning hour and what must have been a punishing few weeks, he was immaculately dressed, looking like he could walk into any boardroom in the Western world and command respect.

Upon entering the office, Jochen was directed to sit at the smaller table near the window. The room was silent. Aldo Lange was staring out the window. His eyes focused on some far distant object that only he could see. Jochen had heard this referred to this as a thousand-yard stare.[134]

While Lange was staring out the window, Jochen sat perfectly still, not wanting to be the one to break the moment. He moved only his eyes to the bookshelf.

At that moment, Jochen felt he knew where the meeting was going and what he believed about Aldo Lange. The photo of Lange, standing alone in front of the *Schlosskirche* – the castle church – was still on his shelf. Lange's visit to the place where Martin Luther had begun the Reformation spoke of a man who had a moral compass and a concept of values.

---

[134] From a medical standpoint, the thousand-yard stare represents that a person has experienced such significant trauma that they have had to dissociate or disconnect from the world or from other people. By going numb, by not feeling, they may still be functional in their environment.

Aldo Lange suddenly turned from the window and faced Jochen directly. "Sorry for the late-night messenger service. It has become clear to me that all my phones are likely being monitored. I had the office swept for bugs again last night, and this time there were two listening devices. Any form of electronic communication is being monitored for two reasons. You and your team are the first. The analytical work of your team, plus the presence of foreign nationals at the off-site meeting, has drawn attention. Unfortunately, not all the attention was good."

Jochen began to respond, but Lange cut him off with a wave of his hand.

"Do not worry about that. I agree with most of what you have said, and it has been a great service to me and many others. The other reason for all the spying on us is my position on the Great Reset and the attacks. I have been rather direct with a few financial leaders from other corporations, and I have said similar things to our police and intelligence services. My conclusion is that the Great Reset is little more than a coup intended to take over the European Union and turn it into a totalitarian state with the worst aspects of communism, fascism, and bureaucracies all rolled into one. Europe, as the center of Reformation, learning, culture and freedom is finished if this carries on."

Jochen sensed that Aldo Lange was just starting, so he simply nodded and said, "Agreed."

"Today is the last day of normality for Hessen Reinsurance. As with the rest of Europe, the company will now change whether it wants to or not. Unfortunately, my board of directors is full of fools. They are still talking about adjusting our business model until the situation gets 'back to normal.' Years of complacency and wealth have dulled their minds into passivity."

Aldo Lange paused, and Jochen could see something important was coming.

"There are several reasons why you are here today. First, you need to bring me up to speed on your most recent analysis. Second, however, I have a video conference with the Reich Chancellery at 8:00 AM with the Chancellor and the Interior Minister. I managed to arrange this meeting through your former boss at the Deutsche Bundesbank. The meeting will be at the BKA office here in Frankfurt. We will use their secure conference facility."

"My contacts in the financial world and the business world agree on little except for one thing. The Great Reset announcement by Enrica Leclercq has caught everyone by surprise, including most elements of government at the EU and national level."

"It is not something I would usually share with a relatively new employee like yourself, but Hessen has been restructuring over the last several years. Following the 2008/09 recession, it became clear that no lessons were learned from the financial disaster. The government and the financial industry decision-makers simply doubled down on their previous mistakes and kept on going. Synthetic derivatives. Mortgage-backed securities. Quantitative easing. Negative interest rates. Collateralized debt obligations. Massive debts. The financialization of the economy. Corporations were buying their own stock to spike the market price. All these practices are sheer madness. These are the people who believe you can create wealth with more and more debt. The reality is that wealth only increases when you build something. Today's so-called financial experts in the major banks are little more than grifters who have found ways to skim wealth from everyone while putting us into long-term debt and financial servitude."

Aldo Lange looked around the room and smiled. "Sorry for the rant. I have been silently frustrated for years, watching the insanity grow. Notwithstanding all of this, I would ask you and your team to stay with the company for now. There are no guarantees that the company will survive given the destruction. Insurance losses will be staggering, even presuming we still have an intact financial system a few weeks or months from now. However, there is some good news. Since 2016, I have been quietly restructuring the company. We have sold off some properties and rented the office space back. We have been slowly moving profits into holding companies. The upshot is that we have converted a considerable amount of capital over the last few years into precious metals – mostly gold but some silver. The metals have been stored offshore, mostly in Singapore and Canada. Whatever happens over the next weeks and months, we have what most other companies will not have – stored wealth and working capital. Hessen has no debt, so it may yet survive. So will you stay?"

Jochen nodded. "I will stay. I cannot speak for the others, but my belief is they will stay as well. They may stay out of loyalty, or they may stay out of curiosity as to what happens next, but these last few weeks have been the most fascinating time of all of our lives."

Lange leaned in and said, "Is it even possible that the Islamists believe they have a hope of winning? They only make up about seven to nine percent of the population in France[135], five percent in Belgium[136], and about five percent in Germany.[137] So how do they hope to have any real victory or even gain?

"Too many people say that without having a sense of how such things work," said Jochen. "The number of people you need to overthrow society, or so at least

---

[135] Unknown Editors, "France: People and Society - Religions," The World Factbook (Central Intelligence Agency, May 6, 2021), https://www.cia.gov/the-world-factbook/countries/france/#people-and-society.
[136] Unknown Editors, "Belgium: People and Society - Religions," The World Factbook (Central Intelligence Agency, May 4, 2021), https://www.cia.gov/the-world-factbook/countries/belgium/#people-and-society .
[137] Unknown Editors, "Germany: People and Society - Religions," The World Factbook (Central Intelligence Agency, April 30, 2021), https://www.cia.gov/the-world-factbook/countries/germany/#people-and-society .

change it dramatically, is rather small. As the Bolsheviks showed in Russia and the Nazis proved here in Germany, you need less than three percent of the population to take over – given that other social and economic factors are favorable to your position. The Nazis had less than three percent of the population as party members when they seized power. Even at that, many party members were probably members of convenience who joined to get jobs and contracts rather than any real sense of belief in the cause. The same goes for the Bolsheviks. They had way less than three percent of the population as members of the party. It took them years, but they took over and then implemented a most oppressive regime. It lasted 75 years. What is important is that the party members are true believers and willing to act out."

"What about influence in a democracy short of revolution?"

Jochen paused to consider his response for several seconds. "You do not need 50% plus one to take control of democracy. Opinions and circumstances vary, but a minority population of less than 10% can change the entire direction of a society. Of course, that population must have a certain degree of coherence. But, indeed, an active and intelligent 10% minority can fundamentally change the nature of society. It takes a few years and a lot of money, but it can be done."

"So, the Islamists in Europe all work together? Are they are a united force?

"The Islamist leadership works hard to portray the Muslims of Europe as a united group – an ummah. The reality is more complicated than that. The Islamist claim to be the voice of Muslims in Europe, but this is doubtful. What they have done is successfully taken over almost every organized group of Muslims. They use that to convince an array of governments that only they can speak for Muslims. At the same time, they undertake extensive campaigns of coercion and blacklisting to ensure that any Muslim voice that speaks out against them is crushed. As a result, they are not so much united as forced to submit to the will of the Muslim Brotherhood, a few Salafists, and the Diyanet."

"Why did they choose to move now? I have heard it said they were not prepared to take action for another five or so years?"

"This is also a complex question," said Jochen. "It is unlikely that they had any role in initiating the current conflict. The Islamists were likely provoked into doing what they were going to do anyway, but they found they had to move earlier. Another reason for their hard push now also exists. The Muslim Brotherhood and the others have been successful in taking over most of the Muslim community. As a result, a lot of younger Muslims are going in different directions. Some are following the Muslim Brotherhood, while others are moving up to work with groups like ISIS. However, a new pattern is emerging as well. Lots of younger Muslims are simply walking away from the faith – both the moderate and the extremist political versions. It is difficult to say, but senior leaders in the Muslim Brotherhood have been forced into a *now or never* situation. They are at their peak level of strength, and they have to become more aggressive and violent."

Lange picked up his coffee cup and walked over to his desk while he pondered this latest information. "After the formation of the European Union, I had not considered the idea that Europe could be consumed with conflict again. At least not the member states. Following the recession of 2009, however, I began to have doubts. However, the pandemic was an inflection point, and I could see the great forces at work that may now be unleashed. That is, of course, why I stole you away from the Bundesbank with the permission of Sebastian Koehn. By the way, he is an ally and did not want to see you stay at the central bank while this was happening. Yet here we are. My optimistic view is that we face massive violent social unrest. My pessimistic view is that we will have tanks in the street and widespread armed conflict. Once again, the cities may burn."

"I think you are closer to being right about the cities burning that you may care to believe."

"Explain yourself."

"You remember my Dutch colleague from the off-site meeting on the 12th of July? He has communicated that contrary to much of the media speculation, NATO will go ahead and declare that Article Five is in effect. They may do that as soon as today. So if

Berndt is correct, we will see tanks in the street sooner than you believe."

Aldo Lange laughed for a second before a look of resignation covered his face. "Jochen, when I was a much younger man, I believed that I had been cursed by being born in a time of boredom with no great adventures to be had. Now, as an older man, I fear that we live in a time of great adventure."

Jochen nodded in agreement. "While we are talking about great adventures, maybe now would be a good time to tell you who is behind the current violence. We may have cracked the case, so to speak, late yesterday afternoon, and I am awaiting confirmation now." Jochen pulled out his phone and showed it to Aldo Lange.

"It is almost six-thirty. I know what you said about shutting our phones off due to monitoring, but I expect a text message in the next few minutes. It may tell us who was responsible for the terrorist attacks on the 28th of June."

"Who is going to tell us that?"

Jochen reached into his pocket and turned on a small flip phone he had never used before. "It's a rather long story, but the same team we had at the off-site meeting on the 11th and 12th of June have been working on the problem. It has been a painful process, but we have narrowed down the possibilities. Daniel, Isabel, Sergio, and Carsten have been working on nothing but this for the last five days. They now have the answer we need, or at least I think we do. We will know in a few minutes."

"My God, Jochen!" Aldo Lange looked dangerously close to being angry. "We have known since the off-site meeting that all of our communications must be monitored. The BKA officer in my office bragged about his links to the British GCHQ. He also inferred he was dealing with 'the fort' in America. I figured out afterward that this is the NSA! Everything you have said will be in their hands by now."

"I rather doubt that, Sir." Jochen had turned the conversation back from a first name basis and back to a more formal tone.

"Horst may be good at working on the Dark Net, but I doubt he can beat them, especially when they are watching us anyway."

"Horst is not involved in the message traffic when we are discussing the real issue. He keeps up a minimal series of Proton Mail encrypted messages between the team members. He is also sending a few texts on Signal. The information in the messages is purely diversionary. I do not know if the Swiss have handed the encryption keys over to the TLAs,[138] but nothing of any significance will be in their hands even if they have. We are not using WhatsApp.[139] If we were,

---

[138] TLAs = Three Letter Agencies, which refers to the majority of agencies which members of the Intelligence Community, e.g. the CIA, NSA, FBI, DoD, NGA, MI5, CSE etc.
[139] "About WhatsApp," WhatsApp.com (WhatsApp LLC, 2021), https://www.whatsapp.com/about/ .

they would know we are not serious as WhatsApp has been compromised for years.[140]   It is useless as a secure communications tool in the face of the TLAs."

"I don't believe this at all. You are trying to tell me you are smarter than the spy agencies?"

"Not smarter. Simply better. Or maybe different. I doubt the TLAs even know we have a separate communications network. Even if they did, it is highly improbable they could track it. Most importantly, even if they could track it, the coding system is based on a one-time pad[141] (OTP) system. It is unbreakable. After that, we have another layer of coding that only we can use. With certainty, they do not know what we have been talking about, and they will not know what the conclusions of our work will be. When we tell you who started the terrorist attacks, they will not know."

"So, how does this magic network of yours work? Do you have trans-Atlantic carrier pigeons? Does Mata Hari work for us now?"

Jochen thought a moment on how much he should tell Aldo Lange about the network. The most

---

[140] Bruce Schneier, "Changes in WhatsApp's Privacy Policy," Schneier on Security (https://www.schneier.com/ , January 11, 2021), https://www.schneier.com/blog/archives/2021/01/changes-in-whatsapps-privacy-policy.html .
[141] Unknown, "One-Time Pad," en.wikipedia.org (Wikimedia Foundation, May 4, 2021), https://en.wikipedia.org/wiki/One-time_pad

important fact was that he needed Aldo to trust both the analysis of the network plus its security, so he decided to tell him most of it while leaving out a few key details.

"We have a network which is centered on a radio operator here in Frankfurt. He is at the center of the network with nodes in Amsterdam, Rome, Oslo, and Ottawa. The radio operators are all hams or amateur radio operators. I communicate with the Frankfurt node with handwritten messages delivered to him by a dead drop box.[142] He then sends out my message to the others. It is done on High-Frequency Radio using between five to forty watts of power. The genius of the system is that it is based on computer sound cards. Technology has changed over the last five years. There are now at least 70 different sound card modes available to us. The older modes have a limited ability to transmit any volume of data, but some of the more esoteric newer codes have improved that. The programs for this are neither large nor expensive, and some of them are free. They take anywhere from 400K to 40 megs on a hard drive. Even the most ancient steam-powered laptops running Windows XP can handle most of them. For a relatively new laptop, this is nothing."

Aldo appeared to be following, so Jochen pushed on with the explanation.

---

[142] Unknown, "Dead Drop or Dead Letter Box," cryptomuseum.com (Crypto Museum, October 4, 2018), https://cryptomuseum.com/covert/deaddrop/index.htm

"The key to all of this is to use one-time pad encryption; shorten the transmissions themselves; use unique codes in the messages; employ non-standard frequencies and change them every time. On top of that, there have been considerable changes in the solar weather recently. Our operator here knows to watch for changes in the solar flux on an hour-by-hour basis and then determine which frequencies are best for any given moment. The frequencies being used are as far down towards the noise floor as they can be. Consequently, anyone trying to monitor them will have a tough time trying to pick out the actual signal that appears against a background of noise. The signal-to-noise ratio is critical, but the new software is amazing. Only the most experienced monitor would be able to pick out the signal here. This is not new stuff, of course. The concept and ideas trace back to the early work of an American named Joe Taylor, who had the call sign K1JT. Others have followed and improved it. It gets even better. The software now can track the signal strength and noise level. When a response message goes back, it can choose even better frequencies to make this process harder to detect again. Just to be difficult, the tones used in the transmission are inverted. Again, not an unbreakable system, but it makes it that much more unlikely it will be detected."

Aldo put up his hand to tell Jochen to stop. "I will have to take your word for this on the technical stuff. This is well outside of my area. But cannot the TLAs sweep up everything and then go back through it?"

432

"Highly unlikely, but if they do, they will get nothing. The messages we send are structured, so the information transmitted will only have a series of letters or numbers, which will appear meaningless to an outside observer unless they have the message structure outline to go with it. The next layer of defense is the one-time pad system we set up at the off-site meeting. When they are used once, they are unbreakable. If the message has, for instance, the alphanumeric code OTP18, they will know that the following characters are to be understood through the use of the one-time pad coding system. A 'Q' in the right place will indicate the next group of characters should be understood through the Q code systems, and a P means the Phillips code system.[143] Then, to take it one step further, that will only produce more alphanumeric characters. Those characters can only be understood by decoding them with a book that we have all agreed upon. For instance, the five-character set P8W55 would tell the reader to go to page eight of the book and look at the fifty-fifth word. There is another way to identify a geographic location. It is called the Maidenhead locator system.[144] It is well known to radio amateurs, but not so much to others. On top of everything else, the radio operators themselves have no idea of what

[143] Unknown, "Phillips Code," en.wikipedia.org (Wikimedia Foundation, June 5, 2021),
https://en.wikipedia.org/wiki/Phillips_Code
[144] Unknown, "Grid Squares," arrl.org (American Radio Relay League, 1980), http://www.arrl.org/grid-squares

the messages are saying, nor do they fully know what this is all about. But we have agreed to pay for the upgrade of some of their equipment. By we, of course, I mean you and the company."

"Not that it matters at this point, but what is this going to cost me? Hundreds of thousands of Euros? A million?"

Jochen laughed out loud. "No. We did not go overboard as we did with Karl's dinner. Even with some of the software and the promise of a new laptop for each of the radio operators, the full cost of defeating the TLAs will be under five thousand Euros, and we can use this network again at no cost."

"So, how will you find out what the team has discovered? If they phone or text, does that not give away what we are doing?"

"No. I had my sister buy two burner phones a week ago in Heidelberg using cash in a local store with no video cameras. She sent them to me by courier. They have not been used. Last night, I left one at the dead drop box with a note telling my operator to contact me with it by text this morning at 06:45 AM. He will likely drive across Frankfurt to another location, so the cell phone uses a tower that is not near where he lives. After he uses the phone, he will throw it in the river."

Aldo looked at the clock on the wall and walked over to his desk. He picked up the landline and dialed four digits – an internal number. "More coffee, please. Lots more coffee."

They sat in silence for a while, neither one knowing what to do as they waited for what might be the most important message of their lives.

Aldo finally broke the silence. "You mentioned a book used for the coding. Should I ask the name of the book? Or will you have to kill me if you tell me the title?" The last question was delivered with a tired smile, even if it was not yet seven in the morning.

"It was not a book. It was more of a thesis," said Jochen as he pointed to the photo of Aldo Lange on the steps of the Castle Church in Wittenberg.

Aldo Lange looked perplexed for a moment before getting the reference. "The Ninety-Five Theses.[145] Brilliant idea – and amazingly appropriate under the circumstances."

The ensuing silence was broken by the sound of a single ping from Jochen's burner phone. He flipped it open and read the one-word message with no sign of surprise on his face. Next, he turned the phone so Aldo could see the word 'Yes' on the screen. He then turned off the power to the phone and twisted it so the two sections of the phone broke apart. "This will also go in the river later this morning."

---

[145] Unknown, "Ninety-Five Theses," en.wikipedia.org (Wikimedia Foundation, March 31, 2021), https://en.wikipedia.org/wiki/Ninety-five_Theses

"Well?"

"As I thought. The man behind the first wave of bombings is the managing director of the International Monetary Fund. It is CRJ himself."

Aldo Lange's coffee cup hit the far wall and shattered into pieces. His face went so white that Jochen thought about his last dog sledding trip. On a cloudless day, the snow in the wilds of Canada was the purest form of white.

"Impossible!"

"When we left the off-site meeting, we believed that the four attacks on the 28th of June were setups. That much was clear. We also believed that organizing these attacks had to be done by a group of people with considerable financial resources, superior planning skills, and strategic patience. The Great Reset announcement by Enrica Leclercq initially led us to believe that she must be either the mastermind of the violence or at least the leader of a group of senior government officials from multiple organizations. We had considered CRJ as the most likely leader, but we had only circumstantial evidence for that. Large numbers of leading figures in the EU were working towards the Great Reset. That was not a secret. Klaus Schwab's book was even called *COVID-19: The Great Reset*.[146] Yet virtually every senior leadership figure in

---

[146] Klaus Schwab and Thierry Malleret, "COVID-19: The Great Reset," Amazon.com (ISBN Agentur Schweiz, July 9, 2020), https://www.amazon.com/COVID-19-Great-Reset-

the EU appears to have been startled by the turn of events. A variety of indicators, conversations with some of their staffers, and their private emails all expressed astonishment at the Great Reset announcement. They had no idea it was coming – and certainly not from Enrica Leclercq."

"You are saying that CRJ has gone rogue and that Enrica is supporting him in all of this? They are behind the Great Reset, and everything that will now fall out from it?"

"No. He is the master. She is the puppet. We also believe that the Great Reset is not the objective. Rather it is a masterful deception that is working to camouflage a larger goal."

Jochen paused for a few seconds again. He realized that what he was saying was akin to saying the Gnomes of Europe were working with the Order of Knights Templar to take over the world.

"Impossible! Or perhaps I should say impossible again. If the Great Reset is not the objective, then what is happening? Why are all these people dying?"

"Our collective belief is that CRJ is about to pull a Trudeau. He will throw a woman under the bus, in this case, Enrica Leclercq, then blame her for everything. The fear will continue to grow. While that is happening, he may decide to present himself as the rational choice for a new leader in Europe. In short, it is a political coup."

"This is insanity on steroids. Does CRJ believe he can get away with this?"

"We did some digging into the family background, his family's companies, and some of his interests. The books he has ordered, and his research interests, suggest he may have a grievance narrative. His family lost their social positions and property in the collapse of the Austro-Hungarian Empire during World War One. We have tracked the front companies involved in some of the financial transactions. As far as we can tell, his family has substantial financial resources of its own, even though they maintain a relatively low profile. Additionally, Horst seems to think that CRJ has used money from both the International Monetary Fund and the World Bank. The amount of money used to set up the four terrorist attacks on the 28th of June must have run into the millions of Euros."

"How certain are you that it is him? Can he be doing this by himself? It all seems like such a nightmare."

Jochen handed Aldo a printout. "The financial trail has a few holes in it, but there is enough evidence here to lay it out in a courtroom. As for the rest of it, it is a bit thin, but we believe that CRJ is responsible for the four attacks and setting up Enrica. Another interesting fact. The attacks were on the 28th of June, the same day Gavrilo Princip assassinated the Archduke in Sarajevo. That assassination unleashed the events that destroyed CRJ's family and forced them to leave Austria. After that, they set themselves up in France."

"He must have had help. This was a huge undertaking."

"There is little doubt that he had help in setting up the contacts to organize the attacks. But we think you will find that there was only one person who had the whole picture. He told no one below him or beside him. He must have learned from Anders Breivik in this respect."

Aldo was silent for a few seconds. "Breivik, the Norwegian terrorist who murdered all those children on the island?"

"The same one. Breivik wrote in his manifesto that he could plan out two major attacks because he never told anyone what he was doing. Breivik worked on his plan for years, but no one in his family or circle of associates had any idea what he was doing even after the attacks. I would say the same goes for CRJ. He was able to lead a double life for years."

"Who have you told about this?"

"No one outside our team. We just put all of this together over the last 24 hours."

"Good. Does Berndt know as well?"

"He will have found out at the same time we did, plus or minus an hour or so."

"Will he tell his colleagues at NATO?"

"Not sure, but my belief is he will. He has to, given his official position."

"Fair enough. If you can, contact him and say it would be best to share everything as fast as possible. I will also give you a name when I leave. She is a journalist that I trust implicitly. Call her from my desk and tell her everything you know. You do not have to give her the names of your team members but explain everything else."

"Should I put any hold on the story, or do you want her to get it out as fast as possible?"

"Tell her that anytime after 11:00 this morning is good. I doubt she will be able to write up a story like that and get it past her editors any faster."

"Done."

"I expect to be back from the meeting no later than 9:30. You will stay in the office here and talk to only the reporter and your team. Tell your team to stay in their office when they get here and let them know they will get further directions by about 10:30."

"Will you tell those at the meeting about CRJ and how we believe he is behind all of this."

"Yes."

"That should be interesting as CRJ has many well-connected and powerful friends. What you are saying will not be appreciated. You will get resistance."

"Good point, but may I remind you that I am one of those people who you describe as well connected in those circles? I have met him on more than one occasion. Our common friend in the Deutsche Bundesbank warned me about getting too close to him. His private life may have had a few small problems."

"Horst mentioned that. It seems there are some rumors in police circles about CRJ and a willingness to assault vulnerable women. He and the late Prime Minister Trudeau would have got along well."

Aldo Lange's cell phone beeped, and he checked his watch. "Time for me to go. My driver is outside. Like I said, stay here until I get back. Then we will talk more."

* * *

Jochen sat in the office alone for a few minutes, wondering where Europe was going and what role he had just played. Then, a discrete tap on the door announced that more coffee and pastries had arrived. Jochen thanked the staff member, pouring himself another coffee, and moved to sit at Aldo's desk. He leaned back in the chair and took in the office and the view. It would be easy to get used to such comfort and amenities. But would he be happy? All told, Jochen was most comfortable when in the middle of a group of analysts working on complex problems that crossed various intellectual and real-world boundaries.

Jochen pulled out his cell phone and called Karl. "Keep everyone in the office. Tell no one what we have just figured out. Order food if you want, but do not leave. I will call you again around 10:00 this morning."

Karl did not sound impressed. "Are they going to try and gag us and stop the truth from getting out?"

"Quite the opposite. The story is going out later this morning. Meanwhile, the boss is off for a video conference at the building where some of your former colleagues work. More on that later, I suspect. Remember, talk to no one yet."

Karl was going to answer, but Jochen had already hung up.

Jochen then picked up Aldo's desk phone and dialed the number he had been given for the journalist.

The phone was answered on the second ring. "Is this Jochen?"

Jochen, momentarily taken back, said, "Yes, it is. How did you know who would call?"

"Mr. Lange just texted me and said you would call from his office number. He said I should talk to you and take everything you say as though it was coming from him."

"Do you have a pen and lots of paper?"

"Yes."

"Good. This is a bit of a complex story. I know little of journalism, but I believe that your editor is going to give you a raise soon, assuming we are all still in business."

"I am ready."

"Do you know CRJ – also known as Clement Raes-Javier?"

"You mean the managing director of the IMF?"

"That is him. He has been a bad boy lately."

An hour later, Jochen hung up the phone. The journalist's questions had been polite, but she had a hard time believing what she had been told. Nonetheless, she told Jochen that the story would be out later that morning on her paper's website.

With that, Jochen decided to pick up the pieces of the shattered coffee cup, put them in an envelope, and dropped it in the trash can. He then headed back to the chairs and table by the window. The large desk was nice, but he felt more comfortable in the chairs.

He looked at the clock on the wall. It was getting close to 09:30. Looking out the window, there were still a few spirals of smoke rising. All was not well.

* * *

Aldo Lange walked in the door at 09:45. His face was blank and showed no emotion.

"How did the meeting go? Did you tell them about CRJ?"

"We were less than five minutes into the meeting before I told them. Unfortunately, the result was not good. The Chancellor appeared to be either frustrated, angry, or perhaps both. Everyone had lots of questions, but clearly, they either do not, or more likely, will not believe that all of this is the result of CRJ by himself."

"Could we try to provide more evidence? I can call the team. They are probably working on it anyway."

"There is no point in more evidence at this time. But do call the team and tell them to communicate nothing now. We will call again in about an hour or so."

Jochen called Karl, passing on the message. When he hung up, Aldo Lange started to talk.

"For the first time in years, I do not know what to do next. It was made clear that I should not do anything until the Office of the Chancellor calls back. I believe that they may understand what they have been told, in which case we may have further involvement. Both of us will have a future. The other possibility is that they will not believe it, and the company and I are finished. The next step may very well be an orderly wind-down of the business."

"Given all the other shocks that have occurred over the last three weeks, perhaps they will be more receptive?"

"I do not know, Jochen. Here I sit with no idea what to do next. Everything depends on the next phone call. Just as I feel I should be busy, I am forced to sit here and do nothing for more than an hour. Meanwhile, let us have more coffee."

With that, Aldo Lange picked up his coffee cup and turned to look out the window.

Jochen watched the clock mark off the passing of five minutes, which for some reason felt like more than an hour. It was frustrating. He was sitting with one of the best informed and connected people in the financial world. Business leaders would pay a fortune or sell their souls for such an opportunity. Yet they sat in silence.

Finally, Jochen could contain himself no more.

Pointing to the photo on the shelf, Jochen asked, "Mr. Lange. When did you first start to believe that the European project was in real trouble?"

"Why do you ask?"

"The only photo of you in your office is you on the exact steps of the same church where Martin Luther is said to have nailed his Ninety-Five Theses. Whatever happened after, Luther is seen as a pragmatic reformer who based his views on moral grounds. You admired him, which somehow tells me why you are supporting our work, which you could silence in a heartbeat if you wanted. I also believe that your decision to support us did not occur overnight. You have seen problems coming for years. This is why you conspired with Sebastian Koehn at the Deutsche Bundesbank to move me here. When did you first see the problems coming?

"It is a bit complicated. My parents grew up in the shadow of World War Two. My mother was a survivor of the bombing of Dresden[147] and a refugee from East Germany. My father grew up in Hamburg. I have supported the idea of a united Europe as far back as I can remember. Whatever its faults, I believed that we could not afford another war. I supported the Schengen Agreement[148] in 1985 and again in 1990. I supported the Maastricht Treaty[149] in 1993 and the creation of the Euro in 1999. The war in Yugoslavia was an eye-opener. How is it that the European Union could not respond to such a conflict on its borders? But I explained the doubts to myself by saying the EU would get better as it went along. Then came the

---

[147] Unknown Editors, "Bombing of Dresden in World War II," Wikipedia (Wikimedia Foundation, May 4, 2021), https://en.wikipedia.org/wiki/Bombing_of_Dresden_in_World_War_II.
[148] Unknown, "The Schengen Agreement - History and the Definition," SchengenVisaInfo.com (Schengen Visa Information, March 3, 2021), https://www.schengenvisainfo.com/schengen-agreement/.
[149] "Maastricht Treaty," en.wikipedia.org (Wikimedia Foundation, May 31, 2021), https://en.wikipedia.org/wiki/Maastricht_Treaty.

financial crisis of 2008/2009. Again, the EU responded, but the responses were all band-aids, and nothing was fixed, even two or three years later. Do you follow so far?"

"Yes."

"The year 2013 was pivotal for two reasons, both of which were of minor consequence, but forced me to accept that something was wrong. The first event was in early May. I had attended some conferences on the future of the Euro Zone. Dry stuff. But I had lunch with an individual who was a Vice President of Risk at Deutsche Bank. She told me that the European project was beginning to fail on generational lines. For her, those over forty were largely supporters of the EU, fearing as they did a return to war, having grown up around bombed out buildings and hunger. By contrast, those under forty knew nothing of war and deprivation and were becoming increasingly distrustful of the whole European idea. They were more focused on falling living standards, the environment, and being part of the 700 Euro generation. For them, OCCUPY, and Los Indignados[150] were more relevant than the parliament in Strasbourg. It is unfortunate that the bureaucrats and politicians were in such a rush to destroy the OCCUPY movement. They raised several valid concerns in social and financial reform areas that should have

---

[150] Unknown Editors, "Spain's Indignados Protest Here to Stay," BBC News (BBC, May 15, 2012), https://www.bbc.com/news/world-europe-18070246 .

been addressed. Instead, we now have more wealth disparity and a greater potential for social unrest."

Aldo stood up and walked towards the windows. Then, after pausing for a few seconds, he began talking again.

"You are going to laugh at the next part. Less than a week later, I was in Brussels for meetings on the possible expansion of the Euro Zone. Late in the evening, I decided to go out to dinner by myself, a rare privilege in my life. As is common, the waiter first brought me a few slices of bread with some olive oil. The oil, however, was not on a small plate as was the norm, but it was in a small bottle with a screw-on top and a seal. The waiter apologized for having to open the bottle and pour it myself, but he said the 'Eurocrats' had said that all olive oil in restaurants must be served in sealed bottles due to health reasons. He noted that they would likely stop serving oil and bread due to the costs. This struck me as strange. In 2,500 years of recorded European history, had anyone ever become sickened by olive oil in a restaurant? I looked it up on my phone while sitting there, and the waiter was correct. The European Union has stated that new rules would require that oil for bread and salads could only be served from non-refillable bottles. According to the EU spokesman, the EU was 'just protecting consumers.' Yet, there were no similar rules for salt, pepper, or butter. Upon returning here, I asked the staff to check this out. No surprise. As it turns out, the manufacturers of olive oil were bribing certain officials in the EU to put such rules into effect.[151] The obvious consequence was that more olive oil would be wasted, and the costs would go up. This meant more profit for the producers and more costs for consumers. It had nothing to do with safety."

Aldo sat down again and looked directly at Jochen. "The whole olive oil project was simply about putting more and more money into the hands of fewer and fewer people. Strangely enough, I remember the name of the EU spokesman. It was Olivier Bailly.[152] I only remember because his first name is so much like the olive in English. After that, I had my staff dig deep into Brussels. My belief now is that the Eurocrats are employed to create an increasingly large bureaucracy designed to support only itself while concentrating more and more power in Brussels. The same goes for the EU Commission, the EU Parliament, and the EU Presidency. Few of these fools are accountable, and they were accumulating so much power they were becoming untouchable. How strange is it that a tiny bottle of olive oil changed my views on the EU?"

---

[151] Alan Matthews, "EU to Ban Reusable Olive Oil Bottles in Restaurants: CAP Reform," CAP Reform | Europe's common agricultural policy is broken - let's fix it! (Alan Matthews, May 20, 2013), http://capreform.eu/eu-to-ban-reusable-olive-oil-bottles-in-restaurants/ .
[152] Unknown Editors, "EU to Ban Refillable Olive Oil Jugs and Dipping Bowls," BBC News (BBC, May 18, 2013), https://www.bbc.com/news/world-europe-22579896 .

"Perhaps this is an example of the butterfly effect?[153] One tiny action in one location can have a huge effect elsewhere at a different time?"

"The folks who like chaos theory[154] would love that. Those who run the EU, the IMF, the World Bank, and the UN are interested in global governance. It makes sense to them. It means more power in the hands of the elites. It means more power and wealth are concentrated in their own hands, while the rest of their populations can suffer in servitude. They have been able to take the worst aspects of fascism and communism and combine them with crony capitalism. When their favored corporations and financial institutions do well, they all make money on the way up. But if losses occur, it is socialism on the way down, and everyone must share the losses. The small-time retail shareholders take some of the losses, and the taxpayer covers the rest through bailouts. The globalists were not kidding when they said, 'you will own nothing, and you will be happy.'[155] They were well on their way to destroying representative democracy and moving towards a totalitarian system. Still, the pandemic and the

---

[153] "Butterfly Effect," Wikipedia (Wikimedia Foundation, April 28, 2021), https://en.wikipedia.org/wiki/Butterfly_effect .
[154] "Chaos Theory," Wikipedia (Wikimedia Foundation, May 3, 2021), https://en.wikipedia.org/wiki/Chaos_theory.
[155] "WEF: By 2030 You'll Own Nothing And You'll Be Happy," YouTube.com (YouTube, November 15, 2020), https://www.youtube.com/watch?v=IBBxWtKKQiA

Islamists provided the perfect opportunity to advance and expand their agenda. Once they had crushed free speech, no one could resist. Europe would once again become a totalitarian nightmare, setting the stage for more oppression, civil unrest, and war."

Aldo looked across the city and began again. "What we are seeing is the end of science and reason in favor of bureaucratic totalitarian control from the center. The sovereign state was able to manage its bureaucracies to some degree, but the EU did not. One overlooked aspect of the French Revolution was that it was simply the removal of one set of elites in favor of another. They turned out to be more violent than the monarchy. We need sovereign democratic states to defend individual rights. Monoliths always turn out to be totalitarian systems that favor the elites that run them."

Aldo Lange looked at his watch, his face now starting to show the strain of waiting. "When I first heard about Enrica Leclercq making her announcement about the Great Reset, it all made sense. It was the power grab by the globalists and progressives. Therefore, it is easier to see what CRJ has been up to the whole time. He has used the Great Reset believers to do his dirty work for him, and now he wants to decapitate them and take singular power for himself, which in a way is the final product of the whole process – more and more power in fewer and fewer hands. CRJ is, in a twisted way, the logical conclusion of the Great Reset project. Depending on what happens next, he still might get away with his grab for power. He will become the new totalitarian, commanding a system that is neither fascist nor communist, but even worse. A technocracy devoid of any moral compass or belief system."

"Do the Great Reset project supporters have a belief system of any sort?" asked Jochen.

"One of the defining features of the Great Reset is that it is a collectivist movement which is intolerant of any ideology or belief system that does not support them. It lacks a moral compass. You have noticed that Christians were heavily targeted during the pandemic in a variety of countries. The targeting was not an accident. It follows years of government and social pressure to water down belief systems. Christianity supports views that are offensive to the social justice warriors. Christianity believes in men and women. It believes in hierarchy, while at the same time believing those who are strong must support the less fortunate. A belief in hierarchy is, of course, a belief that a selection of individuals may be stronger, more intelligent, or work harder than others. Such an idea is offensive to the woke warriors who believe in the delusion of equity. But most damning is that Christianity believes in the separation of the church and state and supports the sovereign nation system. It is not for nothing that we have the expression "Render to Caesar the things that are Caesar's, and to God the things that are God's."[156]

---

[156] "'Render to Caesar the Things That Are Caesar's, and to God the Things That Are God's,'"

"What effect might the phone call have?" said Jochen.

"If the Chancellery agrees with us, then a pre-emptive move may undercut CRJ and his whole project. If it does not, I suggest your team leave Europe as fast as possible and not return until the conflict is over. That means you as well."

As if on cue, a phone in Aldo Lange's pocket began to ring. When he pulled it out, Jochen realized that it was a satellite phone and not a standard cell phone. Seeing his face, Aldo smiled and said, "A new toy from the Chancellery. It is encrypted or something."

With that, Aldo answered the phone with a business-like "Lange here."

The conversation was completely one-sided. The only words from Lange were 'Yes' and 'certainly.' His final statement was, "It will all be arranged from our end." There was no last exchange of pleasantries.

While putting the phone back in his jacket pocket, Aldo Lange's face suddenly became alive again, now full of energy and confidence. "Finally, we can move. The Chancellery is not completely convinced, but they want to meet again early tomorrow morning outside Zurich in Switzerland. The information was less than clear, but tomorrow's meeting may have more than one head of state. We have been summoned to

https://www.kingjamesbibleonline.org/ (King James Bible Online, 2021),
https://www.kingjamesbibleonline.org/Mark-12-17/.

appear. No reason was given, but we have to be prepared to explain ourselves. Are we ready for this?"

"I am not sure anyone is ready for what is coming. But we will be able to defend our position quite well."

"Here is what you are going to do. Contact your immediate team here and tell them to go home, grab some clothes and be ready to fly to Zurich late this afternoon. We will leave together from here, and we will all travel on the company jet. Tell your international team to be ready to move as well. Those in Europe will fly directly to Zurich, and they will be met on arrival as well. Except for Berndt. Tell him to fly to the Frankfurt Airport, and he will be met there. He is to travel in civilian clothes but tell him to bring his uniform. He will also travel with us. Call Daniel in Canada now. I will arrange a corporate jet to pick him up and fly directly to Zurich; he will be met on arrival there. You can make all the arrangements with Annalise in the travel section. She will know what to do, and it will get done in a hurry."

As Jochen was leaving, Aldo Lange had one more statement. "Let us hope that Europe does not become that which we once feared."

CHAPTER 36: THE GOLD COAST AND A Swiss Host

LOCATION:	Gold Coast, Zurich, Switzerland. Private Conference Center
DATE:	19 July
TIME:	7:00 PM

Upon arrival at the Zurich Airport, Aldo Lange, Jochen, and his team had been picked up by an unmarked black van that approached within a few feet of the aircraft. A Swiss customs official had arrived, did a headcount, smiled politely, and left without saying a word. The driver of the van was equally silent. Upon arrival at the conference site, Jochen noticed a few overt signs of security, such as security cameras and a gated guard booth. What was more interesting was the less overt signs of well-thought-out security. While the property was lush with trees and flowering shrubs, there were none within 25 meters of the main building. Thus, sneaking up on the building would be difficult. There were also recessed lights pointing out and away from the building. Mostly hidden in the shrubs and trees were a series of small guard posts.

As they were descending from the van, Karl nudged Jochen. "Note those small guard huts in the trees. From what I can see, they have intersecting arcs of fire. Anyone trying to approach the building can be shot at from at least two if not three directions at once without the guards hitting each other. Whoever runs this place has done some serious planning."

* * *

Jochen looked around the main meeting room of the private conference center. The hardwood paneling, brass fixtures, and wool carpets spoke of money. Old money. There was nothing glitzy about the room as he had seen in many more modern facilities. The room had large windows that looked like they could open outwards. Upon closer examination, it was clear that the glass in the windows was tempered, and the loose-fitting curtains were designed to catch glass fragments if the windows should be blown in by an externally placed bomb. The fire suppression system had been recessed into the ceiling and was barely visible.

The room appeared to have been recently set up. The seating was limited, given the size of the room. There seemed to be head table seating for four senior persons and eight others, with four on either side. This suggested four heads of state and one assistant for each.

Off to the side of the head table was one other chair with its own small side table. A placement for a host?

Separated by about five meters, there were a further 10 seats in a semi-circle. The arrangement suggested one chair in the center with four on one side and five on the other. Jochen assessed this as being the center seat for Aldo and the rest for the team members.

Behind the semi-circle set up was a wall with two double doors that were slightly open. This adjacent room had seating for 12. There was a side table that was set up for tea and coffee.

* * *

Daniel had arrived last, following a nearly seven-hour flight across the Atlantic. The Bombardier Global 800 private jet, with its range of over 14,000 kilometers, was able to make the 6,500-kilometer flight from Toronto without breaking a sweat. Upon Daniel settling into his suite, Aldo passed the word for the team to gather in the informal dining room.

Once they were gathered, Aldo circulated among them, making small talk while ensuring everyone had a drink. Once everyone seemed relaxed, Aldo nodded to the waiter, who silently left the room.

"My friends. We have gathered again, this time under even more difficult circumstances. Europe is in the middle of an uprising that has the potential to turn into a civil war. Without being overly dramatic, what happens here tomorrow may change the course of history. I regret to tell you that I am not completely aware of who will be here tomorrow or what they will discuss. However, I am reasonably certain that there will be four heads of state here. Most likely, it will be

Germany, France, the United Kingdom, and one other. The other may be the Netherlands, Belgium, Italy, or another European state."

"Why Switzerland?" This from Sergio.

"A reasonable question. This meeting tomorrow is a group of heads of states gathering on their own. The meeting is not being carried out under the auspices of NATO, the EU, the IMF, or any other supranational organization. What you have done by suggesting that CRJ is responsible for the current violence has overturned every structure and normality in their worlds. I cannot speak for them directly, but for myself, I can say there is a great sense of betrayal. The leaders have lost their compasses. This meeting tomorrow is an attempt to regain some sense of initiative. For what might be obvious reasons, the meeting could not be held at any EU facility. NATO is out. A meeting at the IMF HQ would be completely out of the question. Anywhere in the EU would be complicated. So, Switzerland it is. The Swiss will keep quiet about this meeting, at least for a few days. A friend of mine runs this retreat and conference center, and he will remain off the property for today and tomorrow. His staff is discrete, and they have hosted higher-profile meetings than this one with no leaks. Tomorrow, just before the meeting, you will hear heavy helicopters. Again, I am not sure of the logistics, but the leaders will arrive then. The staff and the facilities are well adjusted to such flights. By the way, please stay inside the building tonight and tomorrow until after the meeting. The security staff here are among the best but wandering the gardens after dark might be a bad idea."

"What is our role? What are we expected to do?" This from Carsten.

"Again, I have no directions other than to ensure you are present. Your assessment led to the potential exposure of CRJ as being at the center of this. How exactly you will be asked to contribute is uncertain. These are head of state and their most senior assistants. Their questions may be direct. Blunt. They may even seem rude. Given their current disposition, you should be prepared for aggressive questioning. When dealing with leaders of this caliber, keep your answers short and clear. Answer what you are asked. No more and no less. If you do not have an answer for the question, say you do not know. They will not be upset if you do not have an answer, but they will immediately lose all patience and confidence if they sense you are misleading them. In this forum, when you first address them, use the term Mister President or Mister Prime Minister. After that, speak directly to them without the formalities. This is in the interest of time. Another idea to keep in mind during the meeting. In more normal scenarios, the lower-level staff speaks to the middle-level staff, who speak to the senior staff, who speak to the leaders. In this case, the leaders have asked to speak directly to you. Berndt, in particular, will be aware of how unusual this can be. But the best leaders often want to talk directly to the desk analysts. As such, my role tomorrow will be to guide you into position. I will not answer any questions about the case at hand. Do not look to me for direction or guidance when you are asked a question. Look the leader directly in the eye and answer. From what I have seen of you so far, your part tomorrow will go well."

"What time is the meeting?" asked Bettina.

"You should be in the meeting room by 08:30 AM. There will be audio-visual support if you need it. Be in the seats marked out for you by 08:50. It is best to remain silent until the meeting starts, which is said to be at 09:00. After that, I have no idea, so be prepared for anything. Additionally, I have no idea how long we will be required. There is a small room adjacent to the meeting room available to us if we must wait. Any other questions?"

"No questions, but I do have one observation." This from Karl. "The window in my suite overlooks the grounds next to the entrance. Two men were walking around the perimeter. I may be mistaken, but I swear that one of them was the same person who was with the British diplomat at our off-site meeting in Frankfurt. The one we thought was either SAS or SBS. We have at least one snake eater here."

"This would indicate that one of the leaders tomorrow will be the UK Prime Minister," said Isabel. There can be no other reason."

Aldo then turned to Berndt. "Glad to see you again. Do wear your uniform tomorrow. It will add a bit of color and credibility to our presence. So that you know, the Chancellor's office is responsible for your being here after I requested it. Amazing what a phone call to the NATO headquarters can do. But now that we are all here, what do you think happens next from a military perspective?"

Berndt turned to Isabel, and she smiled back at him. "I should be careful as to what I say, even in this company, but the number of possible options seems limited. The EU has effectively launched itself down a path of violence, and its leadership is in disarray. I cannot see how the process towards the Great Reset can continue now that the press has effectively put the knife in Enrica Leclercq. I also cannot see how the EU can reorganize itself and recover. Portugal, Spain, Italy, Greece, and Finland are already saying they want nothing to do with the Great Reset, and others are talking about leaving the EU.

Meanwhile, the Islamist violence is growing, and they are taking territory. The only way they will give it up now is if they are defeated in combat. This means retaking the territory back from them. This is the worst form of combat – fighting a resistance-style enemy in built-up areas with the best knowledge of the terrain. The future, I fear, looks rather tricky."

"On that note, may I suggest we all retire to our rooms. Tomorrow may be a long day."

Chapter 37: The Swiss Inquisition

LOCATION: Zurich, Switzerland

DATE: 20 July

TIME: 08:15 AM

Jochen arose early after a mostly sleepless night. He skipped breakfast, preferring to head directly to the conference room after reading through the morning news. He entered the room under the watchful eyes of two security guards.

The first thing that caught his eye was the Swiss flag at a prepared position off to the side of the main table. The arrangement indicated that the Swiss government would be represented at the meeting, most likely by the president of the Swiss Confederation. What was his role?

The side table that had the audio-visual support equipment now had two small discretely placed cameras. One camera was aimed at the head table. The other was aimed where Jochen and his team would be sitting. Each of the head of state positions had an iPod Pro with a detachable keyboard. So why the cameras, and who else would be watching the meeting?

The head table now had five flags rather than the four as expected. Germany. France. The United Kingdom.

Italy. The Netherlands. The severity of the situation appeared to be growing.

The rest of the team began to arrive one by one. The conversations were subdued and focussed on the room layout and the increasing levels of violence in cities across Europe. Finally, at 08:45, Aldo Lange entered the room. Like the others, he surveyed the room, slightly surprised at the addition to the head table. He greeted the individual team members, offering his thanks for their presence and a few final words of advice on addressing the leaders.

At 08:50, Aldo suggested they move to their seats. The room fell into silence.

Several minutes later, the distant sound of a helicopter became apparent. After thirty seconds or so, the increasing sound indicated the aircraft was headed for the conference center. The windows began to vibrate, and the trees around the perimeter started to whip violently in the downwash from the main rotor.

Daniel left his seat and walked to the window. "It is a German Army NH90 tactical transport helo. Not the usual ride for a head of state. I can see at least two more helos over the lake. The show is about to start."

While the helicopter arrivals were drawing the attention of most in the room, Aldo Lange felt a tap on his shoulder. He turned to see the President of the Swiss Federation standing beside him. "Good morning Mr. Lange. I understand that you are the reason that my schedule has been re-arranged. The good news is,

I have a few old friends coming to join us in just a few minutes. The six of us will meet in an adjoining room for about 10 minutes before meeting with you. By the way, which one of you has been infiltrating our banking system?"

All eyes turned to Horst, who stood there with his mouth hanging open.

The Swiss President, taking his cue, looked at Horst and said, "A pleasure to meet you."

He then turned to Aldo Lange and said, "Please relax until we join you."

Aldo turned to the team. "That was interesting. It seems like the Swiss President is not just here as a courtesy. He will be an active participant in whatever process is evolving here. For you, Horst, it seems your reputation is known in advance wherever you go. I take it a good sign that the President chose to tip his hand about knowing your work. If there were any legal or national security actions pending, he would not have said anything. Also, make sure your phones have their sound turned off. No pinging while this is happening."

Horst reached into his pocket to turn off his cell phone. He looked considerably more nervous than the rest as they all sat down again.

* * *

The Swiss President opened the double door entryway into the conference room and allowed the other five leaders to enter and take their seats. But, rather strangely, the five seats for their staff remained empty.

With everyone seated, the Swiss President began the meeting. "Greetings to all, especially my colleagues from Germany, France, the United Kingdom, the Netherlands, and Italy. It is a distinct pleasure to have you visit us, and I hope our hospitality and arrangements have been sufficient. After all, we Swiss are just poor potato farmers, and having our prosperous friends visiting is a rare treat."

A few faces in the room managed weak smiles at the well-worn joke about the Swiss being the poor agricultural cousins of Europe.

"In the interests of efficiency, may I suggest that we dispense with formalities and move directly to the issue at hand. My colleagues are gathered to discuss future scenarios for Europe. Our meeting occurs against waves of violence expanding across Europe. Mr. Lange, your statements concerning how this violence came to start with one person have caused certain concerns to understate the case slightly. Would you care to explain how you came to believe this? Perhaps it is best if you ignore the four initial attacks and go straight to the information on Leclercq and Raes-Javier."

Aldo Lange rose to his feet as he began to speak. "Mr. President and esteemed leaders. I have merely provided the time and tools for this analysis. The responsibility for the statement that Clement Raes-Javier is behind this is mine, but others did the hard work."

With that, Aldo sat down and indicated to Jochen that he should speak.

Jochen had been trying to read the room. Each of the other leaders likely held more political and financial clout as individual leaders than the Swiss President. Collectively, they had overwhelming weight in their favor. Nonetheless, they were in Switzerland, and the Swiss President played the role of host and inquisitor. There were high politics at play that he could not fathom. As such, he chose to fall back on his earlier training. Speak directly to the person asking the question.

"Mr. President. As noted, the four terrorist attacks of the 28th of June were coordinated, and each of the four had its own set of circumstances designed to mislead the press and the population. The coincident disappearance of the most influential Islamist in Europe was an indicator and warning of further unrest, such as we saw beginnings of the violence in Paris on the sixth of July. Finally, there was the beginning of the flow of refugees and jihadists from Turkey. When the widespread series of attacks began on the tenth of July, we believed we had the makings of the overall plan. Our assessment is based on a few key factors. First, much of the money trail from the four attacks had common patterns. Each money trail showed at least six months, if not years, of preparation. The money involved, especially in the aircraft hijacking attempt, ran into the millions. We also believed that the Islamist groups such as the Muslim Brotherhood were reacting rather than acting. While they are causing the violence on the ground, they might have been used as part of a larger setup. We believed that the Islamist violence would grow beyond the police's ability to control it if allowed to spread. At our joint meeting on the eleventh and twelfth of June, we were reasonably certain that one hand with considerable access to money was behind this. That person must have a major institution affiliation. We also believe that Enrica Leclercq and the High Representative for Foreign Affairs and Security Policy office were involved. Whether she was the leader was not clear."

The President of France interjected. "At this point, do you still believe that the Islamist violence will continue to spiral out of control without the use of military forces?"

"Yes."

The French President looked at his colleagues. "My generals tell me the same thing."[157]

"At that time, we assessed Enrica Leclercq was involved, but she was backed by either the European

---

[157] "Retired French Military Officers Warn of Country 'Disintegrating'," Retired French military officers warn of country 'disintegrating' (TRT World, April 26, 2021), https://www.trtworld.com/magazine/retired-french-military-officers-warn-of-country-disintegrating-46227 .

Central Bank, the World Bank, or the IMF. The IMF seemed most likely. If you will forgive me, this is where it gets a bit complex. The declaration of the launch of the Great Reset was a surprise to everyone. If you look at it within the framework of the Westphalian concept of national sovereignty, this was effectively an attempted coup against all of the European Union members at once. Quite breathtaking, actually."

Jochen paused for a moment to gauge the reaction of five of the sovereign leaders who were sitting there. He had just stated they were the subject of a coup. The complete lack of response told him he was on track.

"After that, it became a question of who in Europe could envisage such a plan and at the same time have a significant overlap with all the evidence we had of funding and planning. Also, who would have been in a position of institutional power long enough to have done the planning? All the vectors pointed to CRJ. But it was not clear if he was working with Enrica Leclercq or was controlling her. So our final round of analysis on June 17th pointed to CRJ, and we shared it with Mr. Lange in the early morning hours of that day. While it is a time-consuming process, we can walk you through the use of Structured Analytic Techniques such as the Analysis of Competing Hypotheses and the Source Reliability and Information Credibility system we use. It was formerly known as the British Admiralty System," Jochen said while looking at the British Prime Minister.

As the British Prime Minister began to ask a question, there was a notable ping from his cell phone. He did not appear embarrassed or upset as he looked at the phone and began to read a text. While he was reading, the Dutch prime minister's cell phone also pinged, shortly followed by that of the Chancellor.

The British Prime Minister showed his phone to the Dutch Prime Minister, who passed the phone along to the others. Each one nodded in turn and then handed the phone back.

The British Prime Minister looked at his colleagues, and they all looked at him. He then stood up and carried his phone over to the Swiss President sitting at a separate table. He took the phone and read the message, his facing appearing to show agreement with whatever message was on the phone.

Rising to his feet, the Swiss President turned to Aldo Lange. "I believe the time for questions to you has ended. Your views on CRJ have just been confirmed by two rather senior intelligence officials who work for my friends here. Their confirmation seems to put us past the point of reasonable doubt." Then, turning to the other leaders, he asked, "Does this seem to be correct? Are the questions for our invited team members done?"

The British Prime Minister pointed his finger at Jochen. "Why did I learn about this from you first and not from our intelligence services? It also seems that they are only working on it now because of your heads up. Even more concerning is that it seems you may have put most of this information together two or three days earlier. Furthermore, all of this analysis is occurring in a state of crisis. What did you have that we do not?"

Jochen rose to his feet again, counseling himself to remain polite while delivering a direct message. "Since 1995 to 2000, the balance between the value of open-source intelligence and classified intelligence has shifted. If faced with a choice to use only open-source intelligence or to use only classified, in most cases, I would choose open-source. Additionally, the best intelligence analysis at the strategic level occurs when a wide variety of minds and experiences come to work together. The information must cross both geographic and institutional boundaries. We have done that."

Jochen paused and pointed at each of the team members. "Additionally, the analysis cannot be restricted. Governments continuously tell their analysts to be open-minded and think outside the box. Then they crush them or caution them if a sensitive territory is approached. None of us could have followed the evidence trail we did as it wove its way through government figures such as Enrica Leclercq and CRJ. Government intelligence agencies fail as they are too large, they do not share information, and individuals must conform to traditional beliefs or be ostracized from the group. Finally, there must be a leader who understands how intelligence and risk analyses work together. We were fortunate to have Mr. Lange guiding us and protecting

470

us from those who would silence or politicize the work." The last comment was a not-so-subtle shot at the BvF.[158]

The Chancellor waved her hand at the pair of doors at the far end of the room. "Thank you, Aldo. Your team will now move to the adjacent seating area and remain there until otherwise directed. After that, we may have further direction."

* * *

Aldo Lange sat down with the team and looked around the room. "The grown-ups will now have their adult discussion while we sit here in the children's room."

Daniel stood up and walked to the windows overlooking Lake Zurich. "Thanks, Jochen. This has been fun. A trip across the pond in an executive jet. The suite I am in is so large I needed the GPS map on my phone just to find the bathroom. A bunch of what might have been amazing food on the room service menu in German and French – most of which I had no clue what it was. All of that followed up by a meeting with six heads of state and a building surrounded by more guys with guns than I have ever seen. Now, we

---

[158] "Federal Office for the Protection of the Constitution," Wikipedia (Wikimedia Foundation, May 6, 2021), https://en.wikipedia.org/wiki/Federal_Office_for_the_Prot ection_of_the_Constitution .

sit in a room while an unhappy bunch of politicians determines what to do to us after telling them they were so incompetent they may now be at war. Is this the part where we are driven away in a black van with no windows by one of those snake eaters, and we are never seen again?"

"None of the leaders were upset with you, whatever else you may think. On the contrary, the Chancellor seemed rather controlled and diplomatic under the circumstances." This from Aldo Lange.

Daniel laughed, the first person to do so far on this day. "If that is a happy face, I can't wait for the irritated look."

* * *

A discrete tap on the door was followed by the Swiss President entering.

"Could you please join us again? As it turns out, there are a few more questions."

As they were seated, the Chancellor pointed at Berndt. "You are a military officer in a Dutch uniform, and you are wearing NATO insignia. How is it that you are with this band of merry rogues?"

Berndt pointed at Isabel. "This my wife, who is considerably brighter than I am. She does, however, tend to have a circle of friends who are non-linear thinkers. I am here for moral support in these

472

circumstances, and I am also rather good at carrying suitcases."

"Really?" said the Chancellor. "That is not what your Prime Minister just said. He seems to think you are up to your neck in all of this. He also thinks rather highly of you, by the way. SACEUR, however, seems to think you have problems staying in your lane and should not be here."

Berndt chose the silent response, believing that at times it is best to say nothing. He nodded his head while bowing slightly.

After that, the Chancellor looked directly at Horst. "My intelligence liaison officer tells me that your name is familiar. You have had interactions with the Bundesamt fur Verfassungsschutz in the past?"

Horst was ready to panic. At least on the inside. The Chancellor of Germany essentially asked him if he had committed illegal acts on the Internet while working in Germany. At that point, he remembered the voice of Aldo Lange speaking last night. Answer the question. Keep it short. Be honest. He swallowed and then said, "Yes, we have interacted in the past."

For the first time, the Chancellor appeared to almost smile. "The BfV suggested you be barred from the meeting today. I almost agreed, but I did not want to miss the opportunity to meet the man who has upset the head of the BfV so badly. He remains angry. Not today, but it would be amusing to hear the details of what you did to him at some point. It must be quite remarkable."

Taking the example from Berndt, Horst simply nodded his head and said, "Thank you, Chancellor."

The Dutch Prime Minister then pointed at Daniel. "You are Canadian."

Daniel was unsure if this was intended as a statement, an accusation, or a question. He simply nodded and said, "Yes."

The Prime Minister continued. "How is it that a Canadian is mixed up in this? A reliable source tells me that it might have been you that put CRJ in the frame for this? Is this true? How is it that Aldo Lange is flying you around in a private jet?"

Daniel was tempted to look at Aldo, Jochen, and all the extended team, hoping for some guidance as to what he should say or what question he should answer. He resisted the urge. "Sorry, Sir. But we Canadians do seem to show up in European wars. A bit of a bad habit that runs from the Somme to the Scheldt to Sarajevo. In fairness to the government of Canada, they probably do not know that I am here."

"They will by tomorrow morning, lad." This from the British Prime Minister, who had a particular look on his face. The sort of look that a wolf gets while looking at a rabbit just before the attack.

The French President then addressed Bettina and said, "You are the only female on Jochen's immediate team and one of two females overall. You have no intelligence, security, police, or military background. What is your role and your contribution?"

Jochen shuddered. Bettina was prone to making some rather blunt statements at the wrong moment.

Bettina stood up and looked directly into the eyes of the French President. "Someone has to integrate knowledge across boundaries. All knowledge is also contextual, so if there is no context, there is no assessment. As is known, women do this form of lateral tasking better than men who tend to think in terms of hierarchy." Bettina promptly sat down again, looking straight ahead, her faced unchanged.

All eyes turned to Isabel, who simply smiled back at the leaders.

The ensuing silence from the leaders was an obvious clue. They were dismissed. Again.

As they left the room, the Swiss President said, "Please be patient. We will call you again shortly."

* * *

As soon as the door was closed, Karl turned to Aldo. "What is going on? Why are we being called in and out of the room?" Isabel, who was standing next to Aldo, answered. "The first discussion was to see if the leaders believe that CRJ is behind this. They must have already decided they do, or they would not be here. But they wanted to hear it from us directly before moving ahead. I may be mistaken, but when we were recalled into the room for the second time, it was an employment interview. The leaders are making plans, and those plans may involve us. What happens next is being discussed in the room now. My feelings are it will be something good, or at least interesting. Otherwise, we would have been sent away by now." She turned to Aldo Lange. "Does that sound about right?"

Aldo nodded in agreement. "This has been the most exciting morning of my life so far. This meeting will be in the history books one day, and you will all know that you were here when it happened. So how do you all feel?"

Jochen turned to Aldo. "What do you think is being planned on the other side of those doors?"

"This is effectively a council of self-appointed elders who are forming a tribal alliance to fight a war. The planning is being done outside of the hallways of the EU and NATO. The EU is effectively finished today, as are the IMF and the World Bank. NATO might survive in some form, although I am not sure how that will work out. Germany, France, the UK, Italy, and the Netherlands will call the shots today. Tomorrow, Spain, Greece, Finland, Portugal, and the others will be offered a role at the table if they want – but they will be the junior partners. In my view, Berndt is right, and we are going to see tanks in the street."

Horst was still shaking. "The Chancellor knows who I am and told me the head of the BfV hates me personally. I'm done. They will ruin me."

"Not likely," said Aldo. "The BfV will find out that you were here and personally spoke to the Chancellor.

They will be doubly angry at that, but there is nothing they can do now. If you ever talk to them again, just tell them there is nothing you can say as the Chancellor ordered you to remain silent. You are next to bulletproof at this point."

Daniel was worried. "Methinks the British Prime Minister does not like me. This situation may not go well when I get back to Canada. Our governments are rather tightly connected, and I have already had a couple of previous problems with the intelligence community and the federal police."

"None of you have to worry," said Aldo. "If this turns out well, you will be the unsung heroes, and the Chancellor, along with the others, will make sure you are untouchable. On the other hand, if the next few days go poorly, it will be such a catastrophe that no one will worry about the likes of us as they will be fighting a war. Besides that, I think the British Prime Minister likes you and he will have some fun telling your folks at home how you were involved, and they did not even know about it."

The doors opened again, with the Swiss President indicating they should return.

Jochen had been trying to read the leaders. Who was calling the shots? Was it the Chancellor? Were there alliances of opinion being formed among the five (six?) of them? What role was the supposedly neutral Switzerland going to play?

Once again, it was the Swiss President who was speaking. "At the suggestion of our Italian colleague, it has been put forth that your extended team should stay for the immediate future. You are requested to continue to monitor events in Europe with a focus on the strategic implications of unfolding events. You may receive questions at some point. It has been decided that the questions will be sent to you by SACEUR, and you, Berndt, will be the communication liaison with him at this end. All answers will go to him. Your answers will be shared by Flash message precedence[159] with the national leaders you see here, plus others as we invite them. This means most of NATO, minus Turkey, of course, and a select list of others. All accommodations will be here, and you will find the conference center has a rather impressive communications room. Each of you can make a trip into Zurich for clothing or any other necessities as you may desire, paid for by the conference center. Take a few minutes to confer among yourselves and see if you all agree."

Few words were spoken, but everyone seemed in agreement.

The only exception was Daniel. "Will you be sharing this information with the Government of Canada, particularly the Prime Minister?"

The Swiss President looked at the other leaders while answering. "This has not been decided, but it seems

---

[159] "Flash Message Precedence," Wikipedia (Wikimedia Foundation, March 2, 2021), https://en.wikipedia.org/wiki/Message_precedence#:~:text=FLASH%20(Z) .

to be probable that Canada may be involved at some level."

"The thing is, Sir, that is highly probable that Enrica Leclercq and Prime Minister Elishchuk played a role in the murder of our previous Prime Minister."

Aldo looked up at the ornate ceiling. "God help us all."

Daniel looked up to see everyone staring at him in disbelief.

"Sorry. It's a long story. I was doing some digging on the plane during the flight. They have the coolest communication equipment on that plane, by the way. During the early morning hours today, I put another piece of the puzzle together. Prime Minister Elishchuk, Enrica Leclercq, and American President Harris have some explaining to do. Elishchuk and Harris go way back, and Leclercq and Elishchuk have also worked together."

Bettina stood and faced the Swiss President. "I had wondered about the death of the Canadian Prime Minister. It was too convenient. Someone had him killed, and I have my own reasons for believing it was from over here."

The Chancellor turned to the Swiss President. "You have better order lunch. It appears this is going to be a long day.

With that, everyone stared at Daniel, who sat quietly contemplating the ornate pattern of the wool carpet.

CHAPTER 38: INTO THE ABYSS

LOCATION: Zurich, Switzerland

DATE: 21 July

TIME: 12:05 AM

The clock had turned past midnight.

Jochen and the team had spent the afternoon becoming familiar with the conference center's communications room and the other facilities. No additional guests were in the center, and they had observed no one entering the compound except for the staff and guards.

The leaders had all left at about three in the afternoon. Aldo Lange had gathered the team together, explaining that he was leaving. He left another satellite phone behind and told them to use it to contact him directly if they needed anything or wanted to leave the conference center to return home.

With no immediate task at hand, the team had gradually dissipated around 11:00 in the evening, believing that the next day would bring new taskings.

Jochen, who was too tired to sleep, sat in the lounge area, endless flipping through news channels. The reports focussed on the increasing violence in much of Europe. France seemed particularly hard hit. Interspersed with the reports on violence were questions about the location of various national leaders and unconfirmed reports that Enrica Leclercq had privately plotted the Great Reset takeover without the knowledge of the other national leaders in the EU.

Around two in the morning, Daniel wandered into the lounge as well. "I cannot decide if I am a bit jet-lagged or just too frightened to sleep. Events are unfolding so fast you may not recognize the world tomorrow."

The two of them lapsed into silence as they watched parts of Europe beginning to burn, exchanging only brief comments.

Just after three, Jochen prodded Daniel in the ribs. "Wake up. I think something is happening."

"Ya think?" said Daniel.

"The news reports are changing. In the last 15 minutes, they have started reporting that military vehicles' convoys are being seen in Paris and Lyon. Same in Belgium. Reports are saying that troops are being deployed around downtown Paris. So things are heating up."

Daniel headed for the Keurig coffee machine. "France will be the worst. They have known for years that the confrontation between the Islamists and the Fifth Republic was coming."

"The reports are coming in so fast that the channels cannot keep up. Everything tells me we are headed to a major conflict at a time when the leadership is in disarray."

They lapsed into silence again. The scrolling news continued at the bottom of the screen while various reporters and talking heads attempted to keep up.

Among the scrolling text lines on the screen were:

- As France burns, media could not locate French President.

- Tanks on the streets. Are we at war?

- EU Spokesperson denies Great Reset announcement fueled conflict.

- Explosion and gunfights in Manchester Hotel.

- Military forces seen in Lyon.

- Turkish President says Islam will return to Europe.

- Austrian President declares state of emergency.

- HAMAS says it will send fighters to Europe.

- Muslim Brotherhood Supreme Guide declares jihad in Europe.

- NATO says Article Five in effect.

- Trains with armored vehicles seen outside of Brussels.

- EU President calls for negotiations with Islamists.

- European stock markets' futures are crashing.

- Gold futures soaring.

- French troops fighting in Clichy-sur-Bois.

- Attack captures Gare du Nord.

Jochen turned to Daniel. "Get Berndt out of bed. I think he should be watching this."

Daniel returned with Berndt in less than two minutes. "I was already up watching TV in my room. The news reports on troop movements are probably correct. NATO had authorized the use of Article Five on the sixteenth of July, so mobilizations were probably started then. Most of what I have seen on TV is showing wheeled armored vehicles and heavy trucks. This suggests mechanized infantry will be used in built-up suburban areas. Vicious fighting and causalities will occur. Tracked vehicles and heavy armor will be initially deployed defensively around airports, government buildings, and critical infrastructure. The mere presence of a tank is usually enough to discourage attacks by even the most zealous of jihadists. If you see tanks moving in the urban areas, then this means the gloves are off, and a full-scale attack will be underway."

"Is NATO commanding this?" asked Jochen.

"Depends on what you mean by commanding," said Berndt. "My best guess is that it will be the leaders we saw yesterday putting pressure on their Defence Ministers to have the deployments ordered by NATO. It at least gives the illusion that there is some unity in

Europe. There will be no American or British field units deployed on the continent, although they will run parts of NATO's support systems. The reality is, there is nothing and no one that can coordinate this sort of activity, so it goes to NATO by default. The European Union cannot play a role, given that they supported the whole Great Reset project that triggered this mess. I am not sure we can directly blame Brussels and Strasbourg for this if they did not know what Enrica Leclercq was doing, but they own it nonetheless."

"What of Russia?" This from Daniel.

"My guess is they will do nothing. The Kremlin could take advantage of the chaos by moving on the Baltics or Poland. But with NATO already engaged in a sort of civil war, the only real response NATO could provide would be in the tactical nuclear role. That would be good for no one. The other area they might move to is in the Donbas Basin in Ukraine.[160] Many of the Ukrainians who are living there are Russians anyway, and they might support it. That one is hard to tell, but NATO will not go nuclear to defend eastern Ukraine."

Jochen headed the window. "Dawn is coming soon. Let us have breakfast together and then try and figure out what we should be doing today."

"Holy Crap!"

---

[160] "Donbas Region, Ukraine," Wikipedia (Wikimedia Foundation, May 6, 2021), https://en.wikipedia.org/wiki/Donbas .

Jochen and Berndt turned to watch Daniel walking towards the TV. "Check this out. An American news channel is reporting that there have been multiple bombings in New York and Washington DC. It is just around midnight there. At least two bombs went off in Times Square in New York and another in DC near Dupont Circle. This is going to get real if it is the Iranians."

"Does the news say it was Iran?" asked Jochen.

"No," said Daniel. "But the Iranians have been building up their strength in North America, especially in Canada, so they can attack America from the north. This is not new to them. You might remember that one of their diplomats, Assadollah Assadi, was convicted for the attempted bombing in Paris back in 2018."[161]

"Canada let this happen?" asked Berndt.

"Yup. The Prime Minister's brother, Sacha Trudeau, used to work for Iran's Press TV, which is their state broadcaster. While Trudeau was alive and still Prime Minister, he let everyone into the country. Iranian operatives and finance guys. Muslim Brotherhood leaders who had been kicked out of Egypt. Khalistani terrorist supporters. In his first campaign to be Prime Minister, he said he would have a race and religious-

---

[161] "France Bomb Plot: Iran Diplomat Assadollah Assadi Sentenced to 20 Years," bbc.com (BBC News, February 4, 2021), https://www.bbc.com/news/world-europe-55931633.

based immigration policy especially for Muslims and Arabs."

"But why kill him? You said that Enrica Leclercq played a role in having him assassinated. How would she gain from that?"

"Even in his own circles, Trudeau was regarded as an intellectual lightweight and a dilettante, unlike his father, who was rather bright. His personal life was a mess, and he came to be seen as a liability. That was, I think, the reason to get rid of him."

"Check this out," said Berndt. The media is now saying that something called the *General Soleimani Revenge Brigade* claims responsibility for the bombings."

"Makes sense," said Daniel. They were pretty upset when their favorite general in the Iranian Revolutionary Guards got whacked back in January 2020."[162]

"This just gets wilder. Schiphol Airport is being closed to civilian traffic, and so are De Gaulle and Heathrow.

* * *

---

[162] "Assassination of Qasem Soleimani," Wikipedia (Wikimedia Foundation, May 3, 2021), https://en.wikipedia.org/wiki/Assassination_of_Qasem_Sol eimani .

By eight in the morning, the team was all sitting in the lounge watching the news and scanning social media in a vain attempt to keep up with events. Mass arrests were starting. Pitched battles were being fought in various suburbs around Paris, Lyon, Nice, Brussels, Amsterdam, The Hague, and Vienna. The Polish Prime Minister had offered troops for "the defense of Germany." It was not clear if it was a serious offer or a rebuke towards Germany and Europe for their failures in earlier years to address migration issues. Either way, the irony was not lost on many viewers when Poland said it would help Germany defend itself.

By nine, it was clear to all concerned that Europe was falling into an abyss. It was not just Islamists attacking the police. A few groups, self-identified as anarcho-syndicalists, were also joining in. Worse still, various Turkish neighborhoods in Germany were erupting in demonstrations, riots, and blockades.

"It looks like everyone is involved in this," said Isabel. "The seeming collapse of the Grand Reset announcement and the violence is causing a sort of revolutionary collective madness. Any group that has been building up for anti-government riots is now coming out. The next few days will be wild."

As she was speaking, the news announcer indicated that breaking news was about to be reported.

Horst almost laughed with contempt. "What would you have to do in Europe today that could outdo all of this other news?"

The TV screen showed an unsteady video tracking a large airliner as it flew over a city area. The aircraft appeared to be under control as it flew directly into the Eifel Tower and exploded in a cloud of fire and smoke. As the smoke gradually began to dissipate, it became apparent that the top three-quarters of the Eiffel Town was gone. The effect of the images was every bit as powerful as those from 9/11 in New York. The room went silent in response.

Karl finally broke the silence. "This has just become serious. France will now have to go to war on its own territory, and much of Europe will be facing the same uprising."

"Once more into the breach, and all of that," said Daniel.

Bettina looked distant again, and she turned to Isabel. "Europe has no Metternich or Churchill at present. This will result in the complete rewriting of everything we know about European politics, globalization, and the Westphalian system. The Great Reset will fail, of course, and with it the grand socialist experiment of the supranational organizations and their so-called elites. If this goes well, we may see a league of democracies establish itself, and the UN will be finished. If it goes poorly, the conflict could become global and return us to a new dark age."

Isabel contemplated this for a moment and replied, "It is possible."

The team sat in comparative silence for the next hour, with little to focus on other than the endless series of news updates about violence growing everywhere.

Horst looked at Daniel. "Who is Bonnie Crombie?"

"She is the mayor of Mississauga, Ontario. Why?"

"Where is Mississauga?"

"It is just south of Toronto. Toronto's Pearson Airport is in Mississauga, not in Toronto. If you have flown into Toronto on an international flight, you have been there."

"Well," said Horst. It looks like someone just tried to blow up her house. Or at least that is what some folks are saying on social media."

Jochen suddenly jumped in his seat. A rather strange tone was emerging from his pocket. He pulled out the satellite phone and held it up for everyone to see. "It has never rung before."

Everyone watched as Jochen answered the phone. He began to wave his hand, indicating he wanted a pen and paper. Karl opened his notebook and put a pen in his hand.

Jochen's face became paler as the one-sided conversation continued. Finally, the conversation ended with Jochen simply stating, "Yes, Sir, we will. Good luck in Berlin."

Jochen continued to write on the notebook page for almost a minute before finally looking up.

"Well," said Bettina? "What is happening."

"That was Aldo Lange. He is in Berlin rather than Frankfurt, which is a bit strange. The French President will be declaring a state of emergency, and he will announce the death of the Fifth Republic and promises the birth of the Sixth Republic before the end of the year. Belgium may collapse later today, and the Netherlands is also going into a state of emergency. Germany, Austria, and Italy are all mobilizing their militaries."

Jochen paused to read his notes. "Enrica Leclercq will be arrested within the hour, and CRJ cannot be located. He has disappeared."

Jochen waited until that news was digested. Then he began again. "We have been asked to assess several questions. They are as follows:

1.   Did CRJ have a hand in the terrorist attack on the Eiffel Tower? Does CRJ have connections to Iran and China?

2.   Does CRJ have a deeper reach into violent organizations that was earlier believed?

3.   What was the relationship between Enrica Leclercq, Prime Minister Elishchuk, and President Harris? Will it affect Europe now?

4.   Are the terrorist attacks in America related to the violence in Europe?"

"When do they want this?" asked Carsten?

"No rush," said Jochen. "Aldo says he will call back at three this afternoon."

The collective gasp was audible.

Bettina leaned over to Isabel and whispered, "If CRJ has ties to President Xi of China or the Iranian Revolutionary Guards, then we are in for a much larger conflict than we thought."

Isabel nodded in affirmation. "We need to discuss this first."

Daniel called out before anyone could else react. "Hey Berndt, have a look at this. I could be wrong, but that looks a lot like a French Leclercq Main Battle Tank."

All eyes were on the TV screen. A news camera was broadcasting live as a tank was sitting on an unknown street. Dismounted infantry soldiers were lining up behind it. A huge cloud of diesel exhaust poured out the back as the tank charged down the street. The next intersection had been blocked with cars, garbage bins, and piles of wood. As the tank crashed through the barrier, smoke grenades from the tank fired off, adding to the confusion. Following that, the main gun on the tank fired, sending a blast of flame and smoke down the street. The infantry troops poured in behind, mainly covered in smoke. The tank then disappeared out of sight of the camera.

Berndt took the remote control and turned the volume back down. "To the best of my knowledge, this is the first time that heavy armor has been used

491

in Western Europe since the Danish attacked some Serbian guns in Bosnia in 1994. The French Army is using heavy armor in an urban setting. This is an all-out attack. There was no explosion from the round the tank fired. Either it was a dud, or more likely, a blank round. However, the concussion from a 120 mm cannon will kill or wound anyone in front of it. The shock effect of such a weapon in built-up areas is devastating."

Berndt looked around the team. "France is using heavy armor in an urban combat situation. NATO has already declared Article Five."

Jochen looked over. "Does this mean what I think it means?"

"Yes. We are now in a state of war in Europe. May God have mercy on us all."

"More than that," said Daniel. "This is the start of a global civilizational war. Either the Westphalian system of sovereign democracies survives, or we are heading down the path of a New Dark Age."

Bibliography

"33rd Annual ISNA Canada Convention - List of
   Confirmed Speakers." isnacanada.com. Islamic
   Society of North America Canada, July 1, 2007.
   http://web.archive.org/web/20070701222024/ht
   tp:/www.isnacanada.com/Convention/Toronto/3
   3/speakers.html.

"About Qatar Charity." About Qatar Charity - An
   overview. Qatar Charity. Accessed January 6,
   2021. https://www.qcharity.org/en/qa/about.

Abueish, Tamara. "Muslim Brotherhood Is a Terrorist
   Group: Saudi Arabia's Council of Senior Scholars."
   Al Arabiya English. Al Arabiya English, November
   11, 2020.
   https://english.alarabiya.net/en/News/gulf/2020/
   11/11/Muslim-Brotherhood-is-a-terrorist-group-
   Saudi-Arabia-s-Council-of-Senior-Scholars.

Adel, Shaimaa, Khaled Adel, Walaa Bakir, Yasmin
   Musallam, Rana el Hindy, Suze Labib, Zeina el
   Sarrag, et al. "Egyptian Arabic Search." Egyptian
   Arabic Dictionary | Word Search.
   https://www.lisaanmasry.org, 2020.
   https://www.lisaanmasry.org/online/search.php?
   ui=en&language=EG&key=%D8%B4%D8%B1%D9
   %8A%D8%B9%D8%A9%E2%80%8E&action=s.

Al Arabiya News, Staff Writer. "UAE Blacklists 82
   Groups as 'Terrorist'." Al Arabiya English. Al
   Arabiya Network, November 15, 2014.
   https://english.alarabiya.net/en/News/middle-
   east/2014/11/15/UAE-formally-blacklists-82-
   groups-as-terrorist-.

Alexander, Kristian. Extremism and the threat of Muslim Brotherhood in Germany. Trends Research, November 3, 2020. https://trendsresearch.org/insight/extremism-and-the-threat-of-muslim-brotherhood-in-germany/.

Alfaham, Tariq, and Hatem Mohamed. "Muslim Brotherhood Terrorist Organisation, Affirms UAE Fatwa Council." Emirates News Agency (WAM), November 23, 2020. https://www.wam.ae/en/details/1395302889318.

The Avalon Project: Hamas Covenant 1988. Yale Law School - Lillian Goldman Law Library, 2008. http://avalon.law.yale.edu/20th_century/hamas.asp.

Bashir, Hassan. "Muslim Brotherhood a Terrorist Group: Saudi Senior Scholars." Emirates News Agency WAM. United Arab Emirates, November 10, 2020. https://www.wam.ae/en/details/1395302885284.

Bell, Stewart. "Federal Court Upholds Government Stopping Funding to Canadian Arab Federation over Concerns It Appears to Support Terrorist Organizations." nationalpost.com. National Post, a division of Postmedia Network Inc., January 7, 2014. https://nationalpost.com/news/canada/federal-court-upholds-government-stopping-funding-to-canadian-arab-federation-over-concerns-it-appears-to-support-terrorist-organizations.

Bimman, Abigail. "More Details on Torn Ballots: It Happened with the Machine That Opens the

Envelopes. It Is Supposed to Slice Open Just the Envelope, but Was Cutting into the Ballots in a Few Thousand Cases. Those Ballots Needed to Be Re-Marked on Fresh Ballots before Being Fed into Counter." Twitter.com. Twitter, August 24, 2020. https://twitter.com/AbigailBimman/status/12976 88290175442944.

"Brainstorming." en.wikipedia.org. Wikimedia Foundation, May 26, 2017. https://en.wikipedia.org/w/index.php?title=Brain storming&oldid=782442844.

Byrne, Caroline. "Sweden Questions Whether Government Should Support Groups Linked to Muslim Brotherhood." www.thenationalnews.com. International Media Investments, March 17, 2018. https://www.thenationalnews.com/world/europ e/sweden-questions-whether-government-should-support-groups-linked-to-muslim-brotherhood-1.713660.

Carré, Olivier, and Liv Tønnessen. "Hassan Al-Banna." Essay. In *The Oxford Encyclopedia of the Islamic World*, edited by John L. Esposito, translated by Elizabeth Keller. New York, NY: Oxford University Press, 2009.

Chesnot, Christian, and Georges Malbrunot. "Qatar Papers: How Doha Finances the Muslim Brotherhood in Europe. eBook." Qatar Papers: How Doha finances the Muslim Brotherhood in Europe. www.Amazon.ca, March 25, 2020. https://www.amazon.ca/Qatar-Papers-finances-Brotherhood-Europe-ebook/dp/B086DSMKFY.

Cole, William. "Entire Leadership of Britain's Biggest Muslim Charity QUITS over Antisemitic Posts."

Daily Mail Online. DMG Media, DMGT plc, August 22, 2020. https://www.dailymail.co.uk/news/article-8653559/Entire-leadership-Britains-biggest-Muslim-charity-QUITS-antisemitic-posts.html.

Daly, Paul. "Governmental Contracting, Procedural Fairness and Fundamental Freedoms - Canadian Arab Federation v. Canada (Citizenship and Immigration), 2013 FC 1283 (CanLII)." CanLII Connects. Canadian Legal Information Institute, October 21, 2014. https://canliiconnects.org/en/commentaries/302 53

Delattre, Nathalie, Jacqueline Eustache-Brinio, Éliane Assassi, Julien Bargeton, Jean-Marie Bockel, Alain Cazabonne, Pierre Charon, et al. "Radicalisation Islamiste - Sénat." Senat. Government of France, July 7, 2020. http://www.senat.fr/commission/enquete/radica lisation_islamiste.html.

"Devil's Advocate." en.wikipedia.org. Wikimedia Foundation, May 23, 2021. https://en.wikipedia.org/wiki/Devil%27s_advocat e.

"Dr. Henry Prunckun." Henry Prunckun - Australian Graduate School of Policing and Security. Charles Sturt University, June 1, 2021. https://bjbs.csu.edu.au/schools/agsps/staff/profil es/adjunct-staff/hank_prunckun.

"Dr. Lorenzo Vidino." Program on Extremism. George Washington University. Accessed January 7, 2021. https://extremism.gwu.edu/dr-lorenzo-vidino.

Dreyfuss, Bob. "Al Jazeera's Muslim Brotherhood Problem." TheNation.com. The Nation Company

LLC, July 10, 2013.
https://www.thenation.com/article/archive/al-jazeeras-muslim-brotherhood-problem/.

El Houdaiby, Ibrahim. "Applying Shariah." Ikhwanweb. The Muslim Brotherhood, September 23, 2007. https://www.ikhwanweb.com/article.php?id=14143.

Encyclopedia Britannica, Editors. "Muslim Brotherhood." Encyclopædia Britannica. Encyclopædia Britannica, inc., September 11, 2020. https://www.britannica.com/topic/Muslim-Brotherhood.

Esposito, John L., ed. "Hassan Al-Banna." Essay. In *The Oxford Dictionary of Islam*. New York, NY: Oxford University Press, 2014.

Federal Ministry of the Interior, Building and Community, ed. "2019 Annual Report on the Protection of the Constitution (Facts and Trends)." Bundesamt für Verfassungsschutz. Federal Minister of the Interior, July 9, 2020. https://www.verfassungsschutz.de/en/public-relations/publications/annual-reports/annual-report-2019-summary.

Fernando, Spencer. "Terrible Decision By Conservatives To Remove Salim Mansur Creates New Opening For Bernier." Spencer Fernando - News & Commentary. Spencer Fernando, June 12, 2019. https://spencerfernando.com/2019/06/12/terrible-decision-by-conservatives-to-remove-salim-mansur-creates-new-opening-for-bernier/.

Freeze, Colin, and Affan Chowdhry. "Saudi Government Funding Private Islamic Schools in Canada, Documents Show."

TheGlobeandMail.com. The Globe and Mail, Inc.,
July 2, 2015.
https://www.theglobeandmail.com/news/nation
al/saudi-government-funding-private-islamic-
schools-in-canada-docs-show/article25223573/.

"Galal Abdelmessih, P.Eng., FEC, PMP." peo.on.ca.
Professional Engineers Ontario, 2019.
https://www.peo.on.ca/about-peo/awards/galal-
abdelmessih-peng-fec-pmp-0.

Ghoraba , Hany. "The Brotherhood's Fifth Column -
Opinion." Ahram Online. Al-Ahram, July 23, 2020.
http://english.ahram.org.eg/NewsContentP/4/37
5074/Opinion/The-Brotherhood%E2%80%99s-
fifth-column-.aspx.

"Glimpse Into The History of Muslim Brotherhood."
Ikhwanweb. The Muslim Brotherhood, June 10,
2007.
https://www.ikhwanweb.com/article.php?id=794
.

"Government of Canada Lists IRFAN-Canada as
Terrorist Entity." Government of Canada.
Government of Canada, April 29, 2014.
https://www.canada.ca/en/news/archive/2014/0
4/government-canada-lists-irfan-canada-terrorist-
entity.html.

Guitta, Olivier. "France Sends a Strong Signal to the
Muslim Brotherhood." *The Levant*. July 26, 2020.
https://thelevantnews.com/en/2020/07/french-
senate-strong-message-to-the-muslim-
brotherhood/.

"Hamas." Wikipedia. Wikimedia Foundation,
November 18, 2020.
https://en.wikipedia.org/wiki/Hamas.

Harley, Nicky. "German MP Calls for Inquiry into Islamic Relief to Nip 'Seditious Sentiments in the Bud'." thenationalnews.com. International Media Investments, November 30, 2020. https://www.thenationalnews.com/world/germa n-mp-calls-for-inquiry-into-islamic-relief-to-nip-seditious-sentiments-in-the-bud-1.1120641.

"Hassan Al-Banna." Religion and Public Life at Harvard Divinity School. Harvard University. Accessed December 21, 2020. https://rpl.hds.harvard.edu/faq/hassan-al-banna.

"Hassan Al-Hudaybi." Wikipedia. Wikimedia Foundation, December 7, 2020. https://en.wikipedia.org/wiki/Hassan_al-Hudaybi.

Heritage, American. "Fundamentalist." Dictionary of the English Language, Fifth Edition. Farlex Inc. Accessed December 20, 2020. http://www.thefreedictionary.com/fundamentali st.

Heuer, Richards J. "The Evolution of Structured Analytic Techniques." Pennsylvania State University: John A. Dutton e-Education Institute, December 8, 2009.

Heuer, Richards J., and Randolph H. Pherson. "Structured Analytic Techniques for Intelligence Analysis, 3rd Edition." Amazon.ca. CQ Press, December 5, 2019. https://www.amazon.ca/Structured-Analytic-Techniques-Intelligence-Analysis-ebook/dp/B082Z59BKT.

Ikhwanweb. "Establishment of the Muslim Brotherhood." Ikhwanweb. The Muslim Brotherhood, June 10, 2007.

https://www.ikhwanweb.com/article.php?id=796
.

iqradotca. "Masjid Toronto Welcomes New Imam and
    Resident Scholar." iqra.ca. Muslim Association of
    Canada, April 20, 2015.
    http://iqra.ca/2015/masjid-toronto-welcomes-
    new-imam-and-resident-scholar/.
Isitman, Elif. "'Kaag: Geen Nederlands Belastinggeld
    Voor Islamclub' [Islamic Relief Worldwide]."
    Telegraaf.nl. TMG Landelijke Media BV,
    Amsterdam, January 19, 2021.
    https://www.telegraaf.nl/nieuws/1377055849/ka
    ag-geen-nederlands-belastinggeld-voor-islamclub.
"Islamic Relief Worldwide - United States Department
    of State." Office of The Special Envoy to Monitor
    and Combat Anti-Semitism. U.S. Department of
    State, December 30, 2020. https://2017-
    2021.state.gov/islamic-relief-
    worldwide//index.html.
Islamism Map. "Listen to Senior #MuslimBrotherhood
    Leader Saying That Islamic Relief Charity
    (Https://T.co/2Q73SmhtXq) Is Part of the Muslim
    Brotherhood: Pic.twitter.com/xfOqBu3zJy."
    Islamism Map. Twitter, April 5, 2017.
    https://twitter.com/IslamismMap/status/849643
    250583560192?s=20.
Kermalli, Shenaz. "Trudeau: Agent of Change?" Iran
    News | Al Jazeera. Al Jazeera, April 16, 2013.
    https://www.aljazeera.com/features/2013/4/16/j
    ustin-trudeau-canadas-agent-for-change.
Korzinski, Dave. "Trust in Government: Canadians
    Wary of Politicians and Their Intentions."
    angusreid.org. Angus Reid Institute, August 1,
    2019. https://angusreid.org/views-of-politicians/.

Kredo, Adam. "State Department Cuts Ties With Islamic Charity Over Anti-Semitism." Washington Free Beacon. Washington Free Beacon, January 18, 2021. https://freebeacon.com/national-security/state-department-cuts-ties-with-islamic-charity-over-anti-semitism/.

Laub, Zachary. "Egypt's Muslim Brotherhood." Council on Foreign Relations. Council on Foreign Relations, August 15, 2019. https://www.cfr.org/backgrounder/egypts-muslim-brotherhood.

Lawton, Andrew. "Salim Mansur's Battle against Islamism." True North. True North Centre for Public Policy, October 16, 2019. https://tnc.news/2019/10/16/salim-mansurs-battle-against-islamism/.

Lia, Brynjar. *The Society of the Muslim Brothers in Egypt: the Rise of an Islamic Mass Movement.* Reading UK: Ithaca Press, 1998.

MacLeod, Ian. "Beware of the Muslim Brotherhood, Expert Warns." ottawacitizen.com. Ottawa Citizen, June 2, 2020. https://ottawacitizen.com/news/politics/beware-of-the-muslim-brotherhood-expert-warns.

Map, Islamism. "Listen to Senior #MuslimBrotherhood Leader Saying That Islamic Relief Charity (Https://T.co/2Q73SmhtXq) Is Part of the Muslim Brotherhood: Pic.twitter.com/xfOqBu3zJy." Twitter. Twitter, April 5, 2017. https://twitter.com/IslamismMap/status/849643250583560192?s=20.

Mason, Tania. "Islamic Relief's Donation Page Is Removed from CAF Website." Civil Society. Civil

Society Media, September 3, 2014.
https://www.civilsociety.co.uk/news/islamic-relief-s-donation-page-is-removed-from-caf-website.html.

McElroy, Damien, and Nicky Harley. "New Islamic Relief Worldwide Chairman Celebrated Muslim Brotherhood on Social Media." thenationalnews.com. International Media Investments, August 28, 2020. https://www.thenationalnews.com/world/new-islamic-relief-worldwide-chairman-celebrated-muslim-brotherhood-on-social-media-1.1069197.

MEE Staff. "UAE's Fatwa Council Denounces Muslim Brotherhood as a Terrorist Organisation." Middle East Eye, November 25, 2020. https://www.middleeasteye.net/news/uae-muslim-brotherhood-fatwa-council-terrorist-organisation.

"Middle East News." The Levant, November 22, 2020. https://thelevantnews.com/en/the-levant-news-middle-east/.

Milewski, Terry. "Trudeau's 'Star' Candidate in Vancouver Spurs Sikh Walkout on Liberals | CBC News." CBC News Politics. CBC/Radio Canada, December 21, 2014. https://www.cbc.ca/news/politics/b-c-sikhs-quit-liberals-to-protest-justin-trudeau-s-star-candidate-1.2866343.

Ministry of Defence. "Understanding and Intelligence Support to Joint Operations (JDP 2-00) 3rd Edition, Change 1." GOV.UK. GOV.UK, May 15, 2014. https://www.gov.uk/government/publications/jd

p-2-00-understanding-and-intelligence-support-
to-joint-operations.

Mitchell, Richard P. *The Society of the Muslim
Brothers*. Middle Eastern Monographs. New York,
NY: Oxford University Press, Inc., 1960.

"The Muslim Brotherhood Official English Website."
Ikhwanweb. The Muslim Brotherhood. Accessed
December 20, 2020.
https://www.ikhwanweb.com/index.php.

Muslim Brotherhood. Federation of American
Scientists, January 8, 2002.
https://fas.org/irp/world/para/mb.htm.

"Muslim Brotherhood." Wikipedia. Wikimedia
Foundation, November 30, 2020.
https://en.wikipedia.org/wiki/Muslim_Brotherho
od.

"Muslim Brotherhood: Structure & Spread."
Ikhwanweb. The Muslim Brotherhood, June 13,
2007.
http://www.ikhwanweb.com/article.php?id=817.

Muslims for White Ribbon. Cordoba Centre for Civic
Engagement and Leadership, December 14, 2012.
http://muslimsforwhiteribbon.com/.

The National staff. "List of Groups Designated
Terrorist Organisations by the UAE." The National.
International Media Investments, November 16,
2014.
https://www.thenationalnews.com/uae/governm
ent/list-of-groups-designated-terrorist-
organisations-by-the-uae-1.270037.

Norfolk, Andrew, and Ryan Watts. "Islamic Relief
Leader Quits as Times Discovers Antisemitic
Posts." News | The Times. The Times, July 24,
2020.

https://www.thetimes.co.uk/edition/news/islami
c-relief-leader-quits-as-times-discovers-
antisemitic-posts-5dplrw9vv.

Norfolk, Andrew, and Ryan Watts. "Islamic Relief
Leader Quits as Times Discovers Antisemitic
Posts." thetimes.co.uk. news.co.uk, July 24, 2020.
https://www.thetimes.co.uk/article/islamic-
relief-leader-quits-as-times-discovers-antisemitic-
posts-5dplrw9vv.

"Our Story." QED. Al-Qazzaz Foundation for Education
and Development, November 26, 2020. https://q-
ed.org/our-story/.

Prime Minister's Office, 10 Downing Street. "Muslim
Brotherhood Review: Main Findings." GOV.UK.
GOV.UK, December 17, 2015.
https://www.gov.uk/government/publications/m
uslim-brotherhood-review-main-findings.

Prime Minister's Office, 10 Downing Street. "Muslim
Brotherhood Review: Statement by the Prime
Minister." GOV.UK. GOV.UK, December 17, 2015.
https://www.gov.uk/government/speeches/musli
m-brotherhood-review-statement-by-the-prime-
minister.

"Profile: Egypt's Muslim Brotherhood." BBC News.
BBC, December 25, 2013.
http://www.bbc.com/news/world-middle-east-
12313405.

"Projects and Campaigns - IRISE." MAC. Muslim
Association of Canada, June 12, 2019.
https://www.macnet.ca/projects-campaigns/.

Prunckun, Hank. "Scientific Methods of Inquiry for
Intelligence Analysis, Second Edition." Rowman &
Littlefield. Rowman & Littlefield, September 2014.
https://rowman.com/ISBN/9781442224315/Scien

tific-Methods-of-Inquiry-for-Intelligence-Analysis-Second-Edition.

Samet, Michael G. "Subjective Interpretation of Reliability and Accuracy Scales for Evaluating Military Intelligence." DTIC. U.S. Army Research Institute for the Behavioral and Social Sciences, January 1, 1975. https://apps.dtic.mil/sti/citations/ADA003260.

"Saudi Arabia Declares Muslim Brotherhood 'Terrorist Group'." BBC News. BBC, March 7, 2014. https://www.bbc.com/news/world-middle-east-26487092.

"Schools & Learning Centres." Schools - MAC. Muslim Association of Canada (MAC), October 16, 2019. https://www.macnet.ca/our-schools.

"Sharia Definition, Sharia Meaning: English Dictionary." Reverso. Softissimo, LEC, 2021. https://dictionary.reverso.net/english-definition/sharia.

"Sharia." Cambridge Dictionary. Cambridge University Press, 2021. https://dictionary.cambridge.org/dictionary/english/sharia.

"Sharia: Definition of Sharia and Synonyms of Sharia (English)." sharia: definition of sharia and synonyms of sharia. sensagent Corporation, 2012. http://dictionary.sensagent.com/sharia%20/en-en/.

Shari`ah Staff. "Sheikh Qaradawi's First Interview with Onislam.net." www.ikhwanweb.com. The Muslim Brotherhood, November 21, 2010. https://www.ikhwanweb.com/article.php?id=272 33

"Sigrid Kaag Geeft Toch Geen 37 Miljoen Aan
   Omstreden Moslimorganisatie." Metronieuws.nl.
   Mediahuis Nederland BV, January 19, 2021.
   https://www.metronieuws.nl/in-het-
   nieuws/binnenland/2021/01/kaag-omstreden-
   moslim-organisatie/.
Staff, National Post. "Cancelled Debate Highlights
   Tension among Canadian Muslims."
   nationalpost.com. National Post, February 7,
   2011. https://nationalpost.com/holy-
   post/cancelled-debate-highlights-tension-among-
   canadian-muslims.
Staff, The National. "List of Groups Designated
   Terrorist Organisations by the UAE." The National.
   The National, November 16, 2014.
   https://www.thenationalnews.com/uae/governm
   ent/list-of-groups-designated-terrorist-
   organisations-by-the-uae-1.270037.
Staff, The National. "UAE Backs Saudi Arabia on
   Muslim Brotherhood 'Terror'." The National. The
   National, March 9, 2014.
   https://www.thenationalnews.com/uae/governm
   ent/uae-backs-saudi-arabia-on-muslim-
   brotherhood-terror-1.254964.
"Standing Senate Committee on National Security and
   Defence - Evidence." Senate of Canada.
   Government of Canada, May 11, 2015.
   https://sencanada.ca/en/Content/Sen/committe
   e/412/secd/52124-e.
"Terrorist Pursuers Are Looking for New Hideouts,
   Fearing a Change in Doha's Position." Main -
   Policy. Albawabh News, April 1, 2014.
   https://www.albawabhnews.com/494011.

"A Tradecraft Primer: Structured Analytic Techniques for Improving Intelligence Analysis." Amazon.ca. US Government, 2009. https://www.amazon.com/Tradecraft-Primer-Structured-Techniques-Intelligence/dp/1478361182.

"A Tradecraft Primer: Structured Analytic Techniques for Improving Intelligence Analysis." Center for the Study of Intelligence. Central Intelligence Agency, 2000. https://www.cia.gov/resources/csi/books-monographs/a-tradecraft-primer/.

Trinh, Lily. "China's Power Play: Political Entryism & The Conservative Leadership Race." TheNationalTelegraph.com. The National Telegraph, August 11, 2020. https://web.archive.org/web/20210106093104/https://thenationaltelegraph.com/national/chinas-political-entryism-and-hypocrisy-in-the-conservative-leadership-race.

"U.S. Army Field Manual (FM) 2-22.3 Human Intelligence Collector Operations." Washington: Headquarters, Department of the Army, September 6, 2006. Appendix B: Source and Information Reliability Matrix; Table B-1, Evaluation of Source Reliability, and Table B-2, Evaluation of Information Content.

"U.S. Army Techniques Publication (ATP) 2-22.9 Open-Source Intelligence." An Army Introduction to Open Source Intelligence. Federation of American Scientists Secrecy News, September 13, 2012. https://fas.org/blogs/secrecy/2012/09/army_osint/. Table 2-1 Open-source reliability ratings, and Table 2-2 Open-source content credibility ratings

"Useful Idiot." Merriam-Webster.com Dictionary s.v. Merriam-Webster Inc., 2020. https://www.merriam-webster.com/dictionary/useful%20idiot.

"Useful Idiot." Useful Idiot - Wikipedia. Wikimedia Foundation, February 10, 2021. https://en.wikipedia.org/wiki/Useful_idiot.

Various, Unknown. "Sayyid Qutb." Wikipedia. Wikimedia Foundation, December 8, 2020. https://en.wikipedia.org/wiki/Sayyid_Qutb.

West, Charlotte. "Canada's Islamist Seat." web.archive.org. Front Page Magazine, January 31, 2006. https://web.archive.org/web/20090212235014/http://www.frontpagemagazine.com/Articles/Printable.aspx?GUID=92F1D795-9884-4005-817F-3EDFCA1DF78D.

Williams, Dan. "Israel Bans UK-Based Muslim Charity Accused of Funding Hamas." Edited by Louise Ireland. web.archive.org. Reuters UK, June 19, 2014. https://web.archive.org/web/20140622025105/http://uk.reuters.com/article/2014/06/19/uk-palestinians-israel-charities-idUKKBN0EU1FE20140619.

Young, Niki May. "Banking Sector Nerves Blocking International Relief, Says Islamic Relief FD." civilsociety.co.uk. Civil Society Media Limited, November 8, 2012. https://www.civilsociety.co.uk/news/banking-sector-nerves-blocking-international-relief--says-islamic-relief-fd.html.

"Yusuf Al-Qaradawi." Wikipedia. Wikimedia
Foundation, December 7, 2020.
https://en.wikipedia.org/wiki/Yusuf_al-Qaradawi.

zhyntativ. "Hasan Al-Banna and His Political Thought
of Islamic Brotherhood." Ikhwanweb. The Muslim
Brotherhood, May 13, 2008.
https://www.ikhwanweb.com/article.php?id=170
65

الحمادي د. أحمد محمد. "صليت العصر في مسجد
كعادتي،بالدفنة ألقيت بعض فامتدت،خواطري ايادي
خيرة فاستقبلتها بدعاء لهموحصيلة هذا المسجد ١١سهم
Pic.twitter.com/f1fCIPTCIH." Twitter.
Twitter.com, July 28, 2013.
https://twitter.com/DrAl7ammadi/status/361476
465516216325.

"هذه هي قائمة 'الإرهاب' المصرية كاملة (1536 اسماء)
[This Is the Complete Egyptian 'Terrorism' List
(1536 Names)]." عربي21. Arabic 21, January 19,
2017. http://bit.ly/3pVRsdX.

———. "Psychology of Intelligence Analysis." Center
for the Study of intelligence. Central Intelligence
Agency, 1999.
https://www.cia.gov/resources/csi/books-
monographs/psychology-of-intelligence-analysis-
2/.

———. Qatar Papers: Comment L'émirat Finance
L'islam De France Et D'Europe. Neuilly-sur-Seine,
France: Michel Lafon, 2019.

APPENDIX A: CHARACTERS, AIRCRAFT AND SHIPS

REAL PERSONS

Justin Pierre James TRUDEAU

Justin Trudeau is the 23rd Prime Minister of Canada, first elected to that position in October of 2015. His father was Pierre Trudeau, who served multiple terms as Prime Minister from the late 1960s to the early 1980s. Justin Trudeau has garnered international attention for several political statements. In November of 2016, he said he learned of Cuban dictator Fidel Castro's passing with "great sorrow" and described him as a "legendary revolutionary and orator." During his first campaign for Prime Minister, he stated that he admired the "basic dictatorship of China." He also told the New York Times that Canada was the first 'post-national state." As part of his views on immigration, he gave an interview to a pro-Iranian newspaper in Canada, stating he would have a dedicated program of Muslims and Arabs if he was elected.

Alexandre 'Sasha' TRUDEAU

Sasha Trudeau is the brother of Prime Minister Justin Trudeau. He has worked for Press TV, which is the state broadcaster of the Islamic Republic of Iran. He also produced a documentary on Israel/Palestinian issues, which included a glowing profile of Zkaria Zubedi, the leader of the listed terrorist group, the Al Aqsa Martyrs Brigades. Sasha is on the list of official advisors to Prime Minister Trudeau, although it has never been clear what he does.

Omar ALGHABRA

The current federal Minister of Transportation in Canada is Omar Alghabra. He was formerly the Parliamentary Secretary to Prime Minister Trudeau. For most of his adult life, he claimed that Hamas and Hezbollah were not terrorist groups. However, after becoming a Member of Parliament, he said he had now recognized that Canada listed these two entities as terrorist entities. Mr. Alghabra was a supporter of a campaign in Ontario for sharia law. He also put out a statement of mourning for Yasser Arafat. Mr. Alghabra gave Prime Minister Trudeau a pair of "Happy Eid Halal Socks," which drew considerable press attention given the Prime Minister's predilection for unusual socks.

Recep Tayyip ERDOGAN

Recep Erdogan was Prime Minister of Turkey from 2003 until 2014 and has been President of Turkey since 2014. He has been committed to the Islamization of Turkey and has provided shelter to many senior Muslim Brotherhood members who were forced to flee Egypt in 2012/13. Under his leadership, Turkey has become considerably less democratic and is a hostile environment for journalists. In 1999, he was jailed for his pro-Islamist activity. In addition, he gained notoriety for his recitation of a poem that included the verse, "The mosques are our barracks, the domes our helmets, the minarets our bayonets and the faithful our soldiers."

FICTIONAL CHARACTERS

Clement RAES-JAVIER, also known as CRJ.

He is the Managing Director of the International Monetary Fund (IMF)

Clement RAES-JAVIER is a sociopath with a troubled personal history, but he is a strategic thinker, unlike most of those who surround him in prominent international organizations. He believes that the European Union is failing due to the weakness of its leadership class and its inability to act collectively. Therefore, he is determined to (re)build a powerful united Europe using the believers in the Great Reset and the Islamists as his pawns.

In addition to his position at the IMF, CR is also an amateur historian. His family had previously been reasonably well off under the Austro-Hungarian Empire, but all that was lost with World War One. His motto, which he rarely shares, is Viribus Unitis (With United Force) which was also the motto of Emperor Franz Joseph I of the Austro-Hungarian Empire.

Enrica LECLERCQ

High Representative for Foreign Affairs and Security Policy for the European Union

Working with CRJ, Enrica Leclercq is the primary driver for the Great Reset plot. She believes that the Soviet Union could have survived and prospered if they had better managed their central control of the economy. Her mother was from a communist family,

512

and Enrica was active as a communist party member in her youth. She is pro-Iran and pro-Hamas. To her, private property, the family, and Christianity are the obstacles to the future.

Jochen STENHAMMAR

Jochen is the Vice President of Risk at the Frankfurt-based Hessen Reinsurance Group. He is a moral, cautious, pattern-based analyst at a high-value reinsurance company. He had formerly worked for the Bundeskriminalamt (BKA or Federal Criminal Police Office). He comes from a modest but solid family background. Jochen's most noteworthy characteristic is the ability is to sense changes in patterns before others. In addition, he has proven willing to challenge superiors when necessary.

Aldo LANGE

Head of Hessen Reinsurance. As the head of the wealthy and influential Hessen Reinsurance company, Aldo Lange has been wary of social unrest and violence in Europe for years. He hired Jochen Stenhammar for his risk analysis of social unrest in Europe. He believes that technocrats and politicians have been perverting political and economic systems for years to advance the cause of various elitists while impoverishing others. His personal beliefs are well-founded in a historical assessment of modern Europe, starting with the Protestant Reformation. He believes that state sovereignty and freedom of speech have had a profoundly positive effect on humanity's well-being and is wary of those who support Marxism, Islamism, and the Great Reset.

Brenda ELISHCHUK

Brenda Elishchuk is the deputy prime minister of Canada who becomes acting Prime Minister when Justin Trudeau is assassinated. She was formerly the foreign minister. Brenda was raised in Montreal, where she met US President Kamela Harris. Brenda plays an enabling role in the killing of Justin Trudeau, believing he lacks the gravitas to be a leader in the future.

Rory NEWSON

Rory Newson is a close friend and confidant of Prime Minister Justin Trudeau. His family name had originally been Nuinnseann when they had landed in Canada from Ireland on Halifax's famous Pier 21. In addition to having been a close friend of the Prime Minister since their college days, he is also a chronic alcoholic. Rumors of the nature of his relationship with Justin Trudeau arise every few months.

Frank ARSENBERG

As the successful strategic advisor to Justin Trudeau, Frank Arsenberg knows everything about Justin Trudeau's personal and professional life. He has a brilliant mind for Machiavellian politics, but is a physical coward. His obsession with politics has kept him single.

The Special Air Service (SAS)

Major Roy BERIKOFF, SAS

Former Coldstream Guards. The Major comes from a family of London City bankers and lawyers but has chosen military service. He was educated in the 'right schools' and has connections in the rarefied world of

London society. He is known for his sharp dress while in civilian clothes.

Captain Andrew DAVIES, SAS

Former Royal Welsh Fusiliers. The captain comes from modest but respectable family background. He is slightly less than average height and has an average build, with light olive skin. He is known as a 'gray man' appearance in that he never stands out from the crowd. The captain played scrum-half in rugby. His presence of mind under stress in rugby allowed him to feed the backs for regular scoring. He has been with the SAS for about two years.

Staff Sergeant Allen CROSBY, SAS

The Staff Sergeant is known for leadership at the NCO level. He has been with the SAS for several years and will be leaving the SAS within the year. He has had global experience with the SAS and is known as the 'go-to guy' when things are going wrong.

Trooper David SKIFFINGTON, SAS

The Trooper is known for his attitude towards 'leaning into' situations. He has a lifelong interest in tech skills. He remains an active Amateur Radio Operator and is currently experimenting with long-range WIFI transmissions and jamming. He also has an interest in tracking airliners through home-based networks. He is helpful at jury-rigging electronics. He is a relatively new addition to the SAS.

The Hijackers of Flight 406

Ali JOWHARI

The leader of the hijack team. Ali is an Iranian Shia. His role was to set off the bomb on the cockpit door and maintain control of the first class and business class cabin during the hijacking operation.

Qassem RIZVI

The pilot of the aircraft hijack team. Qassem is a non-believer and has a mercenary attitude towards conflicts involving the Middle East.

Hossein JAFARI

Member of the hijack team. Hossein is also an Iranian Shia. His role in the hijacking was to maintain control of the economy class cabin. He is seen as a follower and not a leader.

The Pilots who Take Control of Flight 406 and Passengers

Captain David BAMPTON, RCAF

The captain is a Sea King and Cyclone helicopter pilot. He is known as 'Bam-Bam' for his short temper. Referring to his pilot skills, he often tells people in bars that "I may not be too bright, but I have got golden hands." He is 'old school' in that he believes that piloting skills should take precedence of technology in aviation. He is popular in aircrew circles, but not so much with the leadership levels in the military.

Lieutenant Alan GOLDSMITH, RCAF

The Lieutenant is a Cyclone helicopter co-pilot. He is one of the new breed of pilots who are fascinated with technology. He is smart enough to realize that he and Bampton have a combined skill set that is workable under even the worst of circumstances. His spare time is often taken up with flight control simulators of large airliners.

The Judge on Flight 406

Judge Kapoor's mother died on an Air India flight in 1984 when he was ten years old. The terrorist attack shaped his life and career. He decided to use his love of technology and learn to become a Crown Prosecutor specializing in terrorism. He is later promoted to be a judge in the Federal Court of Canada, which hears terrorism cases such as national security certificates.

The Crew of the MS Nordsee Bliss and Fulfillment of the Seas

Captain Meyer JAGER

Captain of the cruise ship MS Nordsee Bliss. The 168,000-ton ship was built at the famous Meyer Werft Shipyard of German and is owned by the Nordsee Cruise lines. The captain is a former German Navy officer (Kapitän zur See) who had joined the Bundesmarine in 1994, just before it became known as the Deutsche Marine. He was part of Operation Flotilla 2 – 2nd Frigate Squadron, the Sachsen-class F 219 air defense frigate. See selected details for F 219 Sachsen under "Ships."

He serves as Captain of the MS Nordsee Bliss on a two months on/two months off rotation. His naval career soared until an unfortunate accident resulted in his ship, the Sachsen, being damaged during a NATO Standing Naval Forces (Group One) exercise. The accidental ramming of a fishing trawler resulted from the action of JAGER's senior officer, an Admiral who had initially been Volksmarine or East German Navy. Konteradmiral BAUER had been promoted well beyond his abilities due to his political connections and a united German government that did not want to offend the "der Ossi." Konteradmiral BAUER represented everything Captain Meyer JAGER hates – politics, corruption, and nepotism being placed over competence.

Andre RAMOS

A Filipino steward on board the Nordsee Bliss. He serves the captain directly and was promoted after being hired as a bartender in the first class. He is noted for his ability to read passengers and crew while anticipating their demands before they know what they want. He was due to return to the Philippines after one contract term but was convinced to remain for a two-year term to serve with the captain.

Wendy WALLACE

Staff Captain and Officer of the Deck of the Nordsee Bliss.

Captain Warren MARTINDALE

Captain of the Fulfillment of the Seas

The Cash Center Robbery Gang

Gamal al-Badawi

Leader of the crew that attacks the cash center. Gamal is originally from Egypt, raised in France, and briefly educated at an English university. He did a short period of service in the French Army and then joined the French Foreign Legion after some 'complications' with the police in Lyon. He is calm under fire and a natural leader. Few know it, but he is the bastard son of a senior General Intelligence Service (Mukhabarat) official who had an affair with his mother. Despite his claims to be serving the Islamist cause, he is genuinely a mercenary at heart and now works purely for money or interest.

Amin ATTIA

Egyptian. He is the least liked among his peers on the crew that attacks the cash center. His flaws are seen as a weak point for the team.

Yassir HADDAD

Egyptian. Failed engineering student. He is one of the most reliable crew members for the cash center attack and is devoid of any sense of empathy for others.

Wilhelm de Haas

Local Dutch contact who hired Gama for the cash center robbery. He has a lengthy criminal past but is well connected in political circles. He is the go-between for CRJ and the cash center crew.

Islamic Assistance Transnational (IAT)

Ilhan BENHADDARA

Head of the charity Islamic Assistance Transnational. She had earlier replaced the former head of IAT, who had been removed for bragging about his Muslim Brotherhood connections. The former leader had openly glorified Hamas and his growing ties with Hezbollah. She is the victim of the highly public assassination outside the Europa Building. She was due to testify to the European Council on EU funding to the Palestinian cause. Despite her high profile, she is simply the organization's public face when they needed someone who had a clean background. She has little real influence on either the strategic goals of the organization or its day-to-day operations.

Tarek RAMAN

Austrian academic in Islamic Studies. He directs Ilhan and runs interference when the organization is criticized for its links to funding terrorism. He portrays himself as a moderate when in fact, he is a hard-core Islamist. He is the most senior and influential figure of the Muslim Brotherhood in Europe. His father lives in Graz, Austria, and the family had fled from Egypt after the plot to assassinate Egypt President Nasser in 1955. He is the crucial link to Qatar and its funding of the Muslim Brotherhood in Europe. He knows that terrorist groups and Islamists can influence the EU by appealing to the collectivist, authoritarian, anti-capitalist, and anti-free speech nature.

City of London Law Firm Chevalier and Tag

Niles CHEVALIER

Lawyer. He is recently divorced but socially well connected in London circles. His law firm has made a full-time practice of suing former soldiers on manufactured evidence of war crimes or human rights. He has a predilection in his background, which was the cause of the divorce.

AIRCRAFT

Boeing 777 (9 series) aircraft

New aircraft. (349 passengers) Eight first-class. 49 business. 292 in economy. Galley in the middle of the business class section. The Cockpit has 4 x 12-inch LCD touch screens display screens multifunctional. Folding wings. 2 x GE 9x engines with carbon composite fan blades. LED mood lighting. GLS OR Global Navigation Satellite Landing System. IAN or Integrated Approach Navigation System. HUD on each side. HUD can be swung into or out of line of site. Economy class is 3-4-3 configuration.

Boeing MRA1[163] / P-8A[164] Poseidon

Boeing's MRA1 (UK designation) P-8A (US designation) Poseidon is a multirole maritime patrol aircraft, equipped with sensors and weapons systems for anti-submarine warfare, as well as surveillance and search and rescue missions.

Specifications:

- Powerplant: two 27,000 lb thrust (120kN) CFM International CFM56-7 turbofan engines.

- Length: 129 ft 6 in (39.47 m)

- Height: 42 ft 1¼ in (12.83 m)

- Wingspan: 123 ft 7¼in (37.64 m)

- Maximum take-off weight: 189,200 lb (85,820 kg)

- Maximum speed: 490 kt (907 km/h)

- Ferry range: 4,500 miles (7,242 km)

- Service ceiling: 41,000 ft.

---

[163] https://www.raf.mod.uk/aircraft/poseidon-mra1/
[164] https://en.wikipedia.org/wiki/Boeing_P-8_Poseidon

Lockheed Martin F-35B LIGHTNING II[165]

The Lockheed Martin F-35 Lightning II is an American family of single-seat, single-engine, all-weather stealth multirole combat aircraft intended to perform air superiority and strike missions. It is also able to provide electronic warfare and intelligence, surveillance, and reconnaissance capabilities. Lockheed Martin is the prime F-35 contractor, with principal partners Northrop Grumman and BAE Systems. The aircraft has three main variants: the conventional take-off and landing F-35A (CTOL), **the short take-off and vertical-landing F-35B (STOVL)**, and the carrier-based F-35C (CV/CATOBAR).

SHIPS AND BASES

MS Nordsee Bliss

The Nordsee Bliss is loosely based on a real ship, the Anthem of the Seas[166] , a Quantum-class cruise ship owned by Royal Caribbean International. The 168,000-ton ship was built at the famous Meyer Werft Shipyard of German and owned by the Nordsee Cruise lines. The ship has 1500 crew, 2219 suites, and rooms, 4000 passengers at maximum, 4 pools, 18 dining options, 18 high-definition projectors, 23 actors. The bridge features a V-shaped command console. The bridge also has a glass deck panel to allow the bridge crew to see straight down. The propulsion comes from two Azipod five-bladed units.

---

[165] https://en.wikipedia.org/wiki/Lockheed_Martin_F-35_Lightning_II
[166] "Anthem of the Seas - Royal Caribbean," en.wikipedia.org (Wikimedia Foundation, March 29, 2021), https://en.wikipedia.org/wiki/Anthem_of_the_Seas.

The ABB Azipod XO 2500 thrusters have a rated capacity of 20.5MW each. Four bow thrusters have a power output of 3,500 kW each.

MS Fulfillment of The Seas

The Fulfillment of the Seas is loosely based on the Royal Caribbean Symphony of the Seas[167]. The ship displaces 228,000 tons.

German Navy Sachsen class F 219 Sachsen (Saxony) air defence frigate

Lead ship of class. International radio call sign DRAA. 5,800 tons. CODAG (combined diesel and gas) power diesel gas turbine, 29+ knots. Two shafts with 2 x 5-bladed controllable-pitch props. Full reverse to full forward. Two helicopters, either Sea Lynx or NH90. Turning radius of 570 m (1,870 ft). Complement of 230 crew plus 13 aircrew.

RAF Lossiemouth - Moray, Scotland

Fast-air base in Scotland. The base normally operates Typhoons and F-35s. The base also supports P-8A / Poseidon fixed wing aircraft, which operates in the anti-submarine role. The P-8A is a modified 737-800. In addition, the base has fire and rescue capabilities for larger fixed-wing aircraft.

---

[167] "Symphony of the Seas - Royal Caribbean," en.wikipedia.org (Wikimedia Foundation, January 26, 2021), https://en.wikipedia.org/wiki/Symphony_of_the_Seas.

Appendix B: Structured Analytic Techniques

R.L.A. (Rick) Gill, CD

Key Points

- Structured analytic techniques or SATs are debiasing techniques; they assist the analyst in overcoming their cognitive biases.

- Structured analytic techniques do not replace intuitive judgement.

- The role of structured analytic techniques is to question intuitive judgements being made, by identifying a wider range of options for the analyst to consider.

- Examples of commonly used SATs described in the storyline are provided below.

Background

The first use of the term "structured analytic techniques" in the US Intelligence Community was noted in 2005. However, the origin of the concept goes back to the 1980s, when the eminent teacher of intelligence analysis at the CIA, Jack Davis, first began teaching and writing about what he called "alternative analysis."

In 1975, after 24 years at the CIA, Richards J. Heuer, Jr. moved from Operations to the (then) new Analytic Methodology Division.[168] During the annual

---

[168] Heuer, Richards J. "The Evolution of Structured Analytic

International Studies Association (ISA) convention in 1977, Richards J. Heuer was introduced to the ground-breaking research in cognitive psychology by Daniel Kahneman and Amos Tversky. Heuer's review of Kahneman and Tversky's research on cognitive psychology was the beginning of his personal interest in this field of study. Heuer retired in 1979 after 28 years of service with the CIA, continuing his work on analytic and cognitive psychology issues as a CIA contractor.

Heuer's studies and writings over the next two decades included the development in the mid-1980s of an interagency course on deception analysis. He stated in his 2009 presentation The Evolution of Structured Analytic Techniques[169] that his Analysis of Competing Hypotheses methodology was the centerpiece of this course. Heuer's *Psychology of Intelligence Analysis*[170] was first published by the Center for the Study of Intelligence in 1999. Chapter 6, Keeping an Open Mind, Heuer speaks to various aspects of mindsets. On this subject, Heuer states:

"Beliefs, assumptions, concepts, and information retrieved from memory form a mind-set or mental

---

Techniques." Pennsylvania State University: John A. Dutton e-Education Institute, December 8, 2009. **Rated A1.**
[169] Heuer, "The Evolution of Structured Analytic Techniques", 2009. **Rated A1.**
[170] Richards J. Heuer, "Psychology of Intelligence Analysis," Center for the Study of intelligence (Central Intelligence Agency, 1999), https://www.cia.gov/resources/csi/books-monographs/psychology-of-intelligence-analysis-2/ **Rated A1.**

model that guides perception and processing of new information.

A mind-set is neither good nor bad. It is unavoidable. It is, in essence, a distillation of all that analysts think they know about a subject. It forms a lens through which they perceive the world, and once formed, it resists change."

Analysts must maintain an open mind, and constantly be aware of their personal beliefs and mindsets; how they are affecting their judgement, and assumptions they are making at any point in time. In chapter 6, Heuer discusses cognitive biases, which he describes as "mental errors caused by our simplified information processing strategies." He goes on to say that it is important that we distinguish cognitive biases from other forms of bias, such as cultural bias, organizational bias, or bias that results from one's own self-interest. A cognitive bias is a mental error that is consistent and predictable.

The ability to think creatively and critically, combined with the use of structured analytic technqiues, allow the analyst to systematically produce well-developed, rational, and logical answers to analytic problems. It is for this reason that this annex on Structured Analytic Techniques has been included in this work.

In chapter 8, Heuer described his methodology Analysis of Competing Hypotheses (ACH). No doubt, due to his earlier interest in the work of Kahneman and Tversky, chapters 8 through 13 addressed various aspects of cognitive biases, and how they relate to the analysis of intelligence. Heuer's Psychology of Intelligence Analysis is now also commercially available in hardcopy and Kindle formats through Amazon.[171]

The US government published *A Tradecraft Primer: Structured Analytic Techniques for Improving Intelligence Analysis* on 4 May 2009.[172] It is now also commercially available in hardcopy and Kindle formats through Amazon.[173] In 2010, Heuer collaborated with Randy Pherson to produce and publish the first edition of the widely acclaimed *Structured Analytic Techniques for Intelligence Analysis*.[174] This publication, now available in its third edition, is one of the few commercially available references on the subject of structured analytic techniques.

Other methodologies and techniques that are today known as structured analytic techniques come from a variety of other areas. For example, the technique of

---

[171] Heuer, "Psychology of Intelligence Analysis", 1999. **Rated A1.**
[172] "A Tradecraft Primer: Structured Analytic Techniques for Improving Intelligence Analysis," Center for the Study of Intelligence (Central Intelligence Agency, 2000), https://www.cia.gov/resources/csi/books-monographs/a-tradecraft-primer/ **Rated A1.**
[173] "A Tradecraft Primer: Structured Analytic Techniques for Improving Intelligence Analysis," Amazon.ca (US Government, 2009), https://www.amazon.com/Tradecraft-Primer-Structured-Techniques-Intelligence/dp/1478361182 **Rated B1.**
[174] Richards J. Heuer and Randolph H. Pherson, "Structured Analytic Techniques for Intelligence Analysis, 3rd Edition," Amazon.ca (CQ Press, December 5, 2019), https://www.amazon.ca/Structured-Analytic-Techniques-Intelligence-Analysis-ebook/dp/B082Z59BKT **Rated A1.**

brainstorming[175] originated in business advertising and marketing circles. The term "brainstorming" was popularized by Alex Faickney Osborn in the 1953 book *Applied Imagination*. The use of a "Devil's Advocate"[176] originated with the Roman Catholic Church beginning in the late sixteenth century, as part of the church's canonization process.

Analytic Problems

A favorite analogy that aptly describes often complex problems faced by analysts is described in this way:

- An analytic problem is like a thousand-piece puzzle box, with no picture of the completed puzzle on the cover of the box;

- Opening the puzzle box, it is discovered that there are far less then a thousand pieces in the box. The puzzle pieces represent items of evidence or answers to the problem which the analyst is attempting to solve. The apparent lack of many pieces of the puzzle is indicative of the reality that the analyst is highly unlikely to ever have all the answers to his or her analytic problem;

---

[175] "Brainstorming," en.wikipedia.org (Wikimedia Foundation, May 26, 2017), https://en.wikipedia.org/w/index.php?title=Brainstorming&oldid=782442844 **Rated B1.**

[176] "Devil's Advocate," en.wikipedia.org (Wikimedia Foundation, May 23, 2021), https://en.wikipedia.org/wiki/Devil%27s_advocate **Rated B1.**

- Some of the pieces in the puzzle box also have no part of the overall picture on them. This represents a lack of understanding by the analyst of the meaning of these pieces of evidence;

- Many of the pieces in the puzzle box are of a different size and shape compared to most other puzzle pieces in the box. This represents extraneous information which has been collected, ("white noise") that has little or nothing to do with the analytic problem;

- Despite all the above, the goal of the analyst is to provide answers to the questions posed by the analytic problem, and typically within often short time constraints imposed by management, consumers, and decision makers.

Heuer and Pherson state in the third edition of their influential reference publication *Structured Analytic Techniques for Intelligence Analysis*[177] that using structured analytic techniques can reduce errors; help to mitigate cognitive and analytic biases, and assist in overcoming preconceived mindsets. SATs also help analysts think more rigorously about an analytic problem, confront assumptions and test hypotheses.

Selected Examples of Structured Analytic Techniques

A selection of the structured analytic techniques described in the storyline of this book are provided

---

[177] Heuer and Pherson. *Structured Analytic Techniques*, 7.

below. The vast majority of the information on the techniques detailed below has been drawn from:

- Heuer's *Psychology of Intelligence Analysis*, 1999;

- United States Government's *A Tradecraft Primer: Structured Analytic Techniques for Improving Intelligence Analysis*, 4 May 2009, and

- Heuer and Pherson's *Structured Analytic Techniques for Intelligence Analysis*, second edition, 2015.

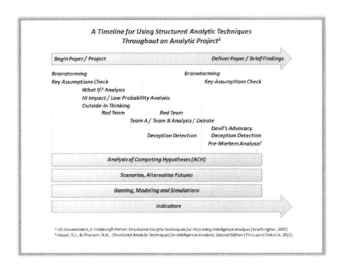

Brainstorming

An unconstrained group process designed to generate new ideas and concepts.[178]

When to Use

Brainstorming is a widely used technique for stimulating new thinking. Typically, analysts will conduct a brainstorming session beginning a new project to help generate a range of ideas and hypotheses about the subject at hand.

Brainstorming, almost by definition, involves a group of analysts meeting to discuss a common challenge. This modest investment of time at the beginning or critical points of a project can take advantage of the range of different perspectives to help structure a problem. This group process allows others to build on an initial idea suggested by a member of the brainstorming session.

Analysts can also brainstorm on their own to produce a range of ideas, without regard for others' egos, opinions, or objections. However, analysts will not have the benefit of others' perspectives in helping to develop their ideas. An individual may have difficulty breaking free of his or her own cognitive biases without the benefit of a diverse group. See Timeline for Using Structured Analytic Techniques graphic above.

Benefits

This technique can maximize creativity in the thinking process, forcing analysts to avoid their personal

---

[178] "A Tradecraft Primer, 27. **Rated A1.**

judgments about their individual ideas or approaches. More generally, brainstorming allows analysts to see a wider range of factors that might bear on the topic than they would otherwise consider. Analysts typically censor out ideas that seem farfetched, poorly sourced, or seemingly irrelevant to the question at hand. Brainstorming gives permission to think more radically or "outside the box." It can spark new ideas, ensure a comprehensive look at a problem or issues, raise unknowns, and prevent premature consensus around a single hypothesis.

Indicators

Periodically review a list of observable incidents or trends to track events, monitor targets, spot emerging trends, and warn of unforeseen change.

When to Use

An individual or a team can create indicators or signposts list of observable events that one would expect to see if a postulated situation is developing; e.g., economic reform, military modernization, political instability, or democratization. Constructing the list might require only a few hours or as much as several days to identify the critical variables associated with the specific issue. The technique can be used whenever someone needs to track an event over time to monitor and evaluate changes. However, it can also be an immensely powerful aid in supporting other structured methods explained later in this primer. In those instances, an individual or team would be watching for mounting evidence to support a particular hypothesis, low probability event, or scenario. See Timeline for Using Structured Analytic Techniques graphic above.

Benefits

By providing an objective baseline for tracking events or targets, indicators instill rigor into the analytic process and enhance the credibility of analytic judgments. An indicators list included in a finished product also allows the decisionmaker to track developments and builds a more concrete case for the analytic judgments. By laying out a list of critical variables, an individual or team also will be generating hypotheses regarding why they expect to see the presence of such factors. In so doing, analysts make the analytic line much more transparent and available for scrutiny by others.

Key Assumptions Check

Analytic judgements are always based on a combination of evidence and assumptions, or preconceived ideas, which influence how the analyst interprets evidence. The Key Assumptions Check is a structured process to clearly state and questions assumptions that guide the analyst's comprehension of evidence and reasoning about the problem at hand. The Key Assumptions Check is one of the most commonly used structured analytic techniques, because the analyst typically needs to make assumptions to fill gaps in his or her knowledge.

When to Use

A Key Assumptions Check is most useful at the beginning of an analytic project. An individual analyst or a team can spend an hour or two articulating and reviewing the key assumptions. Rechecking assumptions also can be valuable at any time prior to finalizing judgments, to ensure that the assessment does not rest on flawed premises. Identifying hidden assumptions can be one of the most difficult challenges some individual faces, as they are ideas held—often unconsciously—to be true and, therefore, are seldom examined and almost never challenged.

A key assumption is any hypothesis that analysts or a group have accepted to be true and which forms the basis of the assessment. For example, a military analysis may focus exclusively on analyzing key technical and military variables (sometimes called factors) of a military force and "assume" that these forces will be operated in a physical environment (desert, open plains, arctic conditions, etc.). Postulating other conditions or assumptions, however, could dramatically impact the assessment. Historically, analysis of Soviet-Warsaw Pact operations against NATO had to "assume" a level of non-Soviet Warsaw Pact reliability (e.g., would these forces fight?). In this case, there was high uncertainty and depending on what level of reliability one assumed, the analyst could arrive at very different conclusions about a potential Soviet offensive operation. Or when economists assess the prospects for foreign economic reforms, they may consciously, or not, assume a degree of political stability in those countries or the region that may or may not exist in the future.

Likewise, political analysts reviewing a developing country's domestic stability might unconsciously assume stable oil prices, when this key determinant of economic performance and underlying social peace might fluctuate. All of these examples highlight the fact that analysts often rely on stated and unstated assumptions to conduct their analysis. The goal is not to undermine or abandon key assumptions; rather, it is to make them explicit and identify what information or developments would demand rethinking them. See Timeline for Using Structured Analytic Techniques above.

Benefits

Explicitly identifying working assumptions during an analytic project helps:

- Explain the logic of the analytic argument and expose faulty logic;

- Understand the key factors that shape an issue;

- Stimulate thinking about an issue;

- Uncover hidden relationships and links between key factors;

- Identify developments that would cause you to abandon an assumption, and

- Prepare analysts for changed circumstances that could surprise them.

Chronologies and Timelines

A chronology is a list that places events or actions in the order in which they occurred. A timeline is a graphic depiction of those events put in the context of the time of the events and the time between events.[179]

When to Use

Whenever it is important to understand the sequence and timing of events; to identify gaps in time or between events, and key events. See Timeline for Using Structured Analytic Techniques graphic above.

Benefits

Chronologies and timelines assist in pattern analysis and the relationship between events. These techniques assist the analyst in making connections between events and the bigger picture. Multiple-level timelines or "swim lanes" allow analysts to track concurrent activities or events that may influence one another. Chronologies and timelines can lead an analyst or analysts to hypothesize the existence of previously unknown events. A series of known events may only make sense if other previously unknown events have also occurred. Finally, chronologies and timelines can be useful in organizing information in ways that can be easily understood in a briefing.

"What-If?" Analysis

Assumes that an event has occurred with potential (negative or positive) impact and explains how it might come about.

When to Use

---

[179] Heuer and Pherson, Structured Analytic Techniques, 138. **Rated A1.**

"What If?" analysis is another contrarian technique for challenging a strong mind-set that an event will not happen or that a confidently made forecast may not be entirely justified. It is similar to a High-Impact/Low-Probability analysis, but it does not dwell on the consequences of the event as much as it accepts the significance and moves directly to explaining how it might come about. See Timeline for Using Structured Analytic Techniques graphic above.

Benefits

By shifting the focus from whether an event could occur to how it may happen, analysts allow themselves to suspend judgment about the likelihood of the event and focus more on what developments - even unlikely ones - might enable such an outcome. An individual analyst or a team might employ this technique and repeat the exercise whenever a critical analytic judgment is made.

Using this technique is particularly important when a judgment rests on limited information or unproven assumptions. Moreover, it can free analysts from arguing about the probability of an event to considering its consequences and developing some indicators or signposts for its possible emergence. It will help analysts address the impact of an event, the factors that could cause or alter it, and likely signposts that an event is imminent.

A "What If?" analysis can complement a difficult judgment reached and provide the policymaker a thoughtful caution to accepting the conventional wisdom without considering the costs and risks of being wrong. This can help decision-makers consider ways to hedge their bets, even if they accept the analytic judgment that an event remains unlikely.

Analysis of Competing Hypotheses (ACH)

Identification of alternative explanations (hypotheses) and evaluation of all evidence that will disconfirm rather than confirm hypotheses.

When to Use

Analysis of Competing Hypotheses (ACH) has proved to be a highly effective technique when there is a large amount of data to absorb and evaluate. While a single analyst can use ACH, it is most effective with a small team that can challenge each other's evaluation of the evidence. Developing a matrix of hypotheses and loading already collected information into the matrix can be accomplished in a day or less. If the data must be reassembled, the initial phases of the ACH process may require additional time. Sometimes a facilitator or someone familiar with the technique can lead new analysts through this process for the first time.

ACH is particularly appropriate for controversial issues when analysts want to develop a clear record that shows what theories they have considered and how they arrived at their judgments. Developing the ACH matrix allows other analysts (or even policymakers) to review their analysis and identify areas of agreement and disagreement. Evidence can also be examined more systematically, and analysts have found that this makes the technique ideal for considering the possibility of deception and denial.

See Timeline for Using Structured Analytic Techniques graphic above.

Benefits

ACH helps analysts overcome three common mistakes that can lead to inaccurate forecasts:

- Analysts often are susceptible to being unduly influenced by a first impression, based on incomplete data, an existing analytic line, or a single explanation that seems to fit well enough.

- Analysts seldom generate a full set of explanations or hypotheses at the outset of a project.

- Analysts often rely on evidence to support their preferred hypothesis, but which also is consistent with other explanations.

Essentially, ACH helps analysts to avoid picking the first solution that seems satisfactory instead of going through all the possibilities to arrive at the best solution.

Devil's Advocacy

Challenging a single, strongly held view or consensus by building the best possible case for an alternative explanation.

When to Use

Devil's Advocacy[180] is most effective when used to challenge an analytic consensus or a key assumption

---

[180] *A Tradecraft Primer*, 17. **Rated A1.**

regarding a critically important intelligence question. On those issues that one cannot afford to get wrong, Devil's Advocacy can provide further confidence that the current analytic line will hold up to close scrutiny. An individual analyst can often assume the role of the Devil's Advocate if he or she has some doubts about a widely held view, or a manager might designate a courageous analyst to challenge the prevailing wisdom to reaffirm the group's confidence in those judgments. When a group of analysts has worked on an issue for a long period of time, it is probably wise to assume that a strong mindset exists that deserves the closer scrutiny provided by Devil's Advocacy.

Benefits

Analysts have an obligation to policymakers to understand where their own analytic judgments might be weak and open to a future challenge. The Devil's Advocacy process can highlight weaknesses in a current analytic judgment or alternatively help to reaffirm one's confidence in the prevailing judgments by:

- Explicitly challenging key assumptions to see if they will not hold up under some circumstances.

- Identifying any faulty logic or information that would undermine the key analytic judgments.

- Presenting alternative hypotheses that would explain the current body of information available to analysts.

Its primary value is to serve as a check on a dominant mindset that can develop over time among even the best analysts who have followed an issue and formed a strong consensus that there is only one way of looking at their issue. This mindset phenomenon makes it more likely that contradictory evidence is dismissed or not given proper weight or consideration. An exercise aimed at highlighting such evidence and proposing another way of thinking about an issue can expose hidden assumptions and compel analysts to review their information with greater skepticism about their findings.

Some Intelligence Community agencies are known to have established a permanent "Devil's Advocate" analytic challenge process as part of their final review of analytic products that are published and released to consumers and decision makers.

Premortem Analysis

Used to reduce the risk of surprise and the subsequent need for a post-mortem examination of failures. It is an easy-to-use technique that allows analysts working on any future-oriented analysis of project to effectively challenge the accuracy of their own conclusions.

When to Use

Premortem Analysis[181] should be used by analysts who can devote a few hours to challenging their own conclusions about the future to see where they might be wrong. It is most effective when used by a small group. A premortem as an analytic aid was first used in the context of decision making by Gary Klein in his

---

[181] Heuer and Pherson. *Structured Analytic Techniques*, 211. **Rated A1.**

1998 book Sources of Power: How People Make Decisions. See Timeline for Using Structured Analytic Techniques graphic above.

Benefits

The Premortem Analysis approach helps analysts identify potential causes of error that previously had been overlooked. There are two creative processes at work here. First, the questions are reframed; this exercise typically elicits responses that are different from the original ones. Second, the premortem approach legitimizes dissent. For various reasons, many members of small groups suppress dissenting opinions, leading to premature consensus. Research has documented that an important cause of poor group decisions is the desire for consensus.

> It is not bigotry to be certain we are right; but it is bigotry to be unable to imagine how we might possibly have gone wrong – G.K. Chesterton, English writer.

The primary value of Premortem Analysis is that it legitimizes dissent. Group members who may have previously suppressed opinions, questions, or doubts because they lack confidence are empowered by the technique to express previously hidden divergent thoughts. If this change in perspective is handled well, each group member will know that they have added value to the exercise for being critical of the previous judgement, not for supporting it.

Nominal Group Technique

A process for generating and evaluating ideas. It is a form of brainstorming, but Nominal Group Technique[182] has always had its own identity as a separate technique. The goals of Nominal Group Technique and Structured Brainstorming are the same – the generation of good, innovative, and viable ideas. The Nominal Group Technique was developed by A.L. Dulbecco and A.H. Van de Ven.[183]

When to Use

The Nominal Group Technique prevents the domination of a discussion by a single person. Use it whenever there is concern that a senior analyst, executive, or outspoken member of the group will control the direction of the meeting by speaking before anyone else. Conversely, it is also appropriate to use the Nominal Group Technique rather than Structured Brainstorming if there is concern that some members of the group may not speak up; the session is likely to be dominated by the presence of one or two well-known experts in the field, or the issue under discussion is controversial and may provoke debate.

Benefits

The Nominal Group Technique can be used to generate ideas, and to provide backup support in a decision-making process where all participants are asked to rank or prioritize the ideas that are

---

[182] Heuer and Pherson. *Structured Analytic Techniques*, 98. **Rated A1.**

[183] A.L. Delbecq and A.H. Van de Ven, "A Group Process Model for Problem Identification and Program Planning," Journal of Applied Behavioural Science VII (July-August, 1971): 46-491, quoted in Heuer and Pherson. *Structured Analytic Techniques*, 101. **Rated A1.**

generated. If necessary, all ideas and votes can be kept anonymous. Unlike Structured Brainstorming, which usually intends to generate the greatest possible number of ideas, the Nominal Group Technique may be used to focus on a limited number of carefully selected opinions or options.

The technique allows participants to focus on each idea as it is presented by the facilitator, rather than having to think simultaneously about preparing their own ideas and listening to what others are proposing. This situation often occurs with Structured Brainstorming.

Appendix C: Revised Admiralty Rating System for Source Reliability and Information Credibility

R.L.A. (Rick) Gill, CD

Key Points

- Since its initial development in the 1940s during World War Two, the original UK Admiralty rating system for source reliability and information credibility has remained unchanged in its original form until 2006.

- Little or no details have ever been provided on the use of the UK Admiralty rating system. Coupled with users' tendencies to correlate source reliability ratings with information credibility ratings, these factors have led to little or no use of this rating system in recent years.

- Revisions to this rating system first began appearing in 2006 in U.S., NATO and other national military doctrinal and open-source publications have begun to make useful improvements to this (now) seven-decade old rating system.

- This revised and updated version of the original UK Admiralty rating system serves to allow users to better choose and identify the reliability of their sources and credibility of those sources' information for readers of their reports and publications.

Recent Events

The first noted changes to the original 1940s era UK Admiralty rating system were published in 2006, in a new and publicly available U.S. Army Field Manual (FM) 2-22.3 "Human Intelligence Collector Operations." The changes included questions and issues to be considered by users when selecting source reliability and information credibility ratings.

In 2010, Canadian analytic methodologists (including the author) began to make further revisions to the original UK Admiralty rating system, based on the questions and issues mentioned in FM2-22.3 to be considered by users when selecting source reliability and information accuracy (credibility) ratings. Our intent was to provide an improved process allowing users to make better choices for ratings to be applied in analytic products.

In his 2010 book, *Scientific Methods of Inquiry for Intelligence Analysis*, Dr. Hank Prunckun[184] addressed

---

[184] "Dr. Henry Prunckun," Henry Prunckun - Australian Graduate School of Policing and Security (Charles Sturt University, June 1, 2021),
https://bjbs.csu.edu.au/schools/agsps/staff/profiles/

the issue of rating information believed to be either "misinformation" or "disinformation." A revised and updated Admiralty rating system was published in 2012[185], in a new U.S. Army publication dealing with Open-Source Intelligence (OSINT), in which the modified rating system appears to have been influenced by the work of Dr. Prunckun. These additional questions and issues to be considered by users when selecting ratings, as seen in the U.S. Army's FM 2-22.3 and later ATP 2.22-9, began to appear in NATO and other allied nations' doctrinal publications.

In the second edition of *Scientific Methods of Inquiry for Intelligence Analysis*[186] published in 2015, Dr. Prunckun expanded upon his earlier work, addressing issues related to the potential for deception by the source, in addition to misinformation and disinformation. He did this by including additional

---

adjunct-staff/hank_prunckun. **Rated A1.**
[185] "U.S. Army Techniques Publication (ATP) 2-22.9 Open-Source Intelligence," An Army Introduction to Open Source Intelligence (Federation Of American Scientists Secrecy News, September 13, 2012), https://fas.org/blogs/secrecy/2012/09/army_osint/ **Rated A1.**
[186] Hank Prunckun, "Scientific Methods of Inquiry for Intelligence Analysis, Second Edition," Rowman & Littlefield (Rowman & Littlefield, September 2014), https://rowman.com/ISBN/9781442224315/Scientific-Methods-of-Inquiry-for-Intelligence-Analysis-Second-Edition , 53-54 **Rated A1.**

ratings in both source and information categories to indicate:

- A source that is either "unintentionally misleading" or "deliberately deceptive," and

- Information which is either "misinformation" or "disinformation."

In this second edition, Dr. Prunckun included new source ratings of F-G and information ratings of 6-7, pushing back the original "F" and "6" ratings of "Cannot be Judged" to "H" and "8", respectively. I believe that this change causes issues of backward compatibility with the original Admiralty rating system, for its many long-time military and other users, who easily remember the meaning of a rating of "F6" as "source reliability and information credibility cannot be judged."

My initial thoughts on adopting Dr. Prunckun's additions to the Admiralty rating system were to leave "F" and "6" where they were in the UK Admiralty rating system and added his additional ratings for "Unintentionally Misleading" (F) and "Deliberately Deceptive" (G) for source reliability, and "Misinformation" (6) and "Deception" (7) below "F" and "6". These modifications would retitle his additional ratings to "Unintentionally Misleading" (G) and "Deliberately Deceptive" (H) for source reliability, and "Misinformation" (7) and "Deception" (8). This modification to Dr. Prunckun's revised UK Admiralty rating system would now keep his revisions backwardly compatible with the original UK Admiralty rating system.

Subsequent discussions with colleagues in Canada's Defence Research and Development, and Security and Intelligence communities led me to conclude that Dr. Prunckun's ratings and descriptions of "Unintentionally Misleading" (F) and "Deliberately Deceptive" (G) for source reliability, and "Misinformation" (6) and "Deception" (7) were in fact regarded as subsets of the categories "Unreliable (E) and "Improbable" (5). Dr. Prunckun's descriptions for his additional ratings of "Unintentionally Misleading" and "Deliberately Deceptive" for source reliability, and "Misinformation" and "Deception" have now been included under "Unreliable" (E) and "Improbable" (5) in the revised UK Admiralty rating system used in this publication.

Background

The first known source reliability and information accuracy (credibility) rating system was developed by the UK Royal Navy's Admiralty staff during the Battle of the Atlantic in World War Two. The Admiralty staff needed a method by which they could systematically evaluate, and rate mass volumes of reporting being received from a wide variety of sources. What quickly became known as the Admiralty Source Reliability and Information Accuracy rating system (shown below) was developed at that time, and subsequently adopted for use in subsequent years by British and other NATO military forces.

Evaluation of Source Reliability		Evaluation of Information Accuracy	
Code	Description	Code	Description
A	Reliable	1	Confirmed
B	Usually Reliable	2	Probably True
C	Fairly Reliable	3	Possibly True
D	Not Usually Reliable	4	Doubtfully True
E	Unreliable	5	Improbable
F	Cannot be Judged	6	Cannot be Judged

A report or information received would be rated for source reliability and information accuracy by a combination of the letter-number codes shown above. For example:

A report or information received from a source that is "**usually reliable**" and whose information provided at that point in time is believed to be "**probably true**" would be rated as "**B2**".

Since its initial development, the original Admiralty rating system shown above has been published in British, U.S., Canadian and other NATO nations' doctrinal publications "as-is" for nearly six decades. Other than one or two examples like that provided above, the Admiralty rating system in these various doctrinal publications were accompanied by little or no explanation on how to effectively select ratings using this system.

Research, Revisions, and Updates

U.S. Army research[187] conducted in 1975 on the use of the Admiralty rating system conducted found:

"About one-fourth of the [37] subjects treated reliability and accuracy as independent dimensions; the majority treated reliability as highly correlated with accuracy, and their judgement of a report's truth was influenced more strongly by its accuracy rating. Numerical (probabilistic) interpretations of scale levels were consistent within individuals but varied widely between them. Development of a new scale is suggested."

This revised and updated Source Reliability and Information Credibility rating system provided below is an amalgam of the U.S. doctrinal publications discussed above, and rearranged additional elements of that published by Dr. Prunckun in 2015. This source reliability and information credibility rating system is backwardly compatible with both the original UK Admiralty rating system, and recent military doctrinal updates to the UK Admiralty rating system. Source reliability and information credibility ratings used in this, and subsequent publications will be indicated in bold, to clearly delineate ratings from a document's content, citations, footnotes, or endnotes. Examples of this are "**rated B2**" (source is usually reliable;

---

[187] Michael G. Samet, "Subjective Interpretation of Reliability and Accuracy Scales for Evaluating Military Intelligence," DTIC (U.S. Army Research Institute for the Behavioral and Social Sciences, January 1, 1975), https://apps.dtic.mil/sti/citations/ADA003260. **Rated B1.**

information is probably true), "**rated C4**" (source is fairly reliable; however, this information is doubtful), and "**rated F6**" (source reliability and information credibility cannot be judged). This revised source reliability and information credibility rating system tables will be included as an annex or appendix in all publications and other products.

Implications

These enhancements to the original UK Admiralty rating system and its use in publications are intended to provide:

a. Analysts with a more consistent method of applying this rating system, and

b. Consumers of analytic products with the best possible understanding of analysts' deliberations on their sources being cited and the information provided by those sources.

Updated Admiralty Rating System: Source Reliability

Code	Description	Issues to be considered by Users when selecting a Rating
A	Completely Reliable	**No doubt** of source's authenticity, trustworthiness, or competency; source has a history of complete reliability.

Code	Description	Issues to be considered by Users when selecting a Rating
B	**Usually Reliable**	**Minor doubt** about source's authenticity, trustworthiness, or competency; source has a history of valid information most of the time.
C	**Fairly Reliable**	**Doubt** of source's authenticity, trustworthiness, or competency, but source has provided valid information in the past.
D	**Not Usually Reliable**	**Significant doubt** about source's authenticity, trustworthiness, or competency, but source has provided valid information in the past.

Code	Description	Issues to be considered by Users when selecting a Rating
E	Unreliable	**Lacking authenticity, trustworthiness, and competency**; the source has a history of invalid information. Alternately, the source is **unintentionally misleading** or **deliberately deceptive**, having been contradicted by other independent and reliable sources on the same subject.
F	Reliability Cannot Be Judged	**No basis** exists for evaluating the reliability of the source.

In every instance, the ratings above are based on previous reporting from that source. If there has been no prior reporting this source, the source must initially be rated "F". **NOTE:** An "F" rating does not mean that the source cannot be trusted, but that there is no reporting history and therefore no basis for making any other determination.

Updated Admiralty Rating System: Info Credibility

Code	Description	Issues to be considered by Users when selecting a Rating
1	Confirmed by Other Sources	<u>Confirmed by other independent sources</u>; logical by itself; consistent with other information on the subject.
2	Probably True	<u>Not confirmed</u>; logical by itself; consistent with other information on the subject.
3	Possibly True	<u>Not confirmed</u>; reasonably logical by itself; agrees with some other information on the subject.
4	Doubtful	<u>Not confirmed</u>; possible but not logical; no other information on the subject.
5	Improbable	<u>Not confirmed</u>; not logical by itself; contradicted by other information on the subject. **Alternately, the information is** <u>unintentionally false</u> or <u>deliberately false</u>, having been **contradicted by other independent and confirmed information** on the same subject.
6	**Truth Cannot Be Judged**	No basis exists for evaluating the validity of the information.

The highest degree of confidence in reported information (1) is given when confirmed by other independently verified sources. The table above provides the evaluated ratings for information credibility. The degree of confidence decreases if the information is not confirmed, and/or is not logical. *The evaluated rating of 5 means the information is evaluated as false: unintentionally or deliberately.* A rating of "6" does not necessarily mean false information but is generally used to indicate that no determination of credibility can be made since the information is new and not previously received from other sources.

About The Authors

Tom Quiggin

Tom is a court expert on jihadist terrorism in the Federal Court of Canada and the Ontario Superior Court. He has testified both for and against followers of the Islamic faith in terrorism cases. He flew as an Airborne Electronic Sensor Operator in CH-124 Helicopters in both the Anti-Submarine Warfare and Search and Rescue roles. He also served as an Intelligence Officer in the Canadian Forces in Bosnia, Croatia, Albania, Russia, and other areas. The RCMP Integrated National Security Enforcement Team (A Div) employed him as a contract intelligence analyst on matters of terrorism and national security for six years. He also was employed in Singapore at Nanyang Technological University on research related to intelligence and national security. Contract work has included the Intelligence Assessment Secretariat of the Privy Council Office of Canada, Citizenship and Immigration Canada and the International War Crimes Tribunal. He is currently the primary contributor to the podcast "The Quiggin Report."

Rick Gill

Rick joined the Canadian Forces in 1974. In 1980 after serving in Canada and Europe, Rick transferred to the Canadian Forces' Security Branch and subsequently the newly formed Intelligence Branch in 1982. Rick has served in a variety of domestic and international positions, ranging from the strategic to the tactical, including deployments to Bosnia-Hercegovina, Kosovo and Afghanistan. In 2009, Rick transferred to the Primary Reserves. At the Canadian Forces School of Military Intelligence, Kingston Ontario, Rick taught analytical methodologies, and served as Sergeant-Major, Standards and Training Development Division. In 2013, Rick retired from the Canadian Forces after 38 years of service, and joined Communications Security Establishment Canada, where he co-developed and delivered intelligence analyst training. Rick also volunteered as adjunct faculty with the Privy Council Office's Intelligence Analyst Learning Program, serving Ottawa's Security and Intelligence community. In 2017, Rick joined the Canadian Security Intelligence Service, instructing on analytic training courses; mentoring Service analysts and training development. In 2018, Rick left the Service and now provides consulting services in the Security and Intelligence field.

Manufactured by Amazon.ca
Bolton, ON